This book is dedicated to J.J. and B.E.
who have showed me the true meaning
of the words love and inspiration

I want to say thank you to my family for all of the love
and support throughout my long journey in writing this book.
I also want to thank the Manahawkin, NJ Book Club (Eileen,
Felicia, Sharon, Christina, Kari and Kathleen), Professor
Rosemary Hardie and her students, Frank Bianchetti (website),
Design 446 (social media), Hampton Lamoureux (cover), David
Provolo (interior formatting) and Beth Dorward (editing). There
are so many more people I should thank for their support and
assistance, but for fear that I might inadvertently miss someone, I
will say thank you to all of you. You know who you are and I will
be sure to thank you all personally. I am forever grateful.

PROLOGUE

November 6, 2043
Friday, 7:00 PM
Outside of Augusta, Georgia
*A little more than a year before the event
that would change the world*

Silence blanketed the Georgia cemetery like a heavy fog as United States Army General, Eric Hyland, kissed the soft petals of a freshly cut red rose. Alternating currents of love and guilt coursed through him as he laid the flower at the base of his wife's monument.

The crescent moon did little to provide illumination so he held up a lantern. He had designed and built Amanda's headstone himself, and he alone knew the secrets it held. Even his only child, his daughter Sara, whom he was closer to than anyone else in the world, did not know. It was a lot for him to carry, and the lantern grew heavy in his hand.

He slipped a large skeleton key into his pocket and stared at the decorative rose pattern that adorned the top half of the tombstone's face. In the lantern light he could see that the granite itself looked as fresh as the day it was carved, but the red color had started to fade from being in the elements for more than eighteen years. Suddenly the phone on his hip started ringing. Checking the screen, he cringed upon seeing that the caller was the United States secretary of defense. Before answering, General Eric Hyland touched the stone rose with his fingertips and whispered to his deceased wife, "One day honey, I swear, Sara will know the truth."

I:
LIQUIDATION

CHAPTER 1

December 26, 2044
Monday, 9:30 PM
New Jersey coast
The evening of the event that would change the world

The air at the ocean is never still.

Or so he had always believed, until this very moment.

The black clouds were still distant on the horizon, so Kid Carlson tried to rationalize. *It is just the calm before the storm.* The words rang empty and he found no comfort in them. To the contrary, his body shivered from a spasmodic chill. There was something more, something he could not pinpoint. In truth, he had felt uneasy since dinner earlier that night with his girlfriend, Sara Hyland, and her father. He knew the food was not the culprit. The disturbance radiated from a point deeper inside than his stomach.

From his beach chair under the pier, Kid stared into a tunnel framed by rows of weathered pillars that ran out to sea. The encroaching darkness hovered beyond the silhouette of a tide that was rolling in, but hardly cresting. Were it not for the deep, muffled rumble, Kid would not even know he was at the Atlantic Ocean. He pulled his maroon knitted hat tighter on his head to fend off the bite of the sub-freezing, stagnant air and turned his eyes. The sky over the deserted beach was like a dome of solid concrete.

A log in the fire pit crackled and popped, creating a small explosion. Kid looked up, afraid that the spark would reach the Casino Pier above them. Convinced that the pier was safe, he turned to his girlfriend of nearly nine months sitting next to him. Sara was so lost in thought that she did not even react to the loud pop. He grabbed her hand as she stared at the gift-wrapped jewelry box on her lap.

Sara smiled at him, but could not hold it. Her mood was atypical, at least for her, and it caught Kid off-guard. She always found the positive in life, and people and even tough circumstances. He caressed her gloved hand, and just wished that he could take away her pain and sadness. He would shoulder it if he could. It would be hard for him to explain, but he sometimes felt like her guardian. It certainly wasn't because Sara was mentally or physically meek. Quite the opposite.

Kid glanced at one of the other couples, who were fighting over the last 12-ounce bottle of hard lemonade. His friend Jessie Kellen, known simply as Jess, had barely taken a sip when his girlfriend, Maria Stefano, snatched the bottle from his hand. Jess and Maria had been dating for four years now, since they were both juniors in high school, but they already acted like an old married couple. Kid had been friends with both of them for a long time, and he marveled at how opposites attract. Maria was fun-loving and boisterous, while Jess was grounded and low-key, and didn't smile much. But they had a level of comfort with each other that was admirable and often humorous.

"I still can't figure out why there were military checkpoints set up at the bridge," Jess noted. "I've never seen that before."

"They checked all of our driver's licenses," Maria responded as she took a swig of the hard lemonade, "so they must be looking for someone."

"I wonder who, and why? Just another waste of government resources," Jess bemoaned as he snatched the bottle back.

Although he appeared to be grumpy all the time, Jess seemed particularly agitated tonight. That tended to happen when Jess felt the presence of the government in any form or fashion. Kid could not count how many times his friend had complained about the taxes being taken out of his paycheck to fund what he referred to as the bloated bureaucracy of government. His friend seemed content with his position as the night crew chief of a local supermarket, so Kid could see Jess lodging the same complaints 20 years from now.

"Speaking of government resources, listen to this one," Brian Mitchell started. "Yesterday, I got off at the wrong exit in New York City with Heidi…"

Shame you didn't leave her there, Kid thought, and then reprimanded himself for his negative reaction. Brian was a long-time friend and Heidi Leer was his first serious girlfriend. They had been dating for six months, but Kid still had a hard time dealing with her.

"… and we were stuck in traffic for hours because of a huge demonstration in Central Park," Brian continued. "More than 300,000 people were there to protest that Utopia Project."

"We didn't even know they were having a protest. We should have just skipped going to the city." Heidi's Brooklyn accent emphasized the disgust in her voice.

"I'm just tired of hearing about it with every news feed, and having to listen to that big-mouth reporter, Lily Black. She thinks she is all that," Jess blurted out as he poked a log in the fire. "For the last week that's *all* we've heard about. Can't we talk about the new line of Sea Rays that are coming out in the spring? One of them even had a flex-skeg. You can turn it on a dime. "

Kid knew that Jess would rather talk about boats. Jess's entire family lived to do three things when not at work- camping, hunting and boating. Jess grew up on a lagoon with ocean access and always had boats, so he regularly used nautical terms that Kid, and most of the group, had never heard before.

"A flex what?" Maria asked as she tried to grab the lemonade bottle. Jess jerked his hand away before she could secure it.

Ignoring Jess's attempt to divert the conversation, Brian continued, "I hate to say it, but the hullabaloo about the Utopia Project is not going to simmer down any time soon. Not since they've discovered that other countries were participating in that project with us, including Russia, Britain, China, India and Japan."

"Three large ships with more than 20,000 people." Jess shook his head. "Did they really think that project would stay hidden forever, even off the coast of Greenland?"

"I don't know, but it did for nearly 20 years. Anyway, it wasn't hidden. More like disguised. Even the Prime Minister of Greenland believed the ships were being used for experiments with vegetation, and climates and atmospheres. Not people."

Jess shrugged. "I'm not even sure what they are doing to the people on those ships, or if it has been verified."

"The memo that got in the hands of that reporter Lily Black came from someone *inside* the project, and the authenticity of that document *has* been verified," Brian responded. "They published the entire memo, and basically, the people in that project are raised as mindless zombies, like the walking dead."

Brian was a good friend, but he sometimes sounded like a know-it-all. And now that he was working toward a bachelor's degree in political science and was so in tune with world events, he was more of a know-it-all than ever. Somehow Jess didn't come off that way, even when he used nautical terms Kid had never heard before.

Heidi asked Brian, "Didn't those protesters say they were going to march on Washington, DC, tomorrow?"

"Say it? They were screaming it! Since that controversial presidential election in 2020 there have been many civil crises in our country, but their goal is to recreate the one from 2025, which worked in shutting down a similar government project."

Sara muttered, "The CCP."

"What?" Brian asked.

"Oh, nothing. Just mumbling to myself." She sat forward in her chair and stabbed at the sand with the toe of her shoe.

Kid didn't know what was bothering his girlfriend, but she appeared uncomfortable, so he thought she might want to get away for a few minutes. He abruptly stood up. "Not that I don't want to hear this, but I need to stretch my legs. I'm going on top of the pier." He offered Sara his hand.

Brian waved to acknowledge Kid's words and kept telling the story to the others, "Anyway, when we were in New York I realized the truck was almost out of gas and…"

"Leaving in the middle of the story Kid? That's kind of rude." Heidi rolled her blue eyes and crossed her arms.

"You would know rude." He did not miss the irony that Heidi had also interrupted. "I wasn't really paying attention anyway. I'm a little out of it tonight. Is that alright with you?"

"You know, if you weren't a friend of Brian's, I'd tell you to go to... never mind." She failed to disguise the loathing in her voice.

"I have to say, Brian," Kid glowered at Heidi, "you really know how to pick 'em." For no reason in particular, there had been friction between Kid and Heidi since the day they met. Heidi claimed that she just wanted to be accepted among Brian's friend group, but yet she could not help being combative, especially toward Kid. It came as no surprise when Brian noted that she didn't have many friends, and that she was even alienated from most of her family.

Sara jumped in and said, "If y'all don't mind, I'll go with Kid. I could use the walk myself."

Kid's growing contempt was instantly diffused by his girlfriend's polite, southern accent. It had that effect on him.

"No problem. He's all yours," Maria answered as she swiped the lemonade bottle from her boyfriend's hand.

"Lucky me," Sara responded.

Maria chuckled and lifted the bottom of the bottle to the sky over her waiting mouth. Not even a single drop came out. As the smile evaporated from her face, Jess laughed for the first time that night.

Sara took Kid's hand and stood up. Her other glove still held the jewelry box.

Walking together, he asked, "Why don't you just open that box now? It's been weighing on you all night." He didn't use the word melancholy, but that was the most accurate description of her mood.

"I can't. You heard my father at dinner. He was adamant, really adamant, that I can't open it until the exact moment that he proposed to my mother on December 26 at the beach a long time ago."

"I know. Not 11:02, not 11:04, but *exactly* 11:03 p.m." Kid smirked. "He's so particular and to the minute. Like his coffeepot being set on auto-brew for 5:56 a.m. So what do you think is in there?" He pointed.

"I don't know. Maybe Mom's wedding ring?" She gazed at the box, almost reverently.

Kid didn't know either. But more than anything, he knew that the jewelry box held the spirit of her mother, who died the day she gave birth to Sara. "Why don't we put it in Brian's glove compartment for now, so that you don't accidentally drop it off the pier?"

She seemed reluctant to let it out of her sight. "Will it be safe there?"

"Yes. It will be fine."

She relented and handed it to him.

"Just don't forget it." Kid walked over and opened the passenger door of the truck. The small box, covered in red rose wrapping paper, fit perfectly in the glove compartment.

"Trust me, I won't," she said as he closed the vehicle door. "I know I am kind of lost in thought tonight, but so are you. Are you alright?" Sara asked as they held hands and walked up the beach toward the boardwalk.

"Yeah, I really wanted to check out the ocean from the top of the pier. It's hard to see through the pillars underneath." He thought he sounded convincing.

"Right." She sighed. Translation: I don't buy it for a second.

"And I wanted to be alone with you, even if just for a few minutes," he added.

"I don't know how long we want to leave the crew under the pier without their fearless leader." She nudged him with her elbow.

He looked at her with one raised eyebrow. "Don't think so. We don't have a leader."

"I don't have to be a psychologist to diagnose the one affliction you clearly suffer from."

"What's that?"

"Denial!" she blurted out.

He paused. "I don't see it."

"That's the problem," she said and chuckled.

Kid also laughed, but mechanically so. Her comment resonated and he felt a discomfort somewhere deep inside. It was true that everyone seemed to look to him, whether it be friends, family, teammates or even bandmates. But he always worried about letting people down.

On top of the pier, the various amusement rides, game booths, and food stands were all boarded up and closed for the winter. "This place is a frozen ghost town," Sara whispered, as if worried that someone might overhear. She turned and leaned on the wooden rail at the end of the pier, which extended nearly 200 feet out to sea.

"It's off-season." Having grown up in a small town just across the bay, Kid knew the extremes of this shore resort, which was around 45 miles north of Atlantic City, New Jersey. Although quiet in the winter, Seaside Heights was an overcrowded madhouse every summer. He shivered as he also leaned on the rail, and said, "I guess it's a far cry from sunny Augusta."

"I might still be there, were it not for that satellite project my father got roped into," she noted.

Just a few years prior, Sara's father, United States Army General, Eric Hyland, had been transferred from Fort Gordon in Georgia to Fort Dix in New Jersey. After having spent her entire life in Augusta, Georgia, Sara had to enroll in a new school, in a different part of the country, for her junior year of high school. Kid could only imagine how difficult that transition must have been. He knew that she still sometimes got homesick. She had many friends in Augusta, and kept in touch with almost all of them. That included members of the theater group, teammates from volleyball and softball and co-workers from the restaurant she worked at, among others. She was such a good person, and such a caring person, that she established bonds very naturally, and very deeply. Kid knew that firsthand.

"But I think we've talked enough about government projects tonight," she added.

Kid smirked. "Brian is probably still going down there."

For a long minute they both stared out from the edge of the continent. The ocean loomed before them like a massive audience in a large dark auditorium.

"I recognize that one," she noted. Kid turned to her, uncertain what she was referring to.

Sara brushed his long, brown hair off of his shoulder and face. His cheekbones, which everyone described as prominent, were numb to the casual petting of her gloved hand. She finally clarified, "You were humming a song, that new one you were working on. I think you called it 'Angels Never Cry'."

"Sorry. I didn't even realize I was humming it."

"Sorry? Don't be sorry. I love that one. I know you are working on getting your business degree, but I just hope you finally give music a shot. You've really got it in you. I see it and feel it. So does Bull the Bouncer and he sees bands all the time."

Kid smirked. "Love that guy." Bull was the big, Greek bouncer who guarded the door at the Stone Pony music club in Asbury Park. Over the summer, Kid played there a few times and was featured on the holograph circuit. His band, Airstrip One, was on stage in New Jersey, but with the holograph technology, it appeared as if they were concurrently playing live in several clubs around the country. The quality of the image was stunning. Kid's cousin in Virginia had gone to a club in Richmond to see Airstrip One and said the hologram was so vivid that the band members looked more real than half of the live patrons in attendance. But Kid and the Greek bouncer had become fast friends, and for Airstrip One's second gig, Bull ran on stage and introduced Kid as, 'the Jersey Shore's next musical legend.'

"Thanks Sara, but even if someone really has the music in them, that alone doesn't guarantee success."

"But you have such a conviction for it. And you'll never know if you don't give it a shot."

"True. Wait, *I* have conviction?" he asked. "How many full academic scholarship offers did you pass up to follow your dream?"

He was transfixed by her hazel eyes. They, along with her full, red lips, were a perfect offset to her pale, yet somehow healthy-looking, skin. Her father, General Hyland, more than once had quipped that she could thank the Irish wing of the family for her fair complexion.

"Well, technically four." Sara was majoring in Drama and Theatre at school in Maryland. Her number three class rank in high school had afforded her several academic scholarship opportunities, but she remained guided by her love of the arts. When she wasn't acting or performing, she was painting.

"But you have to pursue what makes you passionate." Leaning up and bridging the gap between her five-foot seven-inch frame and his six-foot frame, she planted a gentle kiss on his lips.

Under the pier, the embers in the fire sizzled and started blinking out.

Mike and Mark Norris, two stocky identical twins, finally returned after having left to go to the bathroom. They were accompanied by Mike's girlfriend, Cathy Conroy.

Jess glanced up. "What took you guys so long?"

Mike was quick to point at his brother. "I told him not to eat that cheap burrito from the Quick-Fix."

Turning to Cathy, Jess asked, "How do you put up with those two?"

She just smiled and looked away, reminding him of why Kid called her 'Chatty Cathy.' The girl hardly ever said a word. But Mike had told Jess in confidence that Cathy was quiet and socially awkward because she was physically and emotionally abused as a child.

The connection between Cathy and Mike made sense to Jess, because both Norris brothers were also abused, at least physically, by their father. The dad wanted his sons to be tough football players, and took it too far. Jess couldn't count how many times both brothers came to football practice with bruises and cuts they did not get playing football for the school team.

"Alright, I'm freezing now." Heidi stood up and stretched her five-foot-eight, slender frame. She rubbed her cheeks with her gloves and warm, visible breath shot out of her mouth in wisps.

Brian pointed. "And we went from two-foot waves to five-foot waves in just a few minutes."

Jess turned to look and jumped to his feet. "Jesus! When did that change? We need to get out of here and fast."

CHAPTER 2

December 26, 2044
Monday, 10:00 PM
New Jersey coast
The hour of the event

On top of the pier, Sara wrapped her arms around Kid's neck. "Did you miss me this week?"

She had only spent three days at her grandparents' place near Rutland, Vermont, but to him it seemed a lot longer.

"Hey guys!" Jess yelled up from below the pier, sounding grumpier than ever. "Kid, Sara, are you ready to go?"

"You were gone this week?" Kid whispered.

Sara smacked his shoulder and yelled, "We're coming down Jess!"

Jess responded without hesitation, and his voice conveyed an urgency. "We need to move! The storm is coming in faster than we thought!"

Kid's moment of humor dissipated as he peered out to sea. The horizon had been swallowed by a blackness that was rolling toward shore, devouring the gray sky in its path. He looked down over the rail. Ferocious, churning whitecaps roared in an angry cacophony. Right then, a frigid gust of wind whipped his face so hard that his teeth hurt. Closing his mouth and taking a deep inhale through his frozen nostrils, the characteristic scent of the sea penetrated enough to finally register, and reminded him of his grandfather's freezer full of salted fish.

He actually felt some measure of relief that he was standing nose to nose with a storm. The earlier period of calm had been so deep, and so absolute, that it had not felt like a simple precursor to a weather event. It had felt like a warning.

Kid and Sara hustled back under the pier. They had to stop short as the incoming tide almost kissed their shoes before it made a hasty retreat.

"Where's Heidi?" Kid asked as he approached Maria.

She brushed her straight dark hair off her olive colored face. "Under the pier, over that way," she said while pointing. "I think she wanted a few minutes to herself. Let's go get her." She wrapped her arm around Kid's.

"And quick. You won't want to be outside when this storm hits," Jess grumbled. "And don't you have work tomorrow morning?"

Maria shrugged. "Yeah, but no big deal. If I'm late, I'm late."

Kid smirked. Maria was so aloof at times, and unfortunately that extended to most areas of her life, including work. She had not lasted at any job for more than six months. The only thing that kept her grounded in life was her autistic younger brother. She was his primary caretaker and was always there for him.

Sara turned and started folding up her beach chair.

"Want to come, Sara?" Maria held out her other arm.

"That's alright. Y'all go. I'll help out here."

"I wouldn't leave us alone. I'm a little tipsy."

Sara smirked. "Just don't leave any marks."

Maria turned away laughing. As they walked, she said, "I love that girl. I'm glad Sara's not insecure, like that last one you dated."

Kid was also thankful that his long-time friendship with Maria wasn't threatening to Sara. He was one of the first people Maria met after her family escaped her violent, alcoholic father and moved into town from southwest New Jersey. That was back in fourth grade when they were both nine years old. They had grown up akin to siblings, and their relationship had always been platonic.

"The last one I dated?" He turned to her. "What did you call her, the Prom Queen? Hey speaking of…"

"Stop there, Kid," she warned.

He started laughing. "You could have been a Prom Queen. That is, if you didn't threaten to kill anybody who voted for you." His comment earned him an elbow to the midsection.

In all the years he had known Maria, senior prom was the only time he could remember her getting dolled up to the hilt. Her dark hair was slightly curled and her make-up was applied to perfection. Kid, like every other person in the room, was awestruck. She seemed a bit uncomfortable wearing anything other than blue jeans, but she carried herself well for the entire event. He even approached her at the end of the night and asked in the most formal of tones as he bowed, "May I have this dance... beautiful lady?" Maria's formal response was, "Sure... dirt-bag," as she grabbed him by the tie and walked him out to the dance floor.

"My feet still hurt from those pumps I wore," she said as they took a few steps back from the rising tide. "Speaking of Prom Queens..." She pointed to Heidi, who had her arm around a pillar and was staring out to sea. Waving a hand, Maria called over, "Hey, Miss Wander-Off! Come on. Time to go."

After they hustled back to the vehicle, Kid climbed in and sat against the back door next to Sara. Jess and Maria were also in the back, sitting across from the Norris brothers and Chatty Cathy. They all had to cram in and sit on the floor since Brian had removed the back seat in preparation to transport some furniture the next day.

"Thought you guys ran away," Kid said to Mike Norris.

"I almost did. You should have smelled the deuce he dropped in a hole in the sand," he said as he pointed to his brother. Mark raised his middle finger.

Kid laughed. "Wait until some poor kid digs that up next summer. A souvenir from the Jersey Shore."

"It couldn't be worse than when Mark used to clear out the entire football locker room," Jess said. Turning to Kid, he added, "You are lucky you stuck with baseball."

"Maria, you are a piece of work," Heidi blurted out from the front passenger seat while fastening her seatbelt. "Why do you always give people crazy nicknames? Tonight I am Miss Wander-Off. The other day I was Miss Priss, and just because I combed my hair?"

"No, you were Miss Priss because I had to repeat the same question three times since you were so preoccupied with that long, beautiful, blonde hair of yours. Anyway, I don't know why I do what I do, and say what I say." Maria turned to Kid and added, "Miss Analyst up there."

Sara got on her knees and crawled forward. "Heidi, can you please hand me the gift-wrapped box that is in the glove compartment?"

Pulling it out, she muttered, "Pretty," as she handed it back.

"Thanks. I have to open it soon. At 11:03 p.m. to be exact." Heidi had an expression of curiosity, so Sara shrugged and said, "It's hard to explain, but that's my father for you. Anyway, Brian, can you wait that long?"

"That's like, 20 minutes."

"I know. I'm sorry. If it's too long, just leave me here and I'll call a car."

"No need for that," Heidi interjected. "That's not much time to kill. We're warm and dry inside the truck."

"I know how to kill some time." Brian put ZZ Top's old classic, 'La Grange,' on the stereo and grabbed the shifter. "It's time for a ride."

"Don't even think about it," Jess warned from the back, but was jostled as the truck was shifted into drive.

Kid's head banged against the back door as Brian put the gas pedal to the floor and started driving along the shoreline.

"At least get us off the beach!" Jess yelled. "Look over the ocean. The sky is pitch black."

"You fixed the drive shaft. We already tested it," Brian countered.

"I know, but now is not the time for a beach ride."

"Who said I was going to drive on the beach?" Salt water shed off of the tires in high arcing sheets as he cut the wheel and turned the truck into the sea.

Kid and Sara braced against the back door as the hungry ocean loomed straight ahead of them outside the windshield. Sara grabbed his arm and held on tight.

"Brian! What are you doing?" Heidi shrieked from the passenger seat, her bright blue eyes piercing, not probing.

"Four-wheeling!" he exclaimed with an ear-to-ear smile. "I've been dying to do this, but I had to wait until we fixed the front drive-shaft."

Water splashed high in the air as he drove in the shallow surf. He then turned the vehicle back toward the beach.

"You're getting carried away," she said as she braced her hands against the dashboard.

Once more he turned the nose of the truck into the surf, and a tall wave splashed over the top of the hood.

"You are a madman, Brian!" Maria yelled, but not disapprovingly, as she slid across the floor in the back of the truck.

While bouncing up and down in her seat, Heidi turned. "Can we stop encouraging him?"

"I'm with her," Mark said with one hand on his stomach.

Not wanting to spoil the fun, Kid stayed quiet but he was worried as he grabbed Sara's hand. Brian did not have a good track record when it came to four-wheeling. It rarely ended well.

Driving further into the sea, he stopped short and put the truck in reverse. The tires spun, but the vehicle wouldn't move. He lowered his window and popped his head out. "I can't see my back tires! They are completely submerged!" Gunning the engine, the vehicle didn't lurch a single millimeter. Turning to face the storm looming over the ocean, he uttered, "Holy shit."

"Four low!" Jess yelled out from the back.

"No good."

"Why not?"

"I'm already in four low."

Jess looked out the window and barked, "This is not the time, or the place!"

Heidi glared at Brian, and did not even need to say the words, *I told you so.*

Kid groaned. "Come on Jess, we have to bail Brian out... again." Opening the back door, he jerked back as he realized that the water level was almost even with the bumper. Half of the tail pipe was submerged. "Keep the idle up or else you're going to stall!"

With a sharp audible inhale, Sara scooted her rear end away as some salt water sloshed into the back of the truck.

Kid jumped into the ocean. A second later the cold registered with his senses and he shook with a quick, spasmodic chill. Jess followed him out, and gasped as the water splashed halfway up his midsection. Running up the beach, Kid was frantic to find a solution. Without hesitation, Jess starting pulling out sections of dune fence. "Come on, grab some slats!" he urged.

While wrestling with a slat and sliding it out of the flimsy metal wire frame, Kid could only marvel at Jess's quick thinking and ingenuity. Jess was not 'book smart,' but through their long-time friendship, it opened Kid's eyes to the reality that there are different measures of aptitude. His friend was 'earth smart,' and was supremely proficient when it came to living and surviving outdoors. Kid used to joke that he could send Jess into the woods with a butter knife and a couple of rubber bands, and the guy would somehow build a house with a working waterwheel.

He and Jess took off their coats and shirts and handed them through the window to Heidi. Then following Jess's plan, they crouched until the frigid water was up to their chests as they wedged fence slats under both of the back tires.

Standing up, Jess said, "We need to push toward the beach with the incoming tide, and hold the truck in place when it heads back out."

They slogged through the thigh-deep water and came around to the front of the truck. Out over the ocean, Kid could see only blackness. *Not good*, he thought. The tidal storm surge was close to making landfall. "Everyone be ready to bail if we can't save the truck!" he yelled.

"Save the truck?" Brian cried out in a panic. "I can't lose the truck!"

Kid yelled, "Put it in reverse and hit it! Go!" While facing the hood and the beach beyond, they started pushing as the next band of waves ran ashore. Brian depressed the gas pedal and the truck started reversing.

"Stop! Hold!" Jess called as the waves retracted and tried to suck the vehicle out to sea. Both of the guys extended their arms and held with all of their might, but lost a few feet of progress.

"Go!" Kid shouted as the next swell of waves broke and rolled toward the beach. Gaining traction, the truck reversed with growing speed and finally escaped the jaws of the ocean. Brian kept going until he was halfway to the boardwalk. Kid and Jess were both drenched and out of breath as they approached.

Brian popped his head out. "Thanks guys, I…"

"Just get us out of here. Enough screwing around," Jess snapped.

As they opened the back door and climbed in, the guys took off their soaked pants and threw them in the middle of the floor. They put their shirts and coats back on and climbed under their respective blankets.

"You should hang these so they start to dry." Maria picked up their pants and hung them on hooks. "Hey, the least you could do up there is crank up the heat!" Brian complied without hesitation.

Sara's mobile device started ringing, so she looked at the screen. "Private caller. There's no number listed."

Kid would have ignored it, but having been trained by her father to always answer her phone, he knew she would pick up.

"Hello? Hello?" Sara put down the phone. "Nobody there."

Shrugging his shoulders, Kid exhaled as he rested his head against the back door.

"Anyway, it is getting close to 11:00 p.m.," she noted as she pointed to the jewelry box sitting on her lap.

With smoke still coming from under the hood, Brian jumped out. He paused as Heidi said, "This night is just not ending well."

Between the blanket and the blasting heat, Kid was just beginning to thaw out. "We're lucky. That was a disaster in the making."

Sara's phone started to ring again.

"You are a popular girl at this hour of the night," Maria quipped. She paused for a second and added, "That didn't sound good."

This time the call-in number activated a picture from her contact list. Sara was quick to answer. "Karen? Are you alright?" She held the device against her ear, but on an angle so Kid could hear.

Karen Stone, their good friend up near Rutland, Vermont, planned to deliver a cease-and-desist ultimatum to her unstable ex-boyfriend that night. Kid could tell that Sara was worried sick about Karen, who was a year younger and like a little sister to her.

"Hey Sara. Sorry to call you so late, but you told me you would be out late."

"No problem. Are you crying?" She sat up straighter. "Did Scott Sherman do something to you?"

"No, no, I haven't met him yet," Karen responded. "It's my mother. She has me so upset right now. We got into an argument and…" Sara sat and listened, but did not say a word.

Jumping back in the truck, Brian exhaled. "The smoke is dissipating. I think it was just burning off the sea water that got inside the engine compartment. Just give it another ten minutes and we should be good to go." He leaned back in his seat and exhaled. "Well Sara, you don't have to worry about still being here at 11:03."

Sara, while still on the phone with Karen, held up the jewelry box and gave a thumbs up.

From the rear of the vehicle, Kid was staring out the front windshield at the black sky over the ocean. The silence became all-consuming, as if a whisper in the wind could shatter an eardrum. Kid was lost in the stillness of that moment when out of nowhere, he had a sinking feeling. He shuddered. There were people who swore that they sensed something a second before it happened…

Suddenly, and without any warning, the sky turned blinding red. A collage of rapidly moving red lines painted the sky in every direction. Everyone screamed and covered their faces as Brian's truck vibrated.

A searing pain registered in Kid's eyes and he reached up to cover his face. Sara's phone fell onto his lap, and he heard Karen's panicked voice. "Oh my God Sara, something is wrong. My room is red, from some strange light…" And then the phone cut out.

A humming sound swept over the truck in quick pulses, and Kid felt his chest cavity being hollowed out. With a pain and sickness like he had never felt before, he concluded, *I am dying, right here and now.*

CHAPTER 3

December 26, 2044
Monday, 11:00 PM
New Jersey coast
The hour of the event

Touching his own face, Kid realized that he was still alive. He rubbed his eyes and tried in vain to focus. He was unable to see anything but a curtain of red in every direction. His heart was beating violently, with his breaths shallow and rapid. Regaining full awareness of his surroundings, he heard a repetitive beep inside the truck. He reached out for Sara and she yelped at his touch, but she was thankfully alive. He heard Brian crying out in pain, while the others in the vehicle were all yelling in panicked fear.

Kid barked, "Hold on everyone. Let's calm down!" The incoherent screaming stopped, but one person was still moaning. "Brian, are you alright?"

"My eyes are burning! I was staring out the windshield when the sky just... exploded," he strained to reply.

"Heidi, how about you?" Kid asked.

"My eyes aren't burning but I'm blind! All I can see is red."

"Me too. Can anyone see anything but red?"

A chorus of desperate and scared voices answered, "No!"

Everyone started talking at the same time, prompting Kid to yell again. "Hold it! Stop! Freaking out isn't helping!" A repetitive pulse blared in the silence inside the truck. "What the hell is beeping?"

Feeling around blindly, Sara grabbed a box and held it to her ear. "It's in this jewelry box that my father gave me!"

"Can you stop it?" Usually a beeping sound would be nothing more than a nuisance, but given the present chaotic circumstances, it invoked sheer panic. It didn't help that nobody could see.

"I don't know!" He heard the crinkle of wrapping paper as she opened the box. "There's a… slip of paper and, it must be an old watch. I'm just pressing every button." Finally, the noise stopped. He heard her stuff everything in the box and shove it into a compartment in the back of the truck.

Heidi's voice was shaking. "What just happened out there, and why can't we see?"

"Must've been an explosion of some kind," Mike Norris replied. "But a blinding one. I can't see anything!"

"None of us can yet," Kid said. "Give it a minute. Maybe it will pass."

"It didn't sound like an explosion," Sara jumped in. "It sounded like it was sweeping over us from side to side."

"She's right, it seemed to be moving back and forth," Kid noted.

"What do you think it was, Sara?" Heidi asked. "If anyone would know weaponry it would be you, since you grew up on military bases."

"I'm not sure. But they looked like neutron beams."

"What!" Heidi replied in horror. "I've heard what those do to people. Don't even tell me…" She was starting to bawl.

"No, no, wait, it couldn't be," Sara interjected.

"Why not?"

"Because we would be dead."

For a couple of seconds, there was complete silence in the vehicle.

"Sara, try calling your Dad," Kid said as he grabbed her phone from his lap. Without the aid of sight she tried, but did not even have a signal. Nobody's device had a signal.

Grabbing the edge of his blanket, Kid began to tear off material to make blindfolds for everyone. "I think we're just flash blind." He hoped the effect was temporary.

Kid tore and dispensed blindfolds for everyone in the back and then crawled forward. "Here Heidi, take these blindfolds. Put one over Brian's eyes, and one over yours."

The group waited in the truck for more than half an hour, blind and helpless, but expecting police or emergency vehicles to arrive. To combat the bitter cold, Heidi would occasionally reach over, turn the vehicle on and blast the heat.

"I hope we're far enough away from the ocean. The storm sounds pretty bad outside," Sara remarked.

"We're far enough back. We were more than halfway up the beach," Kid replied.

He sat listening to the drops of freezing rain pecking at the roof of the truck, wondering if his sight would return soon. He lowered his blindfold and tried to focus, but he saw only a red collage. His mind kept replaying Karen's last panicked words, '...something is wrong. My room is red, from some strange light.' Whatever had happened was obviously not limited to the beach in Seaside Heights, New Jersey.

After another hour, the ice pellet parade ended.

"Maria, can you hand me my pants?" Kid asked. He couldn't stand waiting any longer.

She pushed a pair into his arms. "I think these are yours."

Although it was not usually a difficult task, even putting on pants was awkward without the aid of sight. His blue jeans were remarkably dry, with only limited areas of dampness. Feeling a specific area of moisture against his calf, it seemed to him that his sense of touch was heightened. He then turned around and tried to find the door handle. "I'm going outside. I'll see if anyone's around to help."

"Can you see?" Sara asked.

"No, but I can feel my way to the Quick-Fix. I just need to find the curb and follow it for a few blocks."

"Few blocks?" Jess scoffed. "It's further than that."

"Two blocks in and eight blocks over to be exact," Kid said.

"It's the middle of the night, and you can't see," Sara noted. "And the weather is pretty shaky."

"I can't just sit here. Anyway, it's a 24-hour convenience store, so someone should be there. Probably the same guy who gave me a pocketful of change since he was out of dollar bills. The weather seems fine now, but if it turns, I will just take shelter where I can until it passes."

He found the handle for the back door and said to Sara, "I'm opening the door. Lean forward." To the entire group, he added, "Hang in there everybody. I'm going to find out what is happening here."

It was a meaningless consolation, one that faded as quickly as it arrived, but for a split second Kid actually felt vindicated. The sense of foreboding he had felt in the absolute calm before the storm was not unfounded after all. Now he wished it was. Flash blind, he misjudged the distance to the ground when jumping out and his knees buckled. Lying on his side, he cursed the sand because his pants were soggy again. As he stood up, he reached out and touched the bumper of the truck to reorient himself. "Move back. I'm closing the door, in three, two, one…" he warned. The slam echoed in the night.

Walking cautiously, he moved up the beach until he reached the boardwalk. He ran his hand over the old wooden boards, pulled a splinter out of his numb index finger, and climbed up. The frigid ocean breeze whipped him with a vengeance, accentuating the dampness of his pants.

Kid stopped as his feet contacted the road, and he listened for cars or any sound that might indicate life. He heard the gusty wind, the tide, and nothing else. As he started to walk, his foot began to slide on the icy asphalt. Catching his balance, he stutter-stepped across the street until he stumbled on the curb on the other side. He followed it and headed west up the beach block. As he crossed an intersection, he shuffled his feet until he picked up the curb on the other side of the road. At the end of the second block, he turned south. He continued forward and tapped the curb with his shoe every few steps to make sure he was going straight. Despite stepping with caution, he nearly tripped and twisted his ankle several times. At the sixth intersection, he bumped his forehead into a metal sign that was mounted near eye-level. He jerked back and the sign vibrated, like someone vigorously shaking a thin piece of sheet metal.

Traversing the eighth block, he turned when he reached a curb cut-out, right where he had estimated the store would be. He could not believe how difficult it was to find the place without the aid of sight. Sensing that he had gone too far, he stopped and turned around only to find the side of the building at his fingertips. He followed the wall, came around to the front, and opened the door.

Kid almost fell backward as a wave of the most disgusting smell hit him. He covered his nose and jumped back. "What spoiled in here?" He took a deep breath and again walked into the store.

"Hello." Nobody answered, so he tried again a little louder. "Hello!" Still no answer.

Taking small steps, he made his way to the back of the store. Using his fingertips, he found a door, opened it and reached in. He discovered a ball on a lower shelf. After unraveling a loose piece, he determined that it was string. Immediately he thought of a good use for it, and kept it in his hand.

Going out the front door, he tied one end of the ball of string to the door handle. He unwound it as he headed across the parking lot. Despite the chilly temperature, it felt good to breathe fresh air and get away from the stench inside the store. He intended to case out the area and try to find someone to help them. He wasn't even halfway across the parking lot when freezing rain and hail started coming down in buckets. "How about a break here?" Kid said aloud as his clothes absorbed the falling precipitation.

He was thankful for his forethought in using the string as a guide. Without the aid of sight, he followed the twine and hustled back to the door. Feeling his way to the back of the store, he sat down in a corner. With his arms folded over his knees, Kid shivered as cold and damp clothes pressed against his skin. The stress of the night's events was weighing on his mind and body, so when he buried his nose in the sleeve of his shirt in an effort to escape the smell, he fell asleep.

■ ■ ■

"Kid, wake up!"

Startled, Kid arose. His face became involuntarily contorted as the foul smell in the store again registered with his senses. "Jess?"

"Yeah, I can see now. Take your blindfold off, maybe you can too."

Kid took his blindfold off and tried to focus. He could see shadows, although they still had a tint of red. He rubbed his eyes. "Everything is still kind of blurry."

"It took me a few minutes to focus, but the haze clears pretty quickly."

Jess breathed through his nose. "Something's freakin ripe in here." Breathing again and wincing, "That's just nasty."

"Check the meats in the deli case. What time is it anyway?"

"8:00 a.m."

At this point Kid could see well enough to get up and walk around without having to feel his way. He also realized it was daylight. "How are the others?" he inquired.

"Everyone can see again, except Brian," Jess noted.

"Where are they?"

"At a house down the beach, warming up in front of a wood stove," he answered as he peered into the case holding the deli meats.

"I could use that myself. I need to thaw out," Kid said. "Are you ready to drive back?"

"I didn't drive. I walked because Brian's truck was on fumes when we pulled up to Old Man Drexer's house."

"Old Man Drexer's house?"

"That's what Heidi calls it. She said that when she was down the shore last summer, her and her boyfriend at the time met an old guy named Mr. Drexer who lived there. He told them he used to be an attorney, but he quit and took up surf fishing instead."

"How noble."

Jess stared into the deli case. "These meats haven't gone bad. Anyway, it's cold enough in here for them to keep for at least a few days."

Though his vision was still somewhat cloudy, Kid saw lip balms on a shelf behind the counter. Desperately needing one, he went to reach over and stopped as he noticed the counter was a mess. Taking a handful of napkins from a nearby dispenser, he wiped away what appeared to be a clump of food on the counter. It reminded him of the cheap burrito Mark Norris made the mistake of buying there. He stretched to grab the lip balm and was overpowered by an even more pungent wave of stench.

He looked down and froze, staring in horror.

December 26, 2044
Monday, 11:00 PM
New Jersey coast
The moment of the event

John Patel was bored beyond belief while working the night shift at the Quick-Fix convenience store. He couldn't understand why the place stayed open in the winter. With almost everything on the shore closed for the winter, he would be lucky to have two customers all night. Sure, the job was easy, but the nights seemed endless. To amuse himself, he made the mistake of playing some scratch-off lottery tickets. He could not stop, and after losing $300, he was determined to keep playing until he found enough winners to cover his loses.

Otherwise, even though his uncle owned the store, he would be unemployed tomorrow. And at 24 years of age, his parents wanted him out of the house once and for all. That was the only reason he was working at his uncle's shithole store.

After grabbing yet another lottery ticket and scratching it off, he blinked as the world turned a blinding red. First a strong wave of nausea passed through him, and then he screamed in agony as his insides turned to liquid. The last thing he saw as his eyes melted was yet another losing lottery ticket in his trembling hand.

He collapsed to the floor. As his arm dragged against the counter top, a clump of skin and muscle scraped away, like the meat of a slow-cooked spare rib falling off the bone.

CHAPTER 4

December 27, 2044
Tuesday, 8:15 AM
New Jersey coast
The morning after the event

K id's stomach churned, and he felt weak and nauseous as his brain combined the awful sight with the rotten smell.

On the floor behind the counter was a bloody, lumpy, grotesque mound with a skull, a ribcage, other large bones and entrails. Clearly discernible was a scratch-off lottery ticket, which seemed to be floating on top of the pile. It appeared as though this person had simply melted, with a stream of blood and guts running into one corner of the space behind the counter.

Seeing the expression of disgust, Jess asked, "What's the matter?"

Kid pointed at the floor behind the counter. Maybe his eyes were playing tricks on him.

Jess leaned over and his face too become deathly pale. "Is that…" he started to say and jumped back from the counter, "Damn!" He put his hand over his mouth and nose and tried to stifle the sudden gag reflex.

Grabbing Jess's arm, Kid said, "Let's get out of here."

Jess nodded and ran for the door.

Kid hurriedly gathered snacks and drinks, stuffed them in a bag and dashed out.

As they walked down the boardwalk, Kid could not escape the pungent olfactory recollection of the carnage in the convenience store.

He also couldn't escape the feeling that this was not an isolated incident. "Listen, don't say anything about what we saw back there. Not yet. They'll flip out and jump to all kinds of conclusions."

Jess inhaled a lungful of fresh air. "Fine by me." The walk seemed to be helping him. His face was a little less pale, although his hand still rested across his stomach.

When Kid had heard 'house down the beach,' he was thinking of the multi-million dollar homes monopolizing the shoreline. He was surprised when they walked up to a weather-beaten and unkempt small shack, which appeared to be teetering as it rested on crooked wood pilings. Even more odd, it was the only house on the beach side of the boardwalk. "Went for the diamond in the rough?" he quipped.

"Went for the closest place that had a chimney since we were running out of gas. We were lucky to make it this far. It's actually pretty air-tight and has running water."

"The place looks abandoned," Kid said as he walked up the warped and soggy wood steps.

Jess followed, saying, "I know. But someone was living here."

Sara opened the door, and hugged Kid. "I guess you had to hunker down somewhere?"

"Yeah, the convenience store. I would've called if our phones were working."

"It's better you took shelter. It was bad outside. The storm eroded away half of the beach."

Kid cased out the dusty and dirty dwelling. It had a large open living room, a small bathroom with a toilet and a shower, and a third room with a closed door. He approached the shut door of what he assumed was a bedroom and reached out his hand.

"Locked. We already tried," Maria said as he jiggled the doorknob.

He turned and noticed that she was tending to a wood stove in the back corner of the shack.

"You must be freezing. Come warm up," she offered.

The floorboards creaked with every step as Kid walked over and rubbed his hands in front of the stove.

Lying on a plaid couch, Brian was still blindfolded. Kid stepped over and put his hand on his friend's shoulder. "Eyes still burning?"

"Not really, but I can't see anything."

"Here, drink some water." He placed a bottle in Brian's hand.

"You guys alright?" he asked the Norris brothers and Chatty Cathy, who were sitting on the floor.

"Yeah," they all mumbled.

Maria stabbed at the smoldering embers with a bronze-topped poker. "Fire's dying."

"We'll get some more wood," Kid offered.

"Why would you do that? Now that we found you, let's put some gas in the truck and get Brian to a hospital," Heidi suggested as she sat atop a barstool. "We can't even call an ambulance because nobody has a cell phone signal."

Kid swallowed hard. Nobody having a cell phone signal was telling, but seeing the grotesque pile of flesh and bones inside the Quick-Fix, after they were blinded by some red light from the sky that extended to at least Vermont, was already more than enough cause for suspicion. Of course, Heidi did not know about the dead body inside the convenience store.

"Heidi, I don't know what, but something really strange happened last night. I'm afraid it is bad out there."

"With the military guarding the bridge, we should have known there was some credible threat," Jess noted.

"Let me and Jess get gas and take a quick ride to see if everything is alright first. You guys just look after Brian."

"She's right, Kid. We should get him to the hospital. On top of it all, we're starving to death," Maria added. "And you know I have to watch my blood sugar."

"It's not much but here." Kid threw the bag with assorted snacks and drinks from the Quick-Fix over to her.

"I'll be fine," Brian said. "I'm not in pain and the red I see when I open my eyes, it's fading a little. Let them go."

Heidi sighed, "You guys will be quick?"

Kid knew that an inspection of the local area would not be bene-

Kid knew that an inspection of the local area would not be beneficial to her since her mother lived in Long Island. "Yeah, we won't be
long. We'll throw some more wood on the fire and go. If cell service is
restored we'll call."

Relenting, but clearly not happy about it, Heidi took Brian's truck
keys from the counter and flung them over to Kid.

"Hey Jess, do you remember how to siphon gas?" he asked.

"I'm on it." He grabbed the keys from Kid's hand and walked out the
door. "I'll have her filled up by the time you get more wood in the stove."

Kid took the time to break up a wood chair and feed the fire.

He kissed Sara on the cheek. "Hold down the fort and keep everyone…" Kid moved his eyes over to Heidi, "calm."

As he walked out the door of the shack, Jess was coming across the
street with a gas can in his hand. "Not fueled up yet?"

"Hey, cut me some slack. There aren't many cars over here to steal
gas from in the winter."

December 26, 2044
Monday, 11:00 PM
New Jersey coast
The moment of the event

Edith Dalton hated driving in three particular situations: when it
was dark outside, when the weather was wintry, and when a bridge was
involved. Tonight, she was confronted with the convergence of all three.

And the capper came when she approached the bridge and found it
blocked. In all of her 65 years, she had never seen the military guarding
the Tunney Bridge. Not being the person they were looking for, and not
revealing why they were there, she was waved on. She mumbled a prayer
with the ominous span dead ahead.

With her rosary beads woven through her fingers, she strangled the
steering wheel and motored over the icy bridge at half the speed limit.
Her husband Hal usually drove over the bridge while she closed her eyes

in the passenger's seat. Had she known her fears would continue to grow as she aged, she never would have chosen a house on a barrier island. The anxiety as she motored up the bridge was overwhelming, but she had to overcome it. Hal, the love of her life for the last 40 years, had just been taken to the hospital in an ambulance because he was having chest pains. If she could not simmer herself down, she might be admitted with him.

Edith had sent Hal's ambulance ahead since she would not leave her Ortley Beach house dressed in a nightgown. She had changed quickly, so she was only 15 minutes behind, but she would not be gaining ground at the speed she was traveling. "Oh Hal," she said, admonishing him for overexerting his already weakened heart as she crossed the arch of the bridge. Seeing the end of the span in the distance, she felt a glimmer of hope that she might make it.

Suddenly the snowy road exposed by her headlights appeared to turn red. The breath was sucked out of her lungs as the sky exploded. Further tightening her death grip on the steering wheel and her rosary beads, she slammed the brakes and started a power-slide. For that split second, she froze with the fear that her silver sedan would careen off the bridge. Edith thought her heart was going to explode.

And then it did.

Hal Dalton sat up on his gurney in the emergency room as a deep hum rattled the walls. He reacted by saying, "Edith?" He saw three nurses collapse hard to the floor as he leaned his head over the side to vomit on the floor. The last thing he saw was his tongue fall out of his mouth as his head approached the ground, yet his lower body remained on the gurney.

In the backyard of a lagoon house in Forked River, an Alaskan Husky awoke. Leaving behind the bunched up blanket he used as a bed, he stepped out of his doghouse. He sniffed the cold air and looked up. His bright blue eyes were met by blinding red and he turned away. The canine yelped once, and tried to again, but his windpipe seemed to have collapsed. As he dropped, his last sight was of his hindquarter spreading across the ground in a hairy mound.

December 27, 2044
Tuesday, 9:00 AM
New Jersey coast
The morning after the event

Kid and Jess drove away from the beach and nothing seemed unusual, until they reached the Tunney Bridge heading over to the mainland. They squeezed past a barricade that had been placed between two olive green Hummers, blocking all but one lane. No military personnel were anywhere to be found.

"I still don't know why the military was guarding the bridge," Jess said as he drove between the Hummers.

They crossed the arch of the bridge and Jess stood on the brakes as they encountered a silver sedan stopped sideways in the middle of the road. There were only three other cars in sight, but they had all come to rest in awkward positions.

"The road is still not plowed, at this hour?" Kid asked with ever-growing apprehension. The street way up ahead was covered with fresh snow. From their vantage point at the top of the bridge, it appeared that the snow accumulation increased noticeably going west.

Jess pulled close enough to see that the silver sedan was occupied, but the driver was a mound of flesh and bones, just like the convenience store clerk. The melted remains were spread across the front seat of the car. Several bones from the driver's severed hand were still affixed to the steering wheel, as if clinging for dear life. Something was dangling from the bony fingers.

"Are those... rosary beads?" Kid was horrified, but couldn't break his stare.

Hitting the gas and speeding away, Jess weaved in and out of the other stopped cars.

Kid turned on the truck radio and heard nothing but static all across the dial. As if painfully crying out, the speakers hissed as he continued to change stations. "This is not a good sign." He tried all of the New York and Philadelphia stations. "Nothing on the air in the whole tri-state area."

They drove west on Route 37 through the town of Toms River and came upon their local hospital. "Wait!" Kid pointed. "Turn there."

Jess cut the wheel and the truck slid through the intersection. He pulled under the covered Emergency Room entrance, which abutted a multi-story parking garage.

"If you can't find help at a hospital, where can you find it?" Kid reasoned as he got out.

Running to the door, Kid had to dodge the carcasses of many dead pigeons on the ground. He remembered seeing them roosting in the rafters of the parking garage every time he had been there before.

Although it was usually the busiest part of the hospital, the Emergency Room was still and quiet. Just inside the door, human puddles were visible in the dim emergency lighting. Formerly white nurse uniforms were discernible in three mounds of human remains. A gurney held half of the remains of a patient, as the other half had oozed down onto the floor.

"Help! Anyone here?" Jess yelled, desperately. "Help!"

Silence.

"This is bad. Worse than bad. Come on." Kid turned and ran back to the truck on legs that felt like rubber bands. "I guess we should go by your house first?" he suggested as they climbed in.

"Why mine?" Jess snapped. "Most of you live in the same town as I do," he said, referring to their hometown ten miles to the south.

"We'll go by all of our houses, but yours is the closest. I don't care what order we hit them."

Jess exhaled. "We can go by my house first. I'm just sick thinking about it."

Pulling up the street where he lived in the town of Forked River, Jess could no longer hide his nervousness. In front of his house, the truck came to a sliding halt. "Let me go in," Kid insisted.

After putting his head against the steering wheel for a moment, Jess conceded. "Go in through the back door."

Kid walked to the back of the house and opened the gate. He was waiting for Jess's Alaskan Husky to come running and snarl at him, as he always did. This time, he was met with silence. He stepped into the backyard and winced as he spotted the hairy remains of Jess's dog in front of his doghouse. As a formality, he opened the back door of the house and was again assaulted by the same foul smell of death. He couldn't shut the door and get out of there fast enough. Slowing his pace as he walked up to the truck, Kid tried to regain his poise as he opened the door.

Jess was looking straight ahead at the road.

Clearing his throat, Kid climbed in and said quietly, "Sorry, Jess, but I think we're going to find the same at all of our houses. Let's go."

Jess put the pedal to the floor and sped up the street. He stared straight ahead and his face twitched as he fought back tears. The truck slid and fishtailed in the snow going around the corner. Driving past Brian's house, Cathy's and then the Norris's, Kid and Jess never even got out of the truck. There were no signs of life anywhere. The same was true when driving up the street to Maria's house.

After passing Maria's small Cape Cod, Jess said, "Hold on a minute." He put the truck in reverse and stopped in front of her driveway.

"What are you doing?" Kid asked.

"I am going to bust into her house." He grabbed a crowbar. "I just have to hold my nose and get her two diabetes medications from the kitchen counter where she always leaves them. The first time she feels faint, she will thank me for thinking of it."

A few minutes later, Jess returned with the medications in his hand, and a grimace on his face.

"Are you alright, Jess?"

"Yeah, and I didn't see anything or even breathe out my nose, but I felt it everywhere."

"Felt what?"

"Death."

They stopped in front of Kid's house and both stared straight ahead in silence. For several minutes they waited. Kid knew his mom would've opened the door by now, and asked them what they were doing parked outside. This time, his front door stayed eerily still. He knew he was delaying the inevitable, but he reflected as he looked around at the houses of the old neighborhood kids. In his pre-teen days he was pushed around and excluded from most neighborhood sports and activities because he was a few years younger than most of the kids on the block. Finally, as he hit his teenage years, he started fighting back, both verbally and physically when he had to. Although he didn't always win the fight, the other kids came to respect him. From that time forward, he vowed to confront his fears head on, and never let them keep him down. But he had never felt the degree of fear he felt right now. He forced himself to open the truck door. "I'll be back."

Jess grabbed his arm. "Wait, are you sure you want to do this?"

"No, I don't want to, but I am going to."

"Do you want me to go?"

"I appreciate the offer, but I got it Jess."

Walking up to his front door, Kid heard something crunch under his foot. He used his shoe to brush away the layer of snow, and stared down at the carcass of a small black bird. Taking another step, he heard the same sound. Shuffling his feet as he moved forward, he kicked aside what seemed to be an entire flock of dead birds.

Reaching his front door, he slid his key in the lock and turned the knob. He stepped inside the foyer and forced himself to inhale through his nose. He dropped to his knees as bile rose in his throat. The smell was overwhelming. Struggling to his feet, he closed the front door, jogged to the truck and got back in. Kid knew his expression told Jess all he needed to know.

"Same?" Jess mumbled, seeming unsure of what to say.

"Same," he echoed somberly.

"What the hell is going on around here?" Jess started up the road. "Where else can we go?"

"Sara's. I know it is a haul, but maybe things are different a little further west." He tried to sound optimistic, but faltered.

CHAPTER 5

December 26, 2044
Monday, 11:00 PM
Joint Base McGuire–Dix–Lakehurst
(Fort Dix Army Base), New Jersey
The moment of the event

In a guard booth at the gate of the Fort Dix Army Base, Tom Murphy sat in a raised chair, rubbing his beer belly. As usual, after being starved for so long he had eaten too much for dinner during his 10:00 p.m. break. His wife was going to be angry with him. With the new diet he was supposed to be following, his belly should have been flattening, not expanding.

But even bloated, he was excited and couldn't wait for tomorrow night. He was taking his grandson, Nicky, to see the Philadelphia Flyers hockey game. After being estranged for three years, Tom and his daughter had finally made amends. He missed his child, but more than that, he missed his only grandson. He had no choice but to forgive his daughter because he would never see, let alone be part of, Nicky's milestones and life events—one of them being his first professional hockey game. Tom was thrilled to be the one who was going to make it happen.

Without warning, the sky turned a blinding red. He felt violently ill and fell to the floor as he tried to escape the small booth. Despite his torn rotator cuff, he raised his hand to grab the doorknob and mumbled, "Sorry Nicky." He fell on his back and a few seconds later, his protruding stomach deflated like a popped beach ball as his flesh spread across the floor.

"This isn't a quick ride anymore," Jess noted as they drove 40 miles per hour west on the unplowed Route 530.

"No, but with the news we have to bring, are you in a rush to get back?" Kid settled back into his seat.

The truck bounced up and down violently and Jess slammed the brakes. The vehicle slid sideways in the snow as he fought to keep it on the road. After fishtailing a couple of times, he coasted to a stop and turned to Kid. "Now what did we hit?"

"I'm afraid to look," Kid said as he opened the door.

Walking in the snow, which had been shredded by the swerving vehicle, the guys both stopped dead in their tracks upon seeing the carnage. It appeared that a whole family of deer had been crossing the road when the destruction came. Through the few inches of snow, Kid counted four separate ribcages of varying sizes. A smaller one had been partially crushed when it was run over by the vehicle. Over the next few minutes, the guys went through the disgusting and painstaking exercise of dragging the dead carcasses off of the road.

"That is just nasty," Kid noted while washing his hands with virgin snow.

"I know, but at least we won't have to worry about hitting them on the way back," Jess responded.

They jumped back in the truck and 20 minutes later they reached one of Fort Dix's guard posts. It appeared deserted.

"Possible problem. What if there isn't any power?" Kid said as he spotted the heavy security gates, which were eight-foot high with razor mesh and rolls of electrified razor wire on top. A guard booth straddled both sides of the fence marking the entryway.

"It's a military base. If anyone would have backup power in case of an emergency, it would be them. Look!" Jess pointed. "The guard house light is on."

Kid jumped out of the truck and used a crowbar to pry open the door to the booth. As it popped open, a human puddle started oozing out. Repulsed, he coached himself to only breathe in and out of his mouth so the smell would not register. He stepped over the carnage and examined the rest of the booth. Below the window was a control board. He simultaneously hit a button on top while pressing another one hidden underneath the counter top. The security gates opened.

"How did you know to do that?" Jess asked as Kid jumped back in.

"Hit two buttons simultaneously? I came through here all the time with Sara, and the guard's face would always cringe as he reached for the button under the counter while hitting the button right in front of him. He must've had a bad shoulder or something."

At General Hyland's living quarters, a quaint boxy ranch, Kid stepped out of the vehicle.

"Every time I come here I think the same thing. You would think a general's house would be more... dramatic," Jess commented as he held out the crowbar they had been using to open doors.

"I don't know if he had choices, but Sara's father wasn't really into *dramatic* anyway." Kid waved off the crowbar and held up his keys.

"He actually let you have a key to his house? I'm surprised."

"Why wouldn't he?"

"Nothing against you. It's just that Mr. Hyland didn't seem like the trusting type."

"Not by nature, no. But it wasn't an issue after he got to know me well enough." Kid was quick to ascertain that trust meant everything in the Hyland house. It took him some time to earn Sara's trust, and longer still for him to earn her father's. Finally, last month over the Thanksgiving holiday, the general had asked him to stay at the house with Sara for a few days since he had to leave on urgent military business. With pride born of the general's trust in him, he shook her father's hand and said, "It would be my honor."

While gripping his hand, the general had pulled Kid closer and peered at him. "You sleep in separate beds. Got it?" The general had a way about him. It was the eyes. He could see right through people.

"Oh Dad, stop," Sara had chimed in.

"Got it," Kid had answered, and he made sure they did, at least when they were actually sleeping.

Inserting the key, Kid turned the knob of the front door. "Mr. Hyland?" he called out. No answer. No smell, yet. A laptop computer bag was sitting in the middle of the dining room table, so he figured that the general must have been home when it hit. As he headed through the living room, he passed the picture of Sara and the general at the fifth grade father-daughter dance.

Walking up the hall, he stopped and pushed open Sara's door. His eyes adjusted to the dim light and he spotted the familiar and mesmerizing mural that Sara had painted on the wall behind her bed. He saw the woman standing on a dock, facing a full moon, and he swore he could simply step into the scene and enter another world. Every time he saw it he marveled. He had encouraged Sara to present her mural because he was convinced it would win awards, but she chose to keep the work, and its meaning, to herself.

Pulling the door shut, he continued up the hall and stopped to look at the large, framed picture of Sara's mother's tombstone in Georgia. It was too dark to see it clearly, but the large decorative rose adorning the top half of the slab was unmistakable. When Kid first came over, he had found it odd, if not downright macabre, to have such a picture on the wall. But Sara explained that when they moved to New Jersey, her father said he needed his wife's grave close by since he could not visit it every week as he was accustomed to doing in Georgia.

He approached the door to the master bedroom and pushed it open, waiting for a wave of stench to hit him. To his surprise there was no smell, and no human remains.

Sara's house was empty.

On the drive back to Old Man Drexer's beach shack, Kid stared out the window and watched the trees race by. The snow clinging to the branches left a white visual trail. As they reached more populated areas, many of the houses sported holiday decorations. With the snow cover, the ambiance would've usually been one of joy and good spirit, but in the shadow of doom the houses seemed as dead as their darkened holiday lights. With every home and business that passed by, the stillness became more and more disturbing. He felt like death was watching them from every window.

Closing his eyes, Kid thought of his family. He tried to subdue the emotions swelling within him, but the onset of grief was sudden and ferocious. He fought not to visualize individual family members as tears rolled down his cheeks. He wiped them away and shook his head. For the sake of helping the others deal, he would have to find strength. Like blood from a stone, he would squeeze himself. "We'll have to tell everybody as soon as we get back. No false hopes," Kid said solemnly. He tried to mentally prepare for the breakdown that would invariably follow.

"We have to find out what happened here, and see how far this went. We have to keep driving until we find some other people. If we can't find them here, we'll go to another state, or another country. We should start by driving over to Pennsylvania or New York," Jess suggested.

"The rest of the day is going to be brutal, so tonight we should just stay at Old Man Drexer's. Then we can take a road trip tomorrow." Although he didn't say it, Kid doubted things would be any different in Pennsylvania, New York, or even Vermont where Karen had encountered the same strange red light from the sky.

They arrived at the shack and parked. Kid trudged up the splintered wooden steps and took a deep breath. He reached out, but before he could grab the knob, the door swung open.

Heidi erupted. "A quick ride? Where the hell did you go? You've been gone over three hours!" Kid and Jess entered with their heads down. "Is everything alright or what?" she continued with her heavy Brooklyn accent as she slammed the door behind them.

"No, everything is not alright. Everyone in the area has… perished," Kid said, trying to keep his voice steady.

"Perished?" Maria stood up. "As in…"

"Dead. Except for us, everyone in the area is dead."

Maria stared at them in shock, with her hand over her mouth. "That can't be. Did you check…"

"We went by all of our houses, except Heidi's since she lives in Long Island," he added.

Kid and Jess told them about everything they had seen, notably the horrible mounds of flesh and bone.

"That's disgusting. I'm getting sick just thinking about it." Maria cringed as tears started running down her face. Jess took her in his arms.

Mark Norris ran out the door, leaned over the railing, and vomited.

"Maybe New York is fine…" Heidi started.

"There is not a single New York radio station still on the air. Everything, everywhere is just… dead," Kid added.

"I want to go there and see for myself!" she snapped bitterly. She sat on the floor and hugged her knees.

"Wait, this afternoon I'm helping my Dad pick up some furniture…" Brian said as reality came crashing through.

Needing every last ounce of strength, Kid tended to his own fragile facade of strength and composure. Sara buried her head into his chest, and his heart broke with every convulsive heave of her teary outpouring. He wished he could take away her sorrow, even though he was drowning in his own already. Kid didn't want to mention that Sara's house was empty and give her any false hope. Her father, General Eric Hyland, must have been at the base headquarters when the destruction came.

The next few hours were a time of solitude and silence, with each person dealing with the tragedy in his or her own way. The couples spent much of the time just holding each other, letting the tears fall, but not saying many words. Mike Norris had his arm around the shoulder of his doubled-over brother. Brian's vision finally returned as he continued to wipe his watery eyes. Kid grappled with waves of grief and shock, but also the need for answers. *Who did this, and why did they do it?*

Maria whispered, "Uh-oh. I'm shaking like a leaf, and I don't have my medications."

"Yes you do." Jess handed her the two diabetes medications he had secured from her house.

She took them and kissed his cheek. "Oh, thank God."

Heidi jumped to her feet and blurted out, "Can someone tell me what the hell happened last night?"

"Everything points to neutron beams," Sara concluded as she sat on the plaid couch. "But we survived. That weapon system was supposed to be foolproof, with no chance of survival, zero,"

"That weapon system was the modern equivalent of the old neutron bomb, right? It destroys people but not structures?" Kid sat down next to her.

"Yes."

He shook his head, bewildered. "Well, that's pretty much what we saw out there."

She muttered, "If this was a neutron beam attack, then Professor Cofflin was right."

"Who is Professor Cofflin? And right about what?" he asked.

Sighing, she said, "He was the man who invented that weapon. And he had nothing but fear and regrets from the start."

"How would you know that?" Heidi cut in.

Sara went to speak, but paused. The words seemed to get stuck in her throat. Sighing, she took a deep breath. "Because I was there the day he gave his plans to the military to develop it."

November 6, 2043
Friday, Midday
Boston, Massachusetts
A little over a year before the event

As Professor Cofflin was summarizing lab results and concluding three months of quantum chemistry research in Boston, his stomach would not be settled or quieted. It dawned on him that in his haste to get to the lab that morning, he never made his usual two eggs for breakfast. When he was in his twenties, his body never would have minded. Now in his late forties, missing a morning meal could wreak havoc on his stamina all day.

Despite being in the final day of a project and being pressed for time, he stopped by the university's staff cafeteria. Someone had left a science publication on the table so he flipped through it while eating his turkey sandwich. If he appeared busy he might be left alone. Turning a page, an article piqued his interest and he started reading. It described in detail the chemical reaction when detonating a neutron bomb. The purpose of that type of explosive device was to bombard an area with just enough neutrons to destroy living beings, but not enough to damage structures. The article described the most recent neutron accelerators.

While his mind processed the information, he peered up at the video screen which ran a news channel all day. The reporter presented a teaser about an upcoming story exposing the exorbitant cost of deploying military satellite weapons with modern laser beam technology. She closed by indicating that the only thing being zapped by lasers were the dollars in the wallets of the taxpayers.

With the mention of lasers, his thoughts turned to a laser distribution model he had worked on several years ago. The design of that particular model allowed for different elements to be funneled as a core, surrounded and enclosed by laser beams, to an exact target. Glancing down at the article about the neutron bomb, he pondered, *What if neutrons comprised the core within the laser beams?* The lethal neutrons could be distributed within a barrel made of laser beams and could quickly, yet repeatedly, be swept over land areas, like coloring in a shape on a piece of paper with a pencil. The effect would be the same as a neutron bomb, but with pinpoint accuracy. All the while, the beams would sweep so fast that there wouldn't be any structural damage from the lasers or from too much neutron saturation. The problem was finding a viable, and realistic system of deployment. The laser beams would have to come from above…

He looked up as the reporter covered the full story she had teased earlier.

"In just one year, all 48 satellites comprising the United States Global Positioning System have now been replaced with laser-equipped satellites ten times the size, yet 100 times the cost…"

The sandwich dropped from the professor's hand. It was as if the reporter was speaking directly to him.

"Of course, the GPS satellites!" he said and ran out of the lunchroom.

He pleaded with his superiors for more lab time and explained what he was trying to conceive. Since they had no funding for additional research, they reached out to the United States Department of Defense to see if there was any interest in sponsoring such an experiment. Late afternoon, they received a call from United States secretary of defense himself. Not only was there interest, a contingent of high-ranking military officers was being sent to Boston the very next day. With the pressure on, the professor spent all night developing a satellite laser neutron beam design.

The next day Professor Cofflin found himself surrounded by high-ranking military personnel, including three army generals. After being offered a research team-leader position, including relocation costs, the professor had agreed to provide the United States Department of Defense with his satellite laser neutron beam design. Needing time to copy and assemble the information, he said he would provide it by no later than 9:00 p.m. that evening. Time was of the essence since an emergent meeting had just been scheduled at the Joint Base McGuire–Dix–Lakehurst in New Jersey for 10:00 a.m. the next morning with the three generals and the United States secretary of defense.

Based on the interactions throughout the day he could already surmise how the meeting would go tomorrow. Two of the three army generals favored developing the satellite neutron beam weapon.

At 9:00 p.m., the professor provided copies of all of his documents and files to each of the officers. Two of the generals left as soon as they had the information in hand.

The third, General Eric Hyland, was still waiting for his ride. He had called his daughter, Sara, three and a half hours earlier and asked her to come down from Vermont and pick him up. He had noted that she was heading back to New Jersey anyway, so with his meeting scheduled for early the next morning, Sara would just have to leave a bit sooner than she planned. General Hyland described his daughter's reaction to leaving early as, 'less than pleased, to say the least,' because she had just met a guy she was interested in.

Sara arrived in Boston an hour later than expected. Professor Cofflin stood at a window and watched the general affectionately hug his young and vibrant daughter. Even from a distance, he felt the love between them. Watching them, the professor's stomach became unsettled again, and this time not from missing a meal. It was a sudden and momentary realization, but once he had it, he knew it would consume him. It was like the adage about not being able to unsee something once it has been seen. He had not considered the potential risk of his satellite laser neutron beam design to humanity; the impact on real people, and not just variables in an equation.

The professor found himself second guessing whether he should have turned over the weapon plans. Like so many scientists before him, he might succeed in the name of science, but fail in the name of humanity. That night he had the nightmare for the first time. It would not be the last.

After the United States secretary of defense met with the generals the next day, and given that two of the three supported it, he decided to proceed with developing the weapon. Within a week the military had moved Professor Cofflin to the Joint Base McGuire–Dix–Lakehurst, and specifically the Fort Dix Army Base, in New Jersey. A research laboratory with the highest security level was established for the satellite laser neutron beam project.

A weapon was developed in earnest using the professor's plan and designs, which started with a series of laser beams, emitted from the GPS satellites in a circular pattern, resembling the barrel of a gun. When initiated, specific elements were fired down through the beam enclosure. The proliferation of neutrons from an accelerator, coupled with the addition of the mysterious red mercury, transformed the shot into a fast-moving stream of neutrons. The laser beams surrounding this lethal mixture served as a strong and accurate barrel that would, in essence, sweep the neutrons repeatedly over a designated area—just as the professor had envisioned. Maybe most innovative, and deadly, was that the neutrons were delivered in a way that allowed them to pass through solid surfaces and structures, including wood, concrete, brick, water, and even steel. There was no way to escape them.

The professor stayed for the duration of the project, but his remaining days were spent trying to convince everyone that the weapon could never be used, so it should not be built in the first place. The risk would be too great. In the wrong hands, the weapon could extinguish the entire human race in the blink of an eye.

Despite the professor's protests, by the fall of 2044, all 48 GPS satellites were modified in space by the United States at great cost, but this time to include the laser neutron beam system.

The day in October 2044 when the military celebrated going live with the weapon system, Professor Cofflin choose to mark the event by sitting alone in his vehicle inside a dark parking garage. He remembered the moment in Boston when his fears were born, and with the death warrant for the human race now signed, those fears would now be realized.

"What have I done," he whispered with his voice shaking as he held a cyanide pill in his hand. Swallowing the pill, he washed it down with a swig of water and laid back against the headrest. He could not make peace with this world so he was leaving for the next, and he wanted to stay ahead of the masses who would be close behind. And he could finally escape the recurring gruesome nightmare that now haunted more than just his sleep.

The beach sand turns nearly obsidian under a looming shadow as Professor Cofflin sprints for his life. The roar and rumble behind are closing in. And no matter how fast he moves, he is never able to outrun a viscous, red tidal wave that churns body parts, bones, and entrails. Clearly discernible, but trapped in the gory sludge are General Hyland and his daughter Sara in an embrace. And then the giant wave crests and sucks him under.

CHAPTER 6

December 27, 2044
Tuesday, Midday
New Jersey coast
The day after the event

Sara further clarified for Heidi, "A little more than a year ago, a military contingent was sent up to Boston to meet with Professor Cofflin after he conceived something the military was interested in. My father was one of the officers that went. That same day I happened to be in Vermont, so my dad asked me to pick him up in Boston. I wasn't eavesdropping, but before we left I overheard the professor beating himself up for handing over the plans for that neutron beam weapon system."

Kid turned. "Boston? Wait, when was that?"

"Two Novembers ago. November 7, 2043 to be exact." She gazed at him expectantly. "Ring any bells?"

"The day we met," he responded without hesitation.

Brian paced around inside the shack until he exclaimed, "It can't be a coincidence that this neutron beam... attack, or whatever it is, happened a week after that Utopia Project was discovered."

"How could a discovery like that lead to an attack?" Jess asked. "It's not like they were building some crazy weaponry, or an army of terminator robots or something like that were they?"

"No, but maybe they initiated an attack because they were feeling the heat, and were afraid that their project was going to be shut down,"

Brian offered. With nobody responding, he continued, "But even if it was being shut down, would that lead to an attack? I mean, last night we were talking about that CCP project from 2025—that was shut down after public pressure, and they didn't turn around and attack anything."

Sara got up and tended to the fire in the wood stove.

Kid again noticed her discomfort with the topic, just like the night before. After giving her a few moments alone, he came over and sat on the floor next to her. He gave her some more time before finally saying, "Can I ask you a question?"

"Sure, Kid. What is it?"

"You seem really uncomfortable whenever someone mentions that old CCP project," he said. Sara turned her eyes down. Kid knew he was spot on but didn't know if she wanted to talk about it.

She exhaled. "You noticed?"

"Of course. How couldn't I?"

"Let's just say I will forever have a connection to that horrible project," she said.

Kid remained silent. She would talk when and if she was ready.

While slowly spinning a poker in her hand, she finally asked, "Do you remember what led to the CCP being shut down?"

"I was no ace in history, but I should at least know that." He thought for a second. "An army wife, named Anna Delilah, fell off of a window ledge trying to get her kid and escape the CCP project. Her death became the rallying cry for the protesters who started the Civil Crisis of 2025. They marched on Washington and got the president to stop the CCP."

"Exactly right. And Delilah's kid became the infamous Baby Doe."

"The baby they were forever trying to find, and couldn't," he recalled. He wondered where this was going.

Sara turned to him. "I know I've mentioned that I was born at the Eisenhower Army Medical Center in Georgia, but what I've never told anyone is that it was the same hospital, and even the same floor, as the CCP's Baby Doe, just ten days after Anna Delilah gave birth."

"Are you serious?" His eyes were open wide.

"Yes. Actually, my dad told me that I slept in the same bassinet that held Baby Doe. He had already been promoted to major in the Army at that time, and I would have been taken into that CCP program, but it was cancelled just days before I was born. He said my mother was so adamantly opposed to that awful project that if it hadn't been cancelled, she was going to fight them tooth and nail and was not going to give me up."

"Why was she so against it?"

"Remember what CCP stands for: Child Conditioning Program. They were taking the babies of military mothers for the first three months of life so the child could be 'socially conditioned,' aka, brainwashed while their brains were just developing so that they would behave a certain way for the rest of their lives. My mother told my dad that her baby was not going to be one of 'Pavlov's dogs.' She was having no part of it."

Sara's revelation brought a deep silence, until Kid noted, "I never knew that you had such a close connection to one of the historic events in our lifetime. No wonder the topic makes you uncomfortable."

"Nobody really knew. I've never shared that with anyone. But if you think the topic makes *me* uncomfortable, you should have seen my dad. It was really weighing on him, especially over the last week with the press regurgitating it so much. I know it bothered him a lot, because he was writing like mad in his diary."

"The hauntings continue." His reference to an inside joke was automatic, but he wasn't trying to be funny at that moment.

"With a vengeance." After a momentary pause, she asked while poking a log in the open door of the wood stove, "You know what was most sad?"

"What?"

"After having kids, most parents rehash stories over and over about the day their child was born, and talk about how amazed and proud they were, especially with their first child. But my dad could never talk about the day I was born."

"Why not?" Kid knew he made a mistake the second he posed the question. He already knew the answer.

She said somberly, "Because he could never reflect on the day I was born without being haunted by how that day ended with mom passing away."

Not wanting to stick his foot in his mouth again, Kid was silent as he watched her chip away at a log with a bronze-topped poker.

"Every time I saw an article, or heard a newscaster mention anything about the CCP, it was a reminder of losing my mom, and of growing up without a mother. It always hit home. I went through that when the Civil Crisis of 2025 was covered in my history class in school. It bothered me so much that I spent half of the class period in the bathroom."

"That's awful. And it really is, or was, all over the news in the last week. You couldn't avoid it," he added as he pulled her close. He again wished he could take away her pain as his protectiveness kicked in. Sara leaned into him and latched onto his arm.

Jess stood up in Old Man Drexer's living room and announced, "We need to go look for other survivors. I refuse to believe we are the only ones. We just need to travel further than the first run me and Kid made."

Maria nodded. "I agree, but can we eat some real food first? I took my meds but I'm still feeling weak and from what you guys said you saw out there, it may be a long trip."

"Alright," Jess agreed. "Before we do anything, me and Kid can quickly hit the nearby supermarket and grab some food."

"Isn't that place closed for the winter?" Mike Norris asked.

"Yes, but I'm sure they still have a decent inventory of nonperishables." *Nonperishables.* Kid was amused by the choice of words. Jess sounded like the supermarket night crew chief he was.

Turning to Sara, Kid kissed her on the head. "Be back soon." He turned. "Are we driving over Jess?"

"I was thinking we could walk. It's pretty close, and honestly I could use the fresh air. I've felt queasy ever since we saw the guts of that clerk this morning."

"Wait, we're coming too," Mike said as he jumped to his feet.

Chatty Cathy finally spoke and said simply, "I'll stay. Take Mark."

"Come on Mark."

Kid, Jess, and the Norris brothers left the shack and strolled a few blocks west before turning north.

"I don't get it. How are we still alive?" Kid pondered. "Why would they wipe out everything around here except for a small section of the beach?"

"Maybe they just missed the sliver of land along the shore?" Jess suggested.

Kid thought for a moment. "It still doesn't make any sense to me. You heard Sara. That weapon system was supposed to be foolproof, with no chance of survival from an attack."

Mike Norris said off the cuff, "Then obviously they weren't trying to hit us."

They were so immersed in conversation that none of them looked around while walking. Kid stopped short and glanced up at the supermarket façade. "We're already here." He picked up a large rock in the parking lot and hurled it at the door, shattering a large section of the glass. He kicked out the remaining shards, climbed in, and unlocked it. They grabbed two shopping carts and loaded them with canned goods, spring water, soap, paper towels, toilet paper, and assorted other items."

Walking back, Kid and Jess struggled as they pushed full shopping carts along the snowy roadway. The Norris brothers followed behind.

Kid muttered, "I knew we should have driven over."

"Head for boardwalk," Jess said and pointed. "That will get us out of the snow."

On the boardwalk they passed an arcade, and the low whistle of the wind found every crevasse in the building's structure. Kid paused and peered through the window. In the eerie dim light, he could see rows of Skee-Ball lanes and a hockey game encased in a plastic bubble. The games seemed dusty and decaying, as if they had already accepted a fate that he could never bring himself to accept. In a large painting on a near wall, even the seagulls seemed to be wailing in despair, forlorn. Despite the short time in actuality, the inside appeared as if it had not been touched for 50 years. A pang of nostalgic sadness tingled within

Kid when he realized that 50 years from now, if someone was to peer through this same window, they would probably see things exactly as he was seeing them now.

Making their way along the boardwalk, Jess stopped short.

"What is it?" Kid asked.

He pointed and yelled, "Ships!"

Leaving the shopping carts behind, they all ran to the end of Casino Pier and stood next to a little booth tucked away in the corner. Kid gazed out to sea and sure enough, a few miles out were three huge gray ships. There were others alive on the planet, which was an overwhelming relief. "How did we not see three enormous ships approaching?" he muttered aloud, recalling their oblivion as they walked to the supermarket.

"What are they doing down there?" Mark Norris pointed.

Kid turned to see Sara, Maria, Heidi, Cathy and Brian on the beach. The group was far to the south, and were ant-size from such a distance, but he could tell they were waving their hands in the air. The only one not waving was Brian. He was standing still and seemed uncertain. They were so far away that even if Kid yelled they would never hear him. And it was no use trying to get their attention as they were fixated on the ships.

"What is that?" Jess pointed at a white speck in the distance.

After staring for a moment, Kid stated the obvious. "A boat."

The small vessel was motoring toward the shore, and heading for Sara and the others. As it grounded on the beach, seven men jumped out and walked in the direction of the group. Everyone on the beach seemed to freeze with apprehension. The newcomers looked like soldiers as they marched in a militant fashion, all wearing the same gray uniforms. They even seemed to have the same hairstyle. An eighth person walked behind the others, and seemed to be directing them. He had gray hair and appeared to be a much older man.

"What do they have in their hands?" After staring closely, Kid gasped as he realized that they were all holding a weapon.

"I don't know, but we better get down there," Jess replied and went to run off of the pier. He stopped as the older soldier fired a weapon, unprovoked, at Brian from point blank range.

Kid cringed, but there was no concussive blast. Rather it quietly emitted some kind of bright bolt, which caught Brian right in the chest. His friend fell over sideways and appeared to be frozen in the same position as the very second he was shot. Heidi went to run over to him, but one of the soldiers grabbed her and wrestled her into the waiting boat.

From behind the small booth at the end of the pier, the guys watched in horror as the soldiers grabbed Sara, Maria and Cathy and put them in the boat with Heidi. Kid wanted to run down after them, but they would be greatly outnumbered on a wide-open beach, and with the weapons these people were carrying, he thought the better of it. The Norris brothers were frozen in place, but Jess was ready to attack.

"Stay here!" Kid said as he held Jess's arm with a firm grip. "We'd have no chance! It would be a suicide mission!"

"Alright!" Jess snapped and stopped trying to pull away.

They stood at the rail and watched as the older man spoke to four of the soldiers. He seemed to be giving them orders and suddenly, he pointed to the pier. Kid ducked back behind the booth and pulled Jess with him. "Shit, he looked right at us!"

A minute later, Kid peeked around the corner enough to see the boat speeding toward the three large ships. He squinted and was able to discern who the passengers were. "The girls are in the boat, heading out to those ships!" Kid had a sudden chill as he watched the girls being taken away by an obviously hostile group. His heart skipped a beat and his mind took an involuntary snapshot. He hoped it would not be the last time he would ever see any of them alive.

"We need to see which of those three ships they're taking them to," Jess said. "Who is in the boat with them?"

"Some old dude, and three of those… soldiers." It then hit Kid. *Three soldiers? Where are the other four?* He extended his head out further, and gasped as he noticed that the four soldiers left behind were running on the boardwalk and heading toward the pier.

Jess turned to say, "They went to the middle…"

Kid put his hand over his friend's mouth and pulled him to the ground behind the booth at the end of the pier. "Get down," he hissed and waved down the Norris brothers.

The soldiers had made the turn and were now searching the pier.

■ ■ ■

On the middle of the three ships, the girls were escorted by armed soldiers down to the 29th floor. They were separated and directed into their own rooms. Sara and Maria's rooms were next to each other, while Heidi and Cathy were across the hall.

Sara stepped in and turned as the door quickly, but smoothly, slid across and closed behind her. In the top half of the closed door was a large, square piece of glass. While she was looking out, she stepped back as a uniformed soldier sprayed her window with a substance that made the glass frosted, and opaque. Through it, Sara could only see shadows and light, but no details.

Turning back around, she cased out her holding cell. She had a bed, a small round table with four plush chairs, and a large flat screen monitor. Although the monitor was not on, a fluorescent digital clock in the top right corner displayed the time. In the back of the room, not hidden in any way, was a toilet and sink. "The deluxe jail cell," she muttered and sat down in a chair.

Although still alive, Sara did not know what was in store for her. She thought through the possibilities and a full body spasm as chills ran down her spine. *Torture? Abuse? Death?* She jumped up from the chair and started pacing around the room.

CHAPTER 7

December 27, 2044
Tuesday, Late Afternoon
New Jersey coast
The day after the event

L ying down on the pier, Jess's eyes opened wide as Kid whispered, "They're coming this way! We're trapped!"

The pier was long and relatively wide, but Kid knew that with four soldiers searching it would be hard to sneak past them. He raised his head enough to see a young soldier, maybe 18 years old, wearing a gray uniform with a number embroidered on it. The guy had what appeared to be a gun, but based on what Kid had seen hit Brian on the beach, it didn't shoot ordinary bullets. The soldier was only about 50 feet away and the gap was closing.

Mike Norris suddenly jumped to his feet and rushed the closest soldier. Kid remembered that Mike was a four-year starting linebacker on the football team in high school, and the guy could put a serious hit on someone. The soldier crouched and braced. The Norris brother bounced off of the soldier as if he had charged into a telephone pole. Mike grabbed for his shoulder as he hit the ground. The soldier raised his weapon and shot the Norris brother in the chest. Just like Brian on the beach, Mike was instantly frozen. He had an expression of pain and surprise stuck on his face.

"Jesus! Let's get out of here!" Mark Norris uttered. As he bolted, he pulled off his coat and threw it over the soldier's head before the enemy could turn fully around.

Weaving around the rides and booths, it looked like Mark might actually make it off the pier. But then Kid's stomach soured when he realized that the soldiers obviously had a plan. One of the four soldiers had been left at the entrance, to ensure nobody could get behind the other three who were searching. It dawned on him that when the older soldier had directed the soldiers on the beach and pointed to the pier, he had likely laid out this plan.

Mark ducked and a shot whizzed past him. He charged and threw an elbow, which caught the soldier's chin. Kid thought the soldier would crumble, as any human rightfully should, but the enemy seemed unfazed as he lunged and tackled the Norris brother. Mark was drilled in the midsection and lifted like he was a cardboard cut-out, not the 220 pound man he was. The soldier threw him hard to the ground as a second soldier came over and shot Mark in the neck, freezing him. Seemingly unaffected by the taking of lives, the soldiers turned and continued their search.

Seeing no other means of escape, Kid whispered to Jess, "Jump, but its shallow so do a big-time belly flop!"

Jess rolled over the top of the rail and dropped to the water. A sharp splashing sound followed. Peeking around the corner of the booth, Kid watched for a reaction. The soldiers heard the noise and came running toward the end of the pier, weapons aimed forward.

Kid took a running headfirst leap over the rail. As he flew through the air, a bolt flashed by his hand, barely missing him. Although trying to belly flop, his outstretched arms swiftly touched bottom. He knew by the force of the impact that the partial belly flop likely saved him from a broken neck. As soon as his head emerged from the icy Atlantic, he could hear Jess yelling, "Come on Kid!"

He came ashore and sprinted with heavy clothes. From the pier above, they could hear the hurried footsteps of running soldiers. Kid didn't know if they should make a break for it to the north or south side of the pier, so they went further underneath and hid behind pilings. While they were watching the steps down to the beach, waiting for the soldiers to come down, he said, "If they split up and come down both sides, we split up too."

A second later they heard a splash. They turned to each other in scared bewilderment, and then peered behind at the shallow surf. Between the rows of pilings, they saw two more soldiers hit the water. The first soldier had surfaced, and was holding his grotesquely fractured arm. "What are they doing?" Kid stared in disbelief.

As the fourth and final soldier plunged into the ocean, his arms didn't break his fall. His head hit the bottom hard and fast, and the rest of his body went limp, like a rag-doll. Face down in the water the soldier couldn't help himself. His three comrades ignored him and kept up the pursuit.

Grabbing Kid's arm, Jess ran out from under the pier. Reaching the boardwalk, they sprinted across the street and up the block. Kid turned to see two drenched soldiers running after them with blazing, and nearly superhuman, speed. A third soldier followed behind, struggling to keep up as he cradled his arm.

"Where are we going?" Kid panted as they ran.

"Supermarket," Jess responded.

As they went to turn the corner of the next block, Kid glanced over his shoulder to see all three soldiers still a block behind, but gaining ground. "Damn they're fast. Hurry!" he panted as he pushed himself to his limits trying to keep up with Jess. A couple of bright bolts zipped right past him as he turned the corner.

After they ran for two more blocks, they came upon the supermarket. While ducking in through the busted out section of the glass door, the soldiers unleashed a volley of weapon-fire. Bolts hit the top half of the door and adjacent glass windows.

Inside the store, Jess turned up the Non-Food Aisle. "Look for anything that could serve as a weapon!"

Each picked up a heavy wooden rolling pin. "We need to get out of sight," Kid said as he cleared an opening and climbed onto the top shelf of the aisle before lining up a row of furniture polish cans in front of his body. With the sound of faraway footsteps, he knew the soldiers were now inside the store. Jess climbed onto the top shelf across the aisle. Although moving slow as he lay behind rolls of paper towels, the shelves creaked in protest. Any hope that the soldiers might miss it were trampled by the sound of an approaching stampede.

Kid's chest started pounding so hard that he could actually hear his own heartbeat as the first one came around the corner. The enemy was in striking distance of Jess on the other side of the aisle, so as a decoy, Kid made a sound. "Psst!"

The soldier stopped and turned with his weapon raised. Jess sat up and swung the rolling pin like a baseball bat. He connected with the back of the soldier's head, knocking him unconscious. With a weapon now on the floor, Jess swung his legs over the edge of the shelf to jump down when a second one came around the corner. The soldier snapped around toward him.

Even quicker, Kid lunged. The rolling pin didn't hit square and skimmed off of the soldier's head, but the force was enough to make him crumble to the ground. Kid had almost fallen off the shelf, but even more disconcerting to him, the rolling pin had slipped out of his hand. He adjusted the row of furniture polish cans in front of his body and looked around for any object he could use as a weapon.

Across the aisle, on the shelf below Jess, he saw a product that caught his attention. "Psst," he whispered. Jess sat up, so Kid pointed and waved his hand. Moving some paper towel packages out of his way, Jess leaned down and grabbed a long-nosed candle lighter. As he sat back up straight, the top shelf again creaked.

They heard quickening footsteps coming their way.

With a flick of his wrist, Jess whipped the candle lighter over and moved paper towel eight-packs back in front of his body. Kid caught the perfect throw and opened the package as he laid down. Pushing a slide button all the way up, he hoped he was maximizing the butane output and not minimizing it. He waited breathlessly as the footsteps became louder, and then stopped.

Through the gap between the cans, he could see the back of the last soldier's head. The enemy was staring down at his comrades on the floor and was slowly backing up, but Kid no longer had anything to hit him with. Grabbing one of the furniture polish cans, he put it between his thighs and quietly removed the cap. He returned the cap-less can to the shelf while keeping his finger on the nozzle. His other hand held the lighter, the tip of which he snaked through until it hovered in front of the can. The back of the soldier's head was coming ever closer.

Come on, first try, he pleaded, knowing he may not get a second chance. He hit the igniter button.

"Click."

Nothing.

Upon hearing a noise only inches from his head, the soldier swung around and raised his weapon.

Kid could see eternal darkness down the weapon's barrel, and felt himself being sucked in.

■　　■　　■

After sitting restlessly on the ship for nearly an hour, Sara's ears began to discern something peculiar within the low-level white noise. *Is that a voice?* Glancing around her room, she noticed two tiny speakers mounted on the walls. Switching chairs to get closer, she strained to listen. She was putting her ear closer to the speaker when three uniformed people walked in.

She had spent her time trying to convince herself that if they had wanted to harm her, they would've already. The cold look on these three faces gave her little reassurance. She sat up straight as every muscle in her body tightened.

The first was a Caucasian man and he had a neatly embroidered 'Elder-12' on his uniform. The second, Elder-76 appeared to be an Indian woman, with dark skin and long white hair. The third, Elder-1, was also a Caucasian and was the old man who captured them on the beach and shot their friend. She right away despised him for his actions and sensed that he was evil to the core. Brian wasn't a threat to this guy. Brian wasn't a threat to anybody.

Elder-12 and Elder-76 sat, but Elder-1 continued standing and spoke. "So long as we have your full cooperation, and believe you have the right...potential, you will not be harmed."

Sara gazed at his hardened face, hoping to find a trace of compassion. She found none. His eyes were as black as polished obsidian, and his hair gray and thinning. He had a squared off chin and drawn in cheeks. His voice was monotone and not a word out of his mouth carried even the slightest emotion. She knew he was American, and recognized him, but could not place his name.

"Anything less, and you will be eliminated, killed, without hesitation," he warned. "We are Elder-1, the leader of the group on these ships- the Utopia Project. We are here to make a preliminary evaluation of your future potential, as we have just done with your comrades. With the last one, we could see right off that she did not have any, so she was eliminated on the spot."

Sara inhaled sharply, and felt queasy. *One of the other girls is dead?*

He continued, "Everyone from the old world was supposed to die so our new world would be pure upon its rebirth. And last night, with a well-planned neutron beam attack..."

It was a neutron beam attack! But which girl did they kill?

"...we accomplished just that...almost. 99.9% of the human population was eliminated, but it seems that due to an unlikely weapon system malfunction, this beach area was left unscathed."

Such a malfunction struck Sara as odd. Her father had said that the system was so foolproof that it was 'impossible' to survive a neutron beam attack. Then the words sunk in. *Everyone from the old word was supposed to die...we accomplished just that? 99.9%?* She could not wrap her mind around it. "Everyone died?" she muttered.

"You are only to speak if we ask you a question!" he snapped. Turning to his comrades, he said, "Do we have another one who lacks the right potential?"

Sara jumped. "I am sorry, Sir. My apologies."

Elder-1 stared at her for a moment, the longest moment of her life. *Oh God, I am going to be killed right now.*

To her relief, he opened his mouth rather than reaching for his weapon. But his words were disconcerting enough.

"Here, there is no I," he said as he pointed his finger at the corner of his pupil. "You will refer to yourself as, 'we', one of the collective. Consider this your first and only warning."

She swallowed hard and nodded. *She was still alive, but for how long?*

"Anyway, there should not be any human survivors, anywhere, yet as we can see…" he held his hands up and paused, "…some humans did survive."

But the rest of the world is dead? She had to be misunderstanding his words.

"You four, now three, females were not eliminated because our production of offspring is currently behind schedule and has been quite… disappointing," he paused and glared disapprovingly at Elder-12. His fellow elder turned his head.

Production of offspring? He referred to children as if they were commodities. And as a female, was Sara being kept alive just to have children?

"So you can be useful, but will have to be conditioned." Elder-1 stopped and turned to Sara. "Do you know how many others survived besides you and your comrades on the beach?"

Unable to subdue her rising panic, she turned her eyes down. As hard as she tried, she could not stop thinking about Kid and Jess. She chose her words carefully and avoided referring to herself in the first person. "Well, Sir…we cannot tell, since we do not know how large the beach area in question is." Her voice had a slight tremble and her answer did not sound convincing.

"We left four of our members to search every nook and cranny of the affected area. They have been ordered to find survivors, and then hunt them down step for step and kill them. They have incredible physical strength and endurance, highly advanced weaponry and they never give up until they have carried out their orders. You can be assured, if there are survivors we will find them and kill them." He turned. "We will ask just one more time. How many other survivors were there?"

A shudder went down her spine, but she realized he was trying rattle her, and frighten her into revealing if she knew anything. She also suspected that he already knew the answer, and was testing her. Swallowing hard, Sara summoned her resolve and tried to remain calm. "Sir, we know there were other survivors, we just do not know how many." She was not lying.

He continued to stare at her for several seconds. She felt like he was studying her every move, and he gave no indication of whether or not he believed her. He finally said, "Let's hope the members we left on shore are able to find and eliminate them all."

The walkie-talkie on his belt chirped, so Elder-1 picked it up. "Go ahead."

"Sir, Elder-28 here. We are requesting permission to keep the medical suite open until 6:00 p.m. this evening. We still have a long line of elders to be seen and it will take several hours," came through the speaker of the handheld device.

"We will be right there," he radioed back.

Elder-1 turned toward his comrades in the room. "Elder-76, please continue the evaluation. We shall return soon. If there is any lack of cooperation, we want to know right away." At that, he put his hand in front of a scanning pad, the door opened and he walked out.

CHAPTER 8

December 27, 2044
New Jersey coast
Tuesday, Late Afternoon
The day after the event

id punched the lighter again, desperate for a flame.

"Click." Ignition! He pressed down on the can's spray nozzle. A stream of flame hit the soldier and he dropped his weapon while reaching for his scorched face.

Jess sat up and cocked his arm back, ready to swing.

The soldier suddenly thrust his hands out and darted forward. Still holding out the lighter, Kid couldn't move his hand away in time. The soldier clamped on his wrist and ripped him off the shelf. Like a rag doll, he was tossed in the air across the aisle, crashing hard onto the second shelf from the bottom. As he cascaded to the floor, an avalanche of laundry detergent bottles followed. He was stunned not only by the fall, but by the soldier's strength and disregard for his own injuries.

Having been blinded by the flame-thrower, the soldier turned around and reached out with his hands to grab his prey. He stepped across the aisle and lunged, but Jess was already swinging. The rolling pin caught the soldier in the temple and he collapsed to the ground, with the bangs of his hair still smoldering.

Seeing the soldier was down and out cold, Kid stayed where he was and tried to catch his breath.

"Are you hurt?" Jess asked as he climbed down from the top shelf.

"I'm alright. I just need a minute." Kid rubbed his pained elbow and coached himself to breathe easy.

"That guy only had one hand, and look at how far he threw you!"

"Is this what the seniors do to each other on double-coupon day?" Kid always resorted to humor when he was tense.

Jess helped him up. "Pretty much. Maybe even worse."

"My heart is still racing," he said while shaking his head and trying to get rid of the vision of the gun barrel pointed at his face. Like a black hole, the dark inside of the weapon barrel was still exercising a gravitational pull on his heart.

Kid regarded the bodies on the ground, and made a face when the smell of burnt hair permeated his nostrils. "What do we do with them now?"

"I wonder if they have a crusher in the back of this store, like mine has."

With Jess being the night crew chief at a local supermarket, Kid had stopped in many times, and knew exactly which piece of equipment his friend was referring to. In the back of the store was a large, steel box, and they would often be trying to talk over the loud mechanical hum as a hydraulic plate compressed cardboard into tight square bundles.

"You want to crush them?" Kid asked, taken aback.

"No, trap them, until we figure out what to do with them," Jess clarified. "We'll bring the crusher head down and stop it."

"Don't we need electricity to turn it on?"

"They have backup generators right in the back of the store," Jess replied. "And if it is like my store, they are tested a couple times a month so they should be ready to roll."

Over the next couple of minutes, all three soldiers were put in shopping carts and pushed to the back of the supermarket.

"Be right back." Jess went to another area in the back of the store, and turned on the emergency power.

Kid took all of the soldier's weapons and walkie-talkies.

After Jess came back, they threw the three soldiers into the crusher, which was half full with cardboard already. One of the soldiers was coming to and watched as Jess pushed the *Down* button on the front of the crusher. The powerful mechanical head descended until it was within a couple inches of the top of the steel box, and then Jess stopped it. "Nobody's getting through that gap," he stated confidently.

Trying to fire one of the coal-black, lightweight guns, Kid aimed it toward the ceiling and pulled the trigger. Nothing happened, so he handed the weapon over. "Maybe you can figure it out." He knew that if anyone could figure it out, it would be Jess, who was an avid hunter and had numerous firearms.

His friend took the weapon, examined it, and also tried to fire it. They glanced over upon hearing a sound. The soldier that had come to was now grunting, and was reaching his hand through the couple-inch gap between the crusher head and the top of the steel box. "Don't worry, he can't reach the *Up* button," Jess said as he tossed aside the weapon. "Smart-gun. It won't fire unless it reads a specific individual's fingerprint."

"Which means it is useless to us. What a shame. I don't know what it emits, but it seemed powerful." Kid was overcome by a sinking feeling. "Brian," he uttered.

They turned to leave the store.

"Where exactly did…" Jess started to ask.

Suddenly, the crusher turned on. Kid realized that after making sure the *Up* button was out of reach they had not concerned themselves with the proximity of the *Down* button. They both turned and stood frozen as the crusher head came down and began compacting its contents. For the next few seconds, Kid cringed as the most horrific sounds came from the steel box. The soldiers screamed in agony as bones snapped sharply and body cavities burst, sounding like balloons popping under water. Kid tried to cover his ears and run, but it was too late. His brain had already recorded the sounds. The flat-bottomed head finished compacting and paused. The screaming of the soldiers was silenced, replaced by a mechanical hum as the crusher head began its slow ascent.

Running to the crusher, Jess hit the *Stop* button. "That's a sight we don't need to see."

"Those were the most disturbing sounds I've ever heard." The crack of bone kept replaying in Kid's head.

Jess shuddered and put his hands over his ears.

"They sealed their own fate." Kid walked toward the front door of the supermarket.

Making their way back to the beach to find Brian, they ran behind buildings so that they couldn't be spotted from the ships. They crouched and ran across the street, over the boardwalk, and dropped onto the sandy beach. Dusk had fallen and provided them cover, so they crawled until they found Brian's body closer to the waterline. His body was rigid and still frozen in the same position as the second he was shot. Kid knew it was a formality, but Jess checked for a pulse and said, "We need to give him some kind of burial."

"I don't know if we should move his body."

"We can't just leave him here." Jess sounded disgusted. "He has been our buddy for how many years?"

"I don't want to, but if we move him, the soldiers on those ships will know we are here when they come back and his body is gone!" Kid was frustrated by the circumstances. The truth was that he was having a hard time burying such a close friend. It was making him queasy.

"Yeah, but look!" Jess pointed at the severely eroded beach, "They'll think he was taken out to sea with the high-tide."

Kid could not refute that logic. "And in truth, that could happen. Alright. Let's dig a hole in the sand up by the boardwalk."

"Wait, what about the Norris brothers?" Jess asked.

"We can bury them later. Their bodies are on the pier so we don't have to worry about them being washed out to sea. Come on."

They pushed sand into a pile, and hiding behind it, they used some driftwood to dig a shallow grave. Crawling back to Brian's body, Kid grabbed him under the arms while Jess secured his feet and they dragged the body toward the boardwalk. Brian's six-foot frame was stiff and unbending, which sent chills up Kid's spine. Carefully, they put his body down in the hole. After lying on their stomachs in silence for a few moments, they covered Brian with sand.

Jess kept his head down as he patted the sand mound. "We have to save the girls. I can't do this again," he choked out and crawled away.

Kid and Jess returned to Old Man Drexer's and took some time to regroup. They needed water, food, and a plan. Soon the inside of the shack was almost completely dark, save for the faint streams of moonlight coming through the windows.

"When are we leaving?" Jess sounded impatient and nervous.

"I think we would have the best chance if we tried to get on the ship later, in the dark of night," Kid said. "We should try to get a couple of hours of sleep while we can. We have a long night ahead of us."

It took a minute before Jess seemed to accept what was being proposed. "I guess that makes sense." A moment later he added, "I wish we had some heat in here."

"We can't light the wood stove. They might spot the smoke."

"Then I better get the blankets from the truck." Jess walked to the front door.

Through the edgy gray, Kid walked across the shack and into the small bathroom. Barely able to see, he urinated in the toilet. At least he hoped he was.

After Jess returned, he laid down on the floor. While covering himself with a blanket, he asked, "I know we can find a boat to get out there, but how are we going to get inside the ship?"

"I am working on a plan."

"I figured you were. I just needed that peace of mind," he said. "Let's just hope and pray that the girls are alright."

"They didn't seem to want to harm them, just to capture them."

"Without the girls, what is there?" Jess pondered aloud.

"I don't even want to think about it. I can't think about it."

Kid changed the subject. "I guess we're seeing the prodigies of that Utopia Project first hand."

"Yeah, with three huge ships, who else could it be?"

A few minutes later, Jess sat up. He had an expression of deep curiosity. "You know, I can't figure out why they jumped over the pier chasing after us before. All they had to do was run back to the boardwalk and take the steps down to the beach. They would've had us trapped between them and the ocean. That's what anyone with half a brain would've done."

"You're right," Kid agreed. "They weren't thinking, just following. What we did, they did. Lucky for us, because damn they were fast and strong." He was rubbing his wrist as he walked to the back of the room and grabbed an antique spyglass from a shelf.

"These people are more machine-like than the news described," Jess noted.

Kid stood staring out a dusty cracked window facing the sea. Lifting the spyglass to his eye and fully extending it, he spotted the three ships. They were surrounded by a faint glow, and looked like ghosts in the night. He squinted as he gleaned as many details about the ships as he could, given the vague luminosity. As he stared through the spyglass, the focus changed from the ships at sea to a large crack in the window a couple of inches in front of his face. Collapsing the visual aid, he put it back on the shelf.

"Remember the first time we stayed out on this beach all night?" Jess asked, breaking Kid's train of thought. "You telling us all of those ridiculous stories. Ghosts of black dogs with hatchet wounds in their heads and weeping widows walking the beach."

"Don't forget the moon-cussers," Kid added. In the 18th century off of the New Jersey coast, stalking pirates would curse the moon for providing so much light that they couldn't carry out stealthy attacks on passing merchant ships. As he thought of it, Kid stared up at the half moon in the sky. He guessed that the pirates even cursed half-moons since they couldn't attack with absolute stealth.

"None of us slept that night, not even a wink," Jess said.

"I know, but you have to admit, that sunrise was worth waiting for," Kid recalled.

"It was. Nothing better than having a night to kill with your girl-friend at the beach while waiting for the sun to rise."

Kid continued to gaze out the window. "It's hard to believe this all started out as a harmless night of hanging out under the pier."

"I feel like that night still hasn't ended."

"It really hasn't," he replied. "It's like a nightmare you can't seem to wake up from. All of what we've known, all of who we've known, appear to be gone. Everything that seemed so important just a few days ago is meaningless now."

"And what's the future going to hold for us?" Jess sounded despondent.

"It depends on how far this went. If the rest of the country is like this, when winter breaks and all of the corpses thaw, I see us being sick to our stomachs from a smell that we can't escape, a smell that's become part of the air we have to breathe to live."

Jess grimaced. "Just thinking about it makes me want to throw up."

"And can you imagine the swarms of insects? They may take over the earth."

Kid finally laid down on the floor and covered himself with a blanket. He wished he could sleep for a little while, knowing he would need his energy later, but all he did was toss and turn. He tried to clear his mind, but kept thinking of Sara, and he wondered what was happening on that ship. The possibilities were endless, and each one was more frightening than the next.

CHAPTER 9

December 27, 2044
Tuesday, Late Afternoon
New Jersey coast, Utopia Project
Ship Number One
The day after the event

After leaving the room of the last captive, Elder-1 walked upstairs to the central command center. As he approached the medical suite, he noted the long line of waiting elders. It was then that he realized why they were all there.

Raising his walkie-talkie to his lips, he said, "Elder-28, over!"

"Here, Sir."

"The medical suite shall remain open until all elders are seen."

"Yes, Sir."

The elders were all there to get the tiny, rice-sized tracking device removed from their necks. It was just one week ago that Elder-1 had taken a big risk in inserting them in the first place.

December 20, 2044
Tuesday, Midday
Southwestern Greenland coast,
Utopia Project Ship Number One
Six days before the event

The lead elder of the Utopia Project stood at a dais, flanked by the other members of the Board of Elders. He acknowledged the ten Board members up there with him, and was grateful to have so many powerful countries represented. Directly to his left was Elder-2, a Supreme Officer in the Russian Federation. To his right was Elder-3, a *Shang Jiang* in the People's Liberation Army in China, which was the equivalent of being a general in the United States Army. Elder-1 then lifted his eyes and glanced around the dining room of Utopia Project Ship Number One, which doubled as a meeting room when all of the elders needed to come together. He impatiently waited for the doors to be shut and locked, so they could begin their emergency meeting. Member servers were still placing coffee carafes along all 16 rows of tables facing the dais. Steel push carts loaded with fruits and pastries were being parked in the back of the room, but no elders were partaking.

The room seemed tense as Elder-1 looked at all of the waiting eyes. There had been such mandatory group meetings before, but never one like this. First, all electronic and mobile devices were left on tables outside the door. Then, for any of the more than two-hundred elders to enter this confidential, and world-changing gathering, they had to agree to have a tracking device inserted in the back of their neck. It was small, the size of grain of rice, and was not even noticeable once inserted. This temporary invasive measure was touted as being necessary so that the movement of all elders could be mapped and coordinated using the United States GPS satellites, but for only one week's time. The device would then be removed. Most of the elders raised an eyebrow, but cooperated. They all believed it was just a tracker. But it was so much more.

Only eight elders refused to get the tracker inserted, and were precluded from entering the meeting. Fools. They would be dead before they even returned to their country of origin. Upon leaving, all eight were required to sign a release form. The pen they were given was coated with a poison that took about fifteen minutes to reach the bloodstream, where it would propagate and attack the heart.

He was pleased that almost every elder was in attendance, but knew it would be a difficult meeting. Many might feel betrayed so he would have to choose his words carefully. The fate of the entire world was at stake. And four-star United States Army General, Maximillian, 'Max,' Cramer, otherwise known as Elder-1 in the Utopia Project, had invested too much of his life in trying to save it.

Finally, Elder-10 confirmed that the doors were closed and locked. The member servers hustled through the doors to the kitchen, which were closed behind them. The meeting could now begin.

Elder-1 cleared his throat and started. "As you know, for 20 years, the last 19 being here on the southwestern Greenland coast, we have been developing our new society. The Utopia Project was started by America, and we," he touched his chest, "have been proud to lead this project from inception. But given the ongoing crises around the globe since the controversial presidential election in America in 2020, and the world-wide COVID-19 pandemic, and with no end in sight to the death and bloodshed, even in the once sheltered United States, we were able to secretly partner with many of the largest and most powerful countries in the world. We had all admittedly lost control of our citizens, and the carnage and instability was only growing. The entire world needed a solution. That solution was, and is, social conditioning- the only way to truly control the masses." He stopped and looked about the room.

"The Utopia Project represents the ultimate collaboration of many of the largest countries in world, allies and enemies alike. Most are represented right here," he motioned toward the other ten people, five males and five females, sitting at the dais. "Including Russia, Britain, China, India and Japan to name a few. These nations have been graciously providing financial support and 'loaning' top military, government and civilian leaders to assist in this world-saving initiative."

"But with the rapid expansion of the project, we soon outgrew our first ship and had to build two more. And as you know, another vessel was scheduled to be built next year. But most importantly we perfected our conditioning techniques, as exemplified by the society we built on these ships. And after 20 years were finally ready to start the phase-in of our harmless, yet highly effective, social conditioning in several countries. We were on the verge of the transformation of society!"

He realized his voice was rising, so he stopped for a moment to regain his composure.

An elder in the first row raised a hand and asked, "Sir, what do you mean…were?"

"America's president-elect and his new team do not support our project. We met with them a few days ago, in an effort to make them understand what is at stake, especially given how many countries are participating with us. Our efforts were futile. They clearly have their own agenda and had already made up their mind. They pointed to the CCP and the Civil Crisis of 2025, and to the similarities with using conditioning techniques on human beings, and told us our conditioning phase-in will never happen under their administration."

Murmuring and whispering swelled in the room, prompting Elder-1 to raise his hand for silence.

Another elder raised a hand and asked. "But surely they recognize that something must be done? Our countries have all been embroiled in civil crises for decades, with no end in sight."

"They acknowledged that, but they believe conditioning will take too long to show any marked improvement in society's behaviors and actions. They want more immediate results. His brilliant team has other ideas, captured in an initiative they called, Absolute Truth." He turned to Elder-2.

The second highest-ranking elder stood and cleared her throat. Elder-2 began, "With Absolute Truth…" Her native language was Russian, so she tended to speak slow and enunciate every word. "… the 48 United States GPS satellites would continuously record the planet 24 hours per day using advanced infrared video imaging coupled with thermography. They would be able to see people everywhere, even inside buildings and homes, and they could zoom in on a square-inch anywhere, and from any time, past or present. And as far as the use of thermography, we all know it is far more effective than fingerprinting or retinal scans as a means of personal identification, which is why we use it," she patted the thermographic scanning device clipped to her belt. "But in conjunction with the infrared video imaging, they would use thermography to scan the entire world and locate individuals via satellite within seconds."

Holding up a hand, Elder-1 resumed speaking. "Thank you Elder-2. The president-elect touted Absolute Truth as the ultimate deterrent because most crimes would be captured clearly by the infrared video, and the perpetrators of the crimes would be easily identified, located, and caught using the thermography. With people being tracked and recorded 24 hours per day, Absolute Truth would change people's *visible* behavior and how they act, but would not change what people feel and believe inside. Therein lies the philosophical difference versus our approach—our conditioning actually changes people inside; their perceptions, beliefs and internal responses. After being conditioned, a person truly sees a cobra snake as beautiful. With Absolute Truth, a person says the cobra is beautiful while really finding it repulsive."

An elder in the middle of the room raised his hand. Elder-1 acknowledged him, so he stood. "Why wouldn't the new president just do both until he proved which way was better? If he did, he would see why our approach is superior."

"They cannot afford to do both, and were looking for any excuse or justification to shut us down and free up the billions of dollars that support our project every year, funds that the project cannot survive without. Well," he paused, "they now have that excuse. We have just learned that a confidential memo from inside our project, with distorted but incriminating details, is now in the hands of a reporter named Lily Black at the *Washington Post*. We will be headline news by tonight, and will be for days to come."

Another elder asked, "How did a confidential memo get out? Do we know who the traitor is?"

"The memo was authored by Elder-62, our former lead psychologist who deserted us a few weeks ago. But this plays right into the new president's hands. This will stir up the public and make them hostile, leading to protests and condemnation, before they can even be presented with the facts. The new president has already said this morning, that once the news breaks, his response will be that he will shut our project down as soon as he is sworn in."

That was the flashpoint. A cacophony of angry and incredulous voices erupted in the room. Several elders jumped to their feet. Elder-1 again raised his hand for silence. "Sit. We have a plan."

He waited for the group to quiet down before continuing. "There are already threats to remove us from our government, military and civilian positions in our countries and to press charges based on the information in the memo that was released."

"What is our plan?" asked an elder who was still standing. "We must save this project!"

"Take your seat. Before we discuss the plan, let's first look at our options. It is simple. We let them shut down our project, or we assert our collective power and save it, and the world. If we let them shut us down, the world will soon end. It is already on a crash course with complete destruction. Overpopulation will strangle our planet, but not before the earth is destroyed simply by the behavior of its inhabitants. For decades, the world has seen one civil crisis after another, growing in number and intensity, heading toward a critical mass. We have small, unstable countries with nuclear capability, terrorist organizations, militias, gangs, religious zealots. Members of these groups are gaining power, becoming more implanted and intertwined within the political, corporate, and social structures in many countries, all preparing for the inevitable war. Everyone in this project agrees that the only way to cure the ills of society is through conditioning, otherwise you would not be here. So shutting down the project will result in the end of humanity, and the end of the world, entirely."

Elder-1 took a deliberate pause.

"What makes our group so strong is that we share a common set of beliefs, and a vision of a better world. A simpler one, without the stress the old world lived with and manufactured every day. In our world members are raised with a foundation of innate conformity to rules and expectations. All model citizens. The rise of the Utopia Project has been unprecedented in human history, and our collective power far and away eclipses the individual power of any single country—including America. The only viable alternative is to assert our collective power and take control of the world, and we have the ability to do so. With the advent of the neutron beam system being added to the 48 United States GPS satellites, we can once and for all wipe the slate clean and start to repopulate the earth with the perfectly conditioned 20,000 members we have on our three ships. That will be the start of the new world. It is the only option, otherwise our project is shut down and the world will never be saved."

Elder-155 from Japan raised her hand. Elder-1 acknowledged her and she jumped to her feet. "Sir, to clarify, it is being proposed that we wipe out the entire world using neutron beams?"

Elder-1 gave an assured nod. "Yes. It is unfortunately the only way."

"We are able to access such a secure weapon system and use it for such purpose?"

A knowing smirk came to Elder-1's face. "We already have full and complete access to the satellite system, and tested it this morning when activating the trackers we all have implanted." He turned and nodded at the elder who had helped accomplish this.

Elder-41 looked stunned, and even aghast, that he had unlocked the system for such a purpose.

Elder-1 continued, "We could initiate such destruction right now. They can try to change access codes, but it is too late. We already set up our own technological defenses to that."

"When will this be voted on?" she asked.

Turning to the dais, he nodded to Elder-10, who also acted as the recording secretary for the 11-member Board of Elders. The elder stated, "We already have. Prior to the this meeting, the Board had an emergency executive meeting and unanimously approved proceeding with taking over the United States GPS satellites and eliminating the old world, in just about one week from now." Elder-10 looked up and announced, "The event is scheduled for the evening of December 26, 2044 at 2300 hours, eastern standard time."

Glancing around the room, a couple of elders looked distressed, some others were grinning, but most just appeared stunned.

Elder-155 seemed downright distraught. "So, Sir, at that time, everyone outside of our project will die?"

"Yes. Everyone must die. Remember, with our plans for a phase-in over time, everyone from the old world still would have perished, but it would have taken multiple generations and would have happened through attrition. Instead, we are forced to make it happen all at once. And with the neutron beam weapon, people are eliminated, but structures and technology remain intact, so our rebuild will be very much expedited."

An elder from Britain spoke up and asked, "How will we do that, with just those left in this project?"

"Look around this room. We have more than 200 elders, government, military and civilian, serving in various capacities." Elder-1 swept his hand from left to right in front of his body.

When hand-selecting powerful and capable elders from all over the world, Elder-1 did so using his own psychological manipulations. He gave them their own special number in the project, and he had given the elders nearly king-like status when aboard the Utopia Project ships. Although they still maintained a government, military or civilian rank or status in their home countries, they all came to identify first and foremost with their elder position and number in the project. It became their identity. And it became their life. Elder-1's approach had worked to near perfection. So it was, that the members were not the only ones in the project who were conditioned.

He continued, "Within our team of elders, we have experts in just about every technological, electrical, and industrial application, as well as most utility systems. We will be able to operate just about anything in the world. We have medical doctors covering all disciplines with redundancy, as well as scientists and psychologists. Among the elders with a military background, we have in our project some of the most skilled military commanders, trainers and tactical planners." Elder-1 chose not to add that the majority of the elders were not married, did not have close families and all believed in the project with conviction. Most, if not all, would die for the project.

Still standing, Elder-155 asked, "But, Sir, do we really have to destroy the entire world?"

"On the surface, one might think we are destroying the world, but the truth is, we are saving it. Because now, going forward, the human race will not only survive, but we will finally achieve the impossible goal that has been sought since the dawn of man- a world at peace, without wars, conquest, or conflict. A world where everyone is together as one. A world without divide."

"We are just not sure we agree with going to such extremes." Elder-155 looked around for support, and few would even look her way. A couple of elders nodded their head in agreement, but by and large, the room was against her. Good.

"Take your seat Elder-155. We do not wish to do it, but it is the only option. Otherwise, our project is shut down and the world will end. That is a certainty. We trust that all of you understand these drastic actions and will conform and assist. We promise the new world will be one of peace and beauty, without stress and conflict. You will all be the forbearers of that world."

Now was when Elder-1 needed to choose his words carefully. He could not lose the room. He paused long enough to gauge the expression on his own face. He needed to look somewhat remorseful, and non-threatening. "But to this end, we must inform you that the trackers inserted in your neck, and my neck, are not just trackers. We will remove them in one week, but they have a failsafe built in, given the top secret plan we have shared with you all today. We do not intend to utilize this function, but there is in fact detonation capability for the devices in our necks." He noticed that several elders were reaching back and rubbing their neck. "Again, it is just a failsafe in case anyone tries to betray the project. These devices, just for the next week, will reveal where you are, what you are saying, and it even intercepts vision signals to show us what you are seeing. In the worst scenario, if one tries to reveal or compromise the project, then the tracker will have to be detonated. A spark will fire directly into that person's brain, and fry it in an instant. But, if you are not a deserter or a traitor, then you have nothing to fear."

Elder-155 again bolted to her feet, and seemed quite flustered. "Why would you insert something that dangerous in our neck?"

Waving for Elder-1 to bend down, Elder-2 whispered in his ear, "We have heard rumor that Elder-155 has fallen in love and was secretly married without our knowledge. Her behavior seems to be confirming those rumors."

"Figures," Elder-1 muttered as he stood up straight. "We all have this device in our neck because being compromised by just one person could jeopardize the fate of all. If we inserted it somewhere else, like an arm, a person could simply cut off a limb. And understand, the tracker cannot be removed, or tampered with, without detonating. So be forewarned- and leave well enough alone. Again, we wish such drastic measures were not necessary, but we hope you understand how much is at stake. Not just the fate of our project, but the fate of humanity itself."

Elder-1 looked at the faces of his fellow elders. Many were still stunned, but none moved against him or the Board of Elders. Most of the elders were in the process of accepting their fate and the fact that they had no choice. They will serve the project and stay alive, or they will die. The only annoyingly blind and stupid elder to protest out loud was Elder-155. She was still voicing her displeasure with the device in her neck.

Elder-1 announced, "Understand, you are the fortunate ones being saved. But we will ask just once- if anyone wants to leave the project now, you may do so. But we will require a signed release and you will not be allowed back, and you will die with the rest of the world. So please come forward to the dais if you would prefer to abandon your role as a forbearer of the new world. To the rest of you, let us look forward to the saving the world. We will have additional planning meetings, but this meeting is now…adjourned."

Not surprisingly, Elder-155 came forward to the dais and two other elders joined her. Elder-1 took all three elders to the command center to sign their releases. Or so they thought. As the three elders entered a small office, he said, "This is your last chance to stay in the project."

"We are leaving," Elder-155 stated defiantly, "and the sooner the better."

The second elder followed her in. The third elder stopped at the doorway. Changing his mind, he turned and left.

Pointing at some open chairs along a wall, Elder-1 said, "Sit, and your releases will be brought in momentarily."

Elder-155 remained standing and crossed her arms while the other elder sat down.

Moments later, Elder-1 came to the room with a tablet in his hand. Elder-155 was facing the seated elder, expressing her disbelief at the destruction about to be unleashed on the planet. As she turned, Elder-1 tapped the screen. Elder-155's head shook violently and she screamed. With a panicked expression, her eyes turned blood-red and bulged until one popped entirely out of its socket. She collapsed face-first onto the ground.

The other elder jumped out of his seat and tried to run. Elder-1 tapped the screen again. The fleeing elder also yelped and reached for his head, but he too crumbled.

Elder-2 came up behind him and peered at the two bodies on the ground. "They made a poor choice."

"They had every opportunity to make the right choice," Elder-1 responded. "And Elder-155's decision has turned her secret husband into a widower already. Although he will not be far behind."

Overall, Elder-1 was quite pleased with the response thus far. They had only lost 10 elders, although he suspected they would lose some more. There would be at least handful of elders who would try to stop the destruction and their brains would also be blown.

With the event scheduled for the evening of December 26, 2044, they had only six days to prepare, and there was much to be done. But soon, the world would be reborn.

CHAPTER 10

December 27, 2044
Tuesday, Early Evening
New Jersey coast
The day after the event

Inside the beach shack, Kid and Jess tossed and turned for an hour, but couldn't sleep. They arose and walked back to the same supermarket with a new shopping list. They quickly grabbed food, water, and towels, but it took some time to locate a couple of flashlights and large backpacks. All of the supplies were triple-bagged in plastic trashcan liners before being stuffed into the backpacks.

They made the short walk to a marina on the bayside of the peninsula. At the dock were two boats in the water with winter covers.

"I'm surprised there is no ice buildup under here. The water under this dock must be too turbulent." Jess started pulling the winter cover off of the smaller vessel. "This cuddy is only 24 feet long, and isn't exactly a powerhouse, but it will do." Jumping into the craft, he added, "There's no ignition key. While I'm hot-wiring it, can you check the gas level?"

A few minutes later, Kid said, "Gas tank is almost full, so we're good. I'll be back. There are some important items we need to bring if we're going to have any chance at all."

As Kid walked up to the marina building, he grabbed an eight-inch cinder block and used it to knock the glass out of a window. Climbing in, he scoured around and found thin rope. He also found a steel tow hook. The hook itself reminded him of the one worn in place of a missing hand by Captain Hook in the story of Peter Pan, but with a point that was rounded. Tying the rope securely through the eye at the base of the hook, he wound up the rope and slung it over his shoulder. From inside, he unlocked a back door and walked to the dock, picking up an oar along the way.

Jess touched the right wires together and the boat started. He throttled up and they drove out of the marina and into the main bay channel, pushing aside chunks of ice along the way. Keeping the lights switched off, they cruised at a slow speed, guided only by the glow of the half moon. "Here goes nothing," he muttered as they entered the Barnegat Inlet. "Hold on tight."

Kid kept a firm grip on the top of the windshield as they entered a waterway with a well-deserved reputation for being treacherous. He knew the channel between Barnegat Bay and the Atlantic Ocean had violent and unpredictable currents. Many boats had been chewed up and spit out through the years. Kid had seen many skilled boaters, including Jess, struggle to get safely through Barnegat Inlet on calm days in broad daylight. They were tackling it in the dark of night.

The boat jumped and skipped, mist splashing in their faces as they drove. Kid held on tight as he could see only a few feet in front of the bow. Within this limited sight-distance, it appeared that the water ahead was flowing in a circular pattern. The bottom of the craft suddenly dropped out from under them, leaving their stomachs behind before slamming down. Jess was trying to navigate his way through, but the swift current was making him jerk the steering wheel from side to side. The boat was being thrown around like a cork in a whirlpool.

"Watch the rocks!" Kid warned as the bow swung toward the southern shoreline.

Burying the throttle, Jess turned the wheel. The boat lunged forward, bow in the air, as the starboard rear slammed into a large jetty boulder. A loud scratching sound pierced the air. Jess continued to goose the throttle, trying desperately to turn. He had a death grip on the steering wheel as he passed within a whisker of the last boulder in the line and they burst free from the snapping jaws of the inlet.

Kid walked to the back of the boat to check for any serious damage. "Just scratched up and dented."

"I can't believe we made it in one piece." Jess sounded relieved as he plopped down into the driver's seat.

"And that was the easiest part of the mission," Kid noted as they motored toward the three large ships. "Wait, now what is that?" He pointed at the sea between them and the ships. The dim rays of moonlight had reflected off of something in the darkness.

Jess cut the engine throttle. The choppy water rocked the boat so forcefully that Kid had to break his intent stare. After stabilizing himself, he felt a sudden chill as his ears perked up. He put his hand on his friend's shoulder and whispered, "Jess… there's someone else out here." A mechanical sound was growing louder and seemed to be approaching, so Jess hit the throttle.

A fast moving boat with no lights emerged and aimed for them. As Jess cut the wheel the bows scraped, and the two crafts veered in opposite directions. Kid caught a glimpse and counted two soldiers.

Despite the peril, Kid was grateful that they were alerted by the glimmer of light from the moon. Tonight, the soldiers were the moon-cussers.

Jess turned the steering wheel over hard and the boat canted, almost throwing Kid overboard. "Where are you going?" he yelled as he held on tight.

"We have to get back to land," Jess said. "I only got a quick peek, but I can tell by the size of their engine that we can't outrun them in this."

Looking back, Kid could hardly see anything in the darkness, but he heard the whine of the soldier's boat engine and knew they were giving chase.

Moments later, Jess called out, "Hold on! I am going to ground us." As the boat plowed through the surf, he pulled back the throttle. They came to a sudden halt in the shallows when the engine dug into the sand. The boat fell on its starboard side and the retracting waves flooded the stranded craft.

Jumping out, they sprinted up the sand dune. Kid's heart raced as he glanced back to see the soldiers' boat speeding toward the shore. Turning to the beach block, he saw an amusement park area with two tall water slides that were familiar to him. A large crane and other construction equipment sat idly in the far corner of the property. Making a break for it, he and Jess jumped an orange rubber construction fence and found the steps leading up to the water slides.

Having gone there multiple times, Kid knew this attraction. The tops of the two tall slides met at a large wood platform with a control room. Patrons could choose one of two slides, and both followed winding courses down to the pool. Each slide was a long tube, fully enclosed for most of the descent. The pool was deep, but currently empty and covered with a winter tarp. He noticed two large circular valves on the side of the small building nestled next to the stair tower. That was when an idea hit him. Turning to Jess, he said, "Start unlatching the fasteners holding the pool cover where the slides exit. Get as many as you can. Go!"

Jess took off and Kid ran over to the valves. With considerable effort, he was able to turn and open both of them. He heard water sloshing through insulated eight-inch pipes that ran up to the control room on the platform. With the water partially frozen, it sounded as if the pipes were carrying sand.

Jess came around the corner and yelled, "They spotted us from the top of the dune and are coming this way!"

"Go up the stairs to the top!" Kid instructed.

"Seriously?"

"Go!" he repeated as he ran right behind him.

Ascending the tall, wooden switchback stair tower, Kid asked, "How many cover fasteners were you able to unlatch down there?"

"The first eight on one side," Jess answered as they reached the platform at the top.

Kid easily shouldered open the control room door and in the faint light, he could see a stack of plastic chairs. As he approached them, he noticed the next set of water release control valves in the corner. He turned them on and peeked out the door. Water sputtered out and then shot down the slides, again sounding like sand. At first the water was too viscous to flow with any real force, but it thinned and accelerated as it continued to pump out. Satisfied, Kid turned off the valves.

"They're on their way up!" Jess warned. "Why did we come up here?"

"You'll see." His plan hinged on the soldiers following them step for step, like when the guys had jumped off the pier. He didn't even want to contemplate how dire their situation was if he was wrong.

He gave Jess a plastic chair, and quick instructions. "The slide is steep, and the back of the chair is pretty smooth, so lay down in the chair and push off. When you come out at the bottom, pull back the tarp, even if you have to unlatch more fasteners. I'm assuming they'll follow you down."

Jess laid the chair down at the entrance of one slide, while Kid put a chair in front of the entry to the other. "Just before they come into sight, push this chair down" he continued. "Then you go down and make sure they see you, at least for a second." After leaving additional chairs on the platform behind Jess, Kid ducked into the dark control room and hid next to the water release valves.

As the enemy neared the top of the steps, Jess pushed the empty chair down the slide next to him. The soldiers reached the platform and looked at the covered slide. They could clearly hear something going down. They turned and spotted Jess laying back in a chair, as if he had tipped over backward, so they drew their weapons and ran toward him. But Jess used his hands to push off and started down the slide.

From his dark hiding spot, Kid could see the enemy. They ran across the platform and stared at the slide entrances. Seeming determined to follow, the soldiers holstered their weapons and grabbed the two conveniently placed chairs at the base of the slides. One soldier glanced at the other and a smile appeared to flash across his face. They both laid back in chairs and pushed off.

Perplexed for a split second by the childish grins he had seen, Kid shook it off and opened the valves. A wave rushed down both slides. He knew that by the time the soldiers reached the end of the enclosed tubes, the water would be carrying them at tremendous and uncontrollable speeds. Kid ran out onto the platform and looked over the rail.

Jess had reached the bottom and was working to unlatch more of the pool tarp fasteners. He was already pulling the tarp back when the first soldier exited the tube on his side. As the enemy hit the elevated lip at the bottom of the slide, he was launched high in the air. Jess was able to pull the tarp back just enough so that the soldier flew into the deep and empty concrete basin. A puddle of blood grew around his shattered skull.

The second soldier exited the other tube and landed on the tarp. Trying to stand, he pushed the chair out of his way and pulled out his weapon. Like a newborn deer, the soldier's legs wobbled as he tried to keep his balance on the loosened tarp. He started firing, but Jess aggressively tugged and shook the pool cover to disrupt the soldier's balance.

Seeing Jess's plight, Kid scrambled down from the platform, taking three steps at a time.

As the soldier got his feet under him, his aim was becoming more controlled. Jess was trapped and all he could do was keep jerking the tarp he held in his hands.

Jumping off the final step, Kid ran to the edge of the pool opposite Jess. He was peering at the soldier's back as he started feverishly unlatching the first pool tarp fastener on his side. When it released, the tarp gave way a few inches and the enemy tumbled over, but did not roll into the empty pool. The soldier again stood up and sustained his balance, but Kid was now the target. With nowhere to hide, he tried to stay one step ahead of the next spark of weapon fire as he dropped and rolled.

Jess scrambled to unlatch more fasteners on his side. He released two in quick succession and the soldier finally tumbled off of the edge of the tarp into the deep empty pool. While free-falling, the soldier pulled the trigger and an errant shot fired straight up in the air before his body slammed into the concrete bottom. The water level rose around and over the two unconscious combatants.

Kid ran to the base of the stairs and turned off the water valves and then helped Jess pull the tarp back over and fasten it down.

"We have to get out to the ships tonight. They're going to come looking for all of these guys they've sent out here that never made it back," Kid huffed with heavy breaths. "We've been able to fight them off, but it's just a matter of time before our luck runs out."

II:
EXTRICATION

CHAPTER 11

December 27, 2044
Tuesday, Early Evening
New Jersey coast, Utopia Project
Ship Number One
The day after the event

Elder-76 continued in the absence of Elder-1. She said to Sara, "We will continue your evaluation, but please, relax and do not worry." Her voice was calm, so calm that it almost sounded eerie. She sounded like someone who might be leading a séance. "We are Elder-76, the lead psychologist for the project, at least ever since the prior lead abruptly left the project a few weeks ago. Over the next few days, you will be more fully evaluated by our ten-member team of psychologists."

Sara pursed her lips and nodded, but remained silent.

"You may speak," the elder advised, "so long as you are cooperative and respectful. Should you not be, Elder-1 will not be pleased. You will not get a second chance."

Swallowing hard, Sara squeaked out, "Did you say the entire world was killed off last night?"

"The entire *human* population, except for a few stragglers such as yourself and your friends. We intentionally left certain wildlife tracts intact around the world to ensure the survival of many animal species. Of course, we used pinpoint beam strikes to eliminate all people living in and around these designated areas, so there should not be any human survivors, anywhere."

Sara sat in shock, floating in a zero-gravity somber abyss. *The entire human population.* It was unimaginable. She tried to shake herself out of it.

"Ma'am, it was mentioned before that we were captured, and not killed, because we are females and there was a need for production of offspring. Does that mean we are only here to have children?" She rubbed her arm to confirm that she was not dreaming, or more aptly, was not in the middle of a nightmare.

Elder-76 turned to Elder-12, but he remained silent so she clarified with her mesmerizing voice, "No, but please make sure to only call them offspring. 'Children' and even 'babies' are not recognized words here. You will do much more than produce offspring, especially once your conditioning is complete. Everyone here is a fully productive and conforming member of our society, male and female alike. But unlike the old society, females here do not individually raise their own offspring. Our society does, collectively."

"So women deliver… offspring, and you take them?"

"Precisely," she answered. "Were it not for the problems we encountered in the beginning with cloning and test tube incubation, we would not need females in the actual birthing process at all. In fact, the first 23 members of our society were clones who developed in test tubes. But despite all of our technology, there are certain biological and physiological attributes that could not yet be properly developed or duplicated. We then proceeded to take offspring right from birthing tables as planned, or even unplanned, adoptions, until such time as our own members were old enough to produce their own offspring."

"So your first 23…" Sara started and froze as Elder-1 entered the room.

"Continue," he ordered.

Clearing her throat, Sara asked, "So your first 23 members were clones and look exactly alike?"

"No." Elder-1 interrupted and his lips tightened. "The 23 all look different because they were cloned from different hosts. They were grown from the stem cells of offspring we had in our custody as part of a previous, but similar, project. A project that was unfortunately… derailed. Our original conditioning program in America in 2025 would've been years ahead of its time were it not for the antics of a deranged woman in Georgia who died after the birth of her spawn."

Sara knew he was referring to the CCP and she felt the familiar discomfort. That meant that somewhere on these ships, amongst the first 23 members, was the clone of the CCP's Baby Doe—the child who disappeared and became lost to the world after Anna Delilah's death. She shivered. It was another connection to the CCP. Somehow she knew it would not be the last.

"Her death was blamed on our conditioning project, and was front-page news, where it put us in a horrible and negative light. She alone set the conditioning movement back 20 years," he said, sounding bitter.

"Anna Delilah…" Sara muttered.

Elder-1 paused.

Sara was not about to mention her connection to that event and reveal that she had been born on the same hospital hall just days after Anna Delilah had delivered her baby. Not with Elder-1's obvious disdain about the event.

"Yes, Anna Delilah. As she is known in history," he added as he paced in her room. His tone then turned even more sour "Damn that woman, and that day in 2025. We can only hope she died very, very painfully."

Like a hurricane forming, bands of anger and hurt started circling inside Sara. She had always sympathized with Anna Delilah. The woman fell from a third story window ledge while trying to save her child from being taken into a government project.

"After that woman died, our original conditioning project, the Child Conditioning Program, was stopped in 2025. That, after we," he touched his chest, "had spent so many years developing it. But we were fortunate. We were able to continue the initiative covertly, albeit modified over time, through the Utopia Project."

Sara's shoulders began to sag under the heaviness of his words. After the recent discovery of the Utopia Project, she had not made the connection, or thought about the timing, but it made perfect sense. The public outcry over Anna Delilah's death forced the shutdown of the CCP in 2025, but it was not actually shut down. It was carried on through the Utopia Project.

"Do you realize how little time was really required to achieve a sufficient level of conditioning for a newborn?" he asked.

"No," Sara answered, and almost added, *but I would imagine for most mothers, even one day would be too much.*

Elder-76 jumped in, "We just needed a newborn for the first four hours after birth, and two hours per day for the next 30 days, and then two hours per month for the rest of their life. The offspring could have been with the mother every moment, except during the actual conditioning sessions, even on the very first day."

There was such a stark contrast in the tones of the two elders. Elder-76's voice was soft and soothing. Elder-1 was terse and forceful, and always sounded like he was on the verge of an angry outburst.

Elder-1 continued, "We were scheduled to start phasing this into the birthing process in several large and powerful countries within the next several months, on a voluntary basis. At least at first."

It was the CCP all over again, Sara realized, and even expanded to include the general public and not just members of the military. She felt her face flush and needed to change the subject.

"If this is the Utopia Project, the news said you were stationed off the coast of Greenland. How did your ships get here so fast?"

"We were in Greenland," Elder-1 answered. "But we started heading south when we initiated the world's rebirth, and lucky we did, because the satellite system has been inoperable since late last night. That meant we had to quickly get boots on the ground here to eliminate any survivors."

Sara fought back her fear for the survivors and asked, "So after you are done here, will you move your ships?"

"We will be moving, but not far. We have a cleanup crew at the ready so we can set up our base camp on the barrier island just south of here, Long Beach Island."

"Why there, of all places?" She was surprised.

"Our research had previously concluded that it would be a very good candidate for a home base, and it was on the short list," he answered. "It will not require substantial cleanup since the winter population is quite minimal and since it is an island with only one bridge to the mainland, containment will not be a problem. Most of the power to the island comes from nearby solar panel farms, which can be quickly re-established. The Long Beach Island option became a no-brainer when we realized how close it was to this system malfunction area."

She wrinkled her nose. "Even with a sparse population, we can't imagine the stench with the dead bodies."

He shrugged. "It will not last long. We made as many passes as we did with the neutron beams so that we would expedite the decomposition process. Within a year or maybe two, there will be only skeletal remains."

The walkie-talkie on Elder-1's belt came to life and chirped. "Go ahead."

"Sir, we were asked to inform you the moment the search party retrieval boat was ready to be launched. If they leave now, they should be able to pick up the four members left on the beach, and be back before 9:00 p.m."

"Commence launch," he radioed back.

"Yes, Sir."

Elder-1 said to Sara. "That is enough for now. Rest. Tomorrow morning you will have your first conditioning session. Within the week, assuming you are not in the middle of your menstrual cycle, you will be impregnated. Remember what we said about 100% cooperation. We will tell you what we are doing to ease your immediate fear of the unknown. It is easier for us to overcome a person's will than their fear." As Elder-1 headed toward the door with Elder-76 and Elder-12, he turned and added, "We will answer more questions in the future, but as the conditioning proceeds, you will ask less and less."

How could somebody be so demented and evil? This place is the stuff of nightmares, Sara thought to herself after the elders walked out. She knew she had to escape before this conditioning turned her into a pregnant zombie, or worse.

She recalled that one of the other girls had already been killed. Her stomach felt hollow at the thought that it might be Maria, who Sara feared might be defiant, or at least flippant.

She laid down but her emotions were still too raw to allow her to fall asleep. The death of Anna Delilah and the Civil Crisis of 2025 were still hanging over her, and she was still in shock that the Utopia Project was really a covert continuation of the CCP.

It always resonated with her that Anna Delilah's child, the CCP's Baby Doe, had also grown up without a mother. Sara could feel the child's pain, like a kindred spirit. Tonight, like many nights before, she tormented over the death of her own mother and of the life they would have shared had Mom not died the day Sara was born. Those thoughts swirled in her mind as she rested on her now tear-dampened pillow.

In the hallway, with the door now closed, Elder-12 nodded and left with haste. Elder-1 walked with Elder-76, and he asked her, "What is your snap assessment of this last captive?"

"She seems intelligent and strong-willed. We could sense that based on her questions, her tone and the manner in which she kept herself restrained. Her conditioning, and that for the other captives, will require a modified program since our conditioning plan is meant to start at birth."

"Is that a problem?"

"No," she answered and then paused. "But some of the other lead elders have asked if these captives should just be imprisoned and impregnated until they can no longer bear any more offspring, to save time and resources."

Her words made Elder-1 stop in his tracks. "In the long run, that would require more resources." He turned to her. "Elder-76, how many years do you have invested in the Utopia Project?"

She was hesitant to speak, and even regretful that she already had. "Almost 13 years now."

"More than 20 years," Elder-1 started. "Yes, more than 20 years of my own existence has been invested in this project, as well as the Child Conditioning Program before that, both with the goal of furthering the use of conditioning. And although they are not infants, with these captives we have an opportunity to condition someone not raised on our ships and fully validate and prove the techniques that *we* spent all of those years developing."

"Yes, Sir."

"So we will condition them. And if it is not 100% effective for any or all of the captives, we will simply eliminate them, as well as those who failed in conditioning them," he said and briskly walked away.

Elder-76 glared at Elder-1's back. She whispered, with her teeth clenched through her fake smile, "Yes, *Sir*."

CHAPTER 12

December 27, 2044
Tuesday Evening
New Jersey coast
The day after the event

K id and Jess went back down to the beach in the darkness, grabbed their belongings and commandeered the 26-foot boat left by the soldiers. They took off their pants and shoes and threw them in the boat before they pushed the heavy craft and freed it from the sand in the shallows.

"We have the oar, but do you have the rope with the tow hook?" Kid asked as he jumped into the boat and grabbed his backpack.

"Yeah. Remember, on land it's called rope, but on a boat, it's called line," Jess added as he gave a firm push off.

Kid rolled his eyes. "Get in the boat."

They both grabbed a towel from their backpacks. After patting down their legs and feet, they put their pants back on. Kid was still cold, but thankful to be dry.

After making a path far out to sea behind the large vessels, Jess shut down the boat's engine. They knew the tide approached the beach on an angle to the coastline, and if they estimated correctly, they would drift up to the ships. They also had an oar to help make steering adjustments.

As they drifted closer, both stared up at the vessels in disbelief, amazed at their enormity. The three gray ships appeared to be identical and were lined up in a row with their bows facing the shore. Kid noted that all three had a massive anchor chain descending from a large hole in the hull at the bow, and a smaller anchor chain dropping from the ship's stern. The two outside ships were connected to the center one by rope bridges that sagged, and reminded him of the walkways over deep gorges he had seen in movies. A tall crane stood on each vessel, and above the main deck there appeared to be at least four levels capped by a large bridge.

Jess said, "We have to get in the middle ship. That's where they were taken aboard." Steering them between middle and southernmost ship, he pointed. "They were taken up using one of those davits."

Kid peered up and noticed that each ship had eight tenders on deck, four on both the port and starboard sides, and each was parked under a boat-hoist, or davit as Jess called it. The small boats were dwarfed by the host ships, but still appeared big enough for possibly 20 or 25 passengers. "And they said the Titanic was short on lifeboats," he commented.

"So Kid, how were we planning to get on the ship?"

"I thought we could throw the tow hook up and snag the deck rail, but from shore it didn't look so high."

"The bulwarks all the way up there?" Jess pointed. "There's no way. Even the rope bridges are too high to reach with the tow hook."

So much for that plan! Kid thought.

Glancing down at the water, Jess added, "And we better come up with something quick. Or we are going to drift past the ships and will have to wait until we are close to shore to turn the boat engine back on. Then we'll have to drive all the way around out to sea and try again."

"That will take too much time. Let's find another way to get in, and fast," Kid said, sounding frustrated. As he started back-paddling with the oar to slow their drift, he realized he did not have an alternate plan, and couldn't think of any viable options... except possibly one. "What about there?" He pointed up. "See the round opening halfway up, where the anchor chain enters the side of the hull?"

"The hawsepipe," Jess clarified.

"I figured you would know what it is called. If we can climb the anchor links, we can get in through there. The opening looks big enough."

Jess squinted. "The hole is maybe six or eight feet round, but we have to squirm in and around these monster chain links to get through. We would have a couple of feet of wiggle room at best." He didn't sound optimistic. "That is, if we can even scale up there to get to the opening. Each of those links is as tall as me and they're icy and slippery."

Despite their back-paddling efforts, they continued drifting past the middle ship, and they could not turn on the boat engine without blowing their cover. "We're out of time. I say we try to climb the anchor links and get into the... hawsepipe," Kid said. "Even if we circled around and drifted here again, our options are no different or better. All we would do is lose time. I don't even know if we have enough time to try again tonight."

"What? We have to find a way in tonight!" Jess threw up his hands. "Alright, the hawsepipe it is. We can get in that way."

"Are you sure?" Kid asked.

"Yes. Let's get over to the anchor chain."

Paddling as hard as he could, Kid was making no progress and they were actually drifting further away. "Ahh..." he grunted in frustration. "Either we jump and swim for it, or come back another day."

Strapping on his backpack, but also throwing the coiled line with the tow hook over his shoulder, Jess sat on the gunwale. "The girls may not have another day." He slid over the side into the water, and gasped.

Kid strapped on his backpack and also slipped over the side. The water was so cold that he lost his breath. The pain was instant and excruciating. Swimming briskly, he welcomed pain. What he really feared was numbness. He knew it would not take long for his body temperature to drop and for hypothermia to set in.

They both swam hard, but their clothes and backpacks were drenched, and they were going against the tide. Exhaustion was setting in. Jess was the first to reach the anchor chain at the middle ship. He climbed up on a link and threw the end of the line with the tow hook toward Kid. "Grab on!" he called.

Complying without hesitation, Kid held the line. He was pulled over and helped onto an anchor chain link. The choppy water was lapping the side of the huge vessel, and their feet, as they stood on the lowest link above the waterline. The space was so tight that the guys were almost hugging each other.

Jess turned his head. "Now we need to figure out how to climb these links."

"What the hell were we thinking?" Kid asked as he tried to spot their boat, but it had already drifted away. "Now we *have* to get aboard. Either we die of exposure standing out here drenched, or die of hypothermia swimming for shore."

"We can get in," Jess said, but did not sound quite as sure this time. He took the rope and tossed the tow hook up, over and through the second link above where they were positioned. Holding the line in his hand, he continued to offer slack until he could reach the hook dropping behind the links. As he tied the tow-hook end around the top of the link they were standing on, he pulled the line tight. "I'll take it one link at a time. After each one, you need to untie this so I can reel it in and heave the hook over the link above me. Then each time, grab the end when I let it down, and keep tying it right here," he pointed. "Got it?"

Kid nodded.

"Once I get to the top, untie it one last time and I'll reel it in and tie it somewhere up there. Then you can just grab it and climb up."

Jess climbed hand over hand while walking up the chain link. After he was standing on the link above them, Kid untied the rope. Jess reeled it in and threw the tow hook through the second link above himself and let out excess line until Kid could reach it and tie it off. The process was repeated link after link.

Kid was shivering but he marveled at the efficiency of Jess's work. Methodically, and patiently, Jess scaled a link at a time until he was at the hawsepipe.

Standing on the top link where the chain entered the hull, Jess called down, "Alright, you can untie it now." Kid did so and waited for Jess to reel it in. After peering into the dark hole, Jess called down, "Send up the backpacks first."

With both backpacks securely fastened, Jess pulled them up to the hawsepipe and pushed them into the opening. He tied the line to the anchor link he was standing on, dropped the hook down to Kid, and waved him up.

Find the strength. Tap the reserve bank, Kid coached himself as he wrapped the line around his waist several times and secured the tow hook through a belt loop. He pulled himself up with the line and step-by-step, he scaled the links. *Jess made it look so damn easy*, he thought as he struggled. Halfway up, Kid's foot slipped and instinctively he let go of the line and put his hands out to keep from smashing his face. A panicked gasp shot out his lungs. In a matter of milliseconds, the line around Kid's waist spun him as he dropped like a yo-yo. He clenched his teeth and let out a stifled yell as his shin smacked into a solid metal link. His tumble came to an abrupt end as the tow hook snagged his belt loop, and the line pulled tight.

Kid desperately grabbed the line as his belt loop began to rip under his weight. His hands were wet and he began to slip, but he was able to get his feet on a link. Rubbing his shin, he held up his pointer finger to Jess. He had dropped three links in the fall, but needed to catch his breath as the sudden jerk had knocked the wind out of him. Starting again, he ascended one link at a time until he finally reached the top.

Jess started crawling through the hawsepipe.

Watching intently, Kid put his hand on a link to steady himself as the ship and the anchor chain moved slightly. He wound up the rope with tow hook and slung it over his shoulder. From inside the darkness of the pipe, he heard Jess grunt and then his voice tapered off.

"Jess?" Kid snapped. "Are you alright?" The only response was a faint moan. He started to climb in and although dark and shadowy, he felt a surge of panic upon seeing that Jess was pinned against the cylindrical side of the hawsepipe by a chain link. His friend tried in vain to push the thick metal away from his chest and stomach while desperately gulping for air. Kid grabbed his hand and tried to pull him out.

Jess was barely conscious when the links moved just enough for him to take a few small breaths of air. The ship drifted a little more and the links moved back toward the other side of the hawsepipe. "I got it,"

Jess replied, his voice gruff and strained. He grabbed his backpack and crawled deeper into the opening. After a few tense seconds, he called out, "Come on through. Watch out for the links shifting!"

Grabbing his backpack, Kid entered the large pipe. Squirming in and around the huge links, he had to bend his body in painful positions. In the darkness, he couldn't see where he was going as he crawled, but he could feel the cold steel of the anchor links with his hands. The journey through the hawsepipe seemed never ending. His body chilled with fear and he moved faster upon hearing a deep metal-on-metal scrape in the confined space.

Coming out the other end, Kid dropped down onto a service platform next to the large piece of machinery that guided the chain links through the pipe. He peered around and fully opened his eyes and ears. No soldiers. He exhaled and tried to talk down his anxiety, "We're fine. We made it." Although shaken, bumped, and bruised, they had made it through another gauntlet. Barely. While still panting, Kid was able to whisper, "Are you hurt, Jess?"

"No, but I didn't think I was going to make it for a second there. I knew it looked tight, but I wasn't expecting the chain links to shift," he responded. "How about you? I heard a slam when you fell."

"I'm afraid to feel this when I thaw out," Kid said as he rubbed his raw shin.

They crawled to the edge of the platform and glanced down. Seeing and hearing nobody below, they descended a long metal companionway to the ship bottom.

As Kid stepped, even the slightest sound seemed to echo in the ship bottom's cavernous expanse. It was dark but not completely black, as there was a row of dim lights running the length of the ship up a center walkway. The air had a distinct smell of metal and well lubricated machinery. It reminded Kid of the ferry he used to take to Delaware.

The ship bottom appeared to be a service level, containing engines, piping, machinery, and storage. It was not suitable to be used as living quarters, and wanting to stay hidden, Kid took that to be a good thing. A center walkway extended the length of the ship, which further highlighted its enormity. Kid noted that the bottom of the ship was broken into at least eight sections, with tall, thick watertight doors every few hundred feet that were currently raised.

They tiptoed across the ship, searching for a place to hide. They passed a ladder amidships that went up into a cylindrical, dark shaft. Kid was curious, but kept going. Continuing their exploration, they passed a row of what appeared to be large generators. Ten of them were running, while the other ten sat silent and still. He held his palm close to one, and could feel the latent heat. He then put his hand on the side of a generator and peeked behind.

Jess reached out and absorbed the minimal, but present, warmth emanating from them. "A heated space would help," he whispered, rubbing his hands together.

"No such luck. It's barely a couple of feet wide, and we would probably suffocate back there," he replied and kept walking.

Nearing the end of the walkway, at the ship's stern, they stumbled upon a couple of sizable engines that powered the propellers. Sneaking behind them, they found a large enough space. Kid shed his backpack and the rope with the tow hook and sat down. The area was only four feet wide, and was cold and dirty, but he felt safe. Unless someone was consciously searching, they would never think to look back there.

They proceeded to take off their coats, shirts, and pants. They each had a couple more towels in their backpack, which they wrapped around themselves. Kid was thankful that they had sealed them inside plastic bags. Although not thick, the towels were at least dry. Listening intently for a few moments, it seemed nobody was around so they ran their wet clothes over to the warm generators and laid them out behind the units that were running.

Back in their hiding space, they both nodded off during the next several hours, but every unfamiliar sound would wake them and they would start shivering. Kid's adrenaline was turning on and off like a furnace on a cold day. Unable to fall back to sleep, he checked his watch. 5:30 a.m. "I'm going to check our clothes," he whispered and cautiously stepped out.

Returning with the now dry apparel, Kid wasted no time getting dressed. After Jess also put his clothes back on, they decided to venture around the ship bottom.

Kid headed straight for the ladder amidships. Intrigued by how it went straight up into a shaft, he began to climb the rungs. As his eyes adjusted, he noticed a row of dim lights running up the right side of the enclosure. He came to a hatch and hesitated. "Well, here goes nothing."

He turned the hand wheel, but slowed when it emitted a high-pitched squeak. The slower he turned, the louder the noise seemed to get, so he tried the opposite approach. With a brisk turn of the wheel, the noise disappeared and he felt the hatch seal release. When he pushed it up and open, he saw another ladder ascending in the shaft.

A sudden panic came over him as he heard a faint but audible beep. The dim lights became a notch brighter.

"You must've triggered an alarm! Come on," Jess whispered, standing at the bottom of the ladder.

Frantically jumping down, Kid closed the hatch.

■   ■   ■

Awoken by the audible, continuous beep, Sara yawned and stretched her arms as she lay in bed. She turned her head and saw that the clock on the monitor read 6:00 a.m. Without warning, a face appeared. She inhaled and bolted upright.

The larger than life image of Elder-1 advised, "Breakfast will be delivered to your room shortly, then we will come down and take you for your first conditioning session."

■   ■   ■

Kid and Jess both ran back behind the propeller engines and waited breathlessly for soldiers to come down after them.

Kid stared at his watch for several minutes. 6:05, 6:06, 6:07, 6:08. As the minutes passed, he started to ease up. "I don't hear anybody coming down here. I don't think that was an alarm. I want to go back to that ladder." He stepped out and ran up the center walkway.

Following behind, Jess whispered, "I sure hope it wasn't an alarm."

Heading to the ladder, Kid again climbed the rungs up into the shaft but this time, Jess climbed right behind him. As he went to turn the hand wheel, the echo of a door shutting reverberated throughout the vast ship bottom. Jess grabbed his ankle and motioned for silence with one finger over his lips. Standing still, Kid's heart started rising in his throat as he heard footsteps, and they were growing louder. Jess's foot was on a ladder rung below the shaft enclosure, so he lifted his right leg and held it in the air.

Two soldiers walked past the ladder and never glanced up. Kid heard ten more generators come to life.

Jess clenched his teeth while holding up his leg. He appeared overcome with fatigue.

Finally, the soldiers turned off ten of the generators and walked back across the ship bottom.

Jess's face was bright red and strained. Hearing the door slam closed as the soldiers exited, he groaned and let his leg fall and dangle below him.

"Maybe we shouldn't be running around during the day," Kid whispered.

Nodding his head in agreement, Jess climbed down the ladder and they tiptoed back to their hiding place. In the dark confined space Kid had his back against a freezing cold propeller engine. He wrapped a couple of dry towels around his neck and said, "We'll go looking for the girls tonight, after everyone's hopefully asleep. In the meantime, we should try to sleep in shifts. I'll stay up and keep watch if you want to catch a few winks first."

"Alright. I'll try," Jess agreed. He laid down and kept repositioning himself.

"I know, it's hard to get comfortable," Kid noted.

"It's not that. I could sleep on a bed of nails, you know that. It's like my body is refusing to sleep and I know why. With all of the worst case scenarios that have been running through my mind about the girls, I know I'll have nothing but nightmares."

■ ■ ■

Sara sat on the edge of her bed and rubbed her eyes. She felt a sudden surge of emotion, and thought, *Oh, Kid...sweetheart.*

■ ■ ■

With his ears and eyes wide open, Kid was on high alert. After several moments of silence and stillness, his tension came down just a notch, but it was enough to free his mind. He thought of Sara and at that particular moment in time, he couldn't explain why, but he felt an overwhelmingly strong connection with her. As he settled back and rested his head, the reels in his mind, and memory, began to turn. He thought of all that had transpired with Sara since the day they met. Their hearts had converged instantly, but their path together in life did not.

CHAPTER 13

November 7, 2043
Saturday, Morning
Near Rutland, Vermont
A little over a year before the event

In the fall of his sophomore year of college, Kid was overloaded with schoolwork, but made a last-minute call to leave it all behind and go skiing in Vermont with Jess and Brian.

He was sitting on a bench outside the town of Rutland, waiting for his friends to get out of a store. The air was cold and crisp, but nonetheless refreshing. He was looking around, wondering why the lower elevations still had so many remnants of fall color. Bright multi-colored leaves covered the bases of the mountains yet the peaks were already covered with snow. Fully captivated by the picturesque scene, he thought nothing could compare.

And then she came into sight.

Sara Hyland's beauty was the only thing that could one-up the splendor of that fall morning. At first he glanced over at her, then away. He did a double take and realized she was coming his way. She walked over to the bench wearing blue jeans and a baggy gray sweater. Her natural beauty stunned him. Kid became transfixed and involuntarily uttered, "Wow."

Sitting down, she too seemed to be waiting for someone. He felt an instant attraction to her. She had long, dark hair, which spiraled down her chest in a loose body wave. Her dark red lips were a perfect offset to her fair complexion. Her physical attributes all seemed to fit her medium build perfectly. Kid had to break the ice, "I imagine if you grow up here, you might take the beauty for granted. Do you live here?"

She turned toward him casually and then glanced away. "No, actually I don't."

"You don't huh?" Kid replied, in an effort to further the social intercourse.

"No."

An eternity passed. He wasn't sure if he was still breathing or not.

She finally looked at him. "But my grandparents do. They retired here a few years ago." Her slight southern accent was a clear indicator that she wasn't from Vermont.

Pointing at the mountain, he commented, "It's strange how the leaves at the bottom are still colorful, while the top is all white."

"Yeah, they had a late fall this year, and then a big snowstorm hit this week." She glanced around the area and then her eyes settled on him. "But I'll tell you what, even if I did grow up here, I could never take the beauty of this place for granted."

From the bench, Kid gazed at a large mountain peak, which was close enough to loom over them where they sat. The mound of tectonically raised earth was massive, but beautiful and inviting. It almost had a mystical quality about it, and seemed too beautiful to be real. He turned toward her and as he went to speak, he froze with his mouth open. She had the most beautiful eyes, and prepossessing smile. "No," he uttered, "who could take such… beauty… for granted."

"Why are you here?" she asked, eyes now fixed on his. As she awaited his response, she ran her fingers through her hair, pulling the silk-like strands off her face.

Kid felt an uncontrollable gravitation between them. He couldn't help but notice the body language, as they were starting to lean toward each other. Or was he just dizzy? "I'm here with friends skiing, but only the upper-elevation trails are open at this point. Do you ski?"

"Yeah, but I usually have to go myself. My grandparents don't hit the slopes anymore. Actually, my grandfather is in great shape, so he could ski if he really wanted to, but my grandmother, no chance."

Kid added, "She should hang with me. I've been told I ski like an old lady."

Sara laughed and ran her fingers through her hair again.

Whenever she did that, Kid felt weak. She was stunning, and her disposition only complimented her physical beauty. "I have to get in some serious skiing today," he noted. "I have to get back to New Jersey early tomorrow to get some things and then drive back to college in Pennsylvania, all in one day."

"Where in Jersey?" She seemed interested.

"The shore in Ocean County. A coastal town named Forked River." Pronounced, 'Fork-ed' as opposed to 'Forkd.'

"Is that near the Joint Base, and Fort Dix?"

"Fort Dix? Do you know someone stationed there?" Kid's interest was piqued in an instant.

"Yeah, my father. We moved there a couple of years ago from my hometown of Augusta, Georgia." She squinted her eyes slightly, "Is Fort Dix a long way from Fork-ed River?"

"Not at all. A half an hour or so." He was starting to wonder if he was dreaming. This gorgeous girl actually lived a half an hour away from him.

"Hey, do you want to go skiing today?" he asked after a few seconds of silence. He really wanted to get to know her and was hoping she would come with him. But the way he was feeling, he could've just as well spent the rest of his life with her on that bench.

"I would, but... I can't." She seemed conflicted, and even apologetic. "I really have to spend some time with my grandparents today. I have to go back to Jersey tomorrow myself, before I go back to college in Maryland early Monday."

He wondered if he was getting his feelings mixed up. He felt it was 'there' between them, and they were in the zone together, but was she blowing him off? He searched her eyes and found his answer and more. Sara's alluring hazel eyes perfectly combined sincerity and regret.

"With your friends here, I don't know if y'all have plans already, but can you meet me tonight after you ski?" She turned to him. "My grandparents go to sleep early. I figure I'll go out after they go to bed."

Kid almost jumped off the bench with his arms in the air, but he had to play it cool. He hesitated as if pondering this, but knowing he would run barefoot 100 miles on broken glass to meet her if he had to. "That would be great. By the way, I'm Billy Carlson, but everyone calls me Kid."

"I'm Sara," she said and again pulled the hair off her face, running her hands through it in one smooth, sexy motion, "Sara Hyland."

"Do you want to meet here at this bench tonight at 8:00 p.m. and then we can go from there?" he asked.

"Sure. I'll see you then."

As they went to stand up, Kid realized they were now sitting a couple of inches apart. They started a few feet apart, but it was the attraction, the gravitation. He knew they both were feeling it. It was that warm and fuzzy feeling that can only be felt by two people who have meshed. It's a chemical everyone possesses that is never active until combining with just the right element in someone else, and even then, only if the conditions are right. When it happens, it can be all consuming.

At that second in time, he felt compelled to kiss her. He couldn't resist even though he had just met her. He closed his eyes, leaned forward, and instantly felt the warmth of her lips. She was more than receptive. He would never forget what he felt at that moment, as a warmth spread throughout his entire body. He pulled back in slow motion, and they just stared into each other's transparent eyes.

"I'm sorry. I'm never forward like that." He was shocked by his own behavior.

"Me neither. Never. But I felt the same thing."

"Then... neither one of us was being forward, since we were at the same point?"

"I'll buy that." She smiled.

After standing up, they stared at each other for a moment. Sara was only as high as Kid's shoulders. She waved and started walking away. Kid also raised his hand. He turned around to search for his friends, but felt compelled to look back at her. She also glanced back and their eyes met again. She smiled and resumed walking.

"Ready?" Jess was zipping up his coat as he came over. He stared for a second, and said loudly, "Earth calling Kid…"

"Oh, didn't see you there Jess. You ready?"

"That's what I just asked you. Let's do it."

Kid skied with Sara on his mind all day, and he couldn't wait to meet her later.

At 7:45 p.m., Kid was pacing behind the bench. He was a little nervous, and didn't want to screw this one up. As long as he befriended the butterflies in his stomach they would not become pterodactyls and eat him from the inside out.

It was much colder than during the day, but it didn't bother him. The stars were out and he thought he looked pretty good. In his jacket pocket, carefully protected and wrapped was a single red rose. He had some ideas about what they could do that night. The only definite was that they had to spend some time in front of the fireplace in the rustic lodge where he was staying. In his mind, nothing could be more intimate and memorable.

As Kid waited, he kept checking his watch. 7:55 p.m., 8:00, 8:05. He finally sat down on the bench. He kept squirming as he sat, and kept turning around to see if she was coming. 8:10 p.m., 8:15. Sara was nowhere in sight. He checked his watch one last time, 8:30 p.m. Getting up, he tossed the flower into the snow and left.

He shuffled back to the lodge with his hands in his jacket pockets and his heart dragging on the ground. What bothered him most was that he had really felt like there was something special between them. When he stepped into the room back at the lodge, Jess and Brian saw his face and didn't say a word as Kid grabbed his small suitcase and finished packing.

Jess put his hand on his shoulder, "Didn't go so well?"

"She didn't show."

"Ah, women. Who needs 'em?" Jess patted his back. "Look at you, the long face, garbage stuck to your back," he said as he ripped a piece of paper off of Kid's coat, crumpled it up and tossed it in the open suitcase. "Man, you're a mess."

Closing his suitcase, Kid confirmed, "I am a mess." He wasn't referring to his appearance.

The drive back to Jersey the next day was a long one for Kid. He still couldn't believe she stood him up. Once back in Jersey, he dropped the other guys off and went home. Later that night, he threw his suitcase in the car and went back to school in Pennsylvania.

Despite Kid feeling sour about how it all ended, the magic of their moment on the bench in Vermont continued to linger.

■　■　■

On February 14, 2044, Kid could not take it anymore. He secured Sara Hyland's phone number and called her to let her have it. She claimed that she left a note for him taped to the bench in Vermont. He didn't buy it. The call ended with him hanging up the phone, after telling her that standing him up was a bitchy thing to do.

■　■　■

By spring break a few months later Kid had begrudgingly accepted the fact that Sara was behind him now. It churned his insides when he thought of her, so he tried not to. It helped that the college semester was a tough one, and had kept him busy to that point.

On Friday, April 8, 2044 Kid went back to his dorm room after his final class. He needed to pack for a long spring break trip. Within the hour they would be leaving from eastern Pennsylvania and heading down to Florida. Pulling his suitcase out of his closet, he threw in a handful of shirts and pulled out a crumpled piece of paper. *Where did this come from? Oh yeah, Jess, Vermont.*

He took the piece of paper, struck his best free throw pose, and went to shoot it at the garbage can. It stuck to his hand because it had a piece of tape on it. Stopping dead in his tracks, he thought for a second, and then his heart sank.

The balled-up paper was a small envelope with a piece of tape on each end. He opened it and pulled out a small piece of paper. As he started to read the note, he had to sit on the bed. He was aghast, with his mouth and eyes wide open. Sara really had left him a note. He remembered Jess pulling something off of the back of his coat that night in Vermont, and throwing it into his suitcase. It must have stuck to his back when he sat down on the bench! He fell onto his bed with his arms outstretched.

Sitting up, he smoothed the wrinkled paper on his leg and immediately recognized the phone number. It was same one he had dialed in anger in February. His fingers trembled as he entered the digits and hit talk.

He begged Sara to give him another chance, but she was not interested. After enough of his groveling, she reluctantly agreed to meet him that night at Lakehurst Diner in New Jersey, since she was heading home from college in Maryland. Kid postponed his spring break in Florida just to come back to New Jersey and meet her. He knew he had but one chance to connect with her, or lose her forever.

■　■　■

At ten minutes before 9:00 p.m., the Lakehurst Diner parking lot was all but empty. Kid was desperate in his hope that Sara would show. From the back seat of the car, he snatched the red rose he had picked up on the way.

The inside of the diner was even emptier than the parking lot. The smell of the fresh desserts in the case next to the door permeated the air. A great ploy, Kid thought as he realized he was now craving apple pie. Glancing around, Sara wasn't there yet.

"Dining alone tonight?" asked a middle-aged waitress with a stained apron and a large mole on her cheek. Her black hair was in a bun and looked ready to unravel at the slightest jolt. A good bit overweight, she appeared worn and tired.

"I hope not. A seat for two please, in the corner preferably."

She led him to the booth in the back corner. He put the rose down on the table and sat with his back to the door. He couldn't look. *What if she doesn't show again?* His stomach felt hollow at the thought.

The waitress pulled out a little grease stained pad from her apron pocket. She grabbed the pencil resting atop her ear and aimed the point at the flower. "Is that for me handsome?"

"It might be, check back in 15 minutes." His voice had a nervous edge.

"I guess you'll wait to order?"

"Yeah, I'll order when," he cleared his throat, "if, my party shows."

"Your party is a young lady?" she guessed, smiling.

"Yes."

She put a setting of silverware in front of him and the vacant seat across from him.

"Don't worry," she said in a more serious tone. "If it was meant to be, it will be," she stated as she became a little choked up and walked away.

As Kid sat there, he could sense the waitress was referring more to her own life than his.

Sara took a deep breath, and walked into the diner. She peered around and felt a little anxious.

A server came right over to her. "Young... and gorgeous too. This way." As she led Sara to the booth in the back, the waitress exhaled. "I thought it might finally be my night."

"Excuse me?" Sara asked.

"Oh, never mind, forget it."

Walking half way up the aisle, the waitress stopped and pulled Sara close. "The end booth. I'll be over in a few minutes."

"Thank you," Sara answered. "Why are we whispering?" The woman just waved her hands, directing her to the booth.

As Sara walked up the aisle, she hesitated for a moment. She could see Kid spinning a rose with his fingers and checking his watch. She started to smile, but then reminded herself, *play it tough.*

As she strolled past him, she said softly, "Hi."
That did not sound tough!

Kid was startled but managed to stand up. "Hi…" he reciprocated, drawing out the word as they sat down across from each other. Her beauty took him aback, just like the first time they met. Only this time she was wearing a pretty black and white striped blouse, rather than a heavy sweater. They sat for several seconds just staring at each other. Finally, Kid gazed deep into her hazel eyes and spoke. "I'm truly sorry for acting the way I did when I called you. At the time, I was hurt and didn't deal with it very well." He held out the flower.

"I love roses," she muttered. As she reached for the stem, Kid gently grabbed her hand.

She pulled her fingers back and her voice was stern. "Listen, we need to set some ground rules right now. Don't ever," she slowly shook her head, "ever, call me bitchy and hang up on me, especially when you don't know all of the facts first. I didn't deserve that. Agreed?"

"Agreed." He could tell she was not the kind of girl who would be pushed around or taken advantage of, and he really liked that about her. "I didn't find your note until today when I went to pack my suitcase. How it got there is a long story, but when I called you in February…"

"On Valentine's Day," she pointed out.

He felt like he was shrinking. It never dawned on him that he called her on that holiday.

"But go ahead," she prompted.

He cleared his throat. "Anyway, when I called, I was upset because I thought you had led me on, and then stood me up. That was hard for me to take. I had already started falling for you." Kid was holding onto her fingertips for dear life.

"I know, but the way I saw it, I really wanted to meet you that night but had an emergency situation where I had to hurry down to Boston and pick up my father."

"Boston?" he repeated.

"Yes. But I took the time to write you a note and tape it to the bench where we were supposed to meet. I knew no one else would be sitting on that bench that night in 20-degree temperatures, so I figured you had to get my note, and because I had an emergency and couldn't meet you, you decided not to call? I felt stood up myself," she explained.

She slid her hand into his and together they held the flower.

A spike of warmth reverberated throughout his entire body. "I told you it was one big misunderstanding," he noted.

"Yeah, but I didn't go out of my way to ring you up and call you bitchy!" She squeezed his hand.

"Point well taken." As he stared at her, she smiled. He also grinned. That warm feeling was rushing back. The chemicals were combining in a way that only they could feel. Like sinking into warm bath water, their combined essence enveloped them as they sat together.

"It…" both went to say at the same time.

They put their heads down and laughed.

"Go ahead," Kid said.

"No, really," she insisted. "What were you going to say?"

"It's so nice to see you again. I can't believe we're sitting together right here, right now." Her beautiful eyes seemed to open a little wider and became even more bright. He continued, "What were you going to say?"

"Just about the same thing. Since that day we met I couldn't wait to see you again and get to know you."

"I couldn't agree more," he said. "We kind of got off to a rough start and need to make up for lost time, so why don't we go somewhere quiet and talk? I know a few good places."

"Sure."

"Do you want to eat first?"

"I'm really not hungry," she answered. "I ate a late lunch."

"Me too," he fibbed. He really just wanted to go somewhere and be alone with her. "Let's get out of here."

They got up and walked toward the front of the diner. He grabbed Sara's hand and felt a warmth as she interlocked her fingers with his.

The waitress was behind the counter, wiping it down. Kid handed her a $50 bill. "Sorry, but we have to go. We don't have time to eat."

"That's too much! I'm lucky to make that much in a full shift!"

Before she could continue her protest, he closed her hand and patted it.

"I don't know what to say. Thank you." She pursed her lips. "Such a good man."

She leaned to the side and waved Sara down. Holding a hand to block her lips, the waitress whispered, but Kid still heard her.

"Don't ever let go of his hand. Don't *ever* let go."

■ ■ ■

After leaving the Lakehurst Diner, Kid and Sara parked their car at the Toms River and walked to a gazebo. His shoulders were relaxed and he felt like he was walking on air. At the diner, Sara's rigid shell had softened, she had forgiven his blunder and they had finally been able to connect. A smile came to his face. The magic was again ever-present.

"When did we cross into Mississippi?" Sara asked.

"What?"

She pointed across the river, having spotted the River Lady, which was a replica of a 19th century Mississippi River paddle-wheel steamer.

They sat down close together inside the gazebo. While facing the tranquil river, they were accompanied by the sound of gentle waves kissing the bulkhead. The breeze was cool, but not cold. A mass of cumulus clouds had started consuming the nearly full moon.

For hours, they talked, and they talked. They also kissed and touched, often. Kid knew he was falling in love with her.

He learned that Sara's father graduated from West Point and was now a general in the United States Army. Her father never even dated another woman after the death of Sara's mother, which happened the day Sara was born 19 years ago. He was also surprised to learn that Sara's grandmother in Vermont needed to take a rare medication every day to sustain her life.

"So you are primarily Irish with no Italian, yet you have an aunt in Italy?" he asked, looking curious.

Sara chuckled. "Doesn't add up does it? Actually, she is a family friend and not a blood-relative, but I've always called her 'Aunt' Adele. What are your nationalities?"

"German, Scandinavian, and American Indian- Cherokee."

"That's cool that you are part American Indian. I actually can see that heritage in your cheekbones. They are strong and pronounced," she said as she caressed his face. "Tell me about your family."

"In a nutshell, I'm the middle child of three brothers, my parents have been married for 25 years, which I know is quite unusual, and…I only recently stopped attending church every Sunday."

"Is religion no longer a part of your life?" she asked.

"No, it still is. I am a firm believer in God, but now don't belong to one particular church."

She looked at him with wide eyes. "Same here. When I was growing up, me and my dad went over bible passages almost every weekend at home. He said we didn't need to go to church to be close to God."

He nodded as another puffy cloud crossed the sky and swallowed the moon.

"So," Sara started as she sat upright and turned to face him. "I guess I should ask, are you dating anyone right now?"

"Nobody. Since my last girlfriend, I've shelled up a little. I need to stop being so critical of myself, especially the things I wish I could change."

"If you look hard enough for a negative in anything, you're going to find it. You should see yourself from my perspective. You'd be pretty impressed," she whispered.

He responded by initiating a passionate kiss. Having arrived on cloud nine, Kid tried to sound nonchalant, but he was desperately hoping for the right answer. "How about you? Someone as beautiful as you must be seeing somebody."

"Only three guys right now. But you are already in second place," she tried to put forth a serious expression, but seeing him with his mouth agape made her laugh. "Yeah, right. Actually, I last dated a guy a couple of months ago. He seemed real nice at first, but it wasn't long before his true colors came through."

"So you're single?" Kid asked.

"That depends," she ran her fingers through her hair, "on you."

He was trying to play it cool, but was having a hard time masking his happiness. A grin came to his face as he spoke. "Then I would say, you are *not* single."

She smiled and kissed him, clearly accepting.

Checking the clock on her mobile device, Sara inhaled sharply. "Where did the time go! I wish I didn't have to leave, but I'm already going to be late. I told my dad I would be home by 11:00 p.m."

Kid drove her back to the diner. She got out of the car and went around to the driver's window. Leaning in, she kissed him goodbye.

"What are you doing for the rest of this weekend?" he asked.

"Tomorrow I'm spending the day with my Dad. We have to go shopping for some things for the house. How about Sunday? Are you free?"

"The only thing I was going to do that day is get my disposable camera, since I'm home," he said. "I left it at a cabin in the woods a few months ago after taking some great pictures."

"Cabin?" Her interest seemed piqued.

"Yeah, me and my friends have a cabin in the woods a little south of here, good old Ironside."

"You built your own cabin in the woods? That's pretty wild."

"We didn't build it. When we were in high school my friend Jess found it, way out in the middle of the Pine Barrens. It's over 100 years old."

"What makes you think this camera will still be there a few months later?"

"I guarantee nobody has been there since we were out there last. That cabin is like a needle in a haystack. You should see Jess's map. You wouldn't believe how many turns you have to make through the trails. Hey, do you want to take a ride out there with me on Sunday?"

"Sure, I'd like to see this infamous cabin. Call me." She looked up and huffed, "And maybe this time you actually will."

He went to speak, but sputtered, "Hey, wait…" prompting her to chuckle.

As she turned to leave, Kid grabbed her hand, pulled her back and kissed her. "You realize you are going to be really late getting home?"

"Worth it," Sara said as she walked away.

He did meet her that coming Sunday, and to Kid and Sara it would forever be known as simply, 'the day at the cabin.'

CHAPTER 14

December 28, 2044
Wednesday, Morning
New Jersey coast, Utopia Project
Ship Number One
Two days after the event

N ow awake on Utopia Project Ship Number One, Sara was startled as her door slid open and breakfast was brought in. She sat at her table and looked at a bowl of what appeared to be a creamy wheat concoction, pancakes, and toast. As she fully awakened, she realized she was too nervous to eat anything.

Taking a sip of coffee, she winced. "Piss water," as her father would always say. She also liked her coffee strong.

As she picked at her food, she watched the program on the monitor. It was showing cities and natural wonders throughout the world. Rome, the Grand Canyon, London, and then the scene changed to Times Square in New York City. It dawned on her that there were no human beings in any of the scenes.

A short while later, her door opened and Elder-1 stepped in with his hands behind his back. He said just one word, "Come."

They walked up the spiral staircase for many floors, and then entered a windowless room that resembled a dentist's office. There was a reclining chair and several mechanical instruments, monitoring devices, and capped syringes. Elder-76 was waiting.

"Please, sit," she instructed and pointed at the chair, which had shiny metal buttons in neat rows lining the seat, seatback and armrests.

Sara felt her heart pounding in her chest. "This looks like a torture room."

"It's not," Elder-76 said in her hypnotic voice. "Here we administer positive and negative conditioning, from euphoria to excruciating pain. If used for negative conditioning alone, then our members would become afraid of this room. We can only imagine how problematic and counterproductive that would be."

As she reluctantly sat in the chair, Elder-76 strapped down her arms, legs and head and whispered, "Relax," which only made Sara more uptight.

The lights were dimmed and a large screen came to life and moved toward her. The screen went from the floor to the ceiling, and wrapped around the chair on each side, encompassing even her peripheral field of vision. The person in the video was defying authority by spitting at a uniformed officer and throwing rocks at him. A sudden and painful electric shock ran through her body. Sara shrieked and tried to look away. With her head strapped in place, she tried to turn her eyes down, but the screen was still in her field of vision.

She closed her eyes and was rocked by an even stronger shock. This one lasted a full second. She moaned in pain and was shaking.

"Every time you close your eyes, the video will pause and you will be shocked for a full second." Elder-1 sounded sadistic. "It would be wise to watch the screen, or the session will only be longer and more painful."

Unable to move her head or shut her eyes, she could not escape the images on the video screen. She felt sick and tried with all her might to shake free. Again she closed her eyes and a shock rammed through her body. A blood-curdling cry erupted from her throat and she felt like she was spitting flames.

For a full hour Sara endured a conditioning program to ingrain respect for authority, observance of their society's rules, and discomfort with being alone. The next program called for the desensitization of common pleasant and unpleasant emotions.

The most bizarre and frightening part of the conditioning program, called 'word conditioning,' was left for the end. She was stuck with a needle as Elder-1 snapped the word, "*Ion!*"

Sara tried to maintain focus, but suddenly her mind was floating, as if she had left her body. She went limp like a wet noodle and slumped in her chair. As hard as she tried, she could not move her limbs. Were it not for the straps being tight, she would have slid to the floor.

Next thing she knew, Sara was looking around in a daze, with people and instruments starting to come into focus. "What happened?"

"You were in an extreme meditative state," Elder-1 answered.

"It felt like being under twilight anesthesia, but just for a few seconds." She continued to peer around the room, reconnecting with the real world.

"You were out longer than a few seconds."

"Couldn't have been much more," she said with a little too much confidence. The smirk on Elder-1's face was nothing short of condescending. "How long?" she asked.

"A full 15 minutes."

A short while later Sara had to meet with Elder-76 and three of her psychologists. After undergoing a battery of psychological tests she had seen enough words, shapes and pictures, and had answered enough questions, to make her dizzy. Between that and the morning conditioning she had a headache.

After being escorted to her room by just Elder-76, Sara dropped down onto her bed and an involuntary moan escaped her throat. The first morning on the ship was far more physically exhausting and disorienting than she ever could have imagined. But at least she was still alive, and had not yet been impregnated.

"Are we exhausted?" Elder-76 asked.

"Kind of." Sara did not want to give them the satisfaction of seeing the toll it had taken on her.

Elder-76's voice was borderline compassionate as she said, "Don't worry, all of our members go through the same conditioning regimen. The results have been ideal, although for them it starts right after birth and requires fewer repetitions."

Sitting upright, Sara asked, "What was that drug you injected at the end there?"

"A proprietary narcotic, but do not worry. Narcotics are only used for so long to send a person out and bring them back. Inevitably that person will slip in and out of a deep meditative state just by hearing the specific trigger words, verbalized in specific tones. That is why we refer to it as word conditioning. We have a trigger word to send one out, and a separate trigger word to bring them back."

"You do that to offspring, while their brains are just developing?"

"No. We should have clarified that. The word conditioning does not start until a member reaches the age of 12, and continues every month for the rest of their lives."

"Why would you need any word conditioning at that point? We imagine that by the age of 12, everyone does what they're told around here," Sara noted facetiously. She would not have been so sarcastic with Elder-1.

"The deep meditative state with the word conditioning serves to clear the mind entirely and is quite therapeutic," she said in her bewitching voice. "But there is another purpose, which is simply to reinforce the conditioning process. It is for calibration. Like training dogs, conditioning and training must be regularly reinforced as not to lose the effect. Even if you don't re-condition a dog for every trick, it is advisable that one regularly reinforces conditioning in general."

"Like dogs?" She raised her eyebrows.

"It is the same principle, but it is true that everyone conforms to the expectations and rules of our society, so it would not be used for punishment." Elder-76 paused and then seemed to have a recollection. "Actually, there was one time, the only time we can recall in the last ten years when it was used for something other than routine conditioning. One of our male members had a slight mental disorder, or we had a failure in the conditioning process, which we did not identify early on. He became quite attached to one of the female members, and assaulted another male member during a sexual activity period. When we went to remove him, he resisted violently, so we had to use the word conditioning to put him in a deep meditative state. We decided to pull him out and try conditioning him again."

"You had to pull him out of that meditative state? You mean someone doesn't come out of it on their own?"

"No, we must stop it and bring them back. Otherwise, they will be lost in meditative space for eternity and never return to reality. Soon after, their body just shuts down and they die and there is nothing we can do about it. We learned that the hard way early on. But for this particular maladjusted member, after medical and psychological testing, we developed a conditioning program to cure him of his afflictions—his attachment to one person and his propensity for violence. Since then he has been perfectly conforming."

"We could see violence and hostility being a problem, but an attachment to one person is considered an affliction?" She looked taken aback.

Elder-76 nodded. "Very much so."

Sara contemplated for a moment. "What if one of your members gets mad at another? Can't they just yell that word, Ion?"

Smiling, Elder-76 shook her head and her white hair swayed. "No. Besides the fact that you don't see anger from our members, they are unable to say words that start with the sound…" She pointed at the corner of her eye.

"Sorry," Sara said, realizing she had slipped and used a long 'I.' Thank God Elder-1 wasn't there. "So how many more of these conditioning sessions do we have to go through?"

"For you, about 60. Every day for two months and then on a monthly basis thereafter. It takes twice as long for those not conditioned from birth. For you, the specific techniques are a little different than the ones used for those who were raised on the ships, but please do not worry. The results will be the same and you will find the ultimate peace. With some conditioning techniques, notably the word conditioning, you could be almost 100 percent conditioned after just a handful of sessions."

With this last sentence, Sara shuddered. She felt a sense of dread at the thought of not having control of her own body, or mind, as if she were a zombie. *After just a handful of sessions?* she repeated in her mind. *That quick? We have to get off these ships before it's too late.*

Sara noticed a hand touching the opaque glass from the outside. She heard a scratching sound as a palm ran over the rough surface, and then the door quickly opened. She was caught staring.

Elder-1 entered and said, "You look inquisitive. You are wondering why we frosted the glass on your window?"

Sara nodded.

"We need to limit any potential interaction with our members. We cannot risk you corrupting them."

"Corrupting them?" Sara asked, she feared too abruptly. "Sorry, Sir. How so?"

"Because you are too different," Elder-1 answered. "You are a product of the old society, a society that thrived on stress and conflict. That does not exist here. Utopia only exists when we lead stress-free lives. People in the old society grew up conditioned with expectations and perceived needs that could not be addressed without stress to themselves or others. People in the old world so often felt inadequate, unfulfilled, undesirable, or exactly the opposite. But as long as people valued wealth, land, and material possessions, they would always strive to have more than everyone else. As long as people believed in different religions, or that races were not equal, they would always fight for supremacy over those different from themselves. Here, we do not stress over any of these things because we have no regard for them."

Sara was careful with her words. "We," she pointed at herself, "have no regard for much of that either, but how are you able to keep your people completely isolated from these things?" Sara was convinced that this was not possible in any society.

"They were raised on our ships, without any interaction with the outside world, other than the fully trained elders, and we must keep it that way. That is why we cannot have you interacting with them. Since birth, our offspring have been isolated, and have been conditioned to a different set of societal values and norms. All of their basic needs are fulfilled, and without real stress. Our members just perform their regularly assigned, but important, duties on the ships. They don't have the socially defined bars that existed in the old world."

"Aren't you basically doing the same thing, but just re-establishing the socially defined bar?" Although she was horrified, Sara found herself oddly curious.

"Maybe so, but it is a greatly lowered bar," he held up his open hands, "and it is met every day by all. The needs we have established do not require, or create, real stress for the bar to be reached. The members still feel challenged, but none of them ever feel worthless, inadequate, or lack self-esteem. And why not? Because they simply do not compete with each other and are not attached to each other. Remember, the bar seems low to you, but it is not to them. It is all they know. It is what they've grown up with."

Sara was careful that her tone was not flippant as she asked, "People's *real* needs can be met with this 'greatly lowered bar'?"

Elder-76 jumped in and answered, with a voice much softer than Elder-1's, "Yes, they can, and that is why our members feel fulfilled, and are so much at peace. People's real needs are quite simple, and can be broken down into two areas; mental and physical. The need for mental stimulation is more than provided for here, through many activities and brain challenges with varying levels of complexity. Physical needs are provided for through exercise, games and regularly scheduled group sexual activities. To eliminate attachments and competition between individuals, we always rotate partners for both mental and physical activities, and people interact in groups."

"Why do you eliminate attachments between individuals? If you never give them a chance to choose partners, they will never know the beauty and fulfillment of some attachments." She was thinking of Kid.

Elder-1 shook his head. "One big problem in many cultures in the old world..."

He really despised the old world. She sensed another rant coming.

"... was the formal tying together of two individuals. After the early phases of a relationship, which often included heavy physical stimula-tion, couples were left with primarily companionship. For the sake of this companionship and vows that were sworn to, people would often not seek physical stimulation from others when they really did need and require it. This caused nothing but unhappiness and frustration. Here, companionship and physical stimulation are separated, yet both are enhanced. The members have fulfilling companionship through their interactions with others every day, and separately they have stimulating physical activities. To avoid the common pitfalls of attachments between individuals, we routinely change the member groupings for all activities. That way, they come to rely on the system to meet their needs, and not any other specific members."

He then turned to Elder-76. "Since the halls are clear at this hour, please take her to the small, elder dining room." Turning to Sara, he noted, "Your two comrades have already been taken there. For today, you will be able to have lunch together."

Walking up the hall, Sara was surprised that they were allowed to congregate. *Couldn't it undermine the progress of the conditioning plan?* she wondered.

As if reading her mind, Elder-76 said while striding behind her, "For now, and just for now, it will be beneficial to your conditioning regimen for you to find comfort by commiserating with your comrades, so please, talk freely and openly. Your anxiety and fears should be lessened, which will make our conditioning sessions more effective."

"Of course," Sara responded, not surprised that this had been thought through. It also rang loud and clear that having meals with the other survivors was a temporary arrangement.

As soon as she walked into the small dining room, Sara uttered, "Thank God!" Maria was waiting there, as was Heidi. She hugged both of the girls tightly.

"Poor Chatty Cathy," Maria said.

Sara then lowered her head and through pursed lips whispered, "I'm so sorry Cathy."

The three girls sat alone at a large, round table. Out a tinted window they could see the main deck of the ship where a small group of young soldiers was assembled. It looked as though they were being briefed.

Sara noticed there were many nationalities and races represented. *A true melting-pot*, she thought.

Sara watched as two people walked toward a motorboat. She squinted and could make out, 'Elder-48' on the uniform of an Asian male. The other was a younger Caucasian male and she didn't get to see his uniform number before they climbed into the boat. The tender was raised and the telescopic arms of the davit extended out until the craft cleared the deck rail and was then lowered toward the water below.

More are going ashore! Sara swallowed hard and felt her blood pressure rise instantly. Although concerned and anxious, there was a monitor on the wall in this room as well, so she could not react. At least not visibly. She struggled to hide the fear she felt for Kid and Jess's lives, and wondered where on earth they were at that moment.

■ ■ ■

On the bottom of the ship Kid woke to the distant sound of a mechanical hum. It was faint, but he knew it wasn't coming from the nearby generators. He shivered as he listened closely. A few moments later, he could make out the sound of an engine.

Jess woke up and tuned in. "They must've lowered a boat to the water."

Confirming his assumption, a high-pitched rev peaked and then started diminishing as a boat sped away.

"I'll bet they're going ashore to find their friends on the mainland," Kid whispered.

"Good luck with that," Jess mumbled and put his head back down.

After the noise of the boat motor faded away, they both embraced fitful slumber again.

■ ■ ■

Hearing the boat taking off, Maria started to say, "I wonder where…"

"Where the rest of the people eat?" Sara cut her off, inconspicuously pointing toward the monitor behind them on the wall.

Maria got it. "Yeah…where the rest of the people eat." She then whispered, "Can I say 'I' in here?"

"Don't know, but let's not take any chances," Sara answered. "Hey, did y'all have a conditioning session this morning too?"

Both tensed and flashed expressions of disgust while grumbling a synchronized, "Yes."

"Elder-1 told me they had a hard time pulling me out of my meditative state," Maria said. "Not looking forward to going through that again."

"Me neither," Sara said. The word whispered in her ear before the meditative state echoed in her mind. *Ion… Ion…*

"That was freaky," Heidi agreed.

"Did you hear that there were some areas in the world they intentionally didn't destroy?" Sara asked.

"Yeah, some wildlife tracts. But they said the Seaside beach area was supposed to be destroyed," Heidi noted.

"But was left untouched because of a weapon system malfunction right?"

"Yes!"

"And that the satellite system is currently down," Sara said, "so they can't even go back and try again to wipe it out with the beams?" Making eye contact, she could see the realization hit Maria. If the satellites were operational, nobody on the mainland would have a fighting chance of surviving or escaping, notably Kid and Jess.

"I, we, didn't hear that part but that is good to know. *We* also asked about other areas left that were supposed to be destroyed, and…" Maria stopped as the door opened, revealing the rigid form of Elder-1.

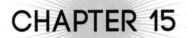

CHAPTER 15

December 28, 2044
Wednesday, Late Morning
New Jersey coast, Utopia Project
Ship Number One
Two days after the event

Elder-1 stood at the entrance of the small dining room as a female member of the society entered and served the girls a dish of pasta smothered in wine sauce. The server wore the same numbered uniform as the male soldiers but had slightly longer hair. Her brown hair came down to her shoulders and was cut straight across. Sara noticed that the server was not expressive, but appeared content; not happy, not unhappy.

"May we speak?" Maria asked.

Elder-1 nodded.

"Hi," Maria said to the female server.

"Hello." 609 put a plate in front of her.

"Thank you!" Maria emphasized her words. "This will hit the spot, especially since my blood sugar feels low."

"You're welcome," the woman answered politely.

"At least they teach them manners around here."

"So, what do you do for fun around here?" Sara asked the server as she put a plate in front of her.

"That will be all," Elder-1 interjected as the server put the last plate down and turned toward the door.

Maria smelled her food. "Hey, these people couldn't be all bad, this sauce has alcohol in it. And at lunchtime?" She glanced over at Elder-1 who looked at her with no particular expression.

"Can't we talk to her?" Sara pleaded with Elder-1, referring to the female server. "We would feel a lot better if we could just talk to one of your members and see what they're like, and know what to expect. We have to get use to the way your people act. You said yourself that you wanted to ease our fear of the unknown," she reasoned.

He went to respond, and hesitated. He appeared to be considering her request. "If it will ease your fears, then fine. It will only help expedite the conditioning process. But we will give you only a few minutes."

Turning to the server, he instructed, "Please, sit with them until we call you. You will then report immediately to the Conditioning Center."

"Yes, Sir." 609 walked back into the room and toward the table.

Elder-1 proceeded to walk out the door, leaving the girls alone to eat lunch and talk with the server. Before the door closed behind him, he hesitated and looked back. He seemed to be second-guessing his decision.

Sara pulled out a chair. "Please, have a seat. We only have a few minutes to talk."

The food server didn't seem nervous or uncomfortable joining them, but she also didn't seem to share any sense of urgency.

"Sit, sit," Sara was repeating. "What's your name?"

"My number is 609."

"That's what they call you, 609?"

"Of course." She pointed at the small, but clear, embroidered numbers on her uniform.

"What do you think of living on these ships?" Sara asked.

"We like it here."

"Why?"

"Why?" 609 repeated, appearing dumbfounded by this question. "Tonight is my sexual activity period," she said with a slight grin. "It's the first since having a week away for menstruation."

"We hear that you have sex in groups," Sara said as she recalled her

135

conversation with Elder-1 about how physical needs are addressed, "but is there ever any one person you like seeing more than others during these activities?"

"We like them all."

Finally, Maria chimed in. "What's with this 'we' stuff?" She looked over at the monitor, cupped her hands over her mouth, and whispered, "You mean to say, 'I' like them all."

"Here there is no…" 609 pointed at the corner of her pupil.

"You're saying there isn't any one special person who really excites you?" Sara pressed, getting back to her question.

"Everybody excites us."

"Have you ever thought about what it would be like to see the same person all the time?"

"No. We don't do that," 609 replied with certainty.

"Is there anyone you hate?"

"What is that?"

"Hate?" Sara asked.

The young woman nodded.

"Is there anyone here who you would like to just slap in the face?" Maria clarified.

"Why would we do that?" She smirked.

"Nobody makes you angry?" Maria continued.

"What is that?"

"She doesn't know what angry means either," Sara concluded. Looking at the other girls, she could tell Heidi was scheming.

"She doesn't know what anger is?" Heidi sat on the edge of her chair and gazed deep into 609's eyes. "What do you expect? With all of the sex, all she does is whore around. Right… slut?"

The server seemed puzzled for a second. 609 then grinned, not appearing offended in the slightest.

Heidi's face flushed with anger. "Look at you, with your stupid hairdo and tight lips. Can't believe any of the guys would want to touch you."

The server continued to grin. "We all really like to touch each other."

Sara turned. "Heidi, it's obviously not working."

"Thick as a brick," Heidi concluded and slid back in her chair.

"Did you have a good time growing up here?" Sara asked.

"Yes, we did."

"What do you remember doing when you were growing up?"

"We were taught so many different tasks and learned so much. We learned a lot of the adult activities. We even got to use the simulators."

"Any one moment in your life stand out to you?"

609 thought for a moment. "No."

"Come on, what was the best moment of your life?"

"Every moment is wonderful, but we especially enjoy the roller coaster simulator, and the sexual activity periods."

"Well, we all have been on real roller coasters," Sara said, "and they-'re more fun than any simulator."

The server smiled, with her eyes wide.

Maria jumped in. "The last time I, we, went on one it broke down halfway through the ride. We kept praying to God until they rescued us."

After reflexively pointing at the corner of her eye, 609's expression made it clear that she did not understand.

"Tell me you don't know who God is."

"We do not."

Sara clarified, "He is the supreme being who created heaven and earth, at least in my religion. People pray to God?"

No response.

"Most people worship God and obey God's commandments?"

"We obey the elders and the rules of our society," the young woman noted.

Heidi and Maria just shook their heads and rolled their eyes.

Sara tried to remain patient. "Listen, here's a story about something that happened in our world." She exhaled and turned to 609. "Have you been the bearer of any… offspring?"

"Two so far." She seemed quite proud. "We hope to contribute many more."

"Maybe you can understand or relate to this story. A few years back, another female member of my society had become pregnant. The week she was due with her… offspring, she was driving home on a road through the forest when she suddenly went into late-stage labor. Her car swerved off of the road and slid down a steep embankment. Do you know what a car and a forest are?"

"Yes, we have heard of these things at our mission meetings in preparation for inhabiting the mainland."

"Well, down in the forest, she delivered the offspring herself."

The young server looked rather surprised, "She wasn't in a Birthing Center?"

"No. She was alone in the forest and her phone had no signal. She was too weak to walk, but she knew enough to cut the umbilical cord and clear the offspring's air passages. She wrapped the offspring up in her shirt and the infant fell asleep. She also fell asleep, right there in the forest with her offspring in her arms." Sara began to get choked up.

609 appeared uncomfortable.

"She knew nothing about caring for an infant. The infant was shivering and she only wanted her offspring to be warm," she continued with her voice cracking.

As she observed Sara, 609 seemed confounded and asked, "She delivered her own offspring, and tried to handle it herself? That task is assigned to others."

"She was alone and had no choice. She held the offspring tight during her nap. A little… too tight," Sara gasped and broke down crying. She kept trying to talk, but was having great difficulty.

609 stared in shock.

"The offspring's face was pressed too firmly between the woman's breasts. She suffocated her own offspring!" she sobbed. Although acting, Sara really could feel the pain of a woman in that situation.

The server appeared shaken by the story, and continued to stare with her mouth open.

Maria also started crying. "Sara! Now why did you have to go and tell that story?"

"Sorry. Maybe we shouldn't have." She avoided saying, 'I' so that 609 wouldn't keep pointing at the corner of her eye.

609 kept glancing back and forth between the girls.

Maria cupped her hand and whispered, "Is that a true story?"

"Yes, it was a story in a military news publication…"

Suddenly, the door opened and Elder-1 walked in. "Come 609, we will escort you to the Conditioning Center."

As the young server went to stand, she stopped halfway up as a teardrop dripped on the table from her face. She stared at the tiny droplet of water, appearing stunned and confused.

"Come, now," Elder-1 commanded. 609 finished standing up and walked out of the room.

After escorting the server to the Conditioning Center, Elder-1 walked back into the girls' lunchroom.

Raising a hand, Maria said, "May we ask a question?"

He seemed a bit perturbed, but nodded.

"With the world pretty much destroyed, how are you able to produce food with wine sauce?"

"The pasta is made right here on the ship, where we have enough grain stores to last for years. As for the wine, we have a significant supply, and the world has left us tons of it on the mainland. Now come. Before the work period is over, we must cut your hair and dress you appropriately." He walked out the door and the girls followed without hesitation.

They walked up the hallway and turned into the hygiene station. After getting her haircut, Sara turned to the other girls. Both Maria and Heidi had their hair shoulder length, and cut straight across. As she ran her fingers through her own hair, Sara imagined hers was no different. Now they looked like every other girl on the ships. "Where's the mirror? We need to see this," she said to nobody in particular.

"We have no mirrors for such purposes," Elder-1 responded.

"And he calls this utopia?" Heidi remarked, but was not joking.

Sara asked, "No mirrors? Why not?"

"Here we don't concern ourselves with physical appearance, although we do ensure proper grooming and each member's ideal weight is maintained for health purposes. We don't want people looking at themselves, individually. Appearance is not a concern, for social or physical, or even sexual, activities." Pulling a device from his belt, he said, "Hold still."

Sara did not move as a handheld scanner was waved over her face. She was then given plain, white undergarments and a gray uniform with a number embroidered on it.

"Now you will shower and change, which we do here on a daily basis. Good hygiene is essential."

"Where do we shower?" Sara asked.

"Right there." He pointed. "Put your uniform on the hook, and once you remove your old clothes we will dispose of them."

She turned to see a row of showerheads against the wall. There were no individual stalls or curtains. "Here?"

"Yes. There is nothing to fear and nothing to hide. Here you are not judged by your physical appearance," Elder-1 assured her.

Sara walked over to the shower area and began taking off her clothes. She was moving intentionally slow, hoping Elder-1 would step out of the room. Instead, he stayed and stared at her naked body, watching every move she made. She folded her arms over her exposed breasts and walked over to a showerhead. She did not lack confidence in her physical appearance, but with him staring, she felt uncomfortable and violated. She hurried to finish her shower and get dressed.

The other girls used the showerheads on each side of Sara. Heidi finished in a hurry, but Maria showered unabashed, as if she could have stood there all day. They all put on undergarments and then put on their individually numbered uniforms, which were one-piece gray jumpers with a soft, dark-green interior lining.

As Sara turned around, Elder-1 was still gazing at her. Finally, he asked, "Have we ever met at any point? We used to spend time on the mainland as well."

"Don't think so. We can't imagine we would've forgotten if we did." She tried not to sound sarcastic.

"Despite your southern accent, there is a certain familiarity about you," he continued as he studied her face.

Elder-1 broke his stare and taking a step back, he examined all three of them. "That's better. Let us know if you require fitting adjustments for your uniforms or undergarments, but now you look just like all of the other females and will fit in nicely. Your integration is proceeding quite well."

After they brushed their teeth and applied some deodorant, he took the girls back into the hallway. As they walked, Sara noticed that both the walls and the ceiling were a soft, light gray color. The floor was covered with a maroon-colored carpet. Most of the rooms on this floor had large windows, and all of the doors also had a large window in the top half. She could again hear a quiet voice and noticed that speakers were mounted every ten feet near the top of the wall. There was also a video camera at each end of the hallway.

Elder-1 led them down the hall and opened an exit door. They were greeted by a cold breeze as they stepped onto the deck at the bow of the ship. The afternoon sun shone brightly over the dark blue water. On one side of the deck, a tall crane cast a long shadow.

"Fresh air." Maria inhaled and put her hands on her wet hair. She shivered as she pushed down. "Wow, cold, fresh air."

The elder put his hands behind his back and gazed at the shoreline, "Our boat has probably reached the beach by now." After a moment, he walked over and unlocked a storage cabinet.

Sara leaned on the deck rail and peered at the shore, pretending to also look for the boat. She was really trying to see if she could spot Old Man Drexer's beach shack. It was too far away to pick out without binoculars. She was wondering if the guys were even still there. As she leaned over the rail, she turned her head and glanced bow to stern. She noted that there were four davits and tenders on this side of the ship—two toward the bow, and two toward the stern. She commented, "Seems like this ship is a little light when it comes to lifeboats."

"Due to project expansion, space needs, and the fact that we were generally moored close to shore, we only needed to keep enough lifeboat tenders to carry the… elders."

The pause in his words made her turn and her eyes opened wide. He was leaning against the rail next to her with binoculars against his eyes. *Damn! Put them down,* she thought.

"Good view?" Sara was trying to break his concentration. "Did you see the historic lighthouse over there?"

"We are not looking for tourist attractions."

"Oh. What are we looking for?"

He did not answer right away. While still holding the binoculars he finally said, "It appears that the body of your dead comrade is no longer on the beach."

Sara swallowed hard. Glancing behind her, she was relieved that Heidi was not within earshot for such a callous reminder of Brian.

"That's strange. Short of another storm, there's no way the tide could have reached his body."

"Are we going to be out here long? It's freezing," Sara said, trying to change the subject.

Elder-1 ignored her. "We need to be on high alert during our search efforts. Back inside!" he instructed as he walked over to the door.

CHAPTER 16

December 28, 2044
Wednesday, Midday
New Jersey coast, Utopia Project
Ship Number One
Two days after the event

The girls followed Elder-1 up the hallway. He stopped in front of a large window and said, "Hold up!"

He pulled the walkie-talkie from his belt and depressed the call button. "Elder-48, come in!"

"Here, Sir. We have already reached the mainland."

"Be on high alert. We highly suspect there are survivors over there moving about in the shadows."

Elder-48 radioed back, "We will be on the highest alert."

"Good. All survivors must be killed. And you are to stay over there until the entire area has been cleared, and even some of the surrounding areas."

"Yes, Sir. We brought supplies and expect this mission to take a few days. We will provide a status report this evening."

"Over, and out," Elder-1 said and clipped his walkie-talkie back on his belt.

Sara was frozen in fear, given Elder-1's conversation. She was staring at a room through a window, but was not comprehending a thing.

"They are all doing their five-hour shifts," Elder-1 noted. "It is much more efficient for all people to work five hours per day, six days per week, than to have some of the population working 12 hours a day and some not working at all."

Shaking her head, Sara blinked until her focus returned. Through the window, she could see men and women cleaning uniforms at a series of washing stations. As the large, industrial sized dryers would finish, a woman would walk the clothes over to a man who would press the uniforms and put them on hangers. The garments were then hung on a mobile rack.

Trying to tamp down her fear, she asked a casual question. "They only work 30 hours per week? Why don't they work more?"

He turned his back to the window and continued, "Life shouldn't be consumed by work. Stop and ask yourself, in the old society, how many jobs or tasks were not truly essential to our survival as human beings?"

Here comes another rant, Sara thought.

"Many. Anything related to money and finances, which is a large pool of workers. Even the legal profession, which was usually about dollars, not justice. And how many professions seemed to exist just to further their own existence or to just make money? If you eliminate useless professions and non-essential jobs, you have more people doing less tasks, and just those that are essential for society to properly function. And in return for performing their assigned tasks, all of our members needs are provided for. There is no need for money or currency."

Sara listened to Elder-1 and watched the workers for a few moments. The repetition was almost mesmerizing. *How can they not be totally bored?* she wondered. They looked like automatons, all set to move at the same speed. Their movements resembled machines on an assembly line.

Elder-1 turned and watched the workers as they continued washing and pressing the uniforms. He seemed pleased. "They are not stressed or hurried, and are very much content while performing essential tasks."

"What about more intense jobs, like researching cures for diseases or something like that?" Sara asked.

"Our members are categorized as Type A, B, or C. The workers you see in there," he pointed in the window, "are Type A, and perform the simpler tasks. Researchers and educators perform more complex tasks and are Type C. Most of the researchers serve as educators as well, and pass their technical knowledge on to the younger members of the same type. We have a matrix of all essential tasks, which includes the member type required to fulfill those tasks, for everything from research to," he held his hands up to the window, "laundry."

"How do you determine a person's type?"

He again turned away from the window and toward the girls. "Throughout every pregnancy and after birth, we perform many tests to determine mental and physical capacity. Members are then categorized by type. We only need to determine their type for our own management purposes. They themselves are not even aware that they are categorized in such a way. They all see each other as equals."

"How can a Type C researcher and Type A laundry worker see each other as equals?" Sara asked.

"The only difference between types is their work location and assigned tasks. They all undergo the same basic conditioning. And all mental and physical activities, as well as sleeping and eating arrangements, do not discriminate as to type."

"Yeah, but if your people are sitting around the dinner table talking, don't the Type A's listen to the what the Type C's are doing for work and wonder why they don't get to do really important tasks?" Although she loathed being on the ship, Sara found herself curious about this society.

"Since all tasks are considered essential, no specific task is regarded as more or less important or mundane than another. They do speak about their tasks, but they are all proud to perform any task that is essential to our society. That is how they have been raised. They all respect and admire each other as pieces of our society's puzzle. The most technical researcher's tasks are no more important than..." Elder-1 again pointed to the uniform washers.

Sara turned and looked in the window. "What happens when people get too old to keep working? Is there a separate type for that?"

"No, but that is where our society's master plan, or blueprint, comes in. It covers every aspect of life from birth through death. Although we are not there yet with our members, the master plan calls for periodic evaluations of all people over the age of 60. As long as they are still able to contribute, even if for a little less time per day or in a different type, they will remain active members of our society. Some will become the next generation of elders. Those who do not become elders and can no longer contribute because of physical or mental deterioration, will be terminated."

"So you send them to slaughter, like dairy cows who have run dry," Maria commented.

Cringing, Sara looked to Elder-1. He did not seem to take offense. "The premise is not so different, nor is it baseless."

Sara tried not to sound disgusted "But we're not animals."

"There should not be such a differentiation. Although we have a higher mental capacity than other mammals, our pure needs are no different than theirs. Food, sleep, physical stimulation? Mental stimulation for species with mental capacity? And those who can no longer contribute are left behind."

"We still have the ability to provide some quality of life, even when people are old, or sick, or can't contribute," Sara noted. "That's what differentiates us from most animals."

"In the long-run, you cannot maintain the production, distribution, and consumption of resources for an entire society when too many members do not contribute to the system due to age, sickness, capacity, privilege or even downright laziness. It is simply an unbalanced equation whereby those who do contribute will inevitably have to contribute too much, to make up for those who don't, causing them to break down, burn out, give up, or even die. This will in turn burden and break down the system as a whole. This is why we terminate all people who cannot adequately contribute to society. We will never have the imbalances the old world had."

"What about disabled or handicapped people? What is their type?" Maria chimed in.

"Members must at least have the capacity to be a Type A."

"But what if they don't?"

"Again, members must at least have the capacity to be a Type A."

"Yeah, but…" Maria pressed.

"We think he's saying they are also terminated." Sara was glaring at Elder-1. She caught herself and looked away.

"Correct," he said. "That is where our highly advanced medical tests come in. Fetuses are tested throughout the pregnancy process and if a serious disability is detected, the pregnancy is immediately terminated. If a disability develops after birth, the member is also terminated, unless they can at least function as a Type A."

Maria's face was bright red. "All of your fetus 'tests' could never measure the depths of someone's heart, soul, or mind. I, fuck, *we* know that. We saw it firsthand with my autistic younger brother."

"All the same, he would have been terminated." He sounded dismissive. "Our member termination policy is quite clear and serves the overall good of society."

Sara reached for Maria's hand to try and calm her down, but she was too late.

Tears started streaming down Maria's face, and her expression turned to one of rage. "You are black-hearted sick, bastards." She swung her open palm at Elder-1's face.

Sara gasped but caught Maria's wrist just in time. She wrapped her arms around her and held tight. "Please, Maria, don't." Her voice conveyed her desperation. "Please…"

Maria finally relaxed her hand and let it fall to her side.

Sara pleaded, "Sir, she won't ever do that again. She got emotional thinking about her brother. Please let it slide just this one time. She is so sorry." Sensing that they had only a split second to push the pendulum, she gave Maria a firm shake. "Right?"

"Such behavior will not be tolerated." Elder-1's eyes were dark. "The risk of having you here may be too…"

"Sorry," Maria offered weakly as she wiped the tears from her cheek. Elder-1 did not react at all.

"Alright. Sorry." Maria sounded a little more sincere. "It won't happen again, Sir."

Come on, let it go, Sara begged in her mind.

Turning his back to them, Elder-1 let Maria's fate hang for the longest minute ever. "Consider yourself lucky that the numbers are what they are, as far as offspring production."

Relieved, Sara let out a deep exhale. She also felt Maria's shoulders loosen.

"And we are surprised that our psychological evaluations have not already identified these violent tendencies. We will take that up with Elder-76 as soon as we are done here, but we have full confidence that our conditioning will cure that," he said with his back to them.

Elder-1 turned suddenly and stepped toward them. "But if we see such hostility ever again, you will be terminated on the spot."

Maria pulled back as if shrinking, and then nodded her head.

"To continue what we were saying, with our member termination policy, we also terminate members with incurable or debilitating sickness. Our policy calls for the termination of anyone who does not contribute adequately to the system."

"No exceptions to the rule at all?" Sara asked, still holding Maria's arm and gently rubbing it.

"None. That was a lesson the old world learned the hard way. Catering to the exceptions to the rule, or the minority, can also burden and break down the system. And by minority, we are not referring to a racial or ethnic minority. So many rules, laws, and programs in the old world were established for the loud and manipulative minorities to which we are referring to, but such special treatment required vast amounts of resources and time. All the while, this caused the majority of people to be stressed, overworked, and to pay the bill, both literally and figuratively. With too many ever-growing minorities not contributing nearly enough to the system, the stress on society was becoming too much, and the societal equation was becoming more and more out of balance."

"We are a little confused. Can you give an example from the old world?" She was hoping her question would further distance him from the member termination policy, for Maria's sake.

"Off the top of my head, the 2035 federal School Security Act, which required a host of extreme security measures for all schools in America. Schools became as secure as Fort Knox. The cost and time involved was incredible, and why was that law passed? Because of a few incidents where unstable offspring became savage and lost control? The cost versus benefit was just not there. The idea of spending vast amounts of money and resources to save one life, or a minimal number of lives, was impractical. With the School Security Act, society as a whole paid, and would've continued to allocate enormous amounts of resources because of the actions of a few unstable individuals; the exceptions to the rule, the minority. This despite the majority, millions, of students passing through school halls every day without incident."

"Guess that was kind of over the top," Sara said. "We remember someone pointing out that if a student is that unstable, they will find a way to cause harm regardless of how secure a school is. If not in school, then they will do their damage at a dance or a football game or something like that."

Heidi seemed surprised that she was agreeing with him. Sara shrugged.

"Exactly. It will not stop, and did not stop, such damage. Now, if they were all conditioned…" He looked at his watch. "The work period is almost over. Let us go while there is nobody in the hallway." Elder-1 escorted the girls back to their rooms.

Back in her room, Sara sat on her bed and rested her cheek against her fist. That was a close call for Maria. She feared her friend would not last much longer before she said or did something to get herself killed.

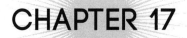

CHAPTER 17

December 28, 2044
Wednesday, Early Evening
New Jersey coast, Utopia Project
Ship Number One
Two days after the event

D inner for the girls was not until 7:00 p.m., but they were again allowed to eat together. After they finished, Elder-76 came to bring them back to their rooms. At this point, Sara was never sure who would escort them, but it is always either Elder-1 or Elder-76.

As they walked past a large room, Maria hesitated for a moment and glanced in the window. "Are they…" and then she cupped her hand over her mouth.

Elder-76 stopped. "Go ahead and look."

Although she should not have been surprised, Sara couldn't believe what she was seeing. The room was full of naked people, most engaged in some sort of sexual activity. The room had plush dark carpet and several couches and futons.

"A planned group sexual activity," she noted, with her enchanting voice.

"It's like a porn movie," Maria countered.

"Not at all. No such negative connotations. These activities are very satisfying to the participants, as well as healthy. Every member has an assigned sexual activity period each week."

"Are those birth control pills?" Sara asked. Inside the door was a metal tray containing pills for people to take as they came in.

"There is no birth control, and there won't be for a long time, if ever. We want every female pregnant so our population will quickly grow. Remember, that's why you three are still alive," Elder-76 said matter-of-factly. "The tray holds Viameen pills, which are sensitivity enhancers, and really make you tingle at every touch. They amplify the intensity of every sexual experience, which is helpful even with our production of offspring. When you are conditioned enough to participate, you will take them and understand."

"The girls here obviously aren't worried about their reputations," Heidi commented as she stared through the window.

"Why would they be? The girls report to no parents, and society does not judge and frown upon their behavior. They are not conflicted, nor do they feel ashamed. To the contrary, being promiscuous and better yet, becoming pregnant, is a joy, not an embarrassment. They do not have to worry about struggling to deliver, or take care of, their offspring. Our society takes care of it all. As you can see," she raised her hands, and her voice sounded sultry, "they are very content and relaxed, and are doing what naturally feels good."

"They certainly look like they're enjoying themselves," Maria said while pointing at the window.

"How are you going to prevent cross-breeding when these girls get pregnant, and down the road their... offspring participate in these activities?" Sara asked.

"We carefully coordinate the composition of participants in our group sexual activities to ensure that will not be a problem."

"Without them wearing uniforms, or anything at all for that matter, how can you even tell your people apart?" she asked. "They all look the same."

"We manage our member database with thermographic technology." Elder-76 grabbed a small device from her belt. "We just wave this device over your face and it reads your individual signature through 65,000 temperature points. And our database..." she waved the scanning device over Sara's face and checked the read-out. "…has recently been updated to include all three of you."

"What do your young people do all day around here?" Heidi asked.

"That depends on the age. Up to three years of age, which is our infant group, all types are commingled together in large rooms. In those rooms, they are constantly cared for by Type B members of our Offspring Conditioning Team who ensure the infants are happy and content 24 hours per day, seven days per week. They feed them, change them, play games with them, and further condition them."

"Like daycare," Maria remarked.

"What we have here is quite a bit more extensive than that," she said assuredly.

"From what the parents expected these days, it couldn't be much more."

Since snapping earlier while discussing special needs children, Maria seemed to be back to her old self. Sara was relieved, but did not want Maria to get out of line either.

Elder-76 turned away and continued with her soft voice, "Then, from the age of three to 12, they work."

"Work? At three years of age?" Sara was astonished. "Y'all are tough."

"Our pre-adults, from age three through age 12, have a five-hour work day that is comprised of training and learning," Elder-76 responded. "They are exposed to just about every task for their type. Their training schedules mirror the adult workday. Of course, teaching them requires much patience since they are easily distracted at the earlier ages. At the age of 13, all members are assigned specific tasks, and begin to actually perform these tasks."

"Like graduating from school," Heidi commented. "What else do people do around here when they're not working or having group intimacy?"

"The pre-adults and adults have planned activities every week-night, and Saturday. Sunday, they have a choice of activities. That is their free day. Within the allowable activities, they are free to do whatever they wish."

"That is the extent of their freedom?" Sara asked.

"Yes, but it is the appropriate level of freedom."

"They have activities every day," Sara started, "but what if your people just want a day to stay in and be alone?"

"None of them ever do. And even if they did, all of our members have a conditioned anxiety response to being alone."

She stared at the elder with raised eyebrows, "How did you accomplish that?"

"There are several techniques. For example, with the infant group, after being starved for a day, they are put alone in empty rooms. Then 3D images come out of the walls toward them. The images vary, but most are of deformed and scary people and creatures. Just as the images are upon the infant, a loud, blood-curdling scream sounds and the frightened infant is given the most painful electric shock."

Sara let out an involuntary gasp, and seemed appalled.

"Then, the images, noises, and shocks disappear. A large group of offspring is placed in the room, surrounding the terrified infant as peaceful music begins to play. The floor is warmed several degrees and the starving infant is fed. Soon the infant feels safe and content. After repeating this conditioning exercise several times, these responses become ingrained in them. The infant forever associates comfort and peace with being surrounded by people, and they are uncomfortable being alone. That is why activities are all done in groups, and why we have ten people sleeping in each room. If they spent time alone, they would become individuals, and as our motto indicates, here there is…"

Sara pointed to her pupil.

Elder-76 nodded and began walking up the hallway.

"What other kind of recreational activities do you have here?" Sara asked.

"There are too many for me to list; virtual reality simulations, exercise periods, games of chance…"

"Like sports?"

"No, games of chance, whereby the winner or loser is not determined by any player's skill. We don't want to foster a spirit of competition based on any member being any better or worse at some-thing than anyone else."

"Like picking numbers and just rolling the dice?" Maria asked.

"We have games just like that."

"Doesn't that get boring?"

"Keep in mind, here, people don't need the same intense, and often stressful, stimulation people thrived on in the old society. Our members have stress-free lives, and therefore can be easily stimulated just by play-ing a simple game." The elder again sounded like an enchantress.

"Their people must be easily amused," Heidi noted.

"Very much so," Elder-76 acknowledged. "At some point in the near future, you too will find these simple games stimulating. That is the way reality should be."

"With the limited reality these people know, it must be easy to create virtual reality that seems exciting," Heidi added.

"They really do enjoy the simulators. The best is probably the roller coaster. It drops your stomach right out, just like the real thing. Then there's one for sailing, automobiles, water slides, sledding, and the list goes on and on."

"Sounds like their lives are all fun and games outside of work," Sara said.

Elder-76 stopped at the door at the end of the hallway. "Their lives outside of work are consumed by more than just games. Once a month after they reach the age of 12, each member has a word conditioning session. Then once a week each member attends a mission meeting. There we show them what the world outside looks like, and what we need to do when we begin to inhabit land."

Sara noted, "We hope they are not squeamish. It's pretty disgusting out there."

"To that end, we have a decaying corpse in a glass encasement at the front of the meeting room. For that part of the mission meeting, we remove the glass to allow the stench of death to waft through the room. We don't want them to be surprised when they see and smell death."

Going through the door at the end of the hall, they went down a spiral staircase for many floors. As she walked them to their rooms, Elder-76 noted, "Until you are fully conditioned, you will have your own rooms. After that time, you will share a room with nine others like everyone else."

Once back in her room, Sara watched the elder's figure disappear from view out the opaque, frosted glass window. She waved her hand in front of the scanning pad and nothing happened. She attempted to manually pull open the sliding door, but it would not budge. Frustrated, she went over to her bed and sat down. She put her fist under her chin with her elbow on her knee, and thought about how they could get off of the ships before being impregnated, and before the *Ion* conditioning took hold. She could think of no viable escape options. The situation seemed dire.

As she waited for the 9:00 p.m. bedtime tone to sound, her thoughts turned to her father. She recalled the gift he had given her the last time she saw him- a box containing a piece of paper and a watch of some type? Her brow furrowed. Something now seemed odd about him giving her a gift to open the same night as the destruction. Could the timing be a coincidence? Suspicions swirled around in her head, but she did not know and given her hopeless circumstances, she might never know.

What Sara did know was that she missed her father and seeing the military-like elders only served as a constant reminder of him. Had she known what was coming, she would have been in less of a hurry the last time she saw him and would have hugged and kissed him one more time. It dawned on her that her father seemed to become more affectionate after he went up to Boston a little more than a year ago. She was late picking him up, and thought he was going to be angry. But when she pulled up and got out of her car, he hugged her for a long time—so long that she was worried he had some awful news to share. That happened on November 7, 2043, a date she would never forget because that was also the day she met Kid.

She recalled getting the call from her father to go to Boston, and being upset, *very* upset, that she was going to have to cancel a first date that she had been so looking forward to all day. Having snagged an envelope, a piece of paper, and tape from her grandparents' house, she had written a note to leave on the bench where she was supposed to meet Kid at 8:00 p.m. As she drove through Killington that night, she considered turning around and not leaving the note after all. She had only met this guy once and talked to him for a while on a bench. He could turn out to be just another jerk. Another master of illusion. But there was something genuine about her instant connection with Kid Carlson. Maybe it was chemistry. Maybe it was truly love at first sight. She kept driving because all the way to the bottom of her soul, she knew from moment one that it was something more, something deeper.

CHAPTER 18

December 28, 2044
Wednesday, Evening
New Jersey coast, Utopia Project
Ship Number One
Two days after the event

Having heard a noise in the bottom of the ship, Kid stood up behind the propeller engines and peeked around the corner. He spotted two soldiers standing in front of the bank of generators further down the walkway. Ducking back, he bumped into Jess, who had also woken up and was standing behind him. Kid held a finger in front of his mouth. "Shh."

For the next few moments, they heard the start and stop of humming machinery. To Kid it sounded like voices in a large chorus dropping in and out but having slightly different pitches. After a moment of baritone harmony, the sound of the collective hum was overridden by the sharp click of a door being shut.

"Note the time. It seems they come down here on a schedule to cycle the generators," Kid whispered.

"The time is… 8:50 p.m." Moments later a tone sounded and the lights dimmed a few notches. Moving his face closer to his watch, Jess added, "9:00 p.m. on the dot."

Alert for soldiers, Kid and Jess again explored the bottom of the ship. They found containers of chemicals and cleaning agents stacked up in a storage closet. They also found a cabinet with tools and spare parts for the engines. After closing the cabinet, Kid again gravitated to the ladder amidships. He climbed into the shaft and opened the hatch with the hand wheel. Jess followed close behind, watching for soldiers below. Climbing rungs which seemed to ascend indefinitely, they came to a second hatch. Opening it, Kid peered into a dimly lit room with various control boards, screens, and machines. Stepping up through the hatch, it appeared they were in the engineer's room. All of the instruments sparkled like they had never been touched. Straight ahead, they could see the stars in the nighttime sky out a large window. To the side of them, through a smaller window, they could see the ship's bridge.

"The ladder must be a quick route down to the engines, in case of an emergency," Kid whispered.

His heart sank as Jess jumped to the floor and waved him down. Kid was flat on his stomach in a second. Pointing at the window to the room next door, Jess held up one finger. He crawled to the corner of the room and prompted Kid to follow him down a spiral staircase.

Going down for several floors, they reached the main deck level. They looked through a window covering the top half of a hallway door and saw a long, dimly lit corridor. There were no soldiers in sight and all appeared quiet.

Kid turned. "What was that all about up there?"

"There was someone on the bridge next door. I guess some kind of night watchman."

"I'm glad you spotted him before he spotted us."

"We're lucky he was looking straight ahead," Jess whispered.

"At least now we know they have someone positioned up there." Glancing around, he re-focused. "Alright, we know they brought the girls to this ship, but where do we start searching?"

Peering down the staircase, Jess said, "There has to be more than 20 levels, and that's just this side of the ship."

"How do you want to attack it?" Kid asked. "Talk about a needle in a haystack."

"Why don't we just take a quick peek up every hallway and look for something unusual on that floor, you know, like additional security measures. Anything that might give us a hint that there are captives."

"That's a good start. I have to say, for such a top-secret project they don't seem too focused on security around here," Kid noted.

"That's because they've probably never had to worry about it," Jess countered.

"Maybe not, but let's stay alert and not get any false sense of security. Follow me."

They descended the staircase and took a peek up all of the floors, which totaled 31. At each level they would peer through the window of the hall-door for anything unusual, such as guards or any other conspicuous security measure. On the bottom floor, they reconvened behind the staircase. "So much for that. I didn't see anything unusual," Jess said.

"Not a damn thing," Kid agreed, agitated. "Wait here for a second."

He stepped out from behind the staircase, opened the door to the bottom floor hallway and crouched down. Stopping to gaze in the window of the first room, his heart skipped a beat. In the dim light he counted ten bunks, and they were all occupied by sleeping soldiers. Ducking down, he ran to the room across the hall and saw the same setup, so he retreated back through the door to the stairwell. "Listen. Here's the deal," Kid started. "The rooms all seem to have windows and low-level lighting, enough to see in once your eyes adjust. So we have to look inside each one and hope we can spot them. Each room seems to have ten bunks."

"Ten? How are we supposed to find them among that many people?"

"Since the girls are captives, I have a hard time believing they would be kept with the masses. I would guess that the girls are being held separately. So let's take a quick peek in each room until we find rooms that don't have the same setup with ten bunks."

"What if we get spotted, or run into someone?" Jess asked.

Hesitating, Kid knew what that would mean. Since they were trapped on the ship, they would be done for. But he wasn't going to say so. Instead, he suggested, "We hustle back down to the bottom of the ship and hide."

Jess didn't appear to be buying it, but Kid kept his focus on what they needed to do next. "We should split up or this is going to take forever. I'll take this floor, you take the next one up. Run up one side of the hall and come back along the other side, and just take a peek in every window. I'll meet you behind the stairwell at the end of your floor. Then we'll tackle the next two floors and keep going until we reach the top, or run out of time."

Jess exhaled, and gathered himself. He nodded and hustled up the spiral staircase.

Pushing open the door, Kid crouched and ran up one side of the long hall, peeking in all of the windows. He reached the end and came back along the other side, moving with haste. Back at his starting point, he slipped through the door and climbed the spiral staircase to the floor above.

Jess was waiting. "Nothing."

"Me neither. Next two," Kid said. "Go."

On the third level from the bottom he stopped and Jess continued up the staircase to the next level. Kid again crouched and started running up the hall and peeking in the windows. Suddenly, he came upon a window where the glass was frosted and looked different from the rest. He stopped and peered in, but saw only blurry shadows. Although expecting to find ten soldiers snoozing in double-stacked bunks, he was able to discern that the room only had one bed. He studied a shadow on the bed, but gasped when it moved. The form was a person sitting upright, so he jumped down and out of view.

Slowly raising his head, the person was now standing right at the window. His heart stopped and he fell backward on the ground.

As he went to run, the person started waving his or her hands. Coiled and ready to dash, Kid squinted. It appeared to be a female, and her mannerisms seemed familiar. As her face came almost against the glass, he filled with excitement and took a step closer. He knew it was Maria, despite her hairstyle being different. He put his face almost against the surface. She waved and pointed her finger at the room next to hers. He waved back and kept crawling.

Staring in the frosted glass of the next room, he could see the outline of a person lying down on a bed. Assuming it had to be Sara or Heidi, he started tapping lightly on the glass. The person got up and walked to the door. His heart started racing with excitement after realizing it was his Sara. Although her hairstyle had also changed, he would know her outline anywhere. She was still alive, and he was overwhelmed by a feeling of relief. With no other way to communicate, Kid used his finger and wrote one letter on the frosted glass at a time. "H E I D I ?"

Sara used her finger to point toward Heidi's room directly across the hall. She also pointed at the room next door, but Kid already knew Maria was there. He acknowledged and again went to write a message, but paused. He realized they needed time to plan an escape, so he spelled out, "R E S C U E   T O M O R R O W   N I G H T   P A S S   O N."

As he went to leave he put his palm on the opaque glass. Sara did the same. He needed to get her out. He was thankful he found her alive, but was worried sick about what they might be doing to her.

He crawled across the hall to Heidi's room and tapped lightly on the glass. After getting no response, he used his fingertips and tried again. Nothing. She had to be in a sound asleep. He was not about to make any loud noises to wake her. Sara or Maria would have to find a way to tell her about the plan for tomorrow night.

He went back across the hall and spelled out the rescue message on Maria's window before running up the hall and climbing the staircase to the floor above.

Jess was crouched behind the stairwell. "This is impossible..." he started, but was cut off.

"I found them!"

"What? Seriously?" He jumped to his feet. Kid nodded and his head wobbled as his friend shook his shoulder. "Talk about dumb luck! Where are they?"

"On the floor below, about halfway up the hall," Kid answered. "A few rooms had frosted glass windows, and looked unusual, so I stopped to check them out."

Jess exhaled. "Thank God. Are they alright?"

"I think so, but I couldn't see them that well because of the frosting on the glass." He then added, "I just hope someone hasn't spotted us."

"What do you mean?"

"Although they don't seem too concerned with security, they must like to keep an eye on their people. You didn't notice the cameras in the hall?" Kid asked.

"Where?"

Crawling over and opening the door to the hallway, they both glanced up. Sure enough, a small camera was positioned above the door, aiming down the length of the hallway. They gently closed the door and went back behind the staircase. Kid said, "Too late now. If someone's watching, they would've spotted us a long time ago."

"So you think they aren't watching?" Jess seemed doubtful.

"They would've already come after us. We've been combing these halls for some time now," he replied, trying to convince Jess, as well as himself.

"What time is it?"

"4:00 a.m. We don't have time to do anything more tonight. Anyway I told them we would rescue them tomorrow night."

Turning around, Kid realized that there was a door behind the staircase on each level. He had a hunch. "Hold on. I want to check something." He turned the handle and pulled the door open. He froze as a light automatically turned on inside. The small room was a closet that contained janitorial supplies. In the back right corner, a rounded metal protrusion ran from ceiling to floor. He approached it, and despite it being painted the same gray color as the walls, he could see it was clearly made of metal. He turned to Jess who was in the doorway watching for soldiers. "The ladder shaft we came up through," he whispered, pointing to the rounded metal protrusion.

Jess gave a thumbs up.

Kid stepped out and said, "Follow me."

He ran down the steps to the girls' floor and opened the same door behind the spiral staircase. Stepping inside, as soon as the light turned on he reached into his pant pocket and pulled out a handful of change and his house keys. Taking the keys, he put the tip of the pointiest one against the metal of the shaft. He pushed with all of his might and slammed the key with his palm a couple of times until it made a small indent in the metal. Jess cringed. Although the sound was still reverberating up and down the shaft, Kid said, "Don't worry. With the emergency doors at the end of the hallway, they can't hear anything."

After Kid closed the closet door, they trudged up the spiral staircase for many levels until they reached the engineer's room. They crawled on the floor to avoid being spotted by the night watchman on the bridge. Silently, they dropped down into the shaft and closed the hatch behind them. Going down the ladder, Kid stopped near the bottom and searched the enclosure wall. It took a few minutes, but he found the indent he had made with his house key. "We have to remember this spot," he whispered. Figuring it was the easiest way to find it again, he counted the ladder rungs from the indent down to the lower hatch.

Once behind the engines, they took out some food from the backpacks and Kid used a small metal can opener to remove the top from a can of tomato soup. He then took saltines, crushed them up and sprinkled them in the can. This made for a quick but filling meal, which was washed down with a few swigs of bottled water.

Jess said, "Wait, you told them we would rescue them tomorrow night? How are we going to do that?"

"I'm working on it. Just give me a little time."

"I'll give some thought as well, but I trust you Kid. We just need to make sure we don't come up short, like when we were trying to throw the tow hook all the way up to the bulwarks." Jess patted him on the arm and then laid his head down to get some sleep.

"No, this time we will not have to worry about anything being too far away," Kid noted. "Just the opposite."

They lay side by side in the tight space, both covered with a handful of beach towels trying to keep warm. The more Kid thought of the impending rescue, the more nervous he became. He knew there was a very good chance they may not live to see another day. All it would take is one shot from one of the soldier's weapons, and that would be the end. What if they don't get the girls out in time? All he wanted to do was get away and spend the rest of his days with his Sara and the other friends. Regardless of the status of the world, if Sara was by his side, he would at least have something, and someone, to live for. He would never feel empty or alone. These thoughts only made him more afraid of losing her, but at the same time they made him more determined to succeed.

As Kid fell asleep, he could still envision Sara's outline behind the opaque glass. He smiled as he slept. He knew it was her, he'd know her anywhere, with her hands on her hips and that confident stance. As the frosting on the glass faded away, more and more details became clear. He became terrified as he realized that the outline was the same as hers, and the mannerisms were the same, but it was not her. The details of her face came into focus, and the horror made his heart beat rapidly. It was the face of a creature of some kind. It had red eyes and its teeth were long, sharp fangs. The creature was beginning to snarl as it realized Kid was staring at it. Its mouth began to open and it let out a bone-chilling hiss. Blood dripped from the tips of sharp fangs. He was frozen in fear at this bizarre image of Sara's body with the face of an evil beast. He began to toss and turn, moaning in distress.

Jess shook him. "Hey!"

"Stop! I'm awake." Kid stared into the darkness, shaken by his nightmare. He figured the anxiety of being on the ship was starting to play tricks with his mind.

Moments later Kid was starting to doze, but his eyes popped open upon hearing the familiar muffled beep. He checked his watch. "6:00 a.m. It goes off at the same time every day, 6:00 a.m. and 9:00 p.m. I guess 6:00 a.m. is the wakeup call," Kid whispered.

"For us, it's the bedtime call." Jess grumbled.

A few minutes later, Kid heard the also familiar audible click of a door as two soldiers came down to cycle the generators. Jess didn't even wake up, but fortunately didn't start snoring. The soldiers finished their work and exited the bottom of the ship.

Kid stretched out and tried to go back to sleep, but was worried that the awful nightmare would pick up where it left off. Though he tried to snooze lightly, he plummeted through the sleep stages and again found himself staring at Sara's outline through the opaque glass. This time, he stared in fear as the frosting on the glass faded and her outline filled in. Wincing as he slept, the details were becoming clearer. It was like he was looking through an out-of-focus camera lens, and the adjustment knob was slowly being turned. With her face becoming clearer, he started to feel warm inside. As the final focusing adjustment was made, he saw his hands reaching toward the glass. Her smile revealed no fangs and her eyes were a beautiful hazel color. He was sure it was his Sara. She closed her eyes tight, and a teardrop squeezed out and ran down her face. In the strange hazy light emanating from the fringes of his dream world, the saline droplet appeared amber colored. Before she could open her eyes, his dreams took a left turn, and he was captaining the crew of an 18th century pirate ship, cursing the full moon.

CHAPTER 19

December 29, 2044
Thursday, Early Morning
New Jersey coast, Utopia Project
Ship Number One
Three days after the event

Thursday morning, Sara endured her second conditioning session, which left her trembling. *I don't know how many more sessions I can take*, she thought to herself. She tried to push back the conditioning by force of will alone, but resistance was futile, and downright painful. Kid's rescue plan had to work, and it could not happen soon enough.

In the late morning, she again had to meet with Elder-76 and now four of her staff. She endured another round of psychological tests, even more intensive than the day before.

For lunch, they had to eat in their rooms alone. Sara hoped that she would have the opportunity to eat dinner that night with the other girls and inform them of Kid's visit, and of his plan to rescue them. With any luck, he got to them last night as well and they already knew.

When it came time for dinner, Sara was distraught that she was again dining alone. As she sat isolated in her room, she picked at her well-prepared meal, never raising her fork to her mouth. Without a knock or any fair warning, her door slid open and Elder-1 yelled, "*Ion!*"

Sara's eyes stared straight ahead, and her arms seemed loose and flimsy. She slumped in her chair and her head seemed too heavy for her neck. She had to rest it on the top of the table. A moment later, she sat up, blinked and took rapid shallow breaths, while touching her body to make sure her physical form actually existed. She didn't hear it, but he must have said the word to bring her back. That word, *Ion*, and the tone of his voice, gave her chills just thinking about it. She really loathed Elder-1, who seemed to enjoy seeing her struggle.

"We wanted to see the progress of our conditioning program, and it seems to be coming along well," he started. "We will not be here tomorrow. First thing tomorrow morning, a large group is going ashore, and we will lead them. But your conditioning program will proceed as scheduled with just Elder-76. We…" His words were interrupted by the beep of the walkie-talkie on his belt. Raising it to his lips he said, "Go ahead."

"Standing by to initiate routine testing and maintenance of all davits and tenders, before the excursion to the mainland tomorrow, Sir. The nylon drop lines have been inspected and seem to be in great shape."

"Proceed, Elder-110, and report back any problems immediately," he instructed.

He turned to Sara, so she asked, "You are going ashore?"

"We must. The four members we left on Tuesday when we captured you at the beach, and the two-person pickup team that went to get them that very night, still have not returned and cannot be reached. We sent two battle-tested military elders ashore yesterday to find them all, including Elder-48 who checked in just moments ago. He has eliminated many survivors, including several at a hotel, but they haven't been able to locate any of our members who we sent ashore. It seems they did not succeed with their mission. We now know our mistake was sending them without elder leadership. The members follow orders to the letter, which is what we want and need here on the ships, but they lack adaptability. They need an elder leader to assess the battlefield and environment, and adjust their orders, which is what we will do when we go with them tomorrow morning. We will not make that mistake again."

After feeling an initial surge of panic about survivors being killed, Sara knew Kid wasn't one of them since he was stowed away somewhere on the ship. "Maybe your people are just lost," she said.

"That… we doubt. They would never disobey an order. Based on their conditioning the anxiety would be overwhelming. Again we will ask, are you aware of any survivors on the mainland?"

"It wouldn't be a surprise if there were survivors, but none that we are specifically aware of," Sara replied, with more assurance than the first time he had asked that same question. Again, she was not lying. Kid and hopefully Jess, were not on the mainland.

He studied her for a moment.

She did not flinch.

"Some of our weapons and walkie-talkies were discovered in the back of a supermarket, so we are beyond suspicious, especially since your dead comrade's body also seems to have vanished from the beach. We suspect there may be a more organized opposition lurking in the shadows, so we will have to step up our efforts to snuff them out, once and for all." Elder-1 turned and walked out of the room.

Sara gazed straight ahead and did not move. But inside, she felt her blood pumping faster and faster. The elders knew something was amiss.

■   ■   ■

Kid and Jess sat up, hearing the same mechanical hum from outside the ship that they had heard the day before, but this time it was louder and they were encircled by it.

"That's more than one davit they are activating," Jess noted.

The rumbling of boat motors soon surrounded them.

"They must have lowered a bunch of boats," Kid said.

The lights hanging over the center walkway started to flicker and then dimmed a few notches. The nearby generators seemed to be straining, as their typical peaceful hum was replaced by a collective labored whine. "Do you hear those generators?" Jess asked. "Something's not right with them."

"Just keep your eyes and ears open for someone coming down here to check them out."

They sat still for a few minutes and listened. The sound of the boat motors did not fade or dissipate, but abruptly ended. Jess turned. "The boats didn't leave."

■ ■ ■

As Elder-1 walked up the hallway, his walkie-talkie again came to life. "Go ahead."

"Sir, we have a problem."

He stopped in his tracks. "Elder-110, advise!"

"The activation of all the davits at one time has drained the generators to dangerous levels on all ships. If we activate all davits now to bring the tenders back up to the deck, we may kill the first set of generators."

"Then why don't we just switch to the second set of generators?" Elder-1 sounded impatient.

"They are not recharged yet, and are at maybe 60 percent. But they cannot be fully recharged if the first set of generators dies on us now. And if the second set is not charged enough, we may lose power and heat on the ships before morning," said Elder-110.

"Why have we never had this problem before during this routine testing?"

"Well, Sir, for all of those years in Greenland, our ships were moored and used supplemental electric power from the mainland, so power wasn't an issue. That is what made it an easy choice to go with electric davits to begin with. Our problem now is this set up with generators, which was not an issue until…"

"What is your recommendation?" Elder-1 cut in. Given that Elder-110 was a master electrician in the United States Navy prior to the world's rebirth, Elder-1 trusted his judgement in this regard.

"Operate at absolute minimum power for the rest of the day to let the second set of generators fully recharge, which means that we should not activate the davits at this time and retrieve the tenders. Activating the davits again now will kill what little power is left. If we modify the generator changeover schedules and adjust some settings, by morning the situation should be corrected."

"Is there any risk to the boats by leaving them in the water?"

"No, Sir. We checked the radar, and although there are some light snow showers coming through, the seas are not expected to be rolling."

Elder-1's lips were pursed. "Proceed as you have outlined. Tomorrow's search and rescue operation must go forth as planned."

"Yes, Sir. We will use rope ladders to retrieve the mechanics from the boats..."

Although Elder-110 was still talking, Elder-1 snapped his walkie-talkie to his belt and resumed walking.

■   ■   ■

"Strange," Jess observed. "It sounds like they lowered the boats, turned on the motors for a few minutes and then shut them off. They didn't leave the ships, but I didn't hear them being hoisted back up to the deck either. Did you?"

"No. I just wonder if they'll pull them up tonight or not." Kid stared down as he processed the implications. "I'm just glad they didn't take all of the boats ashore. One of those boats is our ride out of here later."

"I know, the rest can sink into the sea for all we care," Jess said off the cuff and took a sip of water.

After thinking a moment, Kid concluded, "That would be good."

"What? I see your wheels turning."

"Just more pieces of the plan coming together," he said with a far-away look in his eyes. As he sat, he rolled up his pant leg and gently rubbed a large purple bruise on his shin.

"That has to hurt." Jess had a grimace on his face.

"Yeah, and it's raw. I need to avoid bumping into things."

After spending some more time thinking, Kid laid out some rescue plan options. He knew they had all the tools they would need in the storage cabinets on the bottom of the ship.

A little before 9:00 p.m., on schedule, soldiers came down and cycled the generators and adjusted some settings. Kid and Jess waited in their hiding space for the soldiers to conclude their work.

"Why were you looking behind the generators?" Kid could faintly hear one of them ask.

"We have not."

"There is a clear handprint on the side of generator number ten." Kid tensed as he listened to the conversation.

"We assure you, Sir, we did not touch the side of the generator."

"Someone did. Maybe you did so unintentionally," the soldier said. "Maybe," he repeated.

The generator adjustment and cycling seemed to take forever, so Kid crawled out and took a peek from behind the engines. He ducked back as he saw a soldier coming up the center walkway, heading in their direction. Kid pointed and used his fingers to warn Jess. The soldier was now close enough that they could hear his footsteps. Kid's heart was racing. They had no weapons, and nothing to defend themselves with. The elder was now almost even with their position.

A soldier called out from the bank of generators, "Elder-110, we are done, Sir!"

Kid and Jess were holding their breath, ready to spring

The footsteps of this Elder-110 stopped. He turned and walked back to the generators. Moments later, they heard the door close as the soldiers departed.

When the 9:00 p.m. beep sounded, Kid said with concerned assurance, "That was close. It's just a matter of time until we are discovered down here."

He emptied his backpack on the floor and slung the line with tow hook over his shoulder and across his chest. He felt like he was wearing the bandolier of a Wild West gunslinger.

Jess asked, "Do we really need that? It might be more trouble than it is worth."

Kid went to lay down the line and then hesitated. He had a feeling in his gut so he kept it. "You never know. We would've never been able to scale the anchor chain links and get into the ship without it. If it hinders me, I'll drop it."

They sprinted to the storage cabinet, took screwdrivers, wrenches, pliers, and hacksaws and put them in their backpacks. "Wait, could they raise anchor and move the ships closer to shore?" Kid asked.

Jess thought for a second. "Even if they raise anchor, with the shallow depth of the continental shelf just off of the shoreline, I don't think they could move in closer. At least not much."

Kid said, "Could they get close enough to swim ashore without dying of hypothermia first?"

"No. Not even close. Why?"

"You'll see," Kid noted.

"So where are we going now?"

Kid rummaged through his backpack and pulled out a heavy wrench. Smacking it against his palm a couple of times, he said, "To take out the night watchman."

Ascending the ladder amidships, they crawled along the floor of the engineer's room. The bridge next door was dark and empty. "There is no night watchman up here tonight," Kid noted.

"Go figure," Jess quipped. "At least not on this ship."

"Follow me and keep your eyes open." Kid took off.

They descended the spiral staircase in the engineer's room until they reached the main deck and found a door to the outside. Unsure if he would trigger an alarm, Kid winced as he depressed the horizontal push bar. He heard nothing more than a click, and the low whistle of the wind. Already shivering from nervousness and the cold outside air, his breath was expelled in short, cloudy bursts as they went outside. While he ran along the deck rail, he whispered, "It doesn't look like any boats have been raised to the deck, so we are going with our first plan option. Cut them all free, except for one."

Reaching the first davit, Kid checked his watch. The time was fast approaching 11:00 p.m. They each opened their backpack and pulled out a hacksaw. The heavy nylon drop line was exposed at the elbow where the telescopic davit arm connected to its base, so they inserted their blades and started sawing. Although the cutting took more effort than expected, they were able to sever the line, and they watched as it reeled out of the telescopic arm and fell to the water below. Now free of the davit's hold, the boat drifted slowly away from the large ship and was soon swallowed by the darkness.

For the next hour, Kid and Jess ran from davit to davit, cutting nylon lines. Soon all of the remaining boats attached to the middle boat were cut free, save one. "That boat has our name on it," Kid pointed at the last davit.

Both he and Jess were panting, so they took a moment to catch their breath. "Time?" Jess huffed.

"Midnight. That means we have six hours," Kid answered.

"Can we get everything done in that time?"

"Do we have a choice? You know what you need to do?"

Jess nodded. "That's what worries me about only having six hours. I'll meet you back here," he said as he hunched low and took off for the rope bridge to the northernmost ship.

Kid ran toward the rope bridge to the southernmost vessel. Crawling on the unstable wood planks between the ships, it seemed like even breathing was making the bridge sway. Once across, he peered up. The bridge high above the main deck was dark. This ship had no night watchman. Going from davit to davit, he cut all of the nylon ropes with his hacksaw, which took much longer as a one-man operation. By the last davit, his hand, arm, and shoulder fatigue had become a raging inferno. After all eight boats were cut free on the southernmost ship, he made his way back across the rope bridge.

Sitting in the shadows against the deck rail of the middle ship, Kid restlessly waited for Jess. As he was catching his breath, he wondered what he was sitting on, so he got down on one knee and examined his makeshift stool. Pulling it away from the deck rail, he noted it was a rolled-up rope ladder with narrow wood steps. Based on the circumference of the roll, he assumed it was pretty long.

As he eyed the ladder, Kid's brain sent a warning. Adjusting his eyes, he realized that something in the background of his visual field had triggered this alarm. Studying the northernmost ship, his eyes were traveling upward when suddenly his breathing stopped. He noticed that the light was on in the bridge. "Watchman!" he whispered as he sprinted across the deck, and made his way over the rope bridge.

He reached the bow of the ship and saw Jess standing on the deck, staring at the bridge above. Kid froze as he spotted the watchman using the shadows to sneak up on his friend. At the last second, Jess must have sensed a presence because he dropped and rolled behind the base of the davit with spider-like quickness. Kid saw the roll. Unfortunately, so did the watchman.

Running the short distance along the deck rail, Kid pulled the coiled line with the tow hook from his shoulder. The circumference was close to that of a hula-hoop, which he hoped was enough. The watchman pulled a walkie-talkie from his belt and started after Jess. *No! He's going to blow our cover!* Kid burst forward and slam-dunked the circle of line over the watchman's head and upper body. The walkie-talkie was knocked free and skittered across the deck. Kid held the line tight with both hands as the watchman struggled to free his pinned arms.

Jess sprang from the shadows of the davit base and bowled over the bound adversary, who landed on top of Kid.

Using a chokehold, Kid held with full pressure until the watchman passed out.

Grabbing the line, Jess tied up the limp body, which had a uniform indicating, Elder-187. Finding a large outdoor storage bin, he slung the watchman over his shoulder and threw him inside. Using the laces from the enemy's boot, he tied the latch to keep the top of the bin down. "That was close. He almost reported in."

Nodding, Kid said, "Hopefully that was an initial call, and not a status update."

After making sure all of the boats were cut free, they made their way across the rope bridge back to the middle ship. Looking over the rail, the one boat they left for themselves was in the water ten feet away from the anchor chain on the port side.

"We need to move the boat over, so it is under the hawsepipe opening," Kid said.

"And I should get down there and strip the ignition wires," Jess said. "Unless they were nice enough to leave the key. Every second will count later."

Kid held up a finger, ran along the deck rail, and returned with the rolled-up rope ladder he had been sitting on. "We're in luck." He attached it to the deck rail and let it fall to the boat below. "When you're ready down there, hold the ladder tight and give me a signal. I'll cut the davit lines up here, and then pull you over to the anchor chain."

Nimbly climbing down the long, unsteady ladder, Jess dropped into the boat. Pointing to a key in the ignition, he gave Kid a thumbs up.

On deck, Kid pulled out his hacksaw. He made sure Jess was holding the ladder below and then cut the nylon davit lines. Now free, only Jess's grip on the hanging ladder prevented the boat from floating away. Unfastening the ladder above, Kid held it tight and strained as he walked along the rail. It felt like he was dragging a stalled locomotive. He stopped when he was right above the hawsepipe opening and anchor chain. This would make for a quick escape later. He refastened the rope ladder to the deck rail while Jess tied the boat to an anchor link with a severed piece of nylon line.

Jess ascended the rope ladder while Kid descended it. They met at the familiar port side hawsepipe and both wriggled through the opening and around the mammoth chain links.

"Hold. Take a quick breather," Kid huffed. He ran through the checklist in his mind as he crouched on the platform at the top of the companionway.

"We're all set now. Once we get the girls and launch in the last boat, they have nothing to chase us with," Jess noted.

"Yes, but remember, these are only the pre-fight preparations. The first-round bell hasn't even rung yet," Kid reminded him, as he grimaced while rubbing his bruised shin.

CHAPTER 20

December 30, 2044
Friday, Before Dawn
New Jersey coast, Utopia Project
Ship Number One
Four days after the event

As Kid crouched on the metal grate platform, his heavy breathing subsided. He rubbed his hands together, relieved that there was no longer a cold wind blowing against his body.

Jess asked, "Assuming we do make it out of here alive and get back to the mainland, where should we go?"

"Somewhere they can't find us. Somewhere hidden away."

"Back in the day, that would have been a no-brainer. Where did we always go to hide out?"

"Ironside," Kid guessed without hesitation, referring to their cabin in the woods. "And I've been thinking about that place lately, remembering the first time Sara and I went there together."

Jess nodded. "Do we have enough supplies to last a while out there?"

"Enough to keep us going until we re-group. Even if they found a way to get to shore they would never find us in the middle of the woods. Then again, we'll have a hard time getting there through the snow in the trails."

"Not if we stop by Logan's and borrow Queen Anne."

"The infamous Queen Anne," Kid repeated. Everybody in town knew Logan Murphy's four-wheel drive truck, which was named after his longtime girlfriend. The vehicle was an ancient extended cab pickup truck with a monster lift, but it was infamous because it had conquered all of the deepest quagmires in the woods. "We don't need that exact vehicle, but his house *is* on that road where we used to pick up the trails," Kid added. Logan lived at the end of a lagoon extension in Forked River where the water met the woods. At the end of the block, a dirt road went into the vast forest and connected to the trail system leading to Ironside cabin.

"And I always did want to take that thing for a drive, but Logan would never let me. Don't know why." Jess started walking down the companionway to the ship's bottom.

"He's obviously seen you drive," Kid muttered as he followed him.

The time was 3:00 a.m. They only had three hours to get the girls out before the 6:00 a.m. wake-up tone. Running back to the tool cabinet, Kid grabbed a couple of cordless drills. Pressing the buttons on the handles, both seemed to be fully charged. He used the chuck to fasten a metal drill bit in each. "We'll both need one of these."

Jess took the drill and raised an eyebrow. "We will?"

"Yes. You'll see. We're going to make a short cut."

Climbing the ladder amidships, Kid's muscles were sore all over from the flurry of recent physical activity. His arms ached as he pushed open the first hatch. Continuing to climb up in the shaft and counting the ladder rungs, he used his fingertips to find the indent in the metal he had made with his key the night before. Pulling out the cordless drill, Kid whispered, "We just need to make an opening in the back of the closet on the girls' floor."

In the dim light of the shaft, Jess gazed up and nodded his head. "A trap door. That'll save us climbing down all of those levels."

"Like you said, every second will count," Kid affirmed as he held onto the ladder.

"We still have to make it to the closet. Even that is a long way from the girls' rooms."

"I'm hoping we make it up the hall before anyone knows what's happening."

Jess looked concerned. "Are you kidding? The girls' doors are probably alarmed, and that's a long hallway."

Kid knew Jess had a point. They both pondered for a moment.

"Wait. Check it out." Jess pulled some dimes and quarters out of his pocket and held them up in his hand.

"And?"

"This is how we can keep the other doors on the hall from opening," Jess said confidently. "The old *pennying* trick."

"Pennying?" He thought for a second. "You mean like we used to do on my college hall?"

Seeming flustered that he even had to explain it, Jess rolled his eyes. "Where do you think I learned it?"

"That's right," Kid recalled. "You were there the night they scorched Richard's khakis."

Jess was visiting him when the guys on Kid's college hall wedged pennies between the hinge-side of the door and the doorframe of pompous Richard Allen's room. With the door unable to be opened, the guy was trapped in his room. The pranksters proceeded to fire a volley of bottle-rockets through the gap under the door, and wound up catching Richard's khaki's on fire.

"Do you have any change?" Jess asked as they stood on the ladder inside the shaft.

"Yes! Remember that Quick-Fix clerk had no bills when he gave me change?" He reached into his pocket and pulled out a handful of coins. They had 18 coins, which they split between the two of them. "We'll have to penny as many doors as we can between their rooms and the closet at the end of the hallway, if we can create this short cut. Here goes nothing," Kid said.

Pressing the tip of the drill bit against the metal of the shaft, he gave the trigger a quick squeeze and pushed hard. The bit broke through and made a popping sound. He leaned against the shaft trying to deaden the reverberating clap.

Jess appeared alarmed by the noise, so Kid reminded him, "Don't worry. There's no watchman on this ship tonight. We need to punch holes in a row, very close together here." He used his finger to trace the outline of a square. "You start on that side."

Pulling out his cordless drill, Jess also started making holes in the metal. All it took was a quick press of the trigger and a firm push, and the bit would bust through. They continued to make holes close together in rows, leaning their bodies against the shaft to deaden the sound. Both were trying to keep their balance on the rungs of the ladder while they worked.

"Damn!" Jess snapped a short time later as he depressed the drill trigger and nothing happened. "The battery died."

Kid hoped that his would hold out, but with one side of the square still to go, his drill also went dead. The completed rows of holes made the top and two sides, so he slammed his shoulder into the metal. Only the top left corner gave way, so he hit it again and most of the top tore free. He shouldered it harder and the metal flap tore and pushed all the way in. His inertia sent him flying into the closet over the ripped sheet of metal. The jagged edges cut his jacket, with one piece tearing through to the skin of his right arm. A loud clap, like a thunder strike, resonated up the length of the shaft.

After getting to his feet in the closet and pushing the metal flap all the way down, Kid used pliers to turn away some of the sharp edges. He again checked his watch, partially rolling up his jacket sleeve. Blood was already flowing over his wrist as he looked at his watch-face and noted that it was 5:00 a.m. "An hour left."

Jess climbed through the opening and followed when Kid opened the closet door. They both crouched and ran until they reached the girls' rooms. Kid and Jess stared through the frosted glass into Maria's room. She was awake and jumped from the bed as soon as she saw his outline appear at the window. Kid spelled out on the glass with his finger, "G E T   D R E S S E D   B E   R E A D Y."

Crawling up to Sara's door, Kid tapped very lightly on the window. After a moment she got out of bed and came over. Kid spelled out, "G E T   D R E S S E D   B E   R E A D Y," in big letters on the glass.

Making his way over to Heidi's room, he tapped the window, but she didn't move. He tried again, this time a little harder. She finally woke up and walked over. At first she stood frozen and didn't seem to know who was there, so Kid put his face almost against the frosted glass. As soon as she recognized him, Heidi threw her hands against the window. The thrusting of her open hands made a quick, but loud, smacking sound. Suddenly, the large screen in her room popped on.

Kid dropped to the ground below the window.

Heidi swiveled around as the elder on the screen asked, "Is something the matter?"

"No. Sorry. We tapped the window with our hand while thinking."

"Why are you not in bed?"

"We couldn't sleep."

"You should be sleeping, not thinking. We will send down some sleeping medication."

"No, that's alright. We'll never get up tomorrow if we take anything. We'll go back to bed now." Heidi walked over and laid down. The interactive screen turned off.

Kid, now afraid to stand, reached up with his hand and began writing the same letters on her window as he did with the other girls.

Jess had started pennying the doors nearest the closet at the end of the hall and was working his way back toward the girls' rooms. Kid took out his change and did the same. With how much effort he needed to wedge the coins between the doors and the frames, he was sure the pennied doors would never open. Both continued until they ran out of change with several doors left to go. "It'll have to do," Kid whispered.

Now 5:30 a.m., Kid's heart began to race. There would be no way to keep down his rising fear. No more reasoning or rationalizing. The wake-up beep would sound in a half an hour. He crawled over to Jess. Both pulled out large wrenches and threw their backpacks aside.

"I'll get Sara and Heidi," Kid instructed. "You get Maria. As soon as you get her out, just go. Don't wait for me. Try to get a good head start and get the boat started."

Jess nodded, now visibly nervous.

Putting his hand on his friend's shoulder and holding up his wrench, Kid emphasized every word, "It's show time. Swing as hard as you can."

Jess grabbed Kid's arm and said nothing.

They both knew that nothing more needed to be said.

Jess crawled up to Maria's window. He stood up and motioned for her to stand back as he cocked his arm back. Turning to Kid, he waited for the signal.

Kid became more tense, his hands clammy. He held up three fingers.

Jess tightened his grip on his wrench.

Taking a deep breath, he held up two fingers. He was breathing heavy as the tension swelled. Adrenaline ran through his veins like high voltage. He had to get his hand up and signal, but he paused. Jess cocked his arm back even further. In just a second, alarms and sirens would awaken every soldier on the ship, but there was no turning back now. It was as if the pin had already been pulled from the hand-grenade.

Raising his hand, Kid shot up just one finger.

All in the same instant, he and Jess swung down their wrenches.

III:
OBLIVION

CHAPTER 21

December 30, 2044
Friday, Dawn
New Jersey coast, Utopia Project
Ship Number One
Four days after the event

Kid and Jess simultaneously slammed their wrenches down and both glass windows shattered on impact. The loud crash reverberated up and down the hallway.

Expecting alarms to sound and lights to flash right away, Kid froze when he was confronted with silence. He and Jess turned and looked at each other in bewilderment and then sprang into action.

Quickly knocking out the bigger pieces of the tempered glass from Sara's window frame, Kid saw her standing in a bra and underwear. *Dammit!* He must not have written his message clear enough. He yelled, "Get dressed and put on shoes, quick! And then jump out!"

He ran over to Heidi's window and smashed it. She stared at the broken window, appearing stunned, but fortunately she had grabbed her uniform and was already putting it on. "What the... Kid? What are you doing here?"

"Shoes on, now! We're getting you out!" he barked as she zipped the front of her outfit.

"But..."

"Now!"

Heidi slipped on her footwear and climbed out of the window

with Kid's help.

Turning for Sara, he saw her pulling her uniform over her shoulders. As he scurried across the hall, she zipped it up and put on her shoes. "Hurry, hurry!" He reached in, pulled her top half through the opening and lifted her onto his shoulders. Once her legs were clear, he put her down.

Jess and Maria were running up the hall at full speed.

Kid grabbed Sara's hand and started sprinting. They were halfway up the hall when lights started flashing and a loud alarm sounded, prompting them to all run faster. As he galloped past, Kid saw the shadows of soldiers in the windows of the stuck doors. The pennying trick had worked.

Elder-1 heard the alarms and was on his feet and dressed in seconds. His room monitor came to life. "Sir, alarms originating from level 29. System also detected hatches open in the engineer's service shaft."

"Alert all elders. Get a team armed and to level 29 immediately. Also, get a force on deck to ensure nobody tries to get off of the ship. We will head to the service shaft to determine status there. Go!"

Jess and Maria made it to the closet, climbed over the metal flap and started descending the ladder in the shaft. Heidi was right behind them.

Pushing open the hallway door and then entering the closet behind the staircase, Kid looked back. From several rooms at the opposite end of the hall, soldiers came spilling out. While closing the closet door, Kid peered up to see more soldiers coming down the staircase. He could see their feet as they marched in unison. Gingerly, he closed the door. It didn't appear that any of the soldiers had seen them enter the closet. He helped Sara through the hole in the shaft and directed her to go down the ladder.

As he went to go through the opening, Kid heard noises echoing from the very top of the shaft. Fearing they would need cover while descending the ladder, he strained as he lifted and pushed the flap of sheet metal through the hole. The metal creaked and began to rip at the bend point, but it held as he slid over it headfirst into the shaft. The skin of his forehead was sliced by one of the metal edges as he glided off the flap and caught a ladder rung.

Descending a few rungs, Kid glanced up. The metal flap was over his head in the shaft, but it would only cover the left side of the ladder. Moving his head and peering up, he saw that the top hatch to the navigation room was open. He noticed soldiers scurrying about, but he had to turn away and squint as blood ran into his eye from the cut on his forehead.

Sara stopped at the bottom of the ladder and waited.

Kid went down the ladder in the shaft under the cover of the metal flap. A weapon was fired from the navigation room above. Upon hearing an odd sound, like someone with a deep voice sneezing, he froze. A bolt streaked down right next to him. It was dangerously close, but as long as he stayed under the flap they couldn't get a clear shot. He then felt the vibration of soldiers on the ladder above him. The next shot bounced diagonally from one side to the other down the shaft. Kid realized they had adjusted their shooting angle to reach the covered space. He hugged the ladder as a shot careened behind him, just inches from his back.

"Get out of the way!" he screamed at Sara as the shot made it all the way down. She stepped aside as the shot hit the ground right where she was standing just a second before. "Run Sara! Catch up to them!"

With only ten feet remaining to reach the lower hatch, Kid held the ladder's vertical rails and jumped. He put the soles of his feet against the outsides of the rails and loosened his handgrip. As he plummeted, his palms started to burn. Squeezing his grip to put on the brakes, his feet found a rung and he pulled the bottom hatch down above his head. Dropping to the ground, he grabbed Sara's hand and sprinted across the bottom of the ship.

Standing on a platform, Heidi frantically waved her hand. Sara made her way up the metal companionway, and the girls entered the hawsepipe opening.

As Kid ran up the companionway, he looked behind to see soldiers dropping down to the ship bottom from the ladder enclosure. Without hesitation, he squirmed through the hawsepipe and grabbed the rope ladder. He tugged it to ensure it was still attached to the deck rail above. He peered down as the boat engine coughed and then started. The girls had made it down the ladder and were waiting in the boat. Jess peered up and was waving for him to hurry down. Getting his footing and descending, Kid heard a commotion on the deck above. Suddenly, the ladder went limp and he fell the last eight feet into the boat below. He knocked Maria down and the ladder piled on top of the both of them. With the wind knocked out of him, Kid was on his back, gasping. He met the eyes of a soldier leaning over the deck rail above.

Jess hit the throttle and sped toward shore as the elder aimed his weapon in their direction.

Catching his breath, Kid pulled the rope ladder off of him and Maria and cast it over the side. He put his hand on her shoulder, but she addressed his concern before he could ask. "I'm alright."

Kid struggled to sit up. Spotlights from all three ships were searching the water through the light snow that was falling. The whole scene was one of absolute havoc, with loud alarms and lights from the three ships combing the surrounding waters and illuminating the pre-dawn sky.

Running to the deck rail, Elder-1 heard a boat speeding away. He could not believe this was happening. A number of other elders were already armed and assembled, and he turned to them. "The captives are escaping! Why aren't we firing?"

"We cannot locate them!" an elder called out.

Turning to the comrades beside him, he spotted Elder-91, a competent Lieutenant Colonel in the Unites States Marines. "Elder-91!"

"Sir!"

"Take three boats. Each should have an elder leader and a team of 20 members. Arm the members and insert a tracker in each so we can account for them this time when off of our ships. And then get after that boat! Hurry!"

"Yes, Sir. Keep in mind we can only use the basic tracking chip right now."

"We know! Now go!"

"Yes, Sir," Elder-91 said and ran off.

Remembering that two elders were still on the mainland hunting survivors, Elder-1 raised his walkie-talkie to his lips. "Elder-48, do you copy?"

"Here, Sir. What is going on out there?"

"The captives are trying to escape. We need you to head them off and eliminate them!"

"Yes, Sir. We came down to our boat as soon as we saw the lights and commotion. We are departing now. Out."

Finally, a spotlight found the fleeing craft and stayed on it.

Elder-1 saw the three female captives, but also a couple of males who were clearly not project members. *Where did these bastards come from, and how did they get on our ship?* "There! Fire!" he barked, and shots started raining down from the ships.

"Lay down! Take cover!" Kid yelled to the girls.

A couple of soldiers had taken up positions on one of the rope bridges between ships. They took aim and started firing bolts from their technologically advanced weapons. Sara was standing in the stern of the boat when Kid spotted a soldier training his weapon on her from the rope bridge. The scene unfolded as if it was happening in slow motion. "Down!" he screamed. As he jumped to one knee and leaned forward to reach for her, he flinched for a split second as his raw and bruised shin bumped against a seat.

The soldier pulled the trigger and a shot headed straight for Sara. Through a torrent of pain, Kid screamed but still grabbed her hand. He pulled her hard and watched in horror as the shot grazed the top of her shoulder while she fell. The bolt changed direction, but kept going. Sara hit the boat bottom hard as she landed next to him. "Oh, no! Can you move?" he asked, panicked.

She wiggled her body, and said in a deeper than usual tone, "Yes."

"What happened?" Jess called out.

"Shot grazed Sara," Kid answered as he helped her into a seat in the back. He wrapped his arms around her and held her tight. "She's alright." His voice conveyed the desperate hope is his heart. "She's alright..."

■ ■ ■

A few moments later, Elder-91 was panting as he approached Elder-1. He had in tow three other elders and 60 members. "Sir, there are no more boats!"

"What?"

"They were all at the water, and they have been cut free."

As he was about to explode with rage, Elder-1's walkie-talkie beeped, and it was the channel reserved for the Board of Elders. "Go ahead!"

"Sir, Elder-2 here. Our boats were cut free, but we found one! It was stuck behind the anchor chain of ship number three. We are holding it."

Here was their opportunity. The battle was not over yet. "We will be right there with a team, and we will lead this mission personally. Drop a rope ladder into the boat!"

"Already have, Sir," she answered.

Turning to Elder-91, Elder-1 asked, "Do these members have arms and trackers?"

"Arms, yes. Trackers, not yet, but we are ready." He held up his hand. He was holding a device that looked like a label gun, which was used to slip a tracker under the skin. He also held a couple of sleeves of tracking chips.

"Come with me, and bring 20 members."

After hustling across the deck and crossing the swaying rope bridge between the ships, Elder-1 reached the deck rail where Elder-2 was waiting. After getting a tracker was inserted into the scalp, the members started descending the ladder one at a time.

"The members will all have basic trackers inserted," Elder-1 said. "Since we do not have the aid of satellites, our location can only be monitored within a 50-mile range using the antennas on the ships. But should the chase reach the mainland and we call for reinforcements, then you will have our exact location."

Elder-2 nodded.

The final member, number 801, had a tracker inserted under his scalp and descended to the waiting boat. Elder-1 grabbed the rail, swung his leg over and found his footing on the rope ladder. Holding the deck rail, he said to Elder-2, "Since we are departing, you are in charge until we return."

"Yes, Sir," she said as Elder-1 climbed down the ladder and disappeared.

Dropping into the boat below, Elder-1 felt the old, familiar rush. The chase was on and he was thirsting for blood. There was nothing more exhilarating than catching and slaughtering prey. And since the world was effectively wiped out, this may be his last such hunt. He planned to savor it.

■ ■ ■

Jess, driving all hunched over, turned his head back and then did a double take. "Ah, shit!"

Without even looking, Kid's heart sank. He knew just by the tone of voice, and then his friend confirmed when he yelled, "I thought we cut all of the boats free!"

"So did I," Kid said as he popped his head up and turned back. With the flood of lights coming off of the ships, he could see a boat wedged between the anchor chain and the hull of the southernmost ship. *Damn!* He cursed himself for being so careless. They should've made sure all of the smaller crafts cleared the anchor chain after they cut them loose. The wedged boat appeared to be full and was taking off. "Now they're coming after us!"

■ ■ ■

Elder-2 leaned on the deck rail and watched as the boat sped away.

"Always a field commander at heart," said Elder-3 as he approached and stood next to her. "Elder-1 doesn't want to watch a slaying, he wants to drive the sword himself and taste and smell the blood."

She turned and was always surprised that her elder comrade spoke such perfect English. His words offered no hint that his native language was Mandarin Chinese.

"That is true," she responded, knowing her own words carried too much inflection. She grew up speaking only Russian and never fully mastered the English language, but she did not care. She spoke it well enough. "But we should not be in this position. How did the lead psychologist not identify that these captives were a flight risk, and had the risk tolerance to try an escape?"

"Elder-76 failed us…again," Elder-3 responded. "Remember, she convinced the Board not to fire the former lead psychologist, Elder-62, and look what harm that brought upon us."

Nodding, she stated, "Since Elder-1 has departed and we are in charge, Elder-76 will immediately be demoted and will no longer be the lead psychologist."

Grunting, Elder-3 waved his hand dismissively. "We are too lenient."

"Unfortunately, we must be, for now. Until we get authorization from Elder-1 to administer a more…fitting punishment."

Backing up from the rail, Elder-3 stated, "Elder-76 must pay a much steeper price. And mark my words, she will."

■　■　■

Jess was already at full throttle. As he headed toward the inlet, he said, "They aren't the only ones coming after us. Look!" He pointed to the north.

Kid jumped into the passenger seat and saw a boat in the distance. He realized that it had to be the one sent out by the soldiers a couple of days ago. It appeared that the craft was occupied by two soldiers.

As Jess came into the inlet, he slowed down to avoid crashing into the rock jetty. The boat with the two soldiers came into the inlet a little too hot and their boat spun out of control. Kid watched, hoping they would crash. The soldiers just barely avoided the large rocks lining the inlet and resumed the chase.

Jess made it through the unusually calm inlet unscathed.

Glancing around, Kid tried to figure out how to slow down their pursuers. He remembered what happened when his cousin had hit a sand bar while speeding across Barnegat Bay. He was slowed down alright, and was lucky he wound up with only a broken arm. "Where is the closest sand bar?"

"Right over that way is Tices Shoal." Jess pointed to a large section of the bay abutting the western side of Island Beach State Park.

Kid knew that particular shoal. There the water was shallow, less than waist-high in most places. In the hot months, the place was always filled with hundreds of boaters who would lay anchor and have a non-stop party. "Head for it!" he instructed. "We'll pull the engine up on an angle so we don't hit ground, but hopefully they will."

Looking at the boat's dashboard, Jess put his finger on a button and said, "Power trim!"

The boat with the 20 soldiers had passed the struggling two-man boat and was gaining speed. After coming around the next buoy, Jess cut the wheel hard and veered away from the path designated by the channel markers. "Kid, go to the back and tell me when the engine is almost out of the water."

While heading to the back of the boat, Kid heard crunching noises. "What's that sound?" he yelled over the high-pitched whine of the boat's engine.

"Ice. Bay is partially frozen, especially here in the shallow water. Lifting the engine, now!"

Jess raised the 350-horsepower outboard engine until the propeller was almost entirely out of the water.

"Hold!" Kid yelled, as the barely submerged propeller still powered them forward while avoiding the shallow, sandy bottom. He noticed that Sara was hunched over as she sat in the back of the boat. She seemed aware of her surroundings, but was in obvious discomfort. He was about to check on her when someone screamed.

"Holy shit! Elder-1 is driving that boat packed with soldiers!" Maria yelled as she pointed.

Turning, Kid watched as the boat behind them came around the same buoy and followed. A minute later, Elder-1's fully submerged engine caught the shallow bottom and their boat came to a dead stop. Half of the soldiers were thrown into the water. A few went right over the windshield. One flew between the front seats and hit the windshield headfirst.

Elder-1 seemed unhurt, and even helped in tossing a limp and lifeless body overboard. The elder was giving orders, and Kid watched as the soldiers in the water lifted the boat out of the sandy entrapment. The engine was raised and a puff of smoke shot out when it was restarted. Elder-1 was waving his hand, directing the soldiers in the water to get back in the craft.

Kid spotted the soldier's other craft with the two men. After barely making it through the inlet, that boat had avoided Tices Shoal and were now gaining ground.

As Jess lowered the engine to its normal position, Kid said, "Get as close to shore as you can and drop me off. I'll find a car and try to take them out at the Forked River Bridge. Listen carefully. At that bridge, make sure you go through the right corridor. Not the left or middle… the right." He had a plan. "And then keep going and I'll meet you at your house."

"My house?" He seemed hesitant to go back there.

"The lagoon behind your house." Kid knew that Jess's house was accessible via the Forked River. "I'll just jump in the boat, then we'll go to Logan's and grab his truck."

Jess relented and nodded.

"I'll need time, so circle the entire bay once before you go up Forked River," Kid added. "Remember, at the bridge, go through the *right* corridor."

"Got it. I should be able to stay ahead of the boat loaded with people, but the other one might catch up pretty quickly."

As Jess started getting closer to shore, larger and heavier pieces of ice crunched against the bow. "We can't go much farther," he noted and slowed down when he approached the thicker crust along the shoreline.

"Close enough." Kid kissed the top of Sara's head and then slithered over the side of the boat.

As he plunged into the icy-cold bay, he lost his breath for a moment. Exhaling and inhaling in short, rapid gasps, he watched with his head just above the surface as the boat sped away. Floating chunks of ice surrounded him as he struggled to tread water. The soldiers never even glanced in his direction and kept chasing Jess, so Kid swam with haste toward the shoreline.

CHAPTER 22

December 30, 2044
Friday, Early Morning
New Jersey coast
Four days after the event

Encountering the edge of the sheet of ice, Kid pulled himself out of the water and onto the frozen surface of Barnegat Bay. Knowing not to stand, he army-crawled on his stomach until he reached land and ran for a nearby house. He broke in and found car keys on the kitchen counter. Before running for the car, he ransacked the bedrooms until he found some dry clothes. In the master bedroom upstairs, he found clean sweatpants and extra-large t-shirts. Breathing only through his mouth, he glanced at the bed while changing his clothes and caught a glimmer of light. He turned to see a disgusting, hair-encrusted tiara tilted sideways on the top of a skull. A couple of the fake gems had escaped the gore and shone in the daylight. The blanket was pulled up to the eye sockets as the skull rested on the pillow, with the dark orbs fixed on him. He could only imagine what kind of role-playing had been going on in this room before the destruction hit. Despite now being dry, he shivered as he ran down the stairs, grabbed a heavy winter jacket, and headed out the door.

Jumping into a little blue car outside, Kid sped toward the hardware store. Spooked by the eeriness of the empty roads, especially at a traffic intersection that was usually very busy, he looked around in every direction. He felt like he was driving through a ghost town, except that this was his hometown. What was once a bustling suburbia was now a 360-degree still-photo.

Kid was kicked back into the moment when he passed a gas station and something caught his eye under the expansive awning. The gas station attendant must've been sitting in a chair next to the pumps when the beams burst from the sky. Resting on a ribcage on a folding chair was a human skull. Most of the innards had run off the side of the chair and formed a large puddle on the ground. Facing the road, the skinless head was tilted a little sideways, as if staring at him quizzically. He felt like the dead were watching him everywhere he went. Trying to shake it off, Kid pushed the gas pedal to the floor.

Up the road, he cut into a parking lot and rammed the bumper of the car into the front door of the hardware store. Backing the car up a few feet, he jumped out and wormed through the mangled entranceway. He gathered various items, including a hammer and some masonry nails. He put the items in a bag, and coiled several long pieces of rope and slung them over his shoulder. After throwing the items in the car, he sped away. He knew he didn't have much time.

■ ■ ■

Jess was circling around the large body of water. The soldiers were still giving chase. He was almost back around to where Forked River met the bay.

■ ■ ■

Driving to the Forked River Bridge, Kid got out of the car and ran to the top of the bridge with ropes over his shoulder and the supply bag in his hand. "Please tell me they haven't been caught," he said aloud.

■ ■ ■

As Jess turned up Forked River from the bay, he glanced back at the two boats chasing. Turning forward, the bridge was dead ahead. "Kid said stay to the right," he reminded himself.

■   ■   ■

Kid was relieved to see Jess's boat, which looked like a tiny speck in the distance. But he realized he had to move quickly.

The bridge was supported by columns drilled deep into the river-bed, which created three corridors to pass under the span. He anchored three sets of ropes by tying them securely to the bridge railing over each corridor, and then tied each rope into a large noose knot.

Letting down the first noose over the southern corridor, the bottom of the rope barely touched the water of the flowing river. He then put two masonry nails in the side of the bridge several feet apart, and rested the top of the rope on the nails. This would keep the noose open wide. Although not a perfect circle, the snare spanned most of the corridor. Kid then used the same noose system for the middle corridor.

For the northern opening, or right corridor from Jess's direction, he ducked down and held the noose in his hand. The other end of the rope was tied to the bridge railing. He was ready not a moment too soon as Jess sped through the correct corridor as planned. Kid was crouched and out of sight, but he listened and tried to gauge the speed of the oncoming soldier's boat. The boat with 20 soldiers followed Jess's exact course, so Kid dropped the noose and held the loop open with his outstretched arms.

Falling to the waterline, the noose snagged the bow of the speeding boat. Kid let go as the rope pulled tight. The weight and momentum of the craft was too much for the twine and it snapped, although the initial jerk turned the boat abruptly toward the shore. This forced the soldiers to lose momentum and let Jess get farther ahead.

With the commotion in front of them, the boat with the two soldiers turned into the middle corridor. Coming under the bridge, the hanging noose tightened until the bow was pointing straight up at the sky. With great momentum the stern of the boat kicked out underneath and the craft flipped as it headed for the shoreline. The windshield vaporized on impact as it landed upside down, crashing on a rock embankment.

Running down to the soldier's overturned boat, Kid laid down and peeked under. The two soldiers were dead, with their heads crushed and twisted awkwardly. He noticed the driver had an embroidered 'Elder-48' patch on his uniform. Kid ran back to the car and put the gas pedal to the floor. The vehicle slid around corners and dodged cars parked along the snow-covered roads. He had to get to Jess's house before the boat did.

■   ■   ■

Jess was weaving through the maze of lagoon channels. The water along the bulkheads was also frozen, so he had to drive right up the middle of the channel. This prevented him from being able to keep up his speed and cut the corners when making turns. The soldiers were following the conspicuous wake his boat was leaving behind.

As he drove farther into the lagoon system, the water became more stagnant, and the ice became noticeably thicker. The edges of the ice sheets were creeping closer to the middle from the lagoon sides, and he still had a few more channels to travel before reaching his house.

■   ■   ■

Kid jumped out of the car and ran for the dock behind Jess's house. When he got there, he couldn't see or hear the boat. "Come on Jess, don't let them close the gap," he said aloud. He knew they needed time to break into Logan's house and find the truck keys.

Turning around, he was again repulsed by the hairy, disgusting mound that used to be Jess's Alaskan Husky. Unfortunately, the carnage would also be visible to Jess when he pulled up. Hearing the boat coming, Kid scrambled to get the blanket from the doghouse. He covered the gory remains of the animal and ran down to the dock.

A moment later, the boat made a wide turn around the corner and sped up the middle of the lagoon channel. As Jess approached his house, he slowed down. The ice extending from the bulkhead kept the boat far from the dock. With the craft in the middle of the lagoon, Kid stutter-stepped as he ran out onto the ice. He leapt headfirst across the bow as the ice began to break under his feet. Jess reached over the windshield and grabbed his ankle to keep him from falling into the water on the other side.

"Got it." Kid was quick to stabilize himself and climb aboard.

With a long straightaway in front of him, Jess yelled, "Hold on!" and buried the throttle.

A few turns later, he reached the end of the lagoon and headed into an area that did not even have bulkheads. "We're here! Get ready!" he called out as he turned toward a low-lying empty lot.

Kid saw Logan's house across the street. It was the last house on a dead-end street where the asphalt ended and a sandy trail began through the forest. Having used this trail before, he knew it crossed Route 9 and wound through a portion of New Jersey's 1,100,000-acre Pinelands National Reserve, a forest with the claim to fame that it was the first National Reserve in America. But to Kid and his friends it was famous for only one thing, Ironside Cabin.

As Jess made for the empty lot, even the middle of the lagoon channel had a thin layer of ice. Fortunately, the boat was having no problem breaking through. "Hold on tight! It will be a rough stop." He engaged the automatic trim to raise the motor all the way. "Now!" he yelled as he cut the wheel hard to the right.

The boat's forward momentum pushed it over the thicker ice along the shore of the channel. With the engine out of the water, the boat fell onto its port side and careened along the slippery frozen surface. With the gradual incline of the ground in the empty lot, the craft came to a halt when it hit the sand, and everyone climbed out.

Kid looked back and spotted the soldiers' boat. It had already turned the final corner and was speeding up the lagoon channel. He scooped Sara into his arms and hurried across the street.

Jess kicked open the front door of Logan's split-level house and the group went in.

Kid carried Sara up the front steps and in the door, but the soldiers spotted him as they pulled into the empty lot across the street. "Hurry! They saw me come in!" he yelled.

Elder-1 turned his boat toward the lot opening. He saw the other boat on its side with the engine tilted up. "Hold on!" he yelled, and pulled the throttle all the way back. "Not this time," he muttered.

The forward motion of the boat slowed, but the submerged engine still caught the edge of some thicker ice and the boat jerked to a sudden stop. Some of the soldiers fell forward, but none fell out.

Inside the confines of Logan's house, Kid gagged from the overwhelming stench of rotting flesh. While everyone was scrambling to find the keys, he carried Sara out to the garage and spotted two vehicles. One was an old pick-up truck and the other was Logan's lifted four-wheel drive, with the neatly stenciled 'Queen Anne' on the side. He opened the back door of the extended cab and lifted Sara onto the back seat. Closing the truck's back door, he ran into the house to help the others.

The soldiers jumped out of the boat and marched on the ice. Once they reached solid ground, they quickened their pace.

CHAPTER 23

December 30, 2044
Friday, Morning
Forked River, New Jersey
Four days after the event

"I found the keys. Let's go!" Jess yelled as he ran down the stairs of Logan's house. Everyone hustled to the garage.

Kid was the last one out and he saw soldiers piling in through the front door up the hall. He closed the door to the garage and whispered as he climbed into the truck, "They're inside." He closed the truck door as quietly as he could, but as soon as it clunked, an older soldier opened the door from the house.

Jess hit the power-lock, securing the truck doors.

Heidi breathed in loudly. "Elder-1!"

The older soldier stepped into the garage and stared into the rear driver's side back window. His dark eyes made Kid shudder.

More soldiers started filing into the garage. Trying to open the door to their vehicle, Elder-1 didn't seem surprised or upset that it was locked. Kid, sitting in the back seat on the driver's side, said with growing fear, "Jess…"

Continuing to stare out his window, Jess fumbled with the keys in his hand, trying to find the ignition. Finally breaking his stare, he found the hole in the steering column and inserted the key.

Elder-1 held up a set of car keys with a smirk on his face. "He's got another set of keys! Hit it, now!" Kid yelled.

Turning on the ignition, Jess hit the accelerator. Despite a soldier jumping in front of the truck, he plowed forward and blasted through the closed garage door. Kid felt the vehicle bounce as it went over a body.

Jess drove toward the partially hidden trail entrance at the end of the street. Even shifting into four-wheel-drive he couldn't get much speed on the wet slippery snow. The tires were freely spinning and the rear of the truck was fishtailing from side to side.

"When is this cat and mouse game going to end?" Heidi asked.

"Not any time soon!" Kid answered. "Look behind us. They have the other pickup truck that was in the garage!"

"We need to gain some ground. Hold on," Jess responded as he entered the forest and finally picked up speed, cutting a path in the untouched snow.

After reaching Route 9, they crossed the deserted highway and picked up the trail on the other side of the road. They passed pine tree after pine tree with branches still holding fresh white powder as they drove for miles, making many turns up side trails. Kid stared out the window as the truck crossed a small wooden bridge over a shallow stream, one of many flowing through the Pinelands. He was about to say something, since they had always used the bridge as a marker, but was beaten to the punch.

"Seven lakes, just around the bend," Jess called out. "And then five miles after that to the cabin. We are making good time now. There is no way they are keeping up."

"We have to go through seven lakes?" Heidi asked. "I came out here with Brian and don't remember doing that."

"We just call them lakes. They are really seven puddles in a row, although the seventh one is almost large enough to be considered a lake," Jess noted as he down-shifted.

Kid was holding Sara as they drove, waiting for the effect of the shot that grazed her to wear off.

"What did they do to your hair?" Jess glanced over at Maria in the passenger's seat.

"They made us all look like them. Check out Sara and Heidi." She turned around. "Sara, how do you like your new look?"

Lying across Kid's lap, she didn't respond.

As he drove up the snow-laden trail, Jess asked, "Wait a minute, can't they spot us out here with satellites?"

"No," Maria replied. "We heard on the ships that since the night of the destruction, the satellite system has been down. Hopefully it still is."

"That's good for us," Jess said.

"They don't need satellites to find us," Kid countered.

"What do you mean?"

"They can just follow our tire tracks in the snow." He knew they had to do something, or their tracks would lead right to the cabin.

After a moment, Jess turned to Maria, "I know there are still some turns to make, but do you remember the way to the cabin?"

"With how many times I've been there, I guess I should," Maria answered. "Why?"

"If they're following us, me and Kid need to jump out and do something to stop them, or at least slow them down. Just head to the cabin and stay inside."

"Wait, should we even go to the cabin?" Maria asked. "Since we are being followed, maybe we should just outrun them and keep going."

Kid jumped in and said, "We need to get Sara in a bed and help her. She's in bad shape."

"Anyway, I have an idea to slow them down. Way down," Jess proclaimed as he turned to Maria.

Jess had successfully navigated the first six puddles along the route to the cabin, despite them all being iced over and camouflaged by snow. Around the next bend, the trail widened, and the seventh lake lurked under a blanket of virgin white powder. He drove with caution up the middle of the enormous frozen puddle. The ice creaked as he gingerly held onto the steering wheel. "Come on, just a little more." The truck made it across and Jess stopped.

"Alright Maria, all yours." Jess climbed out. "Kid, I'll check the truck box in the bed and see what tools Logan kept in there. You check back there. We need crow bars and hammers."

Kid squirmed over and let Sara's head rest on the seat. While he searched behind and under the seats in the cab for tools, Maria jumped behind the steering wheel.

"Got one hammer back here," Jess called out.

Stepping out of the cab, Kid held up a crow bar.

Jess nodded and then turned to Maria. "We'll meet you at the cabin later. Don't light any fires, they might spot the smoke. And above all, be on guard."

"Got it. You guys be careful too." Maria blew a kiss to the guys and drove away.

"So what's your plan?" Kid asked.

"For them to not only get stuck, but to sink in the puddle." Jess pointed. "We know that the puddle is deepest left and right of center. So take that side and weaken the surface of the ice by chipping out the outline of a large square. I'll get this side."

They both began hammering away, Jess with the hammer and Kid with the crow bar. After they made their respective squares on each side, he held Jess's ankles while his friend hammered some of the ice inside the large shapes. As they were working on the second square, the surface started to collapse. As he was being dragged back, Jess huffed, "There's no way they'll make it without the ice giving way."

Throwing snow over the seventh lake, they smoothed it out as best they could. Then starting where the tire tracks led up to the puddle, Jess took a long, dead tree branch and continued the tracks by reaching out and carving wide grooves in the snow going over one of the pre-weakened squares. He carefully connected the two grooves to the real tracks that picked up on the other side of the puddle.

"Nice work. The fake tracks almost look real," Kid commented, marveling at Jess's ingenuity. The transition between the real and fake tracks was not perfect, but he hoped the soldiers wouldn't be looking that close. At that moment, an idea hit him. They had more tracks to erase.

They walked backward into the woods, kicking snow over their footprints. When they reached the denser brush, where the uneven landscape made their footprints nearly inconspicuous, Jess stopped. He looked up to the sky for a full minute. "Follow me, we'll take a straight line to the cabin."

Although five miles by trail, Kid knew they could get to the cabin quicker by running in a straight path through the woods. He just didn't know where he was going. Fortunately, Jess did. "I don't know how you can do that without a map and a compass." Kid was always impressed by his friend's ability to navigate so effortlessly through the woods.

"The map is up here." Jess pointed to his head. "I just needed to find some points in the sky for reference, which is harder when it is overcast. I'm tracking some darker clouds, but had to figure out which direction they were moving and how fast. Come on," Jess responded and then started sprinting. Kid followed as they ran through the forest. The branches were pecking at his body and the cuts on his forehead and right arm were being torn open even more. Jess, being smaller and much more agile, did not seem to be having the same problem.

"Hold… up," Kid sputtered after having sprinted for about 15 minutes. At the point of utter exhaustion, he felt weak as he bent over. His legs were rubbery. "Where are we now?" he asked, panting.

"We'll come out at one of the side trails going toward Ironside," Jess replied, also gasping for air.

Kid paused and took deeper breaths. "Once we get to the trail, we need to cut our tire tracks, or even on foot they can just follow us right to the cabin. We need to erase more of our tracks and divert them, but it has to be at one of the turns."

Jess pondered for a few seconds. "I know a good place to do that—the fork in the trail that has that evil looking dead tree in the middle. If they stay to the left, they'll be going the wrong way. They'll eventually hit that intersection where five trails meet. They won't have any idea which trail to take."

"How far past the fork is that five-trail intersection?" Kid asked.

"I don't know exactly, but I'd guess around six or seven miles? The best part is that none of those five trails lead to the cabin, except the one they took to get there, but they would have to completely double back," Jess explained. "Ready to go?"

"Not really, but… after you."

"We don't need to sprint anymore. We can jog. As long as they get stuck at the seventh lake, we'll have enough time to do what we need to do," Jess said. "If they don't get stuck, we're screwed anyway."

As he jogged through the woods with fatigued legs, Kid added, "For all the times it got us back when, that seventh lake owes us one."

■ ■ ■

Elder-1 drove the pickup truck through the winding forest trails, following the conspicuous tire tracks. There were four soldiers in the cab of the truck, and another 14 crammed into the truck's bed.

He crossed over several frozen puddles with ease, but as he approached the next one, he became suspicious. Ahead, he could see the snow was uneven and choppy in places.

Sensing a trap, he opted to drive across the left side rather than going to the right and following the tracks. About halfway across, the ice gave way.

Elder-1 tried to gun the engine and speed across, but the tires spun freely with no traction. The vehicle slid down into a gaping hole until it was half submerged, and then continued to slowly sink.

"Everybody out!" he ordered as he leapt toward the woods along the edge of the puddle. Landing on the ice and sliding on his chest, he turned and watched as the vehicle sank further into the water. About half of the men were able to take very athletic leaps far enough away to escape the cold water. The other half were unable to get out before getting drenched, and they had to climb out of the hole in the ice.

Elder-1 watched helplessly as the vehicle sank all the way to the top of the roof. He stood up, brushed the white snow off of his uniform and shouted, "Let's march! From here, we search on foot. Every inch of these woods if necessary!"

■ ■ ■

After running through the woods for 15 more minutes, Kid and Jess found the fork in the trail with the unmistakable marker. A dead tree's gray, naked limbs stretched above the other trees, resembling a skeleton with outstretched arms. They could see the truck tire tracks where Maria had turned right at the fork, but Kid noticed that the details of the tire tread were smoothed over by the light snow that was falling. "How many miles back do you think those soldiers are?" he asked.

"They must be stuck back at the seventh lake," Jess checked his watch. "If not, they would've driven past this point by now, and I don't see any fresh tracks." Both peered back up the trail. "If they are following, it would now be on foot."

"Then we should have time to get rid of our tire tracks. Let's get some branches," Kid instructed.

He and Jess grabbed large limbs with dead leaves still attached, and used them as brushes to smooth over the tire tracks. They dragged the branches to make the snow appear untouched. The lightly falling snow was helping their efforts by hiding the imperfections of their work. They started at the main trail and erased the tracks Maria made when turning right at the fork. After going around a sharp bend in the trail, Kid jumped into the woods. "Far enough. Follow me."

Moving parallel to the trail, they ran back to a point just before the fork.

"See the outside tire track? Walk out and put your feet side by side within it."

Jess looked askance at him, but obliged.

Kid used his branch to cover their footprints and then threw it in the woods. He put his feet side by side within the closest tire track and reached out toward Jess. "Put your arm straight out, lock it, and grab my arm." Both locked their hands tightly onto each other's forearm. "Now, keep your feet together and shuffle while walking forward," he instructed. They both began to move their feet with short, choppy strides. "Keep your arm locked and stand up straight or the fake tracks won't have a consistent distance between them."

He turned his head and made sure the soldiers were nowhere in sight. Also examining the fake tracks that they were making, there was no obvious break in the continuity with the real ones. The bottom of the groove was a little choppy from the shuffling of their shoes, but Kid hoped the light snow would disguise such imperfections before the soldiers got that far.

"You really think this will work?" Jess asked.

"That depends on us. We need to be pretty precise, so stay with me and don't get sloppy."

Jess continued to use step-count estimates to measure the distances they were covering. After they shuffled for nearly five miles, they stopped and put their arms down to relieve the overwhelming fatigue. They continued on until finally, they reached the five-trail intersection. They made a left turn and went forward for nearly a tenth of a mile before stopping. Both were exhausted. As they stepped into the woods, Jess picked up another branch and covered their footsteps.

Kid sat and had to rest a moment. His shoulder was so sore he could barely move his arm, and he groaned as he grabbed a handful of snow and shoved it into his mouth.

Jess walked over and stood with his hands on his hips. Kid motioned for him to sit, but his friend waved him off and said, "If I sit, I'll never get back up."

A moment later Kid struggled to get to his feet. "I see what you mean." Stretching his arms and legs, he mumbled, "Here we go again," and started a slow jog through the woods parallel to the trails. Given his state of physical exhaustion, he had no idea how he was able to press on. The power of the mind amazed him. He feared that at any moment, he would just collapse. His mind could only keep him going for so long. There must come a point when the body simply shuts down.

They were back near the fork in the trail when suddenly Kid dropped on his stomach and snapped, "Get down!"

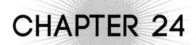

CHAPTER 24

December 30, 2044
Friday, Midday
Pine Barrens of New Jersey
Four days after the event

J ess reacted in an instant to Kid's urgent words, and dove to the
ground.

Kid's breath was shallow as he lifted his head up. One hundred
feet away marching on the trail was the pack of soldiers, led by Elder-1.
The group marched briskly, and did not seem affected by fatigue or the
cold and snow. The pack was going around a bend and actually coming
closer to where they were hiding. Kid put his hand over his face to keep
the thick steam from rising out of his mouth. The soldiers were now
only about 50 feet away, so close that a twig breaking could catch their
attention.

After they passed and were out of sight, Jess crawled over. "That was
close, but the good news is that they're following the fake tracks and they
are past the turnoff to the cabin," he whispered. "Come on."

Kid winced as he stood up and the bruise on his leg bumped into a
stump. The muscles of his legs were burning like a gas-fed inferno, yet
his face was ice-cold from his sweat being slapped by the frigid breeze.
With every deep intake of cold air, he felt like pins were being stuck into
the walls of his lungs.

"We have to keep moving or our muscles will cramp up on us,"
Jess noted.

"Mine cramped up an hour ago."

Still a couple of miles away from the cabin, walking through the woods parallel to the trails, they passed a fire tower. "There she blows," Kid said.

Standing way above the treetops was one of several fire towers out in the Pine Barrens. Kid recalled that Jess had found this 100-foot tower the same day he found Ironside cabin. Since that day, he couldn't count how many times they had climbed to the top of the tower to marvel at the view. They didn't usually stay up there long since the tower swayed noticeably in even the slightest wind, and made them feel uneasy. And only once, during an extended drought, did they find it occupied by a forest ranger.

"We're lucky you can't see the cabin from up there." Jess gazed up at the tower. "In case they happen to stumble upon this."

The tower rose above the treetops, but they knew from experience, a dense wall of tall pine trees to the east kept the cabin out of sight from even the very top of the fire tower. They continued walking for a few miles, making two necessary turns on the way. They crossed another little bridge going over a fresh water stream. Kid looked down to see the steady flow of the water. The snow lining the banks of the stream had a soft, inviting glow. It was surreal to him, given the nightmare they were trapped in.

As they walked up the hill, they could see the silhouette of the cabin against the sky. The large rectangle building was made of cinder blocks and had a sheet metal roof. Except for a section of grass closer to the building, the cabin was surrounded by a moat of deep, fine sand. Now, that moat was filled with snow. From a distance, the structure appeared to be on an island. A faded and worn sign for 'Ironside Gun Club' was still affixed to the door.

Logan's Queen Anne was parked out in front. Maria was standing with her arms folded tapping her foot, waiting for them in the doorway.

When Kid approached the cabin, he stopped for a second as he recalled the first time he brought Sara to Ironside. It was the same weekend during the spring break of 2044 when he finally connected with her after groveling on the phone, meeting her at Lakehurst Diner and then starting to fall in love in a gazebo on the Toms River. It was a weekend he would never forget, and it culminated with, 'the day at the cabin.'

April 10, 2044
Sunday, Midday
Pine Barrens of New Jersey
More than eight months before the event

The midday sun made the forest seem particularly alive as Kid drove for miles through the woods toward Ironside Cabin. He was going there to get his disposable camera, but that hardly mattered to him anymore. What mattered was that Sara was alone with him. After they left the gazebo on the Toms River Friday night, he could not wait to see her again. The Saturday in between seemed to be the longest day in history.

"You weren't kidding about this place being isolated," Sara commented.

Slowing down, Kid inched across an unstable wood bridge over a creek.

"That's what we like about it," he replied as he parked in front of the cabin. "When we found it, it had been abandoned for more than 50 years."

"How do you know that?"

"The old hunting club left a log book inside and the last entry was from more than 50 years before. I guess they left it to die with the club," he remarked.

Stepping out of the vehicle, Sara remarked, "Wow, it's pretty warm out for April."

Walking inside, Kid went over to the corner of the cabin and knelt over a trapdoor in the floor. Lifting up the wood board and peering underneath, it appeared that all of their cans of coffee, soup, and various other items were untouched. He first grabbed the tiny laser pointer Jess kept in there, and put it in his pocket. He then noticed his small disposable camera resting on top of a can of coffee, just as he had left it months ago. Taking it out and inspecting it, he remarked, "Hey, I still have three pictures left. I wonder if this survived the winter out here."

She looked puzzled. "I didn't even know they still made disposable cameras. Why would you not just use your phone camera?"

"Jess worried that the government could access our pictures. In most of them someone has booze in their hand, which is not legal on county property and he didn't want to get fired from his job."

Sara pushed aside a curtain and walked into the adjoining room. After gazing upon a heavy wood framed double bed, she turned toward some newspaper articles pinned to a rectangle piece of corkboard on the wall. "Did you ever read these?" she called out.

"Yes. Which one are you looking at?" he answered from the other room.

"This article is well over 50 years old, late 1980s. They had an original cabin that burned down, and this one was rebuilt on its foundation."

As she was speaking, Kid snuck in the middle room. He came up behind her, wrapped his arms around her waist and kissed her neck. For a moment, she continued to speak, "The original one had…" She stopped as she closed her eyes and tilted her head to expose more of her skin.

When he stopped, he asked, "You were saying?"

"I forget."

As she glanced around the room, she pointed. "So what is in there?"

He opened the door to the third room, and they both peeked in to see a large, galvanized steel tub filled with tools. Kid was used to seeing that tub filled with ice and beer cans.

"What the heck do you need that for out here?" She pointed at a pickaxe.

He was going to make a joke about using it to kill people, but fearing he would creep her out, he just said, "Whatever you need to punch through."

They stood there for a few moments, and then he closed the door. "Come outside. I want to show you something."

Lacing his fingers with hers, he walked her around the back of the cabin. There a metal ladder led to a makeshift wooden deck on the roof with enough room to seat two people. He climbed up and with his prompting, she followed. "Is this thing stable?" she asked.

"Sure, just don't breathe on it and it should be fine." He reached down to help her up.

"Great," she muttered as she took his hand and climbed on the roof.

"This deck was our own addition. We built it last summer."

"What is that stack out that way?" She was looking over his shoulder.

Turning, he pulled the tiny laser pointer from his pocket. With a bright red dot shining on the stack, he asked, "That?"

"Yes. What are you pointing with?"

"My friend Jess's laser pointer. It helps us point things out, especially things far away. Anyway, that is the off-gas stack for the old Oyster Creek Nuclear Power Plant."

"Is it still operational?"

"No, the plant was decommissioned years ago. They've been saying for years that the off-gas stack is going to be torn down, but obviously that hasn't happened. Here, have a seat with a nicer view than a nuclear power plant."

A rolling sea of green pine trees lay before her as she turned and peered east. "Is that the ocean way out there?"

"Barnegat Bay and the ocean. Pretty good view, huh?"

"Yeah." She stared in awe and ran her fingers through her hair. "It's surprising for this part of Jersey. It feels like we're on top of a mountain."

"I guess we are. They call it Forked River Mountain. It's really just a sand hill, but it's far enough above sea level to provide a pretty good view." He still could not get over how sexy Sara looked when she ran her fingers through her hair.

"What are those big warehouses over that way?" Her hand was over her eyes to shield them from the sun, as if she was saluting.

"Remember that diner we were at the other night in Lakehurst?"

"Not ringing any bells. We went out together?" She paused to gaze at him, and then laughed.

He did too as he poked her side and made her drop her arms. "Those are the hangars at the Naval Air Engineering Station Lakehurst, just up the street from the diner."

"Got it. That's the part of the Joint Base I never see," she noted. "Those are the hangars that originally housed dirigibles, like the Hindenburg."

"Here." He handed her the laser pointer. "Put the red dot on the largest structure over there. Just don't shine it too long. We don't need to piss the military off."

"My father would not be happy with me," she said as she took the small device. She went to press the button.

"Wait!" Kid said and turned the tip of the pointer so it faced out. "Don't ever shine it in your eye. It's a laser. It will burn your retina in a heartbeat."

"That would not be good," she stated as she pressed the button and a red dot appeared in the ocean far away.

"We don't need to blind any sea captains either." He took her hand and moved the red dot to a large structure closer and to the north. "There. The Hindenburg went down in flames and crashed right behind that big hangar."

"Interesting." She stood up and handed the laser pointer back to him. "I knew the Hindenburg crashed on the base, but never knew exactly where."

He also stood up and wrapped his arms around her waist. He put his face against hers, and together they marveled at the view for several minutes. Kid then took out his deluxe disposable camera, set it to auto-shoot, and put it on the rail of the deck. "Let's see if this thing still works."

They both sat back down and he put his arm around her.

"Smile…" As he was saying the word, the camera snapped the picture.

Sara chuckled as he got up and set it again to take a picture. Dropping back down, he snapped, "Smile." They sat for a few seconds waiting, with grins on their faces. Nothing happened.

As he got up and took a step forward, it clicked and shot the picture. He froze for a second with his midsection right in front of the lens. Sara started laughing. Kid was ready to throw the camera in the woods. "I can't win with this thing, and there's only one more picture left."

He again set the camera, put it on the rail and sat down. "Last chance. No giggling."

She stopped for a split second, and then began laughing hysterically. She put her arm around Kid, and he also started laughing. The camera shot the final picture. After staying on the deck for a while, he pocketed the camera and they climbed down.

"It's so peaceful out here." She pushed aside the hanging curtain and stepped into the cabin's middle room.

"I know. That's what I love about it," he replied walking behind her.

Kid was starting to feel a little strange, a feeling he had felt before, but never so strongly. He stopped and Sara turned to face him. He was experiencing a warmth at that moment that he felt compelled to explore. As he touched her, it intensified. He put one hand behind her neck and the other around her waist, and gave her a soft kiss. She put both of her arms around his waist, and kissed him back, but more passionately. They both started breathing a little deeper. He was sensitive to the touch of all ten of her fingers on his lower back.

He brushed his lips against hers and pulled away, feeling an electric charge run through his body. Unable to resist, he did it again. It was like touching the tip of a tongue against both posts of a depleted nine-volt battery, but it was a pleasant feeling and reverberated throughout his entire body.

They walked over and sat down on the edge of the lone wood-framed bed in the middle room. As they continued to kiss and breathe deeper, they laid down with his arm still wrapped around her waist. He pulled his hand from around her midsection and it grazed her breast ever so gently, causing her warm breath to quiver as they began kissing more passionately. He felt flush as blood warmer than 98.5 degrees Fahrenheit spread throughout his body.

They shared a slow kiss and he swore he could feel every ridge in her soft, warm lips. The clock seemed to slow as they entered a time vacuum where he was no longer conscious of the world outside of them.

His senses were acute and seriously heightened. Uncontrollable was his compulsion to intimately explore every inch of Sara's existence.

Kid looked into her eyes and was floored by the transparency. Through them, she revealed all of who she was; her desires, fears, and the intense love she had for him. It was a moment so pure and natural that his defenses and fears fell to the floor, also exposing all of who he was. Like never before in his life he was comfortable with his own vulnerability. With their eyes locked, an unbreakable connection was forged between two hearts and souls.

He was fighting the tremble in his voice. "Anything that happens from here on out... is gravy."

"What do you mean?" she whispered, and seemed to also be fighting to keep control.

"This has already been the best moment of my life."

A tingling feeling spread throughout his body, even reaching his extremities, as he realized intimacy was inevitable. Her eyes and surrendering exhale said the same. The chemistry born of their connection then consumed them, entirely. For the next few hours, in the bed in the middle room of the cabin, they would make slow, deliberate love over and over.

With both of them ready to collapse from exhaustion, having been drained of every ounce of energy, Kid got up to make something to eat. Stepping into the main room, he heated up a can of Chicken and Rice soup, which to him was akin to a gift from heaven at that point. After sharing the soup, he lit a candle in the main room and they walked outside to meet the dusk, each wrapped in only a blanket.

Halfway down the grass area in front of the cabin, Sara said, "I have never felt anything like that before. People talk about being taken to the moon and the stars, and I never understood what they meant... until now. I think we did a trip around the entire universe."

"That we did. I'm not even sure we've landed yet."

She stopped. "Do I hear water?"

Kid pointed to a creek running under an old wood bridge.

She inhaled and a smile came to her face. "After the moment we just shared together, the ambiance of this exact spot, the view, the sound of trickling water, the smell of pine, it will be forever etched in my soul."

Standing behind her, Kid slipped her blanket down and kissed her bare shoulder. Leading her to the middle room of the cabin, he grabbed her waist with both hands and softly kissed her neck. That was all it took to prompt another round of love-making. Lying together in perfect contentment on the bed, Sara whispered, "I could stay in this moment forever."

"Me too," he echoed, feeling more tired than he had ever felt in his life.

Propping up on her elbow, Sara leaned over his face and gave him a gentle kiss. "Let's have our own secret code about our experience today, falling so, so deeply in love," she said conspiratorially.

He smiled. She was the cutest girl on earth.

"Only me and you will know what it means when we say," she pondered for a long second, "'the day at the cabin'."

"Perfect," he said as he pushed back the silk-like strands of hair hanging over her face.

They were brought back to reality by the hoot of an owl, reminding them that darkness had descended. Kid checked his watch. "Sara, what time were you supposed to be home for dinner?"

She froze. "We were planning on eating at 7:30. Can I make it on time?"

Kid's eyes opened wide. "That depends. Did you mean 7:30 tomorrow morning?"

CHAPTER 25

December 30, 2044
Friday, Afternoon
The Pine Barrens of New Jersey
Four days after the event

S tanding in the cabin's doorway, Maria waved her hand. "Hurry! Come on!" After they walked in, she closed the door and dropped a heavy wood plank down into mounted brackets to lock it. She hugged and kissed both of them. "I'm glad you're both alright. Where are they now?" she asked.

"Hopefully many miles away," Kid replied.

"How did you do that?"

"We erased your tire tracks coming up here and made fake tracks that would take them far away from here. I doubt if they'll find us any time soon, if ever."

"Good. With any luck they will freeze to death first."

Walking out from another room, Heidi looked relieved and disturbed at the same time. "You made it. It seemed like you guys were out there forever."

"Long enough. We're frozen to the bone." Jess put his cold hand on top of Heidi's.

"You're not kidding," she said as she grabbed his hand and started briskly rubbing it.

"Speaking of frozen." Maria continued to blow her warm breath into her hands. "It's not much better in here."

"I hate to do it, but we're going to freeze to death ourselves if we don't get a fire going." Jess turned to Kid for confirmation.

He nodded his head. "We'll just have to do something so they don't spot the smoke."

Jess shrugged. "That's easy enough. I'll just fray the tops of the flue pipes on the roof so that the smoke doesn't rise in a steady plume."

Heidi added, "I was casing out this place. We should fire up both wood stoves."

"Both?" Kid was standing in the main room of the cabin, which had a large cast iron wood stove and two wood-framed double beds. He stared at the heavy curtain that separated the main room from the middle room. Reflecting on the layout of the rest of the cabin, the middle room had only one wood-framed double bed, but it did have a smaller wood stove. The third smaller room was used mainly for storage of tools. "Oh yeah. I always forget about the one in the middle room because we didn't use it often."

Gazing at Kid's face, Heidi stared at the dried blood. "Are you hurt?"

"I'm fine." He wiped at his face with his arm.

"You're bleeding everywhere." She examined the jacket arm that was torn and stained red also. "Listen, we carried Sara in and laid her down in bed, so why don't you go check on her and then we'll clean you up."

He ran into the middle room, which was lit by only a single candle. Sara was sitting on the edge of the bed, hunched over and clenching a blanket. Her pain seemed to be worsening.

Kid embraced her. "How do you feel?"

"What?" she replied, appearing dazed and confused.

"How are you feeling?"

"Can't move much," she said, her voice not disguising her distress. She appeared spaced out, and her breaths were shallow.

Kid was distraught. They had come too far, and been through so much. She would be fine, he assured himself. She just needed to rest and regain her strength. After all, the shot barely grazed her shoulder.

"Who are you?" Sara asked as she stared at Kid.

He stared in stunned silence for a moment, and then resumed

breathing. "Just lay down for a while and rest. You need it." He took the blanket from her hands and pulled it up under her chin as she lay down.

He looked up to see Heidi standing in the doorway. She must have overheard the conversation because her hand was covering her mouth and her eyes were opened wide.

Kid looked over at her and shook his head. "Still in a little bit of shock," he said and forced a smirk as he left the room.

Stepping out the back door of the cabin, he saw Jess climbing down the ladder. The flue pipes on the roof were already frayed and looked like exploded cartoon cigars. Kid grabbed a bundle of logs from a rack covered by a sheet-metal awning. He took some of the wood into the middle room where Sara was lying down. After lighting a fire, he walked out to the main room.

Jess whispered, "Is Sara alright?"

"She's in pain, and she's a little delirious, but I think she's alright. I'm sure she'll feel better after getting some rest."

"Yeah, I'm sure you're right. Actually, we'll all feel better with some rest. I hope they don't find us tonight. I'm too fatigued to run or fight."

"I think we'll be safe for tonight." Kid was convinced that it would take the soldiers some time to find the cabin. He picked up the candle, walked over to the corner of the main room and lifted the trapdoor in the floor. They had an old-fashioned percolator coffeepot and four big metal cooking pots. A tiny laser pointer and a pair of binoculars rested inside one of the metal pots. At that point, he was torn between hunger and a thirst for coffee. Seeing cans of chicken soup in front of him, it was clear that hunger was winning out.

"Maria, can you please open these?" Kid put three cans of chicken soup and a can opener on the table.

She frantically started opening the first can. "Yeah, I need to eat." She stopped and uttered, "Oh, shit…"

"What is it?"

"My diabetes meds are at that beach shack we stayed in."

"Can you make it without them, at least until the smoke clears and we can get out of the woods?" Jess asked as he walked over.

"Do I have a choice?"

"If it gets bad, we will have to make a run for it and get your meds," he concluded.

Resuming opening the can of soup, she shrugged her shoulders. "I should be alright for a few days, so long as I eat, and watch what I eat. On the ships, they knew I was a diabetic, but I survived on a good diet alone, without needing medication."

Kid took the coffeepot and a large metal pot and went outside. Walking through the light snow that was still falling, he approached the fresh water stream that ran next to the cabin. The friction of the quickly moving water molecules kept the stream from freezing. As far as he could remember, the stream had never once been frozen in all the times they had camped out there. He figured the water from the stream needed to be boiled since they didn't know if there were excessive bacteria counts. He knew the percolator coffeepot boiled the water as part of its brewing process so they would be covered there, but the water he was putting in the metal pot would also have to boil before it could be consumed.

Back in the cabin, Kid added the three open cans of soup to the water in the large pot and left it to boil on the front metal plate of the wood stove. He then put coffee grinds in the percolator and also put it on the hot surface. Walking over to the one and only cupboard in the main room, he took out five ceramic bowls and five tin cups and put them on the table.

Heidi pointed to a chair. "While we are waiting, Kid, take off your jacket and sit."

He complied and took a seat.

She grabbed a roll of paper towels. Tearing off a few sheets, she rubbed snow on them and dressed his wounds. He had two cuts on his forehead and one very deep jagged cut on his right arm. Heidi made a bandage out of dry paper towels and duct tape for his arm.

A few minutes later, Jess looked at the soup on the stove. "Is this ready or what?" He already had a bowl in his hand.

"Almost. I added water from the stream, but it has to be boiled," Kid warned.

"There," Heidi noted as she gently patted the makeshift bandage on his arm. "Sorry about how flimsy it is. I don't have much to work with here."

"It'll work. Thanks. Why don't you get a bowl, the soup should be ready soon."

The coffee and the soup were ready at about the same time.

Kid poured a bowl of soup and went to Sara's bedside. He fed her the entire bowl and said, "Now get some rest and don't worry, you'll be fine."

■　　■　　■

Marching on the trail, Elder-1 came to a halt as the tire tracks in the snow just suddenly ended. "Clever. Fucking clever. Bastards," he muttered as he looked around the area.

One of the members, who had been fully soaked when their truck fell into the puddle under the ice, collapsed. His body was shivering uncontrollably. Although he could be saved, Elder-1 was not going to stop and let his prey escape or get further away. The rest of the members did not seem physically compromised so he ordered them to continue marching, leaving the dying member behind. It was a choice he had made many times before and he did not hesitate for a second.

As a young officer, Maximillian, 'Max,' Cramer had fought side by side with his soldiers in numerous battles for the United States across too many countries to list, from Afghanistan to Iraq to Korea, and he had taken too many lives to count. As a matter of fact, he stopped counting after the first fifty. He had led the rank and file as well as special operations forces. Although considered ruthless by his peers and enemies alike, he saw soldiers as numbers and individual lives were inconsequential. Max Cramer, now Elder-1, did whatever needed to be done to accomplish the mission, regardless of the cost in human heartbeats. That is what made him the ultimate leader.

They left the dying member and started back up the trail, continuing the hunt in earnest.

■   ■   ■

Kid was half-starved when he went back to the soup pot, so he filled his bowl and ate quickly. Afterward, he drank hot coffee from a tin cup and savored every drop. Putting his empty cup down, he took another clean metal pot and walked outside. He skimmed the surface of the snow on the ground until the pot was full, and put it on the wood stove inside.

"So they have no smaller boats to get ashore?" Maria repeated back to Jess, sounding impressed.

"Nope. They're stuck out there."

"For now," Kid interjected. "All we did was buy ourselves some time. It's just a matter of how much."

With the big wood stove all fired up, the main room of the cabin was already warm. For the moment, and for a change, Kid didn't feel uncomfortable. That fact alone made him unsettled. He turned to the girls. "Did they tell you what country was responsible for the destruction?"

"It wasn't one country. Elder-1 said it was individuals in power from several countries, including America," Heidi said as she finished the last of her soup.

"I figured that. How else could they get access to the satellite system? Too many security levels needed to be breached for America not to be involved." Although Kid already suspected this, hearing it sent a wave of anger through him.

"When Sara's up to it she can probably give you more details," Maria offered. "Always the inquisitive one, that girl," she continued as she put her coffee tin down on the table.

"Who is this Elder-1?" Kid asked.

"He's their leader," Maria clarified. "Anyway, in the end, that satellite system wasn't as perfect as they thought. He told us 99.9 % of the world's population was wiped out in the blink of an eye. The reason we're still alive is that the stupid thing malfunctioned and left our beach area untouched."

"But it operated fine for the other 99.9% of the world?" Kid sounded skeptical.

"That's what he told us," Maria answered. She turned to Heidi.

Heidi nodded her head in affirmation.

Jess sounded somber. "99.9% of the world. I still can't comprehend this all. Think of the big cities with melted bodies, like the one we saw the first time in Quick-Fix, but millions of them. Places like New York City, Los Angeles, or London, all with blood and guts running everywhere, in the streets, and out of buildings."

"And remember, it hit us late at night," Kid reminded. "Most of the east coast may have been sleeping, but other areas of the United States, and other areas of the world, were wide awake."

Maria had one hand on her stomach and one hand over her mouth, and she was grimacing. "Do we have to be so... graphic right after we just ate?" Getting up, she started gathering the dirty bowls and cups from the old wood table.

"Let me help you," Heidi offered.

"It's all beyond comprehension, even in thinking about our own lives. I keep catching myself in moments of panic thinking I need to check in at home," Kid said. His emotions swelled instantly. Everyone froze for a moment. It was a harsh reminder of their new reality.

"Your cup?" Choked up, Maria's words came out as a whisper as she held her hand out toward the table. Kid heard her, but was so caught up in his thoughts that he did not respond right away. "Are you going to hand me that or what?" she repeated as she reached for his cup, but then froze and shuddered.

Kid knew why and rubbed her arm. He had asked her once about the small scar over her eye. Maria had explained that one time, when she was a little girl, she had tried to take her drunk father's cup to the sink and he reacted by grabbing the glass from her and breaking it against her face.

"Are you alright?" He held the cup in his hand but did not move.

"Yeah, fine," she said as she reached out and grabbed it. As she turned she lifted her hand and touched the small scar over her left eye.

"Should I go down to the stream to wash the dishes?" Heidi asked Kid.

"No, use the water on the stove. I scooped snow from outside so it could melt in that pot." He pointed to the stove top. "We need to be careful with the stream, it may be contaminated."

"How can we tell if it is?"

"We can't. That's why we have to boil the water," he responded.

Heidi took the dishes, percolator, and dirty pots and went out the back door of the cabin. She cleaned them with soap and the melted snow from the pot on the stove.

"See anything outside?" Kid asked her as she walked back inside.

"All clear."

"Good." Kid sat back. Now warm and fed, he wasn't ready to get up from the old wood table in the main room. At that point, he was so exhausted that he couldn't have moved even if soldiers were at the door.

CHAPTER 26

December 30, 2044
Friday, Evening
The Pine Barrens of New Jersey
Four days after the event

After a few hours had passed, Kid peeked in the middle room and saw that Sara was still sleeping. He closed the curtain and sat down at the table in the main room. The smell of the table's old hardwood entered his nostrils, and he breathed it in. He had always loved the rustic feel of their hidden cabin. It was deep in the woods and many miles away from the nearest inhabited community, which in densely populated New Jersey made the isolation even more of a novelty.

When they stayed at Ironside, he always felt like they were living in Colonial times. The furniture consisted of old wood-framed beds, antique chairs, and an old, bulky wood table. There was no electricity, natural gas, or running water. The bathroom was anywhere one could find in the forest. The only heat was from the wood stoves and the only light was from candles. His group of friends had spent many nights sitting on chairs and beds in the main room where they would talk, laugh, and ponder what the future held for each of them. Every so often, it felt great to warm up by standing right in front of the wood stove. The guys would take turns tending to the fire, saving the biggest logs to throw in the stove right as everyone went to bed. These logs, often rounds that had not been split, were the designated 'all-nighters' since they had the best chance of burning until morning. It struck Kid that the ambiance of those memories is only felt when re-living the moment. When you're in the moment, you don't notice any particular atmosphere.

"Are we ready to turn in?" Maria asked as she laid on a bed.

"Should someone be keeping watch?" Jess responded. They both turned to Kid.

He pondered for a second and then looked out the window. He realized the moon stage was irrelevant. "It's overcast and pitch black out there. Even if someone was to stay up and watch, by the time they spotted them it would be too late anyway."

"I agree." Jess blew out one of the two candles and laid next to Maria.

Heidi jumped into the other double-bed in the main room by herself. "Not to mention, who could actually stay awake at this point."

Picking up the remaining lit candle, Kid noted, "No lookout tonight, but we should have someone doing that during daylight hours."

"They aren't finding this place anyway," Jess muttered, sounding like he was already dozing off.

Kid went into the middle room to sleep with Sara. She stirred and awoke as he climbed in next to her, so he gently massaged her shoulders and neck. His worry for her was growing. He could tell that her breaths were more and more labored. She was very weak and lethargic, and spaced out like someone on heavy drugs. She just wasn't herself at all. *What the hell was in the weapon shot that grazed her?* he wondered.

He blew out the candle, kissed her on the cheek, and wrapped his arm around her midsection. Although weakly, she embraced his arm and pulled it tighter against her body. While she dozed off, he lay there thinking of everything that happened that day. After a moment his mind couldn't deal with the stress of reliving it again, and in self-defense, he too fell asleep.

In the middle of the night, Kid's eyes opened. *What was that noise?* He jumped out of bed, startled. The wood stove door was open and the embers cast the room in a faint, orange-tinted glow. Stepping over to the window, at first he couldn't look. He expected to see the whole pack of soldiers standing there. Summoning his courage, he lifted his head up. A chill shot through his body as he saw a pair of eyes staring in the window. The dark eyes were fixed on his. He froze. A moment later he uttered, "No." The enemy also moved his mouth. As he backed away from the window, so did the enemy. He stared and tilted his head sideways. Smirking, Kid saluted, and his reflection saluted back.

Pressing his face against the glass he searched for soldiers. Seeing no eyes in the darkness, he spun around at the crack of wood popping. *There's the noise*, he realized. He fed the wood stove two more logs and climbed back into bed

■   ■   ■

The next day Kid was the first to wake. He sat in bed staring at the ceiling for a couple of minutes. *Did yesterday really happen?* Turning his head, he saw Sara next to him, answering his question. The wood burning in the stove was all but extinguished, and there was a chill in the air. His face could feel the cold, but the rest of him was warm and comfortable under the heavy blanket. There was a faint smell of burning wood, but it was a nice smell. He really didn't want to get out of bed, so he let himself just lay there for a couple more minutes.

Being careful not to wake Sara, he finally sat up and lit a candle on the small table next to him. As he stood up he rubbed his legs and winced when he hit the large bruise on his shin. He put a few logs on the fire, and stood close rubbing his hands together. Laying his warm hands on his scruffy cheeks, he wondered how long it had been since he shaved. As soon as the thought entered his mind, his face started to itch and he felt like he had a hundred ingrown hairs. Putting on his shoes, he grabbed the percolator coffeepot and went outside.

He crossed his arms against the bite of the crisp morning air. The stars were fading in deference to the impending dawn, casting the scene in a soft gray. Kid squinted as he cased out the area. There was no sign of the soldiers, so he walked down to the stream, crouched down, and dunked the coffeepot. The sound of the stream's trickling water was mesmerizing. He put the filled percolator to the side, and using his index finger, he scooped snow from the ground. Although it was an exercise in futility, he brushed his teeth with his finger. Taking the coffeepot, he made his way back up the hill to the cabin.

Putting coffee grounds in the pot, he placed it on the wood stove in the main room and stoked the fire. While waiting, he sat on the edge of Heidi's bed, close enough to the stove to keep warm. As soon as the coffee was done, he poured himself a cup and sat at the table. Outside the window, a dream-like scene was emerging. The deep snow was bright white and glowing in the dawn. Sipping his steaming hot coffee, he noticed that the snow was still clinging to the tree branches. The white powder on the ground and the pine trees, coupled with the stream flowing under the small wooden bridge, created a scene as beautiful as a postcard. *It's just like a coffee commercial,* he thought as his took another sip of his piping hot drink. It was a simple, pleasant thought, and one he knew couldn't last. Not with the heavier and more disturbing ones that were lurking. *Where are the soldiers and Elder-1 now?* he wondered as he shivered, and not from the chill in the air. He was sure the soldiers were still in the woods searching for them. He just hoped they were many miles away, and that they would freeze to death before finding the cabin.

Sara moaned in pain, so Kid ran into the middle room. She was trying to raise herself, but couldn't. He propped her up and brought her in a cup of coffee. With his assistance, she slowly and painfully lifted the cup to her mouth.

"How do you feel today," he asked.

"Bad," she said as she looked around the room.

"At least it's warm in here."

"Yes," she replied and continued to drink her coffee. Once finished, she handed the empty cup back to him. "That was strong, but good." She still appeared to be in a daze.

"Glad you liked it." Kid tried to hide his surprise. He had made the coffee intentionally weak to conserve grinds. *She hates weak coffee. She really must not feel well.*

He heard Maria yawn and her bed creaked as she stirred. Checking his watch, it was only 6:15 a.m. *Why is everyone up so early, especially after the long day they all had yesterday?* he wondered. He then realized he should be asking himself the same question.

Soon everyone was awake and drinking coffee. Jess made a large batch of cream of wheat for breakfast. "How was your food?" he asked Maria.

"Good, but it would sit better if I wasn't worried sick that Elder-1 and his troops might find us at any minute," she responded.

Sara was still not feeling well. She wasn't able to get out of bed, and went back to sleep right after she ate, so Kid climbed up on the roof. From the deck, he looked out at the ocean. He squinted as he noticed the three dots out at sea. He peered through the binoculars he had grabbed from the storage area under the trapdoor, and could see the ships more clearly as they floated side by side. He then scanned the woods in all directions. No soldiers in sight. Jess climbed up the ladder and joined him. "I guess we can take turns keeping watch. I'll take the first shift, if you want to stay with Sara," he offered.

Kid went down to be with his injured girlfriend. He laid beside Sara, who was napping. Concluding that she needed the rest, he didn't talk, but just kept his arm around her.

Throughout the morning and early afternoon, Kid, Jess, Maria, and Heidi took turns serving as lookout. Nobody spotted anything unusual in the woods. When Jess wasn't on lookout duty, he made an alarm system out of ropes and a bell. As always, Kid was impressed by his friend's ingenuity. Jess used the ropes as trip wires, hidden under the snow in the trail leading up to the cabin and the trail going away from the cabin. He laid them over small trenches he dug around the first bend of each trail, and covered them with snow. The ropes were tied to a bell inside the front door of the cabin. Kid helped him finish the alarm, and they successfully tested it a few times.

Midafternoon, Kid was sitting on the bed when suddenly the bell inside the cabin started to ring. Jess hurried down the ladder from the roof. Kid picked up Sara and ran for the truck. Once outside, he turned left, then right, trying to figure out where the soldiers were coming from. Jess was standing with the keys in his hand. Sounding frantic, he asked, "Where's Maria?"

"She must be out back!" Heidi started to run around the side of the cabin.

"Stop! Don't leave!" Maria was screaming as she ran back on the trail, zipping her uniform. "That was me!" she yelled as she approached the cabin.

Jess lifted his arms up in the air, "What the…" he started to say and dropped his hands against his side. The keys jingled as they bounced off of his thigh.

"That was me," she repeated, out of breath from her short sprint to the cabin. "Why did you run the stupid rope for the alarm over there?" She pointed with the roll of toilet paper in her hand. "My bathroom is that way!"

"Ok, Ok. No harm done." Kid carried Sara for a few steps, and headed toward the door.

"Can we sit out here?" she whispered to him.

"What? Outside?" he asked. "That's probably not a good idea. You're already sick."

"Just for a minute?" Her eyes pleaded.

He was reluctant as he looked at Sara in his arms. He sighed and surrendered. "Jess, can you grab a chair from inside?"

"You want to sit out in the cold?" Jess sounded surprised.

She answered, "Yes. Right here."

"Whatever floats your boat," he said and shook his head. He walked in and grabbed a wood chair. He put it down in the path between the truck and the cabin, where the snow was already flattened from the previous foot traffic.

Kid carefully sat her down facing the stream, the little wooden bridge and the forest beyond. Kneeling down and keeping his hand on her to make sure she didn't fall over, he scanned the area. He had to admit, the scene was very beautiful and peaceful. The stream flowed steadily, and the trees were wearing the snow upon their branches like a comfortable white shawl. The trail leading from the cabin seemed to disappear into a single point as the trail made a sharp left turn beyond the little bridge.

He had a recollection that Sara was captivated by this same view the first time she came to the cabin. The only difference was that this time, there was a snow cover. He inhaled and thought he smelled pine. Given that everything was frozen, he knew it had to be an olfactory recollection from being there with her in the spring, when the smell of pine was ever-present. Sara just stared at the scene and smiled. Even in her condition, she seemed to be fully absorbing the moment.

After several long minutes, Kid said, "That's enough, Missy. We'd better get you inside." She had a slight look of curiosity as he picked her up.

In the middle room, he laid her down on the bed and pulled the blanket up over her. "Thank you," she whispered.

"You're welcome." He kissed her on the forehead. "Now let's get back to resting and recovering."

Walking back through the main room, Kid was ready to go outside and climb up on the roof. He paused and headed back to the middle room. He peeked in to check on Sara one more time. She still seemed content, and absorbed in her moment. But it disturbed him that her smile was so pained.

CHAPTER 27

December 31, 2044
Saturday, Midday
The Pine Barrens of New Jersey
Five days after the event

"I couldn't tell which trail Maria was coming from when the bell started ringing," Kid noted as he sat with Jess on the roof. "We should only use the bell for one trail, and use something else for the one going in the other direction."

After a moment, Jess said, "We could tie one of the ropes to a pan, and leave it on the edge of a shelf? The trail leading to the cabin would be the bell, but the trail leading away would be a pan."

"At least we would know which direction someone was coming from."

"Let me go set that up. It's your turn up here anyway." Jess climbed down the ladder.

Alone on the roof, Kid took the binoculars and scanned the area.

"Hey Kid, what can we do down here to help?" Heidi called up from the ground. He shrugged his shoulders. She put her hand on her hip and tapped her foot. Peering in the back door of the cabin, she yelled to Jess, "Hey, do we have anything to take a bath in?"

"Yeah, the stream," he called out from inside the cabin. "You get used to the cold after you're in it for a while."

"Very funny, Jess," Maria jumped in. "I hate to tell you, but you could use one yourself."

"Are you guys kidding? Elder-1 and his militia could find us at any moment, and you're worried about a bath?"

Kid watched as Heidi went to speak and paused. "Jess, I'm tired of feeling so unclean. Anyway, I need to do something. I'm restless, and nervous, and cold and don't feel like just sitting around all day waiting." Her voice was rising.

"Alright, alright, hold on," Jess called out. "Actually, we do have something. Maria, can you send Kid down to help me, and take lookout for a while?"

"Sure."

"And nobody touch the frying pan on the shelf in here," Jess added. "It's now part of the alarm system."

When entering the main room, Kid saw that Jess had grabbed the large, round galvanized steel beer tub from the third room of the cabin where it was stored.

"We just need to fill it with water and heat it up on the stove. Come on Kid," Jess said as he dragged it to the stream. He and Kid, each holding a handle, filled the tub half way and trudged back up the hill with it. "Now we need to lift it and put it on top of the wood stove."

Kid looked skeptical. "Will it hold?"

"Don't worry, the stove is old, but sturdy." Jess kicked it with his foot. "She won't buckle. Lift!" he barked, and they hoisted the tub. Placing it on top of the wood stove and taking a few steps back, he smacked his hands together. "See?"

Heidi sat the table and watched expectantly as Kid added logs and stoked the fire. "It's going to be a while before this baby gets boiling," he noted.

A half an hour later, Heidi said, "I see bubbles!"

"They say a watched pot never boils," Kid commented.

"It's not a pot, it is a tub," she grumbled.

He rolled his eyes.

Jess and Kid grabbed some rags, wrapped their hands, and lifted the scalding hot tub off of the wood stove. Kid's neck veins felt like they were going to pop. "Damn that's heavy."

"Wait, can you guys put the tub in the middle room?" Heidi asked.

"Sara should bathe first, and she'll definitely need us to help her out."

With great effort, they carried the heavy tub into the middle room. Dipping his finger into the now three-quarters full bath, Kid quickly retracted it. "That's hot."

Heidi did the same. "Actually, it's perfect."

Kid walked to the doorway and yelled up to the roof. "Come on down Maria. I'll take over."

I cannot wait to jump in that water, Heidi thought.

Coming into the room, Maria said, "Jess, do you think you can take our clothes down to the stream and wash them while we take a bath?"

"Wash them? With what?"

"There's a bar of soap under the trapdoor in the other room." Pushing him back, she said, "Just wait there Jess." She then closed the curtain between the rooms.

Walking over to the bed, Maria pulled back the blanket and said to Sara, "Let's get those clothes off." Helping her sit up, she unzipped the uniform and rolled the gray jumper over Sara's shoulders, down her back and pulled her arms from the sleeves. Heidi worked the uniform over her feet. Sara didn't seem to have the strength to help at all. She barely even woke up while she was being stripped down, and proceeded to roll over and fall right back to sleep.

Maria and Heidi disrobed and wrapped themselves in blankets.

"Jess!" Maria called out.

"Yes," he responded from behind the curtain.

Maria pushed aside the divider, threw all of the uniforms over his shoulder and put the undergarments in his hand. "There. Now you're all set. Give them a good wash."

"Anything else?" He rolled his eyes.

"No, that's all for now thanks. Hurry back though." She patted him on the head. "Hang the uniforms next to the stove so they dry."

Heidi and Maria lifted Sara and put her in the tub. Although she was thin, Sara's legs had to be crossed for her to fit in the round metal basin. "Let's wake up here." Maria tapped her shoulder. "Wake up!"

Sara, appearing groggy, opened her eyes and stared into space. Her breaths were very shallow and seemed to require much effort.

Heidi finally made eye contact. "You've got to get better soon. We can't stand seeing you this way. You're just not yourself." Her concern was growing exponentially.

There was no response or reaction. Sara's mind was seemingly vacuous.

"Go ahead and say it Sara, 'Leave me alone. I feel like hell'," Maria urged as she rubbed her back with soap.

With much effort, Sara shook her head once, and for just a second was able to raise her hand and point at the corner of her eye with her finger.

"I know, right?" Maria commented from behind her.

Heidi was face to face with Sara, and froze upon seeing her expression.

"Duh, here there is no 'I'," Maria added as she mockingly pointed at the corner of her eye while making a face. "What is that all about?"

Heidi stared with her mouth open until a splash of water hit her hand, snapping her out of it. After the girls washed Sara, they lifted her out and dried her using a soft blanket as a towel. They gently laid her back down in bed and pulled up her blanket.

"I'm worried," Heidi whispered.

"Me too," Maria said in a tone that made them both pause.

Peering down at the still steaming bath water, Heidi snapped out of it. "That looks like heaven at this point." She turned and waited for a response.

"Well don't just stand there, go for it."

"Close your eyes." Heidi dropped her blanket and climbed into the tub.

"Oh please. Like my grandmother used to say, nobody can ever look something off of you."

Heidi's bath was quick. She said, "I'm done. The water is still pretty hot."

"And I get sloppy third's," Maria quipped as she tossed her blanket aside and climbed in next.

"Trust me, you'll feel better."

"I do already." Maria rubbed soap up and down her arms, and then cupped the warm water in her hands.

As Heidi entered the main room, Jess stepped in and started hanging uniforms next to the woodstove. He said, "These will take some serious time to dry, but at least they are clean. I hope the soldiers don't show up now, or you girls will be running in the nude. How was your bath?"

"Surprisingly refreshing," she remarked as she sighed. She wrapped herself in a heavier blanket and pulled the ripped, thin blanket out from underneath and handed it to him. "Can you give this blanket to Maria? She's still in the tub."

"Nice. Sloppy thirds with the towel now too?" she yelled from the middle room.

On the roof of the cabin, Kid kept a watchful eye to the east, while the sun hovered behind him. As he glanced over his shoulder, he noticed the sun was starting its descent, like it did every other day. On the western horizon it looked like a red and gold globe. *Everything looks so normal*, he thought. It was eerie in light of the circumstances.

He looked down to see Heidi, wrapped in a blanket, coming up the ladder. She appeared to be struggling to keep the blanket around her while climbing at the same time.

"What are you doing?" Kid could see nothing but the top of her blonde head, and the cleavage of her breasts.

"We need to talk, and my uniform could take hours to dry."

He offered his hand and helped her up. She sat next to him and gazed at the ocean.

"See anything yet, besides woods and water?" she asked.

"Not a thing."

After a silent moment, she blurted out, "Kid, I'm worried about Sara. I think she's getting worse."

"Why?"

"She's having problems breathing, and can't even sit up in bed without help. Mentally, she's just not there at all."

"The shot didn't even hit her. It just grazed her shoulder. It'll take some time for her to recover. If she was going to die, she would've already," he said, knowing he sounded defensive.

"You're acting like she'll be fine," she said as she put her hand under his chin and turned his head, forcing him to look into her eyes, "but she won't, unless we do something."

"What? What can we do?" He pushed her hand away. "I know we should, but…" Kid was getting flustered and snapped, "Can you do me a favor, and shut up about it?"

In the stillness that followed his outburst, he had a strangely-timed recollection of a traumatic event from two summers ago. For his entire life, Kid was close to his first cousin, Dawn. She was more than a year younger than him, and was like the little sister he never had. He was there when she got her first period. He took her to her first concert. He went to all of her softball games. When her heart was broken for the first time by a boy, Kid spent that whole day cheering her up. But three years ago when she was 17-years-old, after her parent's ugly divorce, Dawn retreated from the world and was soon hooked on heroin. He did everything in his power to help her, but she could not unravel the noose the drug had tied around her neck. And despite her fragile state, her divorced parents could not stop fighting and putting her in the middle. Kid's relationship with her became an emotional roller coaster because time and again she would call and he would have to talk her off of the ledge. He could not count how many times he saved her from overdosing, inadvertently or otherwise.

Finally, he forced Dawn to enter an inpatient program. She came out clean and seemed to have beaten away the demons that had haunted her once and for all. But in the ensuing months, his Aunt Ginny, Dawn's mother, kept calling Kid and voicing her fear that her daughter was doing drugs again. When he would see his cousin, her face would be tight and her eyes would be a little sunken, but he would always rationalize that she was fine and had not gone back down the dark road. He would assume that she just hadn't slept well, or was stressed from life, but he refused to accept that she had gone back to drugs.

She couldn't. She had worked too hard to clean herself up. And he had worked too hard to help her, and was exhausted from his efforts, both physically and emotionally.

But one humid, suffocating night this past summer, he made a phone call that would haunt him forever. Dawn was driving in the early afternoon to Camden, New Jersey, allegedly to look at a used car she was considering buying. Aunt Ginny called him, panicked and fearful that the trip was really for a drug binge. She begged him to intervene, saying, "Kid, you're acting like she'll be fine. Are you blind to what's going on here?" In his worst moment of denial, he choose not to intervene and call his cousin, believing that she was just shopping for a used car.

As day turned into night, he began to feel uneasy. He tried to call Dawn over and over on her mobile device. All of his calls went unanswered, as did his texts. Finally, he called again and some strange man picked up the phone, laughing maniacally. "Sorry. She is unable to... speak!" he had snarled and hung up the phone. Further calls to her phone went unanswered so Kid and his Aunt Ginny called the police. Two days later Dawn's body was found in a dumpster in Camden. Kid had wept on his knees in front of her coffin for almost an hour, apologizing for not protecting her. His denial had cost Dawn her life.

It was then that Kid, sitting on the roof of the cabin, had a moment of frightful clarity and realization. The gravity of the situation was overwhelming.

Heidi began to weep and the muffled words, "I'm sorry," escaped her lips.

Kid rocked in his seat. "No, I'm the one who should be sorry." He knew she was right. His moment of clarity had exposed the true depth of his denial. "You were doing me a favor, and being honest."

He felt horrible for talking to Heidi the way he did, and he tried to affectionately hug her. To his surprise, she didn't resist, and actually reciprocated. They held each other tight for a minute. When they separated, Heidi had tears running down her face. "We can't lose her."

"I was sure she would get better on her own. I guess I just wanted my Sara back so badly that the reality of the situation escaped me. For crying out loud, she still doesn't even recognize me, or know who I am. Me?" he repeated, shaking his head as he looked down.

"I was hoping she would get better too. Especially since the cure…"

"What?" he turned to her, fear and hope showing in his eyes, "What about the cure?"

"Hear me out. When they shot Brian on the beach, he froze in the same position as the second he was shot. When I was first on the ship, I asked Elder-1 if Brian would be alright. I asked if he was just stunned. He told me Brian was initially stunned, but would die within minutes since all of his muscles were frozen, even his lungs. I begged him," large teardrops started streaming again, "begged him to radio back to the ones left on the beach and save him."

Kid put his arm around her, trying to calm her. He needed to hear the rest of this.

"No use. He said that besides too much time having elapsed, the only antidote is on the ships."

"You're saying that an antidote exists, one that could save Sara, but it can only be found on those ships?" He was incredulous.

"Unfortunately, yes."

"Since Sara was grazed, maybe it only froze a few muscles." His response was reactionary, a remnant of his previous denial pattern. Even he didn't buy it for a second.

Heidi looked sad. "At first maybe, but it's obviously shutting down her body a little at a time. She gets worse every hour. It's consuming her like a damn cancer, or poison."

Unable to hide the quiver of panic in his voice, Kid said, "I can't believe it. After all we went through to escape, the only place we can find a cure is back on the same forsaken ships that we just escaped from?" His own words seemed to knock the wind out of him as he stood up.

"Let's talk to Jess and Maria about it. With all of us brainstorming, we should be able to come up with something." She also stood up.

Kid followed her down the ladder. His core had been shaken by his moment of clarity. It had revealed more than just a truth. With no obstructions or filters, such clarity provided a front row view, in vivid and stunning detail, of his deepest fears.

He realized that even in the mind's eye, some images cannot be unseen.

CHAPTER 28

December 31, 2044
Saturday, Early Evening
The Pine Barrens of New Jersey
Five days after the event

As night fell, Kid and Heidi talked quietly with the others in the cabin. The main room was lit by one candle, which was situated in the middle of the table. *Damned if we do, and damned if we don't,* Kid thought. After pacing around the room for a moment, he proclaimed in a forceful whisper, "I have to get her to the ships and fast."

"But how can we get her there without all of us getting killed?" Jess sat with his face close to the window, watching for soldiers.

"Maybe we could take two boats out there, wrap her nice and warm and leave her in one tied up to their ships. We could alert them as we take off, and then they will take her aboard and cure her?" Kid suggested, and then turned on his heel. He was battling conflicting thoughts. "Damn it, I don't want her captured again! It was hard enough to get her off the ship the first time. It's going to be just about impossible to do it again."

"If they even decide to cure her," Maria said. "We are not talking about a compassionate and caring group of people out there and that's what scares the hell out of me. They could care less about one life."

"I really don't think they will save her," Jess whispered.

"It's a chance we have to take. What choice do we have?" Kid sounded flustered.

"When we were captured we found out that they were in desperate need of females. So there is a chance they won't harm her," Heidi said. "After what happened with us escaping, they just may beef up security."

"They also just may kill her!" Jess voiced with frustration.

Kid turned. "They *may* kill her, but staying out here with us, with no cure, will kill her. Not may... *will* kill her."

"Shh!" Maria put a finger over her mouth and pointed toward the middle room where Sara was lying.

Jess opened his mouth to speak, but only sighed and turned away.

"I have no choice. Even if I have to do it alone," Kid added as he pushed aside the curtain and entered the next room.

Sara was staring at the ceiling. Kid got down on one knee next to the bed. She could no longer move at all without help, and could not even raise her hand. She was like a sailboat without sails, sitting on the smooth but stagnant surface of an open body of water. He had to find the inner-strength to maintain his composure and appear in control.

"In a little while, we have to take you back to the ship so they can cure you," he said evenly. "You're getting sicker and sicker from the shot that hit you, and only they can save you. Don't worry though, we'll come back to rescue you as soon as you're well again."

"These last few days... were the best of days," she strained to reply.

Her words chilled Kid to the bone. Her tone resounded like a harsh and definitive foreshadowing. As he grabbed her hand, she whispered, with her lips quivering and her face wincing as she fought back tears, "We can't... go back."

"It's only temporary, and it's killing me to do it but, please," he pleaded. "They are the only ones who can cure you."

She went to respond, but he cut in, "Not another word. We have to leave soon. Please, just rest until we go." He gazed deep into her eyes and gently brushed his hand against her right cheek. Leaning close to her face, Kid whispered, "I love you too much. I'm not going to lose you."

Her arm twitched as she tried unsuccessfully to move it, but she was able to lean forward ever so slightly and give him a tender kiss.

This small act gave Kid a shred of hope, a glimmer. As he pulled back from her, she was smiling with a tear rolling from the corner of her eye. She squeezed his hand weakly but affectionately. He was melted by a sudden swell of emotion as he pulled the blanket under her chin and walked away. He pushed aside the curtain and stepped with purpose into the main room.

Heidi handed Kid a bowl of baked beans. "Eat, please."

Kid was restless and after one spoon, he put the bowl down. He didn't want to lose that glimmer of hope. He didn't want it to fade away. "Alright, I'm going to get Sara and head out."

"We talked while you were in there and we're all going with you." Jess clapped him on the shoulder. "We wouldn't let you go it alone."

Nodding, he said, "Thanks. Let's get her and go."

"Hey Kid." Maria then whispered, "You may want to tell Sara that when she's recovered, we have her rescue planned out already."

"We do?"

"Not exactly, but give her hope. Sometimes that is the only thing that gets you through."

He nodded and put his hand on Maria's shoulder, understanding what she was getting at.

Walking into the middle room, which was eerily quiet and still, Sara appeared to be sleeping. Kid sat on the bed next to her, put the candle on the floor and held her hand. It felt completely limp and... lifeless.

His heart sank. In a frenzied desperation, he began to check her vital signs. He didn't feel a pulse and her chest didn't rise to take a breath. He started shaking her and yelling, "Wake up! Come on Sara, wake up!" Tears flowed out of his eyes as he pleaded. He fell to his knees and screamed, "No!" at the top of his lungs.

The others rushed in.

"Sara!" Maria shrieked and ran over to the bed.

He turned to her for help. With an autistic younger brother who also had medical issues, he knew that Maria was trained in CPR. "Kid, do chest compressions!" She started blowing into Sara's mouth and lungs.

Jess and Heidi stood over Sara's bed. "What can we do? Maria, what can we do?" Heidi asked in a panic, with her trembling hands at the ready in front of her.

After 30 minutes of regimented CPR, Sara was still unresponsive. Maria's voice was barely audible. "Kid..."

"No!" he snapped and continued to do chest compressions, with his arms trembling.

Reaching out and grabbing his arm, she squeaked out, "It's over."

He gave one final push of his palm on Sara's still chest. "It can't be." His voice had a tormented vibrato.

"Kid... it's over." She cupped her hands over her mouth and slid down the side of the bed. He caught her before her knees hit the rock-hard concrete floor. She put her arms around him and they both began to cry.

With no strength to fight off the internal tidal wave, Kid finally broke down completely. He cried oceans of grief and sorrow, as if every sad event in his life was catching up to him at that very moment. He had always put forth a tough emotional front, and up until that moment, that front had never really been compromised. Now, it was completely obliterated. Not slowly stripped away or chipped at, but annihilated in an instant. The pain he was experiencing was so bad that he thought he literally wouldn't live through it. It was as if his insides had turned to mush like the rest of the world. He felt weak and dizzy, and thought he was going to pass out. As he held Maria, even the muscles of his stomach were trembling and he felt like he was going to vomit.

With a Herculean effort, he turned his eyes again toward Sara. He stared at her face, waiting for her lips to part and resume breathing, knowing that was not going to happen. As he continued to stare, his body began to tremble even more. Maria held him tighter. He felt like he was convulsing. He looked up to see Jess pressing his lips together so tightly that they began to quiver.

Heidi, like a mother consoling a young child, took Kid's head and cradled it against her stomach. With his forehead resting against her midsection, he cried without holding back.

Jess put one arm around Maria and one around Heidi. They were all bound together, with Kid in the center. He knew he was not holding them together, rather together they were keeping him from coming apart.

After several minutes of sobbing, Jess said, "Let's go to the other room. We better get some water before we all dehydrate."

He slung Kid's arm around his neck and carried most of their combined weight as he began the slow journey to the main room. He put Kid down on a bed and ran outside. Jess returned and put a full pot of snow on the wood stove. The snow instantly melted and everyone drank except Kid.

"More than anyone, you need this." Jess handed Kid a cup. "It's too late to do anything more tonight. We'll do whatever you feel we need to do tomorrow," he added as he put a hand on his shoulder.

Kid barely nodded, and kept looking down at his untouched cup of water. Abruptly, he stood up and walked out the front door.

"Where are you going?" Heidi asked.

Falling to his knees in the snow, Kid slumped down and put his face in his hands. "No!" he screamed as he turned his eyes toward the sky, and his fingers squeezed into tight fists.

"Kid! What the…" Jess yelled.

"No!!" even louder.

Heidi ran out and as she turned to face Kid, her feet slid out from under her. She scraped and clawed her way on all fours. Without hesitation, she straddled him, pulled his face into her chest and held him tight. "Shh, please don't scream."

He screamed one more time, but right into Heidi's chest. She held him tighter while saying, "Shh."

They shared a long embrace, until his inferno burned down to smoldering embers. Kid and Heidi stood and dragged themselves back into the cabin. Before closing and locking the door, Jess peered outside in every direction.

"See anything?" Maria asked.

"No. Don't see anyone," Jess answered. "This would *not* be a good time for those bastards to show up."

Kid was sitting on the foot of Heidi's bed. She laid down, grabbed his shoulders, and whispered, "At least lay back and rest."

His weakened body did not resist. His back hit the mattress about halfway up, with his knees and lower legs still dangling over the foot of the bed. Maria came over and took his shoes off. She grabbed his ankles and lifted while Heidi pulled, until his body was completely on the bed.

Turning on his side, Kid stared at the stars he could see in the night-time sky through the window. He really wanted to fall asleep, if not for any other reason than to get a break from the pain. His heart was shattered. How was he ever going to live without her? His sadness turned to guilt as he re-lived the past several days. The rescue went so well, and then one shot at the last moment barely hit her. If only he had told her to get down sooner. If only he had pulled her to the bottom of the boat a little harder. If only he had reached out and caught that bolt with his hand! So many things he could've done.

His guilt gave way to a deep anger. *They will pay for this!* he thought as he clenched his fist. The more he thought of the soldiers, the more he was consumed by rage. He saw the maniacal face of the old man outside the truck window in Logan's garage. He could never forget the cold eyes, and the evil smirk on his disgusting face. They had destroyed almost everything in his life that meant something to him, and Sara was the final straw. He put the bent knuckle of his pointer finger in his mouth and closed his eyes. With so much rage, he bit down, not realizing how hard he did until he noticed the trickle of blood running down his fist.

The night seemed never ending to Kid, who was unable to sleep a wink. Finally at 3:30 a.m., he got out of bed. Lighting a candle, he walked into the middle room of the cabin. Although the others had pulled the blanket over Sara's head, he couldn't bring himself to look that way as he walked past. Continuing to the back storeroom, he grabbed a pickaxe and a shovel.

On his way back through the middle room, he again averted his eyes to avoid the pain of seeing the casket their bed had become. He stopped in his tracks as he spotted something on the wall. Putting down the tools, he reached out and touched a picture, which was now visible in the flickering candlelight. It was the photograph of him and Sara sitting together on the cabin's roof deck, both laughing hysterically. "The day at the cabin," he whispered. That day, he had come with his heart, but she had left with it. As he stared at her laughing in the picture, his mind began to play back the rest of their day together. He saw her laughing and running her fingers through her hair, like she always did, as she sat on the roof. He could never forget the level of intimacy they found that day. It was so much more than physical. It would always be the best day of his life.

After staring at Sara in the picture, he looked over his shoulder and saw the outline of her motionless, covered body. With his eyes again swelling, he nuzzled his face in the crease of his arm at the elbow. *How can I go on without my soul mate?*

CHAPTER 29

January 1, 2045
Sunday, Early Morning
The Pine Barrens of New Jersey
Six days after the event

The next morning, Heidi woke upon hearing a strange noise. *You're imagining things, go back to sleep*, she told herself.
Chink.
She sat up in bed upon hearing it again.
Chink.
She jumped to her feet. "Oh no, someone is here!"

Peering out the window, her sigh seemed to roll from relief to pity. Behind the cabin, Kid was swinging a pickaxe and hitting the frozen ground with tremendous force and might. She stepped back to the bed, wrapped herself with a blanket, and returned to the window.

Jess ran over and stood next to her. "What is he doing?" He yawned and rubbed his scruffy face.

"Trying to cope," she answered, and paused. "We're all heartbroken about Sara, but I can't even begin to imagine what he's feeling right now."

Moving his face closer to the dusty and scratched glass, Jess developed a pained expression. "It's killing him. I'll go help."

"Wait." Heidi grabbed his arm. "Let him go for a little while. Let him deal."

Jess rekindled the fire and reheated the small amount of coffee left in the percolator.

As Heidi watched Kid dig, a cold breeze made it through one of the many gaps around the window and her breath turned to steam.

Midmorning, Kid exhaled and tried to shake the fatigue out of his arms. *Have to keep going*, he thought. He looked up as Jess walked outside. His friend never said a word, but just picked up the shovel and as Kid pick-axed the frozen ground, he would scoop away the chunks of dirt. A couple of hours later, they stood over a shallow grave. Kid finally muttered his first words since Jess had come out. "That's good, thanks."

Back inside, Kid secured the blanket around Sara's body. When he carried her out, the others trailed behind him. He carefully laid her in the freshly dug grave and stayed on his knees. Reaching down, he pulled the blanket down just enough to see her face one last time. She looked very much at peace. Starting to get choked up, he pulled the blanket back over her head and stood up, staring at her body for several minutes. He couldn't say goodbye to her. He would never say goodbye.

Overcast skies had settled overhead and a slight breeze rustled the treetops. The air was raw and everyone breathed steam as they stood still with their heads down. The group stood around the grave and not a word was spoken. Kid preferred it this way. He seized the shovel and started filling in the hole. Jess pushed earth with the head of the pickaxe. Heidi and Maria, in a gesture that Kid appreciated despite it being more symbolic than useful, used their shoes to move small piles of dirt. After the grave was filled, they left the slightly rounded mound and trudged back into the cabin.

Kid took a hammer and dismantled the wooden bed frame in the middle room, while leaving the mattress and box spring on the floor. He took a long piece of wood and a shorter piece of wood and nailed them together as a cross. Next, he carved words into the pieces of wood with a pocketknife. The inscription in the longer piece of wood read, 'Her spirit will never die.'

On the smaller piece of wood, he inscribed horizontally, 'Sara Hyland' and then he stopped. He was going to add the date of her birth and death, but being exhausted and disoriented, he had lost track of what day it was. And if they were in January, it would be the next year. "It doesn't matter." He threw down the pocketknife and took the grave marker outside. Just having her name on it was fine. Honestly, he didn't want an end date, or closure. He then put the marker into the loosened soil at the head of the grave and tapped it in with the back of an axe head. With his task finished, he sat staring at the dirt mound for several minutes.

When Kid walked into the cabin, a bowl of grits was waiting for him on the table.

"Eat," Heidi said.

"Maybe later."

"Maybe nothing, eat. And this time it is an order, not a request. You need to keep up your strength." She picked up the bowl and put it in front of him. He pushed it away, but she pushed it right back. He peeked up at her and then started to eat, not wanting to be bothered about it anymore.

Jess walked in from the middle room. "Hey buddy, me and the girls dumped and refilled the basin. You should take a bath while the water is still hot. It felt great, and I know I needed it."

"I'll vouch," Maria offered, "I'm the one who's been stuck sleeping next to him."

"I even shaved. Didn't even know we had disposable razors. Brian must've bought them. Soap doesn't lather up as well as shaving cream, but it works."

As soon as Kid finished eating, Heidi said, "The bath is open, and you need it. You're dirty from all of that digging."

"I'll wait, someone else can go."

"Everybody else already went." She pointed to the middle room of the cabin. "Now, Kid, let's go," she added in a commanding tone, as if scolding a child.

He walked by, sarcastically saluting Heidi as he passed. In the middle room, the water in the tub was still steaming. The disposable razor was on a chair within close reach. He undressed and slipped in, crossing his ankles under the water to relieve the pressure on his tightly bent knees.

The water level was pushed halfway up his chest since his body took up so much of the metal tub's space.

"Knock, knock. Just grabbing your dirty laundry," Heidi warned and came in. She grabbed his clothes and took them to the stream. After washing them, she hung them next to the stove.

Now finished bathing, he realized that he had nothing to dry himself with. He called out, "Heidi? I need a towel."

"Be right there." A moment later she came in. "How's the water?"

"Still warm," he said with complete indifference.

"This is all we have." She held up the ripped blanket they were using as a bath towel. "It's still a little damp from Jess but it'll do. I've had it drying next to the stove."

"Thanks."

"You know, it's hard to believe all this has happened so fast," she began to say and then stopped. "Sorry, I should leave and let you finish in here first."

"I don't really care at this point."

"You don't care that I'm in here, or you don't care about what's happened?"

"Both." At that moment in his life, he really didn't care about anything anymore.

"It's just that, well, why did this destruction have to happen now? Why couldn't this happen when we were old and gray?" she asked, still holding the makeshift towel.

After a moment passed, he finally said, "It doesn't matter now. It happened," as he flicked at the bubbles on the top layer of bath water.

Heidi, seeming more determined than ever, sat on the floor. "So, what do we do now?" After a momentary pause, she answered her own question, "We just survive I guess, and fight when we have to."

"What's left to fight for?" He sounded solemn.

"We've got to find things to fight for. This society on the ships, they plan on inhabiting the mainland," she noted.

"So what." After a moment of silence, he erupted. "Heidi, they had the power to completely destroy the world and alter the course of history. I'm starting to wonder if it was just meant to be, and here we are, the final crumbs left on the floor. All they need to do is sweep us away, and they'll have a clean slate for their new world. Maybe it was meant to be, and we don't belong here now. Maybe we were meant to be swept away. Can't you accept that possibility?"

"I give up," she blurted out and scrambled to stand up. Getting to her knees, she stopped. After hanging her head for a brief moment, she whispered, "No." She paused, and then snapped, "No!"

Looking into his eyes she said, "Maybe so, Kid. And yes, they have altered history, but their history isn't written yet." Her voice was rising. "I've seen their world, and it's scary, really fucking scary. People aren't meant to live that way. Damn it if the world didn't need to change, but they've gone and stripped people of all of their humanity. Why live at all?" With conviction, she added, "Listen, we need you. Whether you realize it or not, you are our leader, and from what I understand you have always been. For us to make it and survive, we really need you."

"It's their world now. We are only four people. At this point, we sit and wait to die."

Heidi responded, "I know we can't go head to head with them, but there must be something we can do. Even if we could kill them all, would we really want to? Nobody would be left at all. They are the world's population."

They both sat in silence for several minutes.

"I wonder…" Kid began to say and paused.

"What do you wonder?" She seemed desperate for his response. Her eyes pleaded.

"What would happen if there was a way to free the humanity that their society has suppressed? Even if one individual at a time." The subject was beginning to catch his interest, and was chipping away at his depression and indifference. "The back-door approach."

She sat up straighter. "You mean if we could somehow infuse humanity into their society?"

"Not infuse, but free, humanity. It's already there within each of them, even if deep inside. It just sounds like this society keeps them so regimented that they don't really know what it means to be alive."

"Not just regimented, but conditioned like Pavlov's dogs," she added.

He sat thinking, engrossed in his thoughts, connecting dots.

Heidi took the moment to add, "And I used to think the society we knew was too controlled and regimented, and in some ways it was. But compared to this?"

"You know… it would be their ultimate nightmare," he continued as he gazed not at her, but through her. "Their people actually becoming human could destroy this 'perfect' society they've created, and that Sara, Brian, and our families died because of."

Trying to find his eyes, she didn't seem bothered by his lack of eye contact. Her optimism actually seemed to be swelling. "Again history could be altered, but for the better," she concluded. Putting her hand on his arm and leaning forward as she knelt, she looked deep into Kid's eyes. "Would that be worth fighting for?"

He raised one eyebrow and sighed. "Well…" As he turned his head, he lost the air from his lungs. He could swear that for just a split second, he was face-to-face and eye-to-eye with Sara. The flash of her presence, like a lightning strike, stunned him. Turning back to Heidi, and matching the intensity of her gaze, he said with a sense of purpose just one word. "Yes."

She shuddered. Taking a deep breath and closing her eyes, she gently squeezed his arm. "Thank you," she whispered, sounding relieved.

As the tone and vibe of his own one-word answer rang in his ears, even Kid was chilled to the bone.

"That will be our mission and purpose. Otherwise, what would we do? Spend our lives hiding, and running…" she concluded.

"It is all we have left to fight for, even if it costs us our lives," he added as he thought of Sara.

Grabbing the razor from next to the tub and soaping up his face, Kid shaved while they continued to talk. For almost 30 minutes they talked about Brian and Sara, and their families, and how hard it was to cope with all the loved ones they'd lost. Jess and Maria had lost their families, but at least they had each other. He began to see a side of Heidi he had never seen before. The more they talked, the more he saw her differently. This was difficult for him, but he imagined it was difficult for her as well. They had hated each other for so long.

"At some point we definitely need to regroup. We have no plans, supplies, arms," he noted as he refocused.

"Probably no hot water either," she added, seeming a little embarrassed by the present circumstance. "I'll bet that water isn't even warm anymore."

Kid got a chill as he realized how cold the water was. He hadn't even been aware of the water temperature.

Heidi threw him the ripped blanket she was still holding in her hands. "I'll check on your clothes and see how dry they are. I got the fire really kicking in there when I hung them up." She walked back in a moment later with a thicker blanket in her hands, but none of Kid's clothes.

"Not kicking enough?" he asked sarcastically as he stood wrapped in the ripped blanket.

"I guess not." She laughed.

Her chuckle caught Kid off guard. She usually sneered at his sarcastic one-liners. He didn't know how to react.

"Just wrap yourself in this for now," she said.

He threw the dry, thicker blanket around his body and pulled the wet, ripped one from underneath and handed it to her. Heidi grabbed the edge of the thicker blanket, and lifted it off of him. For a second, he thought his naked body was going to be exposed, so he instinctively covered himself with his hands.

"Oh, I'm sorry." She pulled the thicker, green blanket around him. "I was just trying to wrap you tighter."

"Thanks. It's definitely better."

She was rubbing her hand on the blanket, saying, "Good… good," when both were suddenly taken back by their closeness. Kid shifted his weight from one foot to the other a few times and pulled the blanket even tighter around his body. She cleared her throat. "Let's go see what Jess and Maria are up to."

Stepping into the main room, he asked, "Where's Jess?"

"Keeping watch up on the roof," Maria answered.

"Still no sign of any soldiers?"

"Nope. And let's hope it stays that way."

Kid, now shaved and clean, laid down on the bed.

Heidi was hanging the ripped blanket next to the stove. "You know, I was thinking. What if…"

Those were the last words he heard before nodding off.

CHAPTER 30

January 1, 2045
Sunday, Early Evening
The Pine Barrens of New Jersey
Six days after the event

K id woke up, and laid still. He turned his eyes and spotted Heidi sitting at the heavy wooden table. While asleep, his brain must've been crystallizing the essence of the conversation he had with her when he was bathing. The first conscious thought he had upon waking was that Heidi had helped bring him back from a steep and dangerous precipice, one in which more than just his life may have hung in the balance. For that, he could never look at her the same way, and could never repay her. She was the last person he would've ever thought could, or would, save him.

With dusk encroaching, Heidi had lit a candle and placed it in the middle of the table. It was then that Kid realized she had the cabin's logbook in her hand.

"Listen to this entry, Maria," Heidi said and started reading.

"February 1987: Can't believe this logbook survived the awful fire over Presidents Day weekend. Cabin was burned to the ground. I reckon the only good thing is that we still have our table and our logbook, both of which we found on the ground outside. This logbook has our whole history in it. The first entry was written in this book, on this table, in 1922. Looking at the logs over the past few months, maybe the arsonists were the kids who

found this place and started having parties here. As I sit here and stare at the smoldering embers of our Ironside Gun Club, I can only hope that the people who did this didn't mean to burn it down, and that they were just stupid and careless."

"They are lucky their logbook even survived," Maria noted.

Kid heard footsteps on the roof, and a moment later, Jess walked into the main room. "Night is falling, so we can't see anymore," he noted.

"Hey, Jess," Heidi whispered "Do you realize this book and this table were from the original 1922 cabin? They survived the horrible fire of 1987 when arsonists burned the original cabin down."

"It wasn't arson, it was an accident," Kid muttered with his face buried in his blanket.

"Oh, I'm sorry. I didn't mean to wake you."

"I was already awake. Anyway, the kids that did it admitted to it many years after. They said the fire was an accident." He yawned. "The flue pipe opening was cracked, so the wall caught fire. They thought they had put it out. They didn't mean to burn it down."

"I was wondering why anyone would to burn this place down," Heidi noted. "From the entries before that one, Ironside had become the premier party spot."

"Maria, could you please hand me those?" Kid sat up and pointed to his now dry clothes hanging next to the wood stove.

She brought them over and sat next to him on the bed. "Are you alright?" she asked in a moment of sincerity as she put her arm around him.

"Hanging in there." He was still not entirely with it.

"Good." Maria punched his thigh, but not as hard as usual.

"See anything outside?" he asked.

She shook her head. "All is clear. Maybe they've given up or they froze to death. We've been out here two days now."

"With them, somehow I doubt it." He put his clothes on and sat back on the bed.

"No, it's possible that they gave up. Elder-1 is with them," Heidi interjected.

"What difference does that make?"

"He wouldn't be that irrational. He lived in the real world before that Utopia Project."

"Not irrational?" Jess asked. "They destroyed the entire world."

"True," she conceded. "But I can't believe he would be so stupid as to freeze to death trying to find us."

"Maybe not, but his soldiers, they are a different story," Jess said as he opened the floorboard. "We've seen enough of them. They just don't give up for anything,"

"No, but if they weren't raised in that environment, things might be different. All they know how to do is follow orders and regimens." Heidi appeared to feel sorry for them.

"Yeah, and right now their orders are to kill us," he countered.

With darkness falling on the Pine Barrens, they lit a few candles and put them on the wooden table inside the cabin. After eating baked beans they made coffee and conversed for a while. Kid tuned in and out, experiencing periods of sudden and painful grief.

"Let me get this straight. They work less hours, don't have to pay for anything, eat good food, and have orgies?" Jess summarized after listening to the girls' description of the Utopia Project society. "Wow. Maybe we should go back."

Maria backhanded his shoulder. "Trust me, you wouldn't want to be there."

"And they plan on inhabiting the mainland on Long Beach Island?" She nodded.

Heidi watched intently as Kid tied a broken rubber band to a nail on the end of a long, skinny piece of wood. "What are you doing?"

"You'll see. It has always been my outlet." He tied the rubber band to the other end of the piece of wood. "I need a bridge-piece," he said aloud and stood up.

The others watched him, looking curious.

"Ah..," He picked up a small roofing nail, hammered it into the piece of wood near an end, and then bent it over. He laid the rubber band over the bent nail and began plucking it. "Sounds like a D note."

He began pressing the rubber band down against the wood with one hand while plucking with the other.

"Nice guitar. And now, for your listening pleasure…" Maria held her hands up toward him.

Kid continued to finger pick notes until he knew the layout of his makeshift fretboard. He quickly found the root-notes to a song he had been recently working on.

Maria's ears perked up. "Oh, I love that one." She whispered to Heidi, "I bust his chops, but I have to admit, he's a pretty damn good songwriter."

"What are you playing?" Heidi asked.

"'Angels Never Cry,'" Maria said without hesitation, answering for him. "Sing it for her, Kid."

"Alright, but just the pre-chorus and chorus, I haven't found the verse notes yet." He cleared his throat.

"I hear an angel crying up above
denying it's the end of love
but to ice has turned the rose and the dove
crushed in the palm of the world's iron glove
and the Angels can't believe their eyes
but the tears that fall don't tell no lies
they just know that love can never die
but they also know that Angels never cry
Angels never cry. Not in Heaven.
Angels never cry. Not in Heaven."

Plucking the root notes on his one-string guitar, Kid started the chorus over again. He was struggling to keep Sara out of his mind, but her presence consumed him.

The second time he sang the chorus, Heidi joined him. Together they sang the words with great conviction.

"Angels never cry. Not in Heaven
Angels never cry. Not in Heaven,
Angels never cry…"

Kid omitted the end of the last sentence, but since Maria had heard the song many times, she whispered the words.

"Unless they're falling down to earth…"

Jess and Maria stared in amazement, and seemed surprised and inspired. Jess uttered, "That was… incredible."

"I didn't know you sang so well," Maria turned to Heidi, and shook her hand. "I've never heard you sing before."

"I don't usually sing, at least not publicly. But I couldn't help myself there. I was really feeling it."

After sitting in silence for a few minutes, Jess said to Maria, "I can't believe what you told me yesterday about that society. They can just say one word and people basically become zombies?"

"Worse!" she said. "They collapse in a heap. Even zombies can walk. And that would have been us with just a few more days of their brainwashing and doping us up."

Kid turned. "What's the word?"

"I. O. N.," Maria spelled out. "I'm afraid to even say it."

"*Ion?* That doesn't sound very scary to me," he noted.

"Don't underestimate its power." Heidi shivered. "It instantly incapacitates a person, until it is reversed."

"What prevents them from saying it to each other all day? I mean, if one guy gets pissed at another, he could just yell this word and put the guy in a zombie-like trance?" Jess asked.

"No. They're all conditioned to not be able to say any word beginning with the long vowel 'I', so they could never even begin to utter the word," Heidi answered.

"They can't say, 'I'?" Kid asked.

"No. Actually, it is one of their society's mottos. 'Here there is no…I,'" she recited and shuddered.

"They live by this motto, but can't say it?" Kid seemed perplexed.

Maria jumped in, "Actually, rather than trying to say 'I', they just point to the corner of their eye." She then abruptly changed the subject. "Hey, are we going to leave here any time soon? I'm feeling kind of cooped up out here. Not to mention, I need to grab my diabetes medicine before I have an episode."

"Let's leave tomorrow morning, alright?" Jess said, turning to Kid.

"I guess so." He was reluctant. He knew they had to go, but a part of him felt like he was leaving Sara behind.

"We can't just sit out here, and wait for them to come forever."

"I know… I know," Kid replied, feeling conflicted as he got up and walked out the door.

The others sat in somber silence.

Kid approached Sara's grave. In the gray cover of dusk, the outline of the grave marker seemed surreal, like an animation. Thinking he could not possibly have any tears left to cry, having drained every last drop from the well, he fell down on one knee as rivers of tears ran down his face. Several minutes later, he dragged himself back inside the cabin.

As he walked in, Jess peeked his head outside. He glanced in every direction and then closed the door. He pushed down the heavy wood plank to lock it. "Let's get some sleep."

"I just can't wait to get back into some normal clothes. I'm sick of this uniform," Heidi said as she began to pull down her zipper. "Makes me feel like a number," she continued as she flicked the neatly embroidered 19796 on the front of her gray jumper. As her modesty kicked in, she slipped under the bed covers and finished taking off her gray jumper. She pulled her uniform out from under the blanket and laid it next to the bed.

Kid picked it up and hung it next to the wood stove. "You'll thank me tomorrow when it's nice and warm."

"Heidi, I can't believe, in light of the circumstances, you're still such a prude. Hey Kid, look the other way." Maria took off her uniform and hung it next to the fire herself. "Miss Priss over there," she said as she nonchalantly walked across the room, wearing just a bra and underwear.

"Hey, I might be the last hope for female decency on this planet," Heidi countered.

"Yeah, can't help you there," Maria said as she climbed into bed.

"See what I go through?" Jess said as he walked toward the bed and slid under the blanket.

Kid and Heidi again bunked together. She was lying on her side facing the window, so he put his hand on her shoulder and whispered, "Heidi?"

"Yeah," she whispered back, seeming startled by his gentle touch.

"Thank you."

"For what?"

"Helping me get through today."

"It's tough, believe me, I know."

"Also, I'm sorry for treating you badly since the day we met. I'm an idiot. I never let myself see you for who you really were, and are," he said.

Heidi smiled. "Alright already, I'm sorry too. Now go to sleep."

After a pause, she grabbed his hand from her shoulder, lifted her elbow and was pulling his arm down across her upper torso. Taking the cue, he moved up against her. His forearm felt the comforting warmth of her breasts, and his body felt the heat of her exposed flesh through his clothes.

"I guess we could start by altering the course of our own history," she whispered as she stared out the window.

Facing the same way, Kid gazed upon the stars, the light of many refracted and distorted by the cracks in the window pane. "We should," he whispered.

"But also for the better," she added.

He absorbed the human tenderness and comfort of the moment. As he drifted off to sleep with his arm around her, Kid felt a warmth their blanket could never provide, and their blanket was doing a damn fine job.

IV:
REVELATIONS

CHAPTER 31

January 2, 2045
Monday, Before Dawn
The Pine Barrens of New Jersey
Seven days after the event

In the wee hours of the next morning, Heidi's dreams came to a sudden end. Wide awake, she listened attentively. All was quiet. No sign of any soldiers. She sat still in bed, absorbing the warmth and comfort of Kid's embrace. She felt secure and protected. His arm was wrapped around her, as it was when they had fallen asleep. He had slept in his clothes, but his manly body felt warm against her mostly bare skin. She wished she could cover every inch of her body with that feeling.

Her mind was not yet fully functioning, and only allowed her to focus on one thought at a time. She wished her mind always worked that way. *Angels Never Cry.* In her head, she was still singing with Kid. What a powerful, and inspirational moment. She finally felt the magic everyone else seemed to feel with his music. She finally got it.

How could she see Kid so differently now? It was as if a switch had been flicked inside of her. *Why did I dislike him in the first place?* She couldn't recall any specific reason. Actually, she remembered finding him attractive when she first met him. She never admitted it, or let on, but she also found him funny. *Then why was I such a bitch to him all the time?* Waiting for her subconscious to chime in, she kept pondering the same question. *Was I a bitch to him in self-defense, because I was really... attracted to him?*

Her subconscious then spoke, but didn't answer the question on the table. It smacked her with one word.

Sara.

Overwhelmed and restless, she gently lifted Kid's arm and sat on the edge of the bed.

Kid's eyes opened. He watched Heidi get up, dressed in only under-garments. His eyes opened a little wider, and he blinked a couple of times.

Heidi put on her uniform, wrapped herself in a thick blanket, and quietly lifted the wood bar locking the door. Leaning the bar against the wall, she opened the cabin door and peeked her head out. Looking left and right, she took a step outside. Although dawn was arriving, she was still stepping into a dark gray.

As the cabin door closed, Kid lifted his head. Checking his watch, he whispered, "Where is she going at 5:30 in the morning?" As he laid his head back down he groaned, "Probably the bathroom."

Walking slowly and tentatively, Heidi approached the fresh grave. She dropped to her knees. "I need to talk to you Sara."

Putting her head down, she exhaled heavy steam. "First off, we all miss you so much. I wish that shot hit me instead. Well, I really wish the shot had missed all of us," she tried to laugh and tears started running down her face, "But if it had to hit someone, I wish it was me. We all loved you so much, especially Kid, of course. He's crushed. His heart is broken into little pieces. That... well... that's kind of what I wanted to talk to you about."

Rubbing her nose and wiping her tears, she peered up at the wood grave-marker. The silence around her was deafening. The cold air was sharp, but not moving. "This is so difficult. Sara, you know I never had anything but respect for you, and looked up to you and cared so much for you. Where you're at now, you can probably see inside my heart, and

I hope you can because you'd know that I'm telling the truth. I guess if that was the case then you would already know why I need to talk to you," she again tried in vain to laugh. It only made her cry more.

"You know I would never betray you, or step on your toes. To the point Heidi, to the point," she reprimanded herself. "It's Kid. I'm so sorry, but it's Kid. I would never go there if you were alive, but… I'm developing feelings for him and I have this guilt, and fear, and it's ripping me up inside. It's all happening too quick and too soon, but the truth is, I can't fight it. I can't believe I'm saying it, but it's true."

Dawn was creeping in and it offered a lighter shade of gray. She glanced at the grave marker and then down at the slightly rounded dirt mound. "I'm not even sure how he feels about me, but I imagine you would want someone to take care of him and love him if we do survive. This might not matter at all since those damned soldiers could find us any minute now."

Pulling her blanket tighter, she glanced around. She then closed her eyes and put her hands together. "Please Sara, let this be alright with you. I promise I'll do my best. I also promise that I will never try to replace you, and I know I couldn't. But only you can free me and take away my guilt. And from the world beyond, please, I'm begging you, set him free."

Taking a deep breath, she momentarily shuddered. "Sara, if you're not alright with this, send me a sign. Just send me some kind of sign."

She opened her eyes and all of her senses were set to acute. Her anxiety level outpaced her growing realization of how alone she really was. Nervous and spooked, her breaths were shallow and rapid as fear pushed her heart into her throat. Her eyes combed her surroundings in every direction, but nothing moved. Even the treetops were deathly still in the looming gray dawn. Her eyes settled on the grave. She wanted to look away from the mound of dirt, but wouldn't let herself.

Still no sign.

She opened her blanket and held it with both arms outstretched. Closing her eyes, she leaned forward, not realizing that her face was now only inches away from the dirt mound. Tears were streaming down her cheeks and her heartbeat was reverberating throughout her entire body. She kissed her fingertips and despite her overwhelming fear, she actually touched the earthen mound. Pressing lightly, her fingertips broke the surface of the soil. She was overcome by an emotional release that made her tremble. She did not move for a full minute.

Pulling her fingertips out of the soil, she clasped her hands together and closed her eyes. Trying to catch her breath, she whispered, "Thank you Sara. Thank you."

Walking back inside, Heidi felt drained. Her emotions were raw and frazzled. She unzipped her uniform, hung it next to the fire and climbed back into bed.

Kid kept his eyes closed as Heidi slowly slipped under the blanket. He could feel her warm breath on his face. She gently brushed strands of hair off of his cheeks and forehead, and continued to stroke his cheek long after there was no more hair to push aside. He then heard deep, rhythmic breathing and knew she had fallen asleep.

Opening his eyes a sliver, Kid stared at her for a few minutes. Her hand was resting under her chin and she appeared very much at peace. Looking down, his brow pinched as his eyes settled on the dirt-stained tips of her fingers.

■ ■ ■

A little past 7:00 a.m., Maria woke up. After putting on her uniform, she grabbed the coffeepot and opened the door. All was clear so she walked down to the stream. She filled the pot with water and made her way back up the hill. Placing it on the wood stove, she stoked the dying fire, threw in a couple of logs, and stepped out the back door. Making her way up to the roof, she brought the binoculars to her eyes and swept the visual aid from left to right

Heidi awoke to the sound of footsteps on the roof. She lifted her head and looked over at the other bed to see that someone was missing.

Just Maria on lookout. As she laid back down, her eyes focused on Sara's uniform hanging next to the woodstove. *That has to go. It will be a constant reminder*, she realized. Climbing slowly out of bed as to not wake Kid, Heidi slipped on her own uniform. She tiptoed over to Sara's uniform, took it down and went to the large metal garbage can just outside the back door. "Sara," she whispered and hugged the uniform tightly. "I guess this is goodbye." She began to fold up the garment, and stopped. She could see Sara pointing at the corner of her own eye while in the bathing tub. Heidi would forever be haunted by Sara's facial expression and mannerism.

As she went to drop the uniform, she again froze, this time paralyzed by the sound of a distant wind charging through the pine trees. Heidi felt unsteady and held onto the garbage can to keep her balance. Her breath was caught in her throat.

Suddenly, Maria screamed from the roof. "Help!"

Heidi dropped Sara's uniform in the garbage can and stumbled out behind the cabin. She yelled up, "What's the matter?"

What the... Kid bolted upright, ran out the door and turned his eyes toward the roof.

Maria's face was as white as a ghost. "I saw them! Come up here, quick!"

This was the moment Kid feared would come. He had imagined it 100 times, but had underestimated the surge of fear he would have to wrangle with. "It was just a matter of time," he muttered and hustled up the ladder. Maria handed him the binoculars and pointed. He carefully scanned the area a couple of times over. "I don't see them."

"They were right out there!" She was adamant.

"I still don't see them!"

"Let me try again." Maria took the binoculars back and put them to her eyes. "Shit! I... I can't find them now!" she huffed, sounding flustered.

"How far out were they?"

"I couldn't tell, but I could see them through the clearing between the trees way out that way. They were right there!" She pointed far in the distance.

"Based on where you're pointing, we could run into them on either trail out of here, depending on which direction they're moving. It's the worst place they could possibly be," Kid stated. "We have to locate them again."

"We'll have a better chance of spotting them from the fire tower. Come down!" Jess yelled from the ground and ran for the truck.

Maria started climbing down the ladder. Kid hesitated for a moment, and then followed her down. The group piled into the truck and sped away.

The fire tower soon came into sight. Kid gazed up at the square tower basket 100 feet in the air at the top of the tall, skinny steel structure. They jumped out of the vehicle and ran in between two of the four concrete block footings that anchored the tower's legs. Kid looked around at the ground and did not see any footprints in the snow, or any evidence that the soldiers had marched by.

They started up the narrow metal treads of the switchback staircase, climbing from one landing to the next. As they neared the top, Kid could feel the tower swaying in the wind. At the final landing he grabbed a diagonal metal crossbeam, one of the many that zigzagged from the bottom of the tower to the top and held the structure together.

Walking past him, Jess ascended the final section of stairs. He turned a handle and pushed open a square wood hatch. Climbing through, they found themselves in the tower basket, which was a small square room with a seven-foot ceiling and large plexiglass windows facing in every direction. Now far above the tops of the trees, they could see for miles.

Kid used the binoculars and searched in the direction of the cabin. From experience, he knew Ironside was due east, despite being hidden by a dense wall of tall pine trees. Casing out the woods in all directions, he couldn't spot the soldiers.

Jess grabbed the binoculars. "I was hoping we could spot them from up here, but I don't see anything." They were all clearly anxious, and weren't sure what to do next.

"This thing could make you seasick," Heidi said, holding on to a tabletop as the tower continued to sway.

"It's never been real steady." Kid sighed and waved his hand. "Let's go. We'll just have to pick a trail to get out of the woods and hope like hell it's not the wrong one."

As he opened the floor hatch to go down, he froze as he saw what lurked below. His eyes were wide open in horror. About halfway down the switchback staircase, he could see the whole pack of soldiers marching upward. Now aware of their presence, he could feel the slight vibration as the soldiers marched up in unison. He slammed the hatch closed and stood on it. "They're here, climbing up the stairs. We're trapped!"

"What? How? I saw them…" Maria started saying.

"Trust me, they're here!" he responded, knowing that Maria had obviously been mistaken.

"Now what?" Heidi asked. Nobody knew what to do. As the vibration from the soldiers' steps intensified, so did their panic level.

Peering down, Kid could not find any lock for the hatch. Casing out the room, there was only a table and two chairs. He yelled, "Jess, pull that table over!"

"It's anchored to the floor!" he called out.

The soldiers reached the top of the tall stairwell and started pushing on the hatch.

Before Jess could break the table free, a sudden forceful thrust caused Kid to lose his balance and fall against one of the plexiglass tower windows.

Jess dove to the floor to keep the hatch down until Kid regained his stance on it.

"It's hopeless. We don't have anything to fight them with!" Jess yelled as the pushing of the hatch continued. "And I don't think you can talk us out of this one Kid!"

With all hope fleeting, Kid knew that words could not save them. They would die in the fire tower. *Words could not save…* Suddenly, it hit him. A long shot, but the only shot they had. Kid turned to Heidi, "What was that word they used, the one that turns them into zombies and makes them collapse?"

"*Ion!*"

"Yell it at them!" Kid said in desperation.

"What?" she asked.

"Yell the word, just like they did on the ships!"

As Heidi yelled, "*Ion,*" the soldiers continued pushing up on the hatch. "*Ion!*" she tried again. The hatch popped up with even greater intensity. "It's not working!"

Kid grabbed at another possibility. "It must be the tone and inflection of the word." He began to shout, "*Ion.*" Jess joined him.

After changing the delivery several times, Jess chanced upon the proper vocal articulation. The pushing on the hatch stopped and they heard a bang and clatter down below. He continued to yell, "*Ion!*" with the same sharp, snappy cadence, overemphasizing the letter 'I'. They heard more thuds and crashes as bodies tumbled down the stairs. Kid changed his voice to match Jess's.

Heidi fell to her knees. Maria also had to sit on the floor. Kid was confounded until he realized, "It's affecting them too!" He then heard Elder-1 yelling some other word.

"You need to say the second word... that one that brings us... back," Heidi huffed.

"What word?"

Kid was trying to listen closely to the elder. He heard him saying a word, but it was not a word Kid recognized. Hearing it again, he tried to repeat it. "S-on. Fess-on"

"There's an 'L' in there," Jess said.

"Fleson. *Fleson!*" Kid snapped.

"That's it!" Jess said and turned to the girls on the floor. He repeated the word with the same tone, "*Fleson!*" The girls started to come to.

The pushing at the hatch ceased for a moment, so Kid peeked under. Five more soldiers had come to the top. He snapped, "*Ion!*"

The soldiers went limp and collapsed, falling down the stairs. Three of them tumbled off of the tower. The other two came to rest on the landing at the base of the final flight of stairs. At them, Elder-1 yelled, "*Fleson!*" and they rejoined the ambush.

Kid lifted the hatch to see more soldiers approaching. He could also see Elder-1 in the back of the line, halfway up the steps. As the next wave surged up, Kid again yelled, "*Ion!*" The soldiers at the front of the line blanked out and fell backward into the ones behind them, knocking one more over the side.

Elder-1 yelled the word to revive those who had come to rest on the steps and the landing. They snapped out of their trance and were again ready to attack.

"They keep coming back!" Kid yelled out with his arms raised in the air.

Jess pulled the girls and himself onto the hatch to add extra weight.

"Keep holding them off!" Kid said. "We'll never stop them with Elder-1 there. He keeps reviving them, so I am going to try and take him out." He picked up a chair, and using it as a battering ram, he knocked out one of the plexiglass windowpanes. A strong gust of wind circled the room.

At the top of the stairs, the last eight soldiers still alive were pushing at the hatch. Elder-1 was right behind them. As Jess would yell the crippling word the elder would yell the antidote. "Hurry Kid! It's not working anymore," he yelled in desperation.

Kid leaned out of the now open window pane. He took a deep breath after looking down and seeing how high he was and feeling the tower sway. Far below, the ground was littered with the dead bodies of miniature soldiers. *Only one shot at this*, he reminded himself as he lifted one leg, and began climbing out the window. Gripped with fear, his heart throbbed in his chest. As the tower swayed, the top of a nearby pine tree wavered in front of Kid, as if taunting him. He put his foot down on a small metal bar on the outside bottom of the tower basket. Getting his other leg out, he had both feet precariously on the metal bar, with his hands holding onto the window frame. He then tried to pinpoint Elder-1's position by following his voice.

At the top of the stairs, the soldiers continued to push on the hatch and Elder-1 continued to shout the word to save them before they blanked out. After a powerful upward thrust, one soldier, had wedged his arm into the opening to keep the hatch from closing. "Kid! They're almost in!" Jess yelled as he slammed his fist repeatedly into the wedged hand.

Kid listened as the elder again shouted, "*Fleson*." Taking a deep breath, he jumped off of the metal bar, let go of the window frame and plummeted toward the ground.

CHAPTER 32

January 2, 2045
Monday, Morning
The Pine Barrens of New Jersey
Seven days after the event

Without a split second for miscalculation, Kid's hands slid down the side of the tower basket and grabbed the metal bar he had been standing on. With the momentum of his body falling and the abrupt jerk as his hands snagged the bar, his legs swung underneath the basket. Leading with his feet, Kid let go of the bar and his forward motion hurled him through the side of the stairwell, with his head just brushing against a steel crossbeam. Elder-1 was a little farther down the stairs than he had calculated, and his feet hit him high, with one hitting the old man's shoulder and the other hitting his head. The elder flew backward down the stairs and skidded across the landing. His body was within inches of rolling off the tall tower.

Kid landed hard on his back on the stairs just behind the pack of soldiers. He was trying to yell the word '*Ion*' from behind them, but the wind had been knocked out of him. Nothing would come out of his mouth.

Fortunately, before the soldiers could turn around, Jess yelled, "*Ion!*" Without Elder-1 to revive them, one by one the soldiers began to crumble and fall down the stairs. As they fell on Kid, who was lying in the stairwell, he would push them over the side, nearly 100 feet to the ground.

Soon, most of the soldiers were dead, but Kid knew the battle was far from over. Despite his terrible fall, Elder-1 was recovering and picking himself up on the first landing, and he was armed.

"Open the hatch," Kid forced out in a strained voice, still trying to catch his breath after his fall. "Jess, let his arm go! Let him drop," he said as he looked up at the soldier who still had his arm pinned.

Jess opened the hatch. The limp soldier started to fall down the stairs as soon as his arm was freed. His upper body slid over a metal crossbeam which wedged firmly under his armpit, preventing him from tumbling off of the tower.

Kid saw Jess peering out of the opening above. His friend had a look of despair upon seeing that the soldier was still hanging on. A second later, the remaining life seemed to drain from Jess's face. "Kid, behind you!"

On the landing below the final flight of steps, Elder-1 was on one knee. He seemed to have recovered from his fall, and had his weapon in his hand. Snapping, "*Fleson*," at the soldier clinging to the crossbeam, the elder then aimed his weapon at Kid from pointblank range.

Instinctively, Kid sprang into action. He felt like a wild animal as he jumped the final ten steps of the stairwell and landed right on the enemy. For a split second, he thought of Sara, and all of his pent-up rage resurfaced. With an aggression like he had never felt before, he reared back and punched Elder-1 in the face, breaking his nose. He then grabbed the hand holding the weapon and held on with all of his might. For an instant, the elder jerked his wrist and turned the weapon toward Kid's shoulder and pulled the trigger. Without a millisecond to spare, he twisted and pushed Elder-1's hand hard enough that the shot went off into the woods. He was desperately trying to stay out of the line of fire.

Jess felt distraught and wanted to help Kid, but he realized he had a big problem of his own. The soldier who was clinging to the crossbeam had lifted himself up and jumped down to the stairs. With great quickness, he sprang up through the hatch before Jess was able to close it. It happened so fast that Jess's only defense was to backhand the gun out of the soldier's good hand.

The weapon slid over by Maria. She snapped it up and threw it with a quick flick of her wrist. The gun hit a plexiglass pane and bounced right back at her. "Shit!" She lunged for it, but was too late.

As the soldier grabbed it and took aim, Jess kicked the gun. This time the weapon flew cleanly out the open windowpane. The soldier attacked and pushed him against a plexiglass windowpane. Jess said, "*Ion*," but the word came out as a gasp and did not have the right inflection to make the soldier collapse. Despite having broken fingers from having his hand pinned by the hatch, the soldier had two hands on Jess's throat, preventing him from uttering any words.

The girls stood up, both appearing unsteady, but ready to rush the soldier. Jess waved them off.

The plexiglass was bowing out as the weight of Jess and the soldier kept pushing against it. The death-grip on Jess's throat was beginning to tighten, so he pointed to the back of the soldier's legs and gave an upward thrusting motion. The girls at first didn't understand what he wanted, and then Maria seemed to get it. She crawled over behind the soldier and Heidi followed close behind.

Jess also pointed at his own legs, giving a downward pulling motion. The girls nodded their heads. His face was turning bright red. Using his trembling fingers to count to three, Jess stopped resisting and pushed backward with all of his might. As he did, he hooked one arm under the soldier's armpit and threw him into the plexiglass. With both of them hitting at the same time, the windowpane busted out and both men started falling out the open window.

Maria and Heidi grabbed the ankles of the soldier. His momentum increased as the girls lifted and gave his legs a forceful thrust. All in one fluid motion, the soldier had flown out of the basket. But as he started his lethal descent, he was able to grab Jess's hair and rip out a chunk.

Jess's midsection teetered on the bottom of the window frame, with his feet flailing in the air inside the tower basket. After the tug to his hair, his momentum had shifted to his upper body. Seeing the ground 100 feet below, Jess's eyes were wide open in sheer panic. He yelled, "No!" and backpedaled with his palms pushing against the outside of the basket, like a scared cat trying to make a hasty retreat. Both girls reached in desperation for Jess's steadily rising ankles. Clinging tightly, they pulled his legs down. Inching himself backward, he dropped his feet to the floor. Bending over, he huffed through rapid breaths, "My life… just passed before my eyes."

Maria continued to hold Jess's leg for a moment. "Thank God," she whispered.

"I should be thanking you, both of you." He put his hand on Maria and Heidi's shoulders. "Is Kid alright?" He crawled across the floor and peered under the hatch.

Tighter! Tighter! Kid urged himself. *If you let go of his wrist, you are dead!*

Elder-1 pulled the trigger of his weapon while wrestling with Kid. Jess reacted just in time, and the shot hit the hatch while he was closing it.

"Keep it closed!" Kid yelled up as he struggled to hold the enemy hand holding the weapon.

Elder-1 was battling hard. With his free hand, the older combatant threw a quick and solid punch that landed square on Kid's jaw and bottom lip. He shook it off, but knew his lip would be gushing blood. As the elder reared back to throw another punch, Kid's instantaneous reaction was to head-butt him before the punch landed. Leading with his forehead, he quickly popped Elder-1 on his already broken nose. The fist, which was intended for Kid's face, unraveled and grabbed at the brutally smashed and repositioned nose as he let out a sharp yell.

After wrestling for a couple of minutes, the embattled elder still maintained a tight one-handed grip on his weapon. But Kid succeeded in turning the wrist so that the weapon was aimed right at the face of Elder-1. "This, is for everyone you've killed," Kid said in a harsh voice with blood steadily dripping from his lip. "Especially Sara Hyland."

The dazed elder gasped, now out of breath.

"Our escape was a split second away from perfect, and you assholes killed… my… Sara."

A look of surprise crossed Elder-1's face, followed by a last surge of anger fueled energy. "Hyland? No!" he yelled as he tried to turn his weapon and for a second succeeded.

Gritting his teeth, Kid viciously twisted the elder's wrist and heard ligaments tear. With the muzzle nearly back in position, he put his finger over the elder's and pressed the trigger. The shot more than grazed Elder-1's right shoulder and his body froze instantly. Leaning over, just inches away from the elder's face and forever panic-stricken eyes, Kid whispered with a pained voice, "How does it feel?" He watched as the enemy's open mouth could not draw in a single breath. Within moments, Elder-1 was dead.

In the eerie stillness, Kid did not move for a long moment. Blood dripped from his lip and rhythmically tapped on the metal platform. "How... does... it... feel?" he repeated with his voice quivering. Taking his hands off of the dead body, he just stared. The elder was frozen with one hand in the air and the other with the weapon aimed at himself. The old man's eyes, although seeing nothing, were wide open.

Collapsing on the landing, Kid lay on his back panting. Putting his face in his hands, he mumbled, "Sara." As his adrenaline level started to come down from maximum plus, he found himself dwelling on Elder-1's apparent recognition of the name Hyland. *Why would the name mean anything to him? Did he interact with Sara on the ship? Did he know who her father was?* A loud voice broke his already fragile concentration.

"Kid!" Heidi yelled with the hatch now open. "Do you need help?"

When he pulled his hands from his face, his palms had bright red smears. "No, he's dead," he yelled up. Holding his shirt-sleeve firmly against his busted lip, he got to his feet and trudged up the stairs.

Back inside the top of the tower, Jess put his hand on Kid's shoulder. "With the hatch open a little, I saw that incredible leap you took. Do you realize how close you were to falling to your death?"

"We were out of options."

"Saved by the flying Mr. Kung-Fu," Maria said as she gingerly hugged him. "Wow, that has to hurt," she added as she pointed at his lip.

"It could be worse." Kid turned and put his arm around Heidi. "You're shaking."

"So are you."

"Is everyone alright?" he asked.

"I think so," Maria responded. "We wound up throwing that last guy out the window. Jess damn near went with him, but Heidi and I saved his ass. He owes us." She looked at Heidi. "Don't worry. I'll make sure he pays that back for a long time to come."

"Ready to get down from this forsaken thing?" Kid stepped back toward the square opening in the floor.

"Just give me a minute to rest first." Heidi sat down. "Still a little dizzy here."

"Me too," Maria echoed.

"I'll meet you all at the bottom. Hold the railings and just yell down if you need my help. I better make sure there are no survivors down there."

Kid labored down the steps. At the first landing, Elder-1's body lay frozen with his arm raised and his weapon trained on himself. Grabbing the raised arm, Kid pulled the body to the edge of the landing. He felt the same discomfort at the rigidity of the body that he felt when he moved Brian, and it made him cringe. Crouching down, he pushed the body off of the tower. The long descent ended with a muffled thud. Continuing down, as he encountered soldiers strewn in the stairwell, he would make sure they were dead, or at least brain-dead, and roll them over the side to the snowy ground below.

As Kid reached the bottom, he approached a body on the ground next to the steps. Soldier number 801, around 18 years of age, had fallen on top of another soldier and was somehow still alive. He did not appear seriously injured from the fall, but was still in a deep trance. Kid knew the soldier would not last long. He would have let the guy just slip away, but much to his dismay, 801 bore a resemblance to Kid's own younger brother. He sat and argued with himself. *Should I save him?* He thought back to what he and Heidi had talked about, and their plans for freeing the humanity in this new society. They needed to learn as much as they could about them and here was a live specimen, but not for much longer. Despite the internal conflict, he made a decision, one that he suspected would have implications. In the proper tone, he snapped, "Fleson!" Almost instantaneously, the young soldier snapped out of it. He returned to reality, but was weak and disoriented.

Standing up, Kid gathered all of the weapons in sight and threw them into the woods. He found a couple of bungee cords in the back of Queen Anne and tied up 801.

A few moments later, a cacophony of hollow clanging emanated from the metal steps as the group came down from the tower. Once on the ground, they walked past the body of Elder-1 in the snow. The girls stopped for a moment, and stared at his lifeless body without saying a word. Snow was stuck to half of his face, leaving one eye staring straight ahead.

Jess walked over to Kid and the soldier. "What are you doing?"

"He's alive. I think he can help us," Kid answered.

"I think he can kill us too. Are you crazy?" he asked, sounding irritated.

"I'll explain it all to you later. I tied him up. He's unarmed and extremely weak."

Jess looked confounded. "But he'll recover."

"Even if he…" Heidi peered at his uniform number and continued, "…801, does, we know the magic word," she chimed in as she walked over.

"That's true, if he makes one wrong move, we yell the word and put him out of his misery," Maria said putting her arm around Jess, trying to calm him down.

"That's reassuring… a word," he quipped.

"Hey, don't knock it. That's all we had when we were trapped up there," Kid retorted as he pointed to the top of the fire tower.

Jess hesitated then gave a conciliatory head nod.

Kid and Heidi helped the weakened 801 up and walked him to the back of the vehicle. The rest of the group piled in and they drove off.

"And I thought my hair looked funny…" Maria stared at Jess's raw, red scalp. He swept other strands of hair over his bald spot, but wasn't doing a good job of hiding it.

Kid sat in the back between Heidi and the young soldier. The miles of trails and scrub pines passed before his eyes, and like his mind, became a blur.

Jess broke the silence. "Well, where to now?"

"Can we at least stop by the beach?" Maria asked.

"And Jess said I was crazy?" Kid quipped.

"Seriously, my diabetes medications are there, and I still feel dizzy. We could find Metformin anywhere, but the other one I take is a lot harder to find and I don't have any more at my house. I've been feeling kind of squirrely, but just didn't say anything."

"I am surprised you've made it this far without it," Jess said.

"And we still have all of that food from the supermarket at Old Man Drexer's. We might as well grab it while we are there," Maria added as she put her hand to her stomach.

Jess seemed to support the idea. "I guess we could make sure our plan worked, and that the soldiers are stuck on the ships."

He and Maria turned toward the back seat.

Too tired and emotionally drained to care, Kid could only muster a simple response. "Fine. But if we see any signs of them having reached land, we grab Maria's medication and high-tail it out of there and get away from the beach."

Heidi, who had been resting her cheek against Kid's shoulder, finally seemed to absorb the present game plan. She jerked up her head. "Wait. The beach?"

Kid leaned back and looked at her. "What's wrong?"

"Brian. The way they left him…" Her voice was laden with despair.

He exhaled and grabbed her hand. "Before we went out to the ship, Jess and I made a grave in the sand up by the boardwalk."

"Can you take me there?" Her eyes pleaded.

"Of course, but we would have to look at it from the boardwalk. We can't risk being spotted on a wide-open beach."

"That's fine. I just want to be able to see it, and pay my respects."

Leaning forward, Kid said, "Speaking of being spotted, when we get there we need to stay out of sight of the ships."

Jess shrugged. "We can park up the block and sneak up to Old Man Drexer's."

"I don't think they know we are still alive," Kid noted. "Let's try to keep it that way."

CHAPTER 33

January 2, 2045
Monday, Late Morning
New Jersey coast
Seven days after the event

Parking a block in from the beach, the group stepped out of Queen Anne to walk the rest of the way to the shack. The residences along the block would keep them out of sight from the ships.

Kid untied 801's feet and helped him out of the vehicle. The captive's hands were still bound and he seemed weak, so Kid did not feel concerned that he would try and make a run for it. Still, he held onto the rope tying 801's wrists together and walked with him up the sidewalk.

Once the group reached the ocean road, they crouched and ran across the street. Hidden by the ridge of sand between the boardwalk and the sea, they ran south until they found the path between the dunes that led to Old Man Drexer's shack. With the house fully exposed on the beach, they again crouched as they made for the rickety wood steps, trying to maintain cover by keeping the stairwell between them and the ships.

Kid walked the bound soldier inside and sat him down on the floor in front of the couch. He could tell that their captive was still spaced out from his prolonged period in a zombie-like trance. "You are not going to try and run are you?"

"No," 801 said assuredly.

"Good. I don't want to have to tie your legs back up."

"Well, it doesn't look like the ships have moved at all," Jess concluded as he peered out a cracked and dusty window. "And I don't see anyone coming ashore."

Kid nodded. "And we didn't see any already ashore when we got here."

"I know we can't stay here, but let's take five." Jess plopped down on the plaid couch, letting out a loud exhale.

Maria found her medications still on the counter. "Thank God." She swallowed a pill and secured the prescription bottles in her pocket. She then joined Jess on the couch and put her head against his shoulder.

Inside the kitchen, Kid rummaged through the bags of food. He then searched the small living room, and even the bathroom. "Where is the instant coffee?" Nobody had seen it or touched it. "Odd. I know we grabbed some from the supermarket," he noted.

"What isn't odd these days," Maria responded.

Walking over to the last remaining room, Kid jiggled the locked knob for a few seconds. "Should I just bust the door down?"

"It might be an improvement," Jess quipped.

Kid threw his shoulder into it and it swung open. He found himself staring into a small bedroom. The missing jar of instant coffee was on a nightstand next to a half full cup. His eyes turned to a lumpy mattress on the floor which appeared to be moving up and down, as if it was breathing. The tips of a pair of shoes were sticking out from underneath, so he kicked them. He heard a quiet, "Ouch."

Couldn't be a soldier, he thought. He felt no fear at that point. After the incident at the fire tower, his anxiety-bank had long since been depleted. Grabbing the mattress, he quickly flipped it up against the wall. An old man lay on the floor looking at him like a deer in headlights. The man's beard and clothes were equally scraggly.

"I can't believe it, there's someone else alive here." Kid offered his hand.

The group in the living room heard the commotion and jumped to their feet.

"Who are you?" the man asked in a high-pitched voice as he tightened his hands against his chest.

"My name is Kid. I'm not going to hurt you. You must be Mr. Drexer?"

"How do you know my name?"

"You must be a legend. A girl from New York told us about you," he commented with his hand still outstretched.

"What?"

"Yeah, told us you were an attorney, and gave it all up to live the life of a fisherman."

"I gave it up because I wanted peace of mind. The fisherman part was an afterthought," he said as he timidly took the hand and stood up.

Kid was unsure as to whether or not the old man was crazy, but was very sure that the guy needed a shave and a bath.

"Which girl from New York were you talking to?" the old man asked.

Heidi appeared in the doorway. "That, would be me."

Mr. Drexer yelled and stepped back, stumbling into the mattress. "It's... one of them!"

"What?" Heidi froze.

It was then that Kid realized that Heidi was still wearing her uniform from the ships. He laughed. "Don't worry. Although she is wearing one of their uniforms, she is definitely not one of them."

She took a step closer and stated, "I remember you."

He shrank back again, as if he had a guilty conscience. "Wait," Mr. Drexer finally said, "I recognize you too. You were with one of the groups that hung around the beach next to my house. Was that last summer?"

"Yes!" She turned to Kid and her shoulders sagged. "That is when I met Brian."

"The place was a crowded madhouse all summer," Mr. Drexer added. "I couldn't wait for the solitude that comes with the cold weather."

"Believe me, you've got more solitude than you probably know," Kid said. "I assume you were here in your house when the destruction came?"

"I was in here for it, whatever it was. I was sleeping when it happened. Kept myself locked in this room because after, some hoodlums decided to break into my house and stay a while. They even broke up my favorite chair and threw it in the wood stove."

"I'll tell you what, that chair burned real nice," Kid said.

"It did?"

"That was us in your house."

"I thought your voice sounded familiar. Sorry about the hoodlum quip. I heard you talking about militant, programmed soldiers and being chased. Figured everyone had gone crazy until I saw the remains of the Quick-Fix clerk, soldiers roaming the streets, and those ships floating out there." Mr. Drexer scratched at his beard. "Like an unholy ark trinity, launched by Satan himself."

"That's a great description," Kid noted. "It's a long story, but first come on out and meet the rest of the group."

"There are more of you?" He followed Kid and Heidi out of the room.

Kid introduced him to Jess and Maria. "I can't tell you how glad we are to see another survivor." Maria shook his hand so briskly that the old man's head began to wobble on his shoulders.

"Please, just call me Drex."

Jess also shook his hand, although not as vigorously as Maria. "Grab a seat. After all, it is your couch." He scooted over.

As Drex sat down, he saw the soldier sitting on the floor. "I assume he is not one of them either?"

"No, now *he's* one of them," Kid said.

Drex jumped off the couch.

"Wait!" Kid waved his hands. "You have nothing to be afraid of. His hands are tied and he has no strength."

"It was a couple of those soldiers, or whatever they are, who went around the entire area and killed every survivor they found, including the 20 people in the hotel up the road," Drex said as he walked over to the lone wall unit in the room.

"There were 20 people in a hotel at this time of year?" Heidi asked.

"Winter-rentals. Low-income housing," he answered. "Yes, 20 people plus three U.S. Army soldiers, all dead. Don't know where the army soldiers came from."

Kid and Jess looked at each other. "The military checkpoint at the bridge," Jess concluded. "They must have taken shelter in the hotel. Surprised we didn't run into any of these people the day after it happened."

"They picked the wrong place to take shelter," Drex said. "The joint was loaded with weapons and drugs. The soldiers were shot and their bodies were just left on a second-floor balcony."

Having opened the door to a cabinet on the bottom of the wall unit, Drex pulled out a handgun. Kid froze for a second, until the old man held out the grip. "Here, we should cover that soldier. Be careful, it's loaded."

"I wish I had this when we were stuck in the fire tower," Kid muttered as he took the 38-caliber revolver.

"I got that from the hotel. As well as these," he added as he swung the cabinet door all the way open, revealing a cache of additional handguns and ammunition.

Jess's interest was piqued and he walked over. "You got all of these from the hotel?"

"Every single one. When I went in there, some of the residents were dead on the floor, but some were sitting around a table in the lobby and they all seemed… frozen. At first I thought they were still alive."

"That's because they were shot by one of the bizarre weapons used by the soldiers from those Utopia Project ships," Jess clarified. "They don't shoot bullets. They shoot some kind of bolt that freezes people instantly."

Drex shrugged. "I guess that explains it. Anyway, when I looked closer, I realized the dead people in the hotel were sitting around a table loaded with drugs, guns, and money. I took the guns, but you would think I would be smart enough to keep one on me at all times. What if one of the soldiers had come into my house instead of you?" He grabbed a pistol with a belt holster and affixed it to his waist.

"When I go outside, I am always armed," Drex continued. "You have to be. To protect yourself from not only those soldiers, but wild dogs."

"Wild dogs?" Jess asked.

"Yes, as hard as it was to do, I shot two of them yesterday. They may have once been family pets, but they are becoming vicious, wild animals. And with mounds of human guts everywhere for them to feed on, I fear they are acquiring a taste for human flesh."

He turned to Jess, who was kneeling next to him. "Take what you want. Make sure you can defend yourselves."

Jess examined the weapons and handed one to Maria, Heidi, and Kid. None of the other handguns had a belt holster, so they had to carry them in coat pockets. Jess took a Glock 9mm pistol with a full magazine. "Drex, how did you avoid getting caught by the soldiers who were searching the area?"

"I stayed in my room, and hid under the mattress when they came in. I obviously did a better job of hiding that time."

"So they took out all of the other survivors in this area?" Kid asked.

"It appears so, unless they missed other stragglers like me."

"What makes that even more tragic is that there are so few of us to begin with." Kid was beside himself as he stood up and paced the floor. Out the window, he noticed the undulations of the beach sand and remembered the unpleasant task he had agreed to. He glanced over at Heidi. "Are you ready to go over to Brian's grave?"

She looked solemn. "As much as I'll ever be."

Seeing them walk to the door, Drex said, "Make sure you are armed."

Patting the pistol in his pocket, Kid gave a thumbs-up.

Kid and Heidi were hunched over as they ran on the slushy road next to the boardwalk. He jumped onto the boardwalk and crawled to the edge. She crawled up next to him. He felt sadness wash over him as he pointed down at the mound on the beach.

Heidi brought her hands up to cover her face. After several moments of silence, she blew a kiss toward Brian's grave and whispered, "Rest in peace my love. You died so others could live."

Again hunched over while they ran, they returned to the shack. As soon as they entered, Maria grabbed his arm. "Kid! Listen to this." She then turned to Drex. "Go ahead and tell them."

Drex cleared his throat, "They were telling me about your fire tower battle in the woods, and mentioned the words those Utopia Project people used for the word conditioning, *Ion* and *Fleson*. I'm always solving word puzzles, so it jumped right out at me. I believe they are anadromes."

"They are what?"

"The simplest of word codes. Spell *Ion* and *Fleson* backward."

"*No I*," Kid said.

"And nose l… f?" Heidi attempted, and then backhanded Maria's shoulder. "Stop snickering. *No self*."

"*No I and No self*," Kid said. "I never would have thought of that. But it wouldn't surprise me with these people."

"From what I can gather, they definitely seemed to frown on… individualism," Drex said. He seemed to be warming up to the group. "So, do we know what happened out there, on that crazy night?"

Kid poured water into a paper cup and added some instant coffee. He exhaled and shook his head. "We are still trying to piece it all together."

"Maybe the guy over there knows what happened?" He pointed to the bound soldier.

"Nah, I doubt he knows much of anything. He seems to be just one of the ordinary, conditioned members of their Utopia Project society," Kid answered as he sat on the floor next to Heidi.

"Then why are you keeping him captive?"

"To learn about them."

"You said yourself he doesn't know anything," Drex noted.

"I don't think he knows anything about the destruction," Kid clarified while stirring his cold cup of coffee with a plastic spoon. "But he knows what their everyday life is like. That's what we hope we can learn from him. Actually, I have a question for 801."

The bound soldier turned.

"When you all were chasing us around the woods, what did you do at night?" Kid asked. "You were out there three nights. Did you sleep?"

"We found several of what Elder-1 called, campers, parked in the woods. We slept inside them every night."

"The Compound," Jess interjected.

"That's what I was thinking as well," Kid affirmed. They were familiar with a property owner in the Pine Barrens who allowed his friends to park their campers, which were mostly travel trailers, on his land. The site was touted as a rendezvous point if the Country ever came under attack, hence the nickname, The Compound. Coincidently, he realized they were not ready for the kind of attack that did come.

"If so, they were pretty damn close to us," Jess said. "Since they caught up to us at the fire tower, they were only a few turns away from the cabin."

Kid continued, "So 801, you slept in campers, but how did you find your way back to them every night?"

"We marked our path when we went searching for the enemy group so we could find our way back."

"You mean us. We were the enemy group you were chasing."

"Yes."

Maria jumped in. "How could you want to kill us then, but not now?"

"We have no current orders to kill you."

"Well that's good to know," she quipped.

"How did you track us down at the fire tower?" Kid asked. 801 seemed perplexed, so he further clarified, "That tall tower in the middle of woods, where you trapped us?"

"We heard a vehicle engine close by as we were marching back to the ships. Elder-1 ordered us to hide and not attack until the enemy had climbed up,"

"So you weren't even hunting us anymore when you heard our truck?"

"Elder-1 had canceled that order."

Heidi sighed. "That is unbelievable. If only we had waited an hour, they never would have trapped us."

"Another 'if only.'" Kid sounded sour.

Drex cleared his throat and sat back on the couch. He glanced at the group. "So, where do you plan to go from here?"

"Somewhere warm, with a hot shower and a nice juicy steak," Jess answered as he picked up a bag of chocolate chip cookies.

"We may have to go really far to get a steak," Heidi responded.

"Why is that?" Drex asked.

"Because despite the destruction, they left a certain number of 'wildlife tracts' intact in America and around the world, to preserve animal species. But I don't think any are that close to here."

Drex looked taken aback. "How far did this destruction go?"

"Global. Everyone in the entire world is dead," Heidi clarified.

"The *entire* world?" he blurted out, sounding shocked. "It's beyond comprehension. How?"

"The USA's neutron beam weapon system."

"That weapon system they built into the satellites?"

"Yes, but don't worry about them taking us out with it now," Heidi added. "When we were captives on the ships, we were told that the satellite system is no longer working."

Drex stared into space and sounded disgusted. "A world covered with dead bodies? I can't imagine the smell when winter breaks. It will be like the stench inside the Quick-Fix times millions, billions..."

Jess winced and added, "And the smell inside that store was sickening enough. Just the thought of it makes me want to toss my..." Looking down at his hands, he whipped the bag of cookies over to Maria, who was already shaking her head.

"Wait, what about any people living within wildlife tracts?" Kid asked the girls.

"Also dead," Heidi clarified. "They cherry picked human beings in those tracts with another beam from the satellites. It sounded kind of technical to me, but they were able to target people using infrared to distinguish them from the animals they wanted to survive."

"Did they say where the wildlife tracts are?"

"All over the world." Heidi appeared deep in thought. "I didn't see any list, but when I asked, Elder-1 gave me some examples. All I remember in North America were areas within the Rockies, the Appalachians and the Everglades. There were more, but those are the areas I remember."

"It's worse than I could have ever imagined." Drex's fingers trembled as he stroked the scraggly white hair of his mustache and beard. "What about here? We survived and this doesn't seem to qualify as a wildlife tract?"

"Oh, no," Maria interjected. "We weren't supposed to live and neither were you, Drex. But outside of the wildlife tracts that they left intentionally, there were a few areas that they just missed."

"Because of satellite malfunctions," Heidi added.

"Wait, a *few* areas?" Kid started as he pulled his coffee cup from his lips, also looking stunned. "Are you saying there is more than one 'malfunction' area, and that this is not the only area that they missed?"

CHAPTER 34

January 2, 2045
Monday, Midday
New Jersey coast
Seven days after the event

"Yes. Besides here, we were told that there were two other malfunction areas," Heidi clarified.

"Do you know what that means?" Kid asked.

"What?"

"Possibly more survivors." He felt a flicker of optimism.

"Assuming they didn't wipe out the survivors there like they did here," Drex noted.

"Good point," Kid acknowledged as his hope was put in check. "Where are the other two areas?"

Heidi shook her head. "They never told me."

"They mentioned another one to me," Maria jumped in. Everyone turned her way. "Elder-1 said that the second area they missed was in North America. I asked him where, and he said it was around the Green Mountains wildlife tract, wherever that is."

"Green Mountains?" Kid sounded surprised. "Up in Vermont?"

"Maria, you don't remember the Green Mountains? Seriously?" Heidi chided. "We were just up there."

She shrugged her shoulders. "I knew it sounded familiar. Hey, Kid drove. I wasn't paying attention."

"That was early December," Jess clarified. "We saw Sara's grandparents and we were hanging out with Karen Stone."

"Yeah, her," Heidi uttered with disdain. "And her crazy boyfriend Scott Sherman and his even more psycho older brother, Sid." Off the cuff she added, "Knowing our luck those idiots survived all of this."

"What about the third area?" Kid asked.

"He never said," Maria answered.

Heidi agreed, "No, and I guess I don't rate because he never even told me about the second area."

After finishing his coffee, Kid stood up and walked to the back window. Peering at the ships for a moment, he turned and noticed the now cold wood stove. He walked over and knelt in front of it. He realized he was in the very spot where he had had his last conversation with a healthy Sara, before she was captured and before she was compromised by the shot that grazed her. Next to the wood stove was the bronze-topped poker she had used to work the fire while she confided in him about being born in the same hospital in Georgia as the CCP's Baby Doe. His fingers trembled as he reached for the poker, and when he touched it, he thought he felt a mild electric current. Days before, she had held this very tool, and touching it made him feel a connection to her.

Kid suddenly felt an overwhelming need for his Sara. It was a crushing and desperate urge. It was then that he decided he had to go back to Sara's house, and her room. Maybe it was part of the grieving process, but he wanted… no, needed, to touch something, anything she had touched, in hopes that he might feel her one more time. He wanted to put her pillow to his face and smell her. He tried to tamp down the empty but growing swell emanating from the pit of his stomach, to no avail. Unable to take it anymore, he jumped to his feet. "I need to take a ride. I need to go back to Sara's house."

"Alright." Jess started, seeming a little taken aback. He hesitated, as if searching for the right words. "Just curious, but what are you looking for there that we can't find somewhere… closer?"

He stared down for a moment, and muttered, "I don't know. Maybe just… closure."

Jess exhaled and paused. "Fine, but we'll all have to go. We need to stick together. I guess we can just wait in the truck while you go inside."

"Is that really necessary? I hate to do that to everybody," Kid noted. The entire group agreed that they needed to stay together, including their new companion, Drex.

"We needed to move anyway. We are too close for comfort here. Everyone grab all of the food." Jess turned to Maria. "And any medications, and let's hit the road. After we go to Sara's house we'll find a new place to stay."

They had to bring along 801, so they just ensured that his hands were still securely bound.

While opening the shack's front door, Maria stated, "I hope we find somewhere nicer to stay than this dump…" She stopped as Drex was standing right there.

"Hey, wait a minute…"

"Sorry," Maria said as she urged Drex down the steps, patting his back all the while. "No offense intended."

After reaching the sand at the bottom of the steps, Kid saw Brian's truck parked next to the shack. With thoughts of Sara flooding his brain, the sight of the vehicle zapped him with a stinging reminder. He waved everyone else on, and crawled over to it. Opening the back door, he searched for the jewelry box containing the tribute to Sara's mother, and found it stuffed into a side-compartment holding the car jack. If he was going to her house, the least he could do was leave it in her room. He grabbed the unwrapped box and almost looked inside, but decided he had no right to. Although Sara would never see it, it was special and was only for her. He stuck the box in his pocket and closed the vehicle door.

When Kid went to leave, he froze upon hearing a dog barking and then howling in the distance. He instinctively touched his pocket to make sure the pistol was still there. The animal seemed quite far away, so he made his way up the road. With a slow jog, he caught up to the others and they all headed toward Queen Anne.

Jess pulled into Fort Dix and parked in front of Sara's house. With everyone waiting in the truck, Kid walked up to the front door and exhaled before opening it. As he stepped inside, he again noticed the laptop computer bag on the dining room table. The bag almost seemed to be ready and waiting for someone, as opposed to being tossed randomly.

He made for the hallway, pushed open Sara's bedroom door and immediately felt short of breath. He saw the dramatic mural on the wall behind her bed. The curtains were opened just enough to illuminate the painting of the woman on the dock. She stood facing the full moon with her arms outstretched to her sides. He never realized how hopeless the woman appeared to be. Maybe it was a projection of his own feelings at that moment. Dropping to a knee, he wept without restraint. He knew he wouldn't be able to contain himself, which was why he wanted to come inside alone. He didn't want to hold anything back.

Turning away from her bed, he pulled the jewelry box from his pocket and put it on top of her dresser. Lifting his eyes, he gazed into her large mirror which was cropped on each side by a vertical column of wedged pictures. Although he had been in Sara's room many times, he had never stopped to look at them all. Many were of him and her, including her copy of the picture tacked on the wall inside Ironside Gun Club. He kissed his fingertip and touched the photograph from 'the day at the cabin.'

His eyes then turned and settled on a picture of a woman with brunette hair who he did not recognize. She was holding up a piece of paper that said, 'Hi Sara!' Colors jumped off of the print—the deep blue water in the background, and the bright green eyes of the woman in the shot.

He turned around and dragged himself over to her bed. He picked up her pillow, hugged it tightly, and buried his face. The scent of his soulmate was overpowering. He could smell her skin, her hairspray, her perfume, and even her essence. The pillow lacked only a heartbeat, but his was beating strong and fast enough for the both of them. He sat on Sara's bed for a solid fifteen minutes, unable to put the pillow down. His mind was scrambled from grief, guilt, regret, and just plain longing. A voice startled him.

"Kid?" Heidi called out from the foyer.

He buried his face in the pillow to smell Sara and absorb her fleeting essence one last time. Exhaling with his eyes closed, he called out, "In here."

"You've been in here a while. We just wanted to make sure you were alright and…" Coming into the doorway, Heidi inhaled sharply. She froze upon seeing the mural on the wall.

"As well as can be expected. Sorry for taking so long." He placed Sara's pillow on the bed.

"No need to apologize," she said as she stepped closer to the wall behind the headboard. Gazing at the mural, she said, "That is what Jess and Maria were talking about in the truck. Sara really painted that herself?"

"Yes, over the course of a month."

"That is so deep, so real, so telling…" She reached out to touch it with her fingertips.

"No!" he snapped, nearly shouting.

She retracted her hand and seemed taken aback.

"I'm sorry, Heidi. It's just that Sara never wanted anyone to touch it. She said the oil from fingers would show up, sometimes weeks later."

She backed away from the wall with her hands raised in the air. "I'm sorry. I didn't know"

Realizing he had been too abrupt, Kid put his arm around her as they made for the door. He told her to wait in the foyer and he stayed in Sara's room a moment more. He needed to say goodbye to his soulmate. "I love you Sara, forever and ever," he whispered as he blew a kiss and gently closed the door to the sacred vault that was her room.

Reaching the foyer, he opened the front door and yelled, "Can you give us a few more minutes?"

Maria popped her head out of the truck window. "Take your time. We are not rushing you."

"Yeah, it's not like we have any plans!" Jess called out.

Waving, he returned to the foyer and then led Heidi out the back door. "Where are we going?" she asked.

"Follow me."

On the back porch, the Hylands' had a wooden swing that Kid always found soothing. He sat and let out a sigh. Heidi seemed hesitant so he patted the seat. "Please, take a load off." She dropped her rear end down, but shimmied away from him. Glancing over, he said, "I know I need another bath, but do I smell that bad?"

"No, what do you mean?"

"Why are you sitting so far away, all pushed against the arm over there? You look uncomfortable."

She seemed unsure how to respond. "I didn't want to crowd you. I don't know, I feel like I'm kind of intruding into your world here."

Kid peered at her with his brow pinched, and then it released. "Oh, I get it." She was referring to his world with Sara. "No, it's fine. Remember, I'm the one who brought you out here and offered you a seat." The muscles of her body and face seemed to relax all at once, and she scooted over. "Better?" he asked.

"Yeah, my arm was actually starting to hurt."

Using his feet, Kid pushed the swing until they had a steady sway. "If I don't say anything, don't think it is you. I just need a few minutes to free-think."

She shrugged. "No problem. I don't mind the silence."

For the next few minutes, Kid thought of Sara, and all that they had been through, from the moment he found her when they met in Vermont until the moment he lost her in the Pine Barrens of New Jersey. He had the olfactory recollection of her scent on her pillow. He had said goodbye, but he knew it was not goodbye. It was his way of finally succumbing to the gauntlet that is the grieving process. He had to let go, but he realized what that meant now. He could never actually let *her* go. What he was releasing was denial and disbelief. It was letting go of the irrational and desperate hope that it is all a bad dream, and that the person is not really gone. It was accepting that she was physically gone, and had passed on. His stomach would turn for a long time with that thought, but he had finally accepted it. He knew he had to move forward, take the pain with him and get through the gauntlet.

Kid stopped the swing and they both stood up. Walking through the house, he stopped in the foyer to ask her a question. Before he could say anything, the front door opened and Jess, Maria, and Drex walked in. They brought 801 along, with his hands still bound.

"How is it going?" Jess asked. "I know you said you needed a few minutes, but that was a half an hour ago."

"Yeah, sorry. I know I am taking forever. I'm trying to come to terms with a lot of things."

"We know. And again we're not pushing," Maria patted his arm. "We can't even imagine what you're going through coming here."

"I felt like I had to come back here. But I think I'm ready to go now."

Maria tried to smile through the expression of sadness on her face. "Do you mind if we just take a minute to show Drex the mural Sara painted on her wall? We were telling him about it, so he really wanted to see what we were raving about. Plus 801 can see real art."

"Sure. We needed another minute to talk anyway."

Looking sideways at him, Heidi seemed curious.

"You know where her room is," Kid added

Tip-toeing up the hall, Maria opened Sara's bedroom door. Drex and 801 followed her in.

As Kid and Heidi headed for the wide-open front door, they heard Drex's one word evaluation. "Incredible!"

Approaching the truck, Kid turned to her. "I wanted to ask you what you are thinking about. You seem pretty lost in your thoughts." Heidi had not met Kid's eyes since they sat on the swing, which concerned him. She mostly gazed at the ground in front of her.

She continued looking down as she answered. "A lot of things, I guess. Growing up, and my father, and how special he made me feel when I was young. When things were perfect. When I really meant something to someone."

Kid was curious about her life and history, but now did not seem like the time to ask. Not wanting to step on a landmine, he just said, "You mean something to all of us."

She lifted her head up and finally made eye contact. "Even you?"

"Even me." His response was genuine.

Upon realizing that Heidi no longer disgusted him, he felt conflicted and was having a hard time understanding his feelings at that moment. It was guilt, but had he really done anything to feel guilty about? His mental defenses then sprang into action, like conscience-activated perimeter doors automatically slamming shut. *It must be the circumstances. There's nobody left, so we have to work together. That is why Heidi, of all people, helped pull me back from the edge when I was dying of a broken heart at the cabin.*

"Do you mean it Kid? Or are you just patronizing me?"

He decided it was time to let go of his defenses. He allowed the perimeter doors that guarded his heart and soul to rise, and reveal his very raw, but very real, emotions. It was then that Kid realized the pitfall of exposing such a core. He couldn't rationalize or deceive himself, or make false assumptions as to what lay inside those confines. Not when he had revealed himself. The truth was, he no longer loathed Heidi's very existence.

"Yes, I actually do mean it." He was an open book as he met her blue eyes.

"Why are you looking at me that way?" She smirked while struggling to put forth a serious expression.

For some reason, Kid could not speak. He opened his mouth, but could not get any words out.

The corner of Heidi's lips straightened and legitimized her serious expression.

He tried to smile as he stated, "It feels like we've moved past hating each other. We might actually be friends one day."

She sighed as they started walking. "Yeah, I guess that's progress. Rome wasn't built in a day either."

As they stepped around the truck, he stopped and hugged her. She really seemed to need it. Maybe he did too. Still trying to shut down the old hate and negative triggers, his action startled even himself. He was so used to avoiding her at all costs. Heidi didn't say anything, but simply reciprocated and wrapped her arms around him, which surprised him even more.

■ ■ ■

Peering out the blinds and seeing Kid and Heidi in an embrace, Jess snap whispered, "Look at that!"

He startled Maria, who was checking out the pictures wedged into the frame of Sara's mirror. She whipped around and her elbow knocked the jewelry box Kid had placed on the dresser. Falling to the floor, one corner of the box hit the ground and the lid came flying off, scattering the contents.

■ ■ ■

For the first moment in a long time, Kid felt the fog starting to lift. His group had endured so much in the last several days. First the world was forever changed. He still did not know how they survived the cataclysmic event, but he accepted the fact that they may never know. Then they had wound up in one precarious predicament after another, and one life-or-death situation after another, and somehow most of them had survived. He knew that life without Sara would be painful and sad for quite some time, and it was going to be a long road. But he was beginning to accept all that had transpired, and was tapping a hidden well to summon the strength to step forward.

And then he was frozen by a word not even directed at him.

■ ■ ■

"Shit!" Maria yelled after knocking the jewelry box onto the floor, and then too late cupped her hands over her mouth.

"Relax!" Jess turned. "I saw Kid hug Heidi, and it caught me off guard, that's all. Who would have thought?"

She scrambled as she placed the empty jewelry box back on top of the dresser.

Jess turned back to the window. "Kid and Heidi are coming back in!" he warned.

Picking up an item that had fallen, Maria said in a low voice, "This was the gift? It's a men's watch." She stuffed it into the box and put the lid back on.

"Why would he give her a men's watch?" Jess blurted out.

"Shh," she hissed, but it was too late.

CHAPTER 35

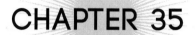

January 2, 2045
Monday, Midafternoon
Joint Base McGuire–Dix–Lakehurst
(Fort Dix Army Base), New Jersey
Seven days after the event

Kid stepped into Sara's room.

Maria had guilt written all over her face. "I was looking at the pictures on the mirror, and Jess startled me because he said… well he startled me, and I knocked the jewelry box off of the dresser when I turned around really fast. I'm sorry Kid. I'll put the box right back where you left it."

"I heard Jess mention a men's watch?" Kid asked.

"Yes, it's in here." She lifted the lid and held the box out toward him.

Walking over, Kid took the watch. What struck him was not so much that it was a men's watch, but that it appeared to be brand new. It did not look like an heirloom or tribute passed down from Sara's mother who died nearly 20 years ago. Thinking the real gift must still be in the box, he took it from Maria and peeked inside. There was nothing else in there, save for a piece of paper. With trembling fingers, he grabbed it and saw it was a note. After reading it, he dropped the paper back in the box, took a few unsteady steps backward, and plopped down on Sara's bed.

"What's wrong?" Heidi asked. "What did it say?"

Kid stared up at her blankly.

Maria picked up the note from the box. "Hard to tell. It's pretty sloppy," she commented but read it aloud, deciphering one word at a time.

'Sara, I know what has happened, and that you are scared and confused, but do as I say. Go home immediately and you will find the answers behind the rose.'

Appearing confused, Maria said, "She had that box all night. How could he know what was going to happen in advance?"

"And what does he mean, 'behind the rose'?" Heidi asked. "I didn't see any roses."

Springing up from the bed, Kid ran into the hallway. He stared at the large hanging picture of the tombstone in Georgia marking the grave of Sara's mother, and General Hyland's wife. The dim light made the picture seem even more eerie than he remembered it. He slid it to the side and reached into the dark pocket behind. He first pulled out a large, old-fashioned skeleton key. The shape was unmistakable. Putting it back, he took something larger out before letting the picture swing back to its original position. "There is a rose. You just have to know where to look," he said as he walked back into Sara's room.

"What do you mean?"

"When I was over here I would sometimes hear strange noises coming from the wall. I thought the house was haunted. But when Sara trusted me enough, she told me what it really was. Her father kept his diary…" Kid held up a black book in his hand, "…in a pocket in the wall, hidden behind the picture of his wife's tombstone."

"What does that have to do with roses?" Jess asked.

"Both her father and Sara referred to the picture in the hall as just, 'the rose,' because of the huge rose that covers the top half of the tombstone. It was Amanda Hyland's favorite flower."

"So the rose he was referring to is actually a picture, and behind the picture, is his diary?"

Kid nodded as he held the black book in his hand.

Drex seemed flustered. "Hold on a second. I know I'm late to the party here, but can we take a step back? First of all, what is the deal with the jewelry box?"

"It was a 'gift' for my girlfriend, from her father," Kid clarified. "She was supposed to open it at exactly 11:03 p.m. the night of destruction. And she did open it, but she was flash blind, so she couldn't see what was inside. She just felt around and pressed buttons until the watch-alarm shut off."

"The gift was an alarm?" Drex looked perplexed.

Shaking his head, Kid concluded, "The gift *had* an alarm, to make her open the box and read the note."

"Why would he direct her to his diary? And in such a secretive, and cryptic way?"

"I don't know, but I suspect we are going to find out." He looked down at the diary in his hands.

"Are you going to open it and see what it says?" Maria asked. "See, it has a tab with Sara's name on it."

At that moment, suspicions were swirling around Kid's mind, each one more frightening than the last. Unable to muster the strength to open it, he put the diary in his pocket. "First things first, we should figure out where we are staying tonight. I can't read it right now anyway."

"Come on then." Jess walked out of the bedroom. "Any ideas on where to go?"

Off the cuff, Kid said, "Somewhere close enough to keep an eye on them, but hidden enough so they can't see us." He thought this would be a tall order, until his friend responded right away.

"It may not be perfect," Jess started, "but the marina in Bayville where I bought my last boat had a view of the bridge to Seaside, and a great view of the bay all the way south to the inlet."

Kid had no desire to weigh his mind down with any more contemplation. "Good enough. Let's go."

Forty-five minutes later, Jess pulled up at the Good Luck Point Marina, which occupied a land area that jutted out into the western side of the Barnegat Bay.

801's wrists were still tied together, so Kid helped him out of the vehicle and then offered a hand to Drex. "I may be old, but I don't need to be coddled." He slapped the helping hand away and jumped to the ground. "Thanks anyway though." Kid loved the old guy's spirit.

Running around a tall marina building which looked like a large red warehouse, Kid saw a house painted the same color, but it had an affixed sign indicating, 'Main Office.' What caught Kid's eye was the octagonal widow's walk on the roof above the second story. The house seemed like it belonged on a beach somewhere, not sitting in the middle of a marina surrounded by shrink-wrapped boats.

Stepping onto the front porch of the office, Kid tried to open the front door, but it was locked. He turned around as Jess came jogging over.

"There's one boat down at the dock. A nice 28-foot Boston Whaler, center console. The key is in it and it has gas," his friend said.

"Why are we worried about a boat?" Heidi stepped onto the porch.

"In case we need to escape by sea," he answered, as if it was obvious. "We would just have to bull our way through the ice that is starting to encrust the hull."

"Stand back." Kid kicked open the front door. The first floor contained a small waiting area with outdated furniture, three small offices, and one larger room with a conference table. The second floor was comprised of offices and storerooms.

Kid and Jess ran up a spiral staircase in the middle of the second floor that led to a fully enclosed cupola with a 360-degree view. Facing north, they had a perfect view of the Tunney–Mathis Bridge going over to Seaside Heights. To the south, they could see the lighthouse and Barnegat Inlet. "We can see everything except the ships themselves," Jess noted.

"But all of the pathways between them and this marina are covered."

When they walked downstairs, everyone was sitting in chairs in the conference room. Seeing Kid, Maria pointed to him and then the chair at the head of the table. "We left that for you. Are you ready to read that diary now?"

Exhaling, he wanted to say, 'maybe later,' but he knew he was just delaying the inevitable. He moved slow, but took his seat. The room fell silent and they all stared at him expectantly. Holding up the black covered diary, he pointed to the 'Sara' tab with trembling fingers and flipped the book open. The first thing he noticed was that the words had an odd and inconsistent spacing between them, and the sentences did not stay on the pre-printed lines. "What the…" he muttered. He flipped back through some entries and noted that the general's handwriting was typically quite uniform and neat. He could not understand why this particular entry was not. "Did he write this entry with his eyes closed?"

The words were legible enough, so Kid read it first to himself. A lump came to his throat and he was frozen in time and space.

"Well?" Maria prodded.

He could not believe what he had just read. The implications made him blank out, as if his brain was an overloaded circuit that had just tripped.

"Are you alright?" Heidi rose and put her arm around his rigid body.

"What the hell could it say that's bothering him so much?" Jess asked. "Heidi, maybe you should read it."

She turned to Kid, and he robotically handed over the diary. He couldn't breathe, let alone speak at the moment.

Heidi sat back down and read the page aloud, gasping several times. When she finished, the silence in the room was heavy.

"Did I hear that right?" Jess stood up and started pacing. "Heidi, can you read that one more time?"

And she did.

It was Maria who finally uttered what they all seemed to be feeling, "Ho… ly… shit."

"No way. There is absolutely no way," Jess stated in disbelief.

"Does this mean what I think it means?" Heidi also seemed stunned.

"And what is that exactly?" Drex threw his hands in the air. "Can someone explain what is going on here?"

It was then that Kid found his voice. "The whole fucking game board just changed."

General Hyland's diary (page tagged, 'Sara'):

Sara,

If you are alive to read this then despite all odds, my plan to make adjustments in the satellite computer program and save a few small areas of the world did in fact work. And your grandparents should have survived as well, although your grandmother is likely running out of her Levonesex 212 (remember, that is the medicine she needs to take every day to live) so she needs to be checked on right away.

I am no longer one of them, but they think I am, so I am trapped/ stationed on one of the Utopia Project ships, but I am alive.

On our dining room table, you will find my laptop bag. The computer is critical, so grab it and don't let it out of your sight. In the side pocket of the laptop bag is a long-range military walkie-talkie with five fully charged batteries. Hit the call button on the walkie-talkie (keep it on channel 5), but do not speak! Only try to reach me between 8:00 p.m. to 9:00 p.m. eastern standard time and keep trying every night until we get in touch. Save battery power and turn it on between 8:00 p.m. and 9:00 p.m. ONLY!

DO NOT go back to the Seaside Heights area for any reason! Stay away from there. If everything goes as I expect it to, after the attack, our base camp will be established on Long Beach Island. That is not set in stone, but I will get to that area one way or another so just remain within 50 miles of Long Beach Island and please, STAY HIDDEN AT ALL TIMES!

For the sake of humanity, and my heart, take care of yourself and survive. I will catch up with you as soon as I can escape myself. I love you and, obviously, have a lot to explain to you.

Love, Dad.

CHAPTER 36

January 2, 2045
Monday, Late Afternoon
Bayville, New Jersey
Seven days after the event

"The game board changed? What do you mean by that?" Drex asked

"Our survival… was no accident," Kid clarified.

"So the 'computer malfunctions' the girls told us about were not malfunctions after all," Jess surmised.

"No, and I should have realized that already."

"How?"

"Look at where Maria said the second 'malfunction area' was—the Green Mountains, right around where Sara's grandparents live in Vermont! Could it be a coincidence that out of the three areas in the entire world that survived, Mr. Hyland's daughter happens to be in one and his parents in another?"

Drex scratched his beard as he contemplated, "How could this Mr. Hyland gain access to a highly secure weapon like that neutron beam system?"

"He was a United States army general, and I know he was involved in the computer programming for satellites and weapon systems," Kid noted. "He didn't talk about it, and neither did his daughter Sara, but she did tell me that much."

"Did he act alone?" Drex asked. "To pull off something like that,

I imagine it had to be a complicated plan, with a lot of moving parts."

"I don't know what his plan was, but in his diary entry he told Sara to stay hidden," Jess said. "I'm sure it threw a wrench into the works when the girls were captured, and again when we rescued them."

Kid responded, "I'm sure it messed up any plan he had, but you can bet he did everything in his power to protect them since he was on the ships. I'm sure he also wanted them to escape and get away."

"I think he was doing more than wanting. We were able to run around the ship, in view of cameras, and we never got caught? And the door alarms were delayed when we started the rescue. I thought we were just getting lucky, but now I'll bet we had help there too, assuming he really is stationed on the ships."

"He is definitely with them," Kid stated as he had another recollection. "When I was fighting with Elder-1 on the fire tower, I said the name Hyland and he recognized it right away."

After a moment of silence, Jess blurted out, "Some things make sense now. There were signs we didn't pick up on, because at the time we weren't looking for signs."

"What are you talking about?" Maria asked.

"Remember the night of the destruction Sara got a crank phone call just a few minutes before it happened? It wasn't a big deal at the time, but I'll bet that was part of the plan."

"In what way?"

"GPS. Her father was calling to pinpoint her exact location, so he could protect her from the beams."

Maria pinched her brow and then her face relaxed. "Ah, I get it."

Kid nodded his head in agreement. "And he obviously wanted her at the beach. The 'gift' was nothing more than a sham to get her there and keep her there."

"She was supposed to read the note in the box right away, but…" Heidi started.

"He didn't anticipate her being flash blinded," Kid finished, with a solemn voice.

"Exactly," Heidi echoed. "He should have considered that. It's not her fault that she didn't see his note sooner."

Kid added, "If she had seen his note, we would have headed back to her house right away to get the diary and she never would have been captured in the first place."

With a voice that seemed to exude more than just sadness and lament, Heidi said, "It certainly would have changed things."

Shaking her head, Maria pointed out, "We were just at Sara's house. I wish we knew we needed to grab the laptop bag." She turned to Kid. "I assume you are going back for it?"

"I'm not in any rush, not with the news I have to give Mr. Hyland." He stared at the ground for a long minute.

"Is anyone keeping watch upstairs?" Jess asked.

Everyone turned and looked at each other.

"Uh-oh. We're all down here." Maria's lips were tight.

The entire group, save 801 and Drex, climbed up to the cupola. With so many eyes scouting the area in every direction, Kid was confident they would spot anyone approaching.

Rubbing her hands together, Maria proclaimed, "There must be a 30-degree temperature difference between this widow's walk and the room downstairs." With an involuntary chill, she added, "That name even sounds cold… widow's walk."

"I wish we knew what those bastards are up to out there," Jess said.

"I guess Mr. Hyland could fill us in," Heidi noted sourly.

Despite the chill in the air, Kid felt numb. For several minutes he was silent as he stared out the window. He was not consciously thinking of anything, but he could tell that his subconscious was a raging maelstrom. Finally some thoughts began to coalesce. With losing Sara, he had been overwhelmed with grief. Now he was also overwhelmed with guilt as he thought of facing Mr. Hyland. He crossed his arms over his stomach at the sickening thought of telling him that his daughter did survive the cataclysm, but he had lost her after all.

Maria seemed to sense his dismay. "Kid?"

He did not move, but muttered, "Her father set it all up so she would survive. And she did, until I got her killed by trying to rescue her."

Heidi whipped around and snapped, "Don't blame yourself."

"She's right. It's not your fault," Maria agreed as Jess nodded his concurrence.

How can't I blame myself? Kid thought, as anger and regret swelled within him. He clenched his fingers in a tight fist. "I should have reached out and caught the bolt that hit Sara with my hand."

"Come on now," Maria huffed and exhaled. "How could you know it was going to hit her? It almost didn't. As a matter of fact, it barely touched her."

As he stared out the window, with dusk encroaching, he thought he could see the glow of the three vessel's lights above the buildings to the east. Somewhere out there was General Hyland. Kid knew he would have a day of reckoning. "I have to face him."

"Why?" Heidi asked as she walked over to him.

"I let him down."

"But…: she started, and abruptly closed her mouth.

"Only now do I know why he was so insistent about it," he continued. A minute later he finally turned to them. "The night of the destruction, after we had dinner, I made him a promise, and I failed to keep it."

December 26, 2044
Monday, Early Evening
Joint Base McGuire–Dix–Lakehurst
(Fort Dix Army Base), New Jersey
The evening of the event

After Sara and Kid had dinner with General Hyland, Brian arrived to pick them up.

Sara was trying to wrap a black scarf around her neck, but it got snagged on her necklace. Taking off her American Indian arrowhead shaped locket, she remarked, "I hate taking this off because it is from you Kid, but it always gets caught in my scarf." She opened the gold locket, kissed her finger and touched the picture of Kid inside. After closing it, she said, "Let me drop this on my dresser and I'm ready to go." She then ran to her room.

Coming back up the hall, she said, "And Dad, before you even ask- I have the gift box to open at 11:03 p.m., and yes, I will make sure my phone is on at all times." She kissed his cheek as she passed. "Love you."

"Perfect. Love you too." He turned to watch her go.

Kid followed her out, and bumped into her as she stopped on the top step. She exhaled and a heavy fog rolled from her lips. She pulled back her hair and put on a hunter-green and black checkered knit hat. She shook her head and let her brunette hair flow down the front of her coat. Putting on her thick black winter gloves, she walked down the steps.

Kid turned and waved to the general. "See you later."

"Bye now," he responded, and then called out as he came to the doorway. "And Kid…"

"Yes?" he asked as he turned back.

"Promise me you'll take care of my little girl."

Sara had just reached the sidewalk and called out, "19, and still his little girl!"

Kid made eye contact with the general and said confidently, "I will. I promise."

The general met his gaze, gave a quick head nod and closed the door to the world, but not fast enough. Something disturbing had shone in the general's eyes, so much so that Kid hesitated at the top of the steps. His momentary trance was broken as a snowball hit him in the chest, while Sara laughed and ran away.

But Kid's feeling of unease would linger for the next several hours. Long after the group had set up under Casino Pier in Seaside Heights, it would culminate in a sudden realization.

The air at the ocean is never still.

As darkness fell on the New Jersey coast, everyone was sitting in the conference room of the marina's office building except for Jess, who was upstairs on lookout duty. Heidi tapped her foot impatiently. How can I get Maria alone?

801 got up and announced that he had to go to the bathroom. He stood waiting for an escort. Heidi had found it odd that one of 801's nuances, presumably from his conditioning, was that he was uncomfortable going to the bathroom alone. The guys had to take turns being his escort. This time 801's quirk provided Heidi with the opportunity she had been waiting for.

Kid stood up. "I got it." He pulled out his flashlight and said, "Come on 801."

As soon as Kid left the room, Heidi got up and sat next to Maria. Leaning close she whispered, "Check this out."

Pulling General Hyland's diary out of her coat pocket, Heidi opened to the passage written for Sara. She held the book at an angle so the swaying candle light could creep across the page. Pointing to the paragraph about using a walkie-talkie to make contact between specific hours, she said, "Maybe we should reach out to Mr. Hyland."

"What?" Maria hissed, a little louder than a whisper.

Drex glanced up at them from across the room. Heidi waved her hand at him. "Just ignore us. Girl talk."

Maria clarified, "I know Kid. For him, this will be a matter of principle, and he may not be ready to do it yet, but he will be seriously pissed if someone else calls Mr. Hyland."

"Maybe so, but he thinks that he let Mr. Hyland down and that Sara's death was his fault. I would rather Kid be mad at me than to take responsibility for something that really wasn't his fault. Mr. Hyland will never forgive him, or worse," Heidi concluded. She did not want Kid to fall on the sword and take the blame for Sara. Mr. Hyland would then hold him responsible and drive the sword even deeper, if not use it to behead him. She could not let Kid be harmed that way. She needed to shield him.

Heidi stared as she waited for a response.

Maria sighed. "Well, I admit he's blaming himself when it wasn't his fault," she conceded. "He is not seeing clearly right now."

"That's what worries me! And that's why tomorrow we should break away and go to Mr. Hyland's house and get the laptop bag with the walkie-talkie. What do you say?" She was going to find a way out there one way or another.

Maria hesitated. "I don't know…" she started, but footsteps sounded in the hall.

Shoving the book into her coat pocket, Heidi stood up as Kid and 801 walked in.

"Everything come out alright?" she asked. It was a stupid and immature question, but while scrambling, Heidi had blurted out the first thing that came to mind. She hoped Kid was not onto the plotting in his short absence.

"That's kind of a personal question to ask amongst mixed company, right 801?" Kid commented, as if offended, and then smirked.

Smiling to hide her relief, Heidi saw no signs that he had picked up on anything.

"We would've been down sooner, but 801 kept staring at himself in the mirror. He does that every time. What is with them and mirrors?" Kid asked.

Heidi said, "He's probably fascinated because he's never seen himself before. They don't have mirrors on those ships."

The group started setting up their makeshift beds. Heidi helped Kid and Drex flip the conference table up against the wall to make more room on the floor. They had enough blankets so that each person had two, which would be sufficient given the two propane heaters they had secured from the workshop building.

"I'll stay upstairs and let Jess come down and get some rest," Drex said. "Poor guy nearly got scalped today."

"Did that all happen today? No wonder we're so exhausted," Maria added.

"Someone needs to be on watch at all times," Kid reminded.

"Drex, in a few hours, come get me. I'll take the shift after you," Heidi offered. She did not feel tired at all. He acknowledged with a wave of his hand and headed up to the widow's walk.

801 lay covered with two blankets. He stared wide-eyed until 9:00 p.m., at which time he dozed off in an instant. Kid looked at his watch. "These soldiers really are like clockwork." Turning to Heidi, as he lay side by side with her, he said, "Try to get some sleep since you only have a few hours until it's your turn upstairs."

"I'll try. Don't worry about me. Get some sleep yourself." Her eyes were wide open as she contemplated getting the walkie-talkie from Mr. Hyland's house.

CHAPTER 37

January 3, 2045
Tuesday, Midmorning
Bayville, New Jersey
Eight days after the event

The exhausted group had a hard time getting up the next morning, including Kid. Just ten more minutes of sleep, he kept telling himself as he dozed. It wasn't until midmorning that Kid woke up and searched for the keys to the marina's small fleet of extended-cab pickup trucks. All three vehicles were painted the same red color red as the marina buildings, but had dull and dirty silver toolboxes mounted in the bed. He went into the conference room and laid the keys on the table.

Walking into the room, Jess saw them through his bleary eyes. "Oh good. We need to take a ride and find propane for the heaters, and an electric hot water heater that we can run using the commercial generator we found in the workshop building."

Without hesitation, Heidi jumped in and suggested, "While you're doing that, Maria and I need to go find some new clothes. I'm not staying in this," she added as she motioned toward her Utopia Project uniform. "We can get fresh clothes for everyone. Then we can grab food from a supermarket on our way back."

Maria opened her mouth to say something, but Kid had already started speaking. "Fine, but grab as much bottled water as you can find. Get those multi-gallon jugs. Take a walkie-talkie, and we should all tune to channel two."

Heidi looked to Maria, who exhaled and said, "Fine. You grab the walkie-talkie, but I'll take the keys. I've driven with Mrs. Formula One over here before, and it wasn't pretty."

"Remember, these cheap walkie-talkies only have a 20-mile range," Kid added as he handed one to Heidi and one to Jess.

After having used the bathroom, 801 walked up the hall. His chaperone Drex was right behind him and asked, "Who should we go with? Who needs help?"

"You can jump in with me," Jess offered.

"I guess I'll stay here and be the lookout," Kid said. "Jess, are you taking 801 or do you want him to stay here with me?"

He shrugged his shoulders. "He can come with us. We could use some muscle with the heavier stuff."

Kid was glad that the anxiety over 801's presence seemed to be diminishing. His hands were no longer bound and he was no longer being treated like a captive. Not only didn't the soldier seem like a threat, but he found him to be quite helpful and did as they asked.

"Listen everyone," Kid started and raised his hands until he had everyone's attention. "Keep your eyes and ears open, and your vehicle headlights off. I will keep watch and if I see anything, I will give a distress call. In that case, hunker down wherever you are until I give you further instructions. Are we clear?"

After getting confirmations from all, he asked, "Does everyone have a firearm?"

Everyone nodded.

Heidi herded Maria out the door.

■　■　■

Heidi checked her watch. *The clock starts now.*

As they approached one of the trucks, she whispered to Maria, "Let's hurry. We have some stops to make before we go to the Hyland house."

"I guess you're still set on doing that?"

"We have to." Heidi jumped into the truck.

Shaking her head, Maria whispered, "Something in my gut is telling me I'm going to regret this."

Heidi gasped upon seeing a multitude of vehicle crashes as soon as Maria reached Route 9. She couldn't believe there was so much destruction in such a small area. Cars and trucks had veered into telephone poles, trees, buildings, or each other. One car had come to rest inside the large front window of a furniture store.

"Hold tight," Maria said as the vehicle started a slow power slide. They had just passed a van parked on top of a fire hydrant that had released enough water to make a lake-sized sheet of ice. She let off the gas and regained control of the truck without hitting anything. As she flexed her fingers and loosened her death grip on the steering wheel, she asked, "I assume you want to make a beeline for the Hyland house?"

"Oh no, we need to hurry, but I was serious about wanting new clothes. We have to lose these uniforms." Heidi feared that she and Maria dressed in a uniform only served to remind them, and specifically Kid, of Sara's final days.

"What a surprise." Maria smirked as she navigated around the obstacles on Route 9.

The girls found a clothes store with a full shoe section in one of the many New Jersey strip malls. The parking lot was empty, save for one car parked with a flat tire. Maria drove up on the sidewalk and used the heavy push bar mounted in the front of the truck to bust open the front door. "This truck is great. It's a battering ram on wheels," she said approvingly.

Casing out the well-stocked store, Heidi and Maria put on new coats, sweaters, socks and blue jeans. Heidi was more than happy to leave her uniform behind. "Finally, real female underwear," she said as she walked out of a dressing room. They proceeded to fill several bags with clothes, coats, and sneakers.

They made haste as they headed toward the Hyland house in Fort Dix. As they went further west, they were surrounded more and more by the pine forest. The ride became quiet and Heidi started to feel the woods closing in on them, until a voice burst from the walkie-talkie.

"Kid, are you there?" Jess radioed.

The girls both jumped and Maria fumbled for the volume knob.

"Go ahead," Kid responded.

"We already picked up propane for the heaters. Now we're trying to find an electric hot water heater and some pipe. See anything? Any problems?" Jess asked.

"No problems. How is it coming along Maria and Heidi?"

Heidi thought for a second and then picked up the walkie-talkie. She knew they would be out of range soon, so they needed to be unreachable without arousing suspicion. "It's coming along fine. We are going to turn the walkie-talkie down and try to finish shopping. But call us if an emergency comes up. Over, and out."

"Will do, Heidi," Kid answered. A few minutes later, his voice came through the walkie-talkie again. "Hey Jess, I assume we'll need... connect... plumbing tape..."

Hitting the gas, Maria concluded, "He's breaking up, which means we're getting out of range, so let's hustle."

■ ■ ■

Out at sea, on the main deck of the middle ship, a group of elders examined the davits.

"Bloody hell," Elder-24 muttered with his British slang. "We cannot reach land without tenders, and as we know, the ships cannot move any closer to shore given the shallow depth of the water."

Elder-2 stood at the deck rail with her hands behind her back. The freezing cold wind rippled her short crew-cut, but her face didn't even flinch. Her early days in Siberia had hardened her with winter blasts far worse. "We will assemble a team to retrieve a fleet of boats from the nearby marinas. And we have other, unfinished business, ashore." She spit over the deck rail in disgust. "There are obviously still survivors to be eliminated, preferably by cutting their throats."

"But, Ma'am, we first need to *get* ashore," Elder-24 noted.

Elder-2 turned and smiled through her gritted teeth. "They were quite crafty in cutting our tenders free, but let's just say they did not leave every stone unturned."

■ ■ ■

Having been on the road for some time, Heidi had fallen deep into her thoughts. *Is Kid going to be mad about this? If so, how mad? And for how…*

"I hope we can get in," Maria blurted out.

The words jolted Heidi back to reality. "What?" she asked as they approached the guard house and entrance to the Joint Base McGuire–Dix–Lakehurst.

"It is a military base. They have gates,"

"Look. Somebody left the gate open!" Heidi said as they got closer.

"Of course they did."

Heidi could tell that Maria would be content to abort this mission. But they could not. It was too important, and frankly, necessary.

Once inside the Hyland house, the girls opened the laptop bag on the dining room table. They found the five batteries and a walkie-talkie that Heidi thought seemed much more sturdy and powerful than theirs.

Maria said, "I'm dying of thirst. Do you know where they would keep bottled water?"

"No idea. Check the kitchen."

As she stepped away, Maria asked, "You need one?"

"Sure," Heidi answered as she stood at the table and glanced around. Her eyes settled on the first bedroom door up the hall. Feeling drawn, she took slow, quiet steps and pushed open Sara's door. She took a deep breath and stepped inside with trepidation.

Heidi's eyes adjusted to the dim light and her mouth fell open as the captivating mural came into full focus. She hadn't had a chance to study the artwork the first time she saw it. The painting depicted the back of a woman dressed in white flowing chiffon as she stood on a weathered dock. Somehow it was clear that the woman was filled with torment and longing, yet her face could not be seen. She had long, brown hair and her arms were outstretched to her sides as she stood before a full moon. The orb was over a deep blue ocean, and its radiance highlighted a small island at sea. Ghostly clouds floated in front of the moon, blocking many of the rays of light from reaching the woman. A small cluster of moonbeams had made it through and were touching her left arm and hand. With her fist clenched, the mysterious woman seemed to be drawing strength and resolve from the rays. Heidi found it strange that the mural initially made her feel a sense of despair and hopelessness, yet after looking closer and falling deeper into the scene, she found embedded signs of hope. Given that it was Sara's painting, she was not surprised. She went to touch the wall, and stopped her finger an inch from the surface. The last time she had reached out to touch it Kid had snapped and made it quite clear that the mural was not to be defiled by the touch of a human hand. Retracting her finger, she abruptly turned around.

Heidi went over to Sara's dresser with the large mirror and was overcome by a sickening feeling. It was a moment of déjà vu, but it was followed by the quick flash of a painful memory. She fought to suppress it, but as she stood in front of the dresser and turned her eyes up, her heart jumped at the reflection. Like a magic mirror, her step-sister Lisa appeared. The image was clear, including the color and detail of the Bobcat on the front of her cheerleading uniform. She then made the connection. Sara's mirror looked just like the one her step-sister had in her room. The dark wood frame was the same, as were the fancy caps on each side, like the tops of two fairy tale towers. The similarity was remarkable. What was different was Lisa's face. She was around Heidi's age, maybe 20 years old, and her skin and features were perfect. Heidi's stomach tensed and she bent over as a chill ran down her spine. The image was all wrong. Lisa was disfigured in a terrible…accident when she was 15 years old.

She shook her head and tried to refocus as she rubbed her sweaty palms together. "I'm freaking myself out. What am I doing in here anyway," she whispered as her eyes wandered. On the right side of the mirror frame was a neat vertical column of pictures. She felt a conflict between her overwhelming curiosity and her fear of what she might see and feel as she looked closer. Some were images of Sara and her father, General Hyland, at various locations with many people she did not recognize. She was familiar with some of the locales, like Niagara Falls and the White House. One picture was of a woman standing on a terrace, holding a piece of paper that said, 'Hi Sara!' The bright green eyes of the woman, a pretty brunette, were offset against the blue body of water behind her. She pulled the picture from the frame to examine it closer. She shivered as she noticed a gargoyle in the corner of the terrace, barely in the picture. It was mounted atop a Roman-style column which made it stand taller than the woman. Turning the picture over, she read the words, 'Adele's incredible house in Anacapri, Italy. Summer 2044.' Underneath that, in parentheses, it noted, '(Sorrento Peninsula in background).' After staring for a few seconds, she wedged it back in the mirror frame.

As she moved her eyes to the photographs along the left-side edge of the mirror, her hand came up and covered her mouth. The pictures all included Kid. There were ones of them together, and some of just him. Her lips trembled as she looked closer. She recognized one of the pictures. Another copy of it had been tacked on the wall inside the Ironside Gun Club cabin in the woods. It was the one of Kid and Sara laughing while holding each other on the cabin's roof deck. She was careful as she pulled the picture out from under the mirror frame and held it in front of her face. Turning it over, in Sara's distinctly neat script were the words, 'The day at the cabin. The day I found my soulmate.' Tears welled up in Heidi's eyes. They were so connected, she thought, and it pained her on some deep level. Could Kid ever hold me that way, and love me that much? Dropping the hand with the photograph down to her side, she gazed up at the ceiling and exhaled a trembling breath.

Hearing a sniffle, she swung around to see Maria standing inside the door with two bottles of water in her hand, and tears running down her face. Heidi handed her the picture.

"We all miss her. I just can't imagine what Kid's feeling," Maria sighed as she read the words on the back of the photograph. "They truly were soulmates…" she added, and then stopped after seeing Heidi's outpouring of emotion.

"I know," she whispered with her hands over her mouth.

Wiping her eyes, Maria handed the picture back and said while walking out, "Come on, we have to go. We've been out of walkie-talkie range for too long. I'll grab the computer bag."

"I'll be right there." Heidi loosely wedged the picture back into the mirror frame. It was then that she noticed a piece of jewelry on Sara's dresser. She picked it up and discovered that it was an arrowhead shaped locket. She opened it and peeked inside and as she expected, it contained a picture of Kid. A pained smile came to her face as she brushed her finger against his cheek in the small photograph. She closed the gold locket and held it tight in her hand, unable to put it down. Feeling conflicted, she eyed the doorway. Maria was nowhere in sight.

CHAPTER 38

January 3, 2045
Tuesday, Late Morning
Joint Base McGuire–Dix–Lakehurst
(Fort Dix Army Base), New Jersey
Eight days after the event

eidi continued to hold Sara's locket in her hand. She knew it was not hers and that she should just put it down. But she could not. It provided an interconnectedness that could not be fully understood or explained in a rational way. She almost felt empowered, as if through it, Sara's deep connection to Kid could somehow transcend. Coiling the thin gold chain and putting the arrowhead locket in the front pocket of her blue jeans, she walked out the door and did not look back.

■ ■ ■

"Hey! Come in!" Jess radioed while driving.

Kid jumped to his feet in the widow's walk. Something was wrong. "Go ahead!"

"Listen to me," Jess started. "After we grabbed the electric hot water heater, Drex wanted to stop by his house and grab a few things. While we were there, I was watching the ships out his window with the spyglass, and I saw them drop a raft in the water and head toward shore. When we were cutting all of their boats free, we didn't see any rafts!"

"No, but I guess it was just a matter of time before they found a way ashore. I just wish it took them longer," Kid said, resignedly. "Where are the girls?"

"Hey Maria, are you there?" Jess radioed.

The answer was taunting silence.

"Listen Jess. I'll keep trying them. You just focus on the road and get back here as fast as you can."

■ ■ ■

Maria and Heidi were driving east on Route 530 when they turned on the walkie-talkie. About 20 miles away from the marina, Jess's voice started coming across, in choppy, fragmented word clusters. "I can't tell what they are saying." Heidi turned up the volume. "Shh."

Maria, who was not talking or making noise, just shrugged her shoulders.

"Anyone there?" Heidi said into the walkie-talkie but got no response. Her hand dropped to her lap as she sighed. "We can hear them, but they can't hear us."

"Get used to it." Maria smirked.

Ten minutes later, Heidi was getting anxious. *Someone better hear us! We've been gone too long and need to check in.* She tried again. "Hello? Anyone there?"

The response was immediate, "Heidi! Get back here now! And be careful. They have found a way ashore!" Kid snapped.

The girls peered at each other with eyes wide, and Maria depressed the gas pedal further while saying, "Hold on."

■ ■ ■

You bastards better keep your distance, Kid thought as he kept a lookout from the widow's walk at the Good Luck Point Marina.

Jess ran up the spiral staircase. "Kid, what are you seeing?"

"Their rafts made it into the bay, but they ditched them after they took a couple of boats from a marina a few miles to the south. Then they drove out through the inlet and I guess went back to the ships. We are lucky to have such a good vantage point up here. We'll see them well in advance if they come our way."

Jess nodded and checked his watch. "The girls better get back soon."

"I know. And from here on out, we need someone keeping watch at all times," Kid noted.

"I'll stay up here for now," Drex said as he walked in. "You guys go do what you need to do."

A short while later, the girls arrived at the marina. Kid turned as they walked in and dropped bags of clothes on the floor.

Jess, who had been pacing, ran over to Maria. "Where the hell have you guys been?"

"Sorry," Heidi interjected. "When we went to go in some stores, I accidently left the walkie-talkie in the truck."

"We need to keep them on us at all times," Kid reminded.

"Do you need help bringing anything else in?" Jess asked.

Heidi shook her head and said, "Nope. That's all of it."

"Where's the food? You were going to stop at a supermarket."

"We never made it," Maria answered.

"Then where the heck were you the whole time? You guys were gone a while."

She went to answer and hesitated, long enough for Kid to glance over. He realized that Jess was right. They were gone a long time. Maria then turned, as if looking for Heidi to chime in, but she had stepped out. "Hey, shopping for clothes and shoes takes time," she said, dismissing the question.

"Oh, that's right. I know how you love to shop," Jess muttered with thick sarcasm and shook his head. "I'm going out to the workshop to set up the hot water heater."

Over the next few hours, Kid helped Jess set up the new shower. They were able to pipe in water from a well, and then used a surprisingly quiet generator to power the electric hot water heater. Everyone took a turn bathing, and then dressed in the clothes that Heidi and Maria had gathered that day.

Keeping a lookout all the while, they ate dinner in the conference room of the marina office building. Kid lit a large 3-wick candle in the center of the table, and the scent of evergreen forest wafted throughout the room. The space was warm enough from the two propane heaters that the group was able to sit in comfort without wearing coats.

After discussing how the soldiers were raised, Drex pointed to 801 and commented, "These poor soldiers are conditioned from birth? That's the same thing they were trying to do with that CCP initiative way back in 2025."

"You remember the CCP?" Kid asked.

"How could I forget?" Drex said. "It was headline news for weeks."

The mention of the CCP reminded Kid of Sara, prompting him to reveal her connection to the project. They were all stunned to learn that in 2025 Sara was born in the same hospital, on the same floor, as the CCP's Baby Doe, but only ten days after Anna Delilah had given birth.

"I wish we knew that," Maria noted. "Now I feel bad that we kept talking about it that last night at the beach."

"That is unbelievable. Any other Hyland revelations we should know about?" Jess quipped.

Heidi had taken the initiative to develop the lookout schedule for the night, paying careful attention to who would be on post from 8:00 p.m. to 9:00 p.m. At 8:45 p.m., she closed the conference room door and ran up to the third-floor widow's walk.

Maria saw her and then turned her eyes back toward the starry sky. "I was afraid you'd find your way up here."

Reaching into her coat pocket, Heidi pulled out General Hyland's walkie-talkie. While Kid was busy in the marina workshop with Jess, she had been able to sneak the computer bag into the office building and hide it in the bottom drawer of a second-floor file cabinet.

"Well, Mr. Hyland did say to try and reach him between 8:00 and 9:00, and I don't think they can hear us downstairs," Heidi said. "They're all in the conference room two floors down, and they're keeping the door closed to keep in the heat."

Holding the walkie-talkie in her hand, she massaged the buttons with trembling fingers. "Are you ready?" She hit the power button and turned it on.

"No," Maria answered. "It still feels wrong side-stepping Kid. Not to mention, we get to be the bearer of the news about Sara? That's going to crush Mr. Hyland. Absolutely crush him."

"I know. That's why I'm delaying pressing the button."

They both sat in silence for a few more minutes.

"What will you even say to him?" Maria asked.

"I'm not really sure. I know what I need to say, but every time I think it through, the script in my mind changes. What time is it now?"

Maria checked her watch. "Almost 9:00."

Heidi peered down the stairwell to ensure nobody was coming. "The window of time is closing. We have to do this. We have no choice," she said with resolve and depressed the call button.

Despite the low-volume of the double-beep, both girls cringed.

■   ■   ■

On ship number one, General Hyland was sitting at a small desk in his room. Deep in thought, he tapped a stylus on his desktop. Hearing a faint double-beep, his eyes opened wide, and he stopped tapping. Pushing his chair back away from his desk, he stood up and went to the large flat screen in his room. He did not have time to jump into the program and insert a still-frame and silence to cover his monitor's video and audio feed. That meant, based on security protocols, he had less than one full minute if he was to avoid being questioned. He nonchalantly turned the monitor off at 20:58:55, but then raced back to his desk. Dropping to a knee, he pulled out the bottom drawer. Wedged inside a leather portfolio case was a thin, black walkie-talkie in stand-by mode. He turned up the volume and depressed the call button. A double-beep sounded. "Hello? Who is this?"

"Mr. Hyland? This is Heidi Leer. I'm here with Maria Stefano, you know... Sara and Kid's friends."

Pressing the call button, he asked, "Heidi? Where are you guys?"

"We are at a marina on Barnegat Bay," she radioed back.

"After all of this time, I'm surprised that you found the walkie-talkie, and I can't believe you are still alive, but thank God." He glanced at the clock. "Listen, I wasn't expecting anyone to call at this point, so we only have a minute before I have to power down. Who else is with you?"

"Kid, Jess, and some others including one of your members who is being cooperative, but listen, Mr. Hyland, about Sara…" she paused.

The general cut in. "Heidi… I know. I'm sorry." His voice was somber. "That will certainly require a very thorough explanation," he added, laboring to get the words out.

He glanced at the clock, and was jolted. He was running out of time. "Listen close. I have to say this quickly. My mother in Vermont should still be alive in another area left untouched. She has a medication she needs to take every day to live. She was running out and will die without it." Looking at the time, the general spoke even faster. "It's a custom medication and is only produced in one place, but it's in New Jersey. Go to the Merck facility in Rahway, Building 34. The medication is Levonesex 212. It'll be hard to find, but it's there. Take as much as you can to my parent's house in Vermont. Kid and Jess know where they live. Merck. Building 34. Rahway. Levonesex 212. Get that medication to her right away! Her life depends on it and I hope you're not too late. Powering down."

He shut the walkie-talkie off, dropped it into the drawer and ran to turn the two-way monitor back on. The clock on the screen said, 20:59:50. When the general turned his back to the screen, he exhaled a breath of relief.

■　　■　　■

Powering down? Heidi felt a surge of panic. She depressed her call button and spoke fast. "Got it, but I need to explain what happened to Sara." Silence. She depressed the button again. "Mr. Hyland?"

Getting no response, she voiced her frustration, "Damn! I didn't get to explain anything!"

Maria kept repeating the general's instructions. "Get some paper, quick. We need to write this down."

"Don't worry. I don't think I'll ever forget a single syllable of that conversation." She turned the walkie-talkie off.

"Levonesex 212. Building 34, Rahway," Maria repeated twice. "I can't believe he already knew about Sara. Saved you from breaking that news."

"I don't know how he knew," she said with a furrowed brow.

"Maybe he saw her get shot. Maybe he was with the soldiers standing on the deck or the bridges between the ships when we were escaping?"

"How else could he know?" Heidi asked. "I guess what matters is that he does. I just hope he doesn't already hold Kid responsible for it."

Maria walked over. "Speaking of responsible, Mr. Hyland now just put his mother's life in our hands. The gig is up. It would've been eating away at me anyway, but now we definitely need to go downstairs and tell Kid."

"I know," Heidi huffed, her voice a high-pitched whine.

Putting her arm around her, Maria said, "You meant well. Come on. We'll go talk to him together."

"No, I'll tell him. I'm the one who got us into this mess. When I bring him up here, step out so I can speak to him one on one." She tried to gather herself. As she went down the spiral staircase to the second floor, Heidi peered up. "Kid's really going to be angry, isn't he?"

Leaning over the banister and looking down, Maria just exhaled. "Does that matter now?" Without waiting for an answer, she waved her hands, indicating that Heidi should move along.

The nervous tension emanating from Heidi was palpable as she stepped into the conference room. She did not even say a word, yet everyone jumped to their feet. "What's wrong? Are they coming?" Kid asked.

"No." She waved her hand in a nervous gesture. "It's not that. Kid, can I talk to you for a minute in private?"

"Come on." He led her out the door.

"Let's go up, and we can send Maria down," she said as they climbed the stairs. Stepping into the widow's walk, she asked Maria, "Do you mind if Kid and I talk up here… alone?"

"Not at all," she said and stood up, avoiding Kid's eyes. Walking past him, she rubbed his back. "The penthouse is all yours."

He stopped and touched his back, seeming surprised at Maria's gesture. Once she was out of earshot, he asked, "What the heck is going on?"

Without saying a word, Heidi pulled General Hyland's diary out of her coat pocket. Kid froze. Bending down in front of the dim light emanating from the propane heater, she flipped through and stopped at the entry written for Sara. She stared at the page for a minute and then held the diary out with her finger on a specific paragraph. Then she stood up and turned away. Holding the diary close to his face, Kid read the words.

Heidi stood facing Barnegat Inlet, but her head was down. She rubbed her eyes and was anxious for him to finish.

Kid closed the book and stood upright. "Alright, I read it… again. What about it?"

"He wanted her to call him on the ship."

"I know. Even though we were just there I guess I'll have to go by his house again and get that laptop bag with the walkie-talkie. I am really dreading that call, but I guess it's time I told him about Sara."

"Any one of us could call," Heidi said sheepishly. "Wouldn't it be easier if someone else told him?"

"Easier maybe, but I need to do it."

"Why you?" She was concerned by the definitiveness of his answer. This is not going well, she realized.

"Because I promised him I would take care of his little girl."

"But it wasn't your fault…" she tried to start.

"Heidi, even if it wasn't 100 percent my fault, it was my responsibility, so I have to make the call."

At that, she turned and walked over to him. She grabbed his hand and gently caressed it. Her eyes were full of tears. "Please, sit down."

His breath stopping for a split second as he seemed to have a realization. "There's something you are trying to tell me, isn't there?"

She froze, and then squeaked out, "Yes."

CHAPTER 39

January 3, 2045
Tuesday, Evening
Bayville, New Jersey
Eight days after the event

Kid sat in a chair in the widow's walk. *What now?* He was afraid to know.

"There is something I need to tell you," she said as she walked over to a window and stared out. "Kid, you're going to be angry. I thought you might be, but I didn't realize how much until this moment. I swear, I meant well…"

He left the diary on his lap as he put his face in his hands. "Heidi, please just tell me."

"Just wait here, one second." She went down the stairs. She returned and put the general's laptop bag on the floor in front of him. "I asked Maria to stop by Mr. Hyland's house when we were running errands today, and I picked this up."

His mouth was frozen open. "Why didn't you tell me?" He started to rise to his feet.

She grabbed his arm and pleaded with him, "Can you stay in the chair here, please, just for a minute? I need to finish."

He moved to the very edge of the chair and looked incredulous. "Finish?"

She faced the window again and exhaled a deep breath. She seemed to be steeling herself for what she had to say. Turning back around,

Heidi got down on one knee in front of him. "I already called him, Kid."

Strong waves of disbelief and anger collided within him and he bolted upright to his feet, knocking his chair over backward. "You what?"

The air in the widow's walk turned deathly still.

Heidi crouched lower, and seemed to be shrinking. She dropped a second knee on the floor and sat back on her heels. She seemed resigned to accept whatever was coming to her. Looking up with desperate eyes, she said, "I'm sorry..."

Pacing in the small space, Kid stopped and felt like he was going to explode. "You called him? How could you do that? You know that was my call to make, or you should have known."

"I was afraid you would lay the blame for Sara on yourself, and that Mr. Hyland would accept it as fact when that's not what happened."

"What gives you the right to speak on my behalf and with something that important?"

"I only wanted to save you from falling on a sword you shouldn't be falling on!" she yelled through tears.

"Save me? I didn't ask to be saved!" he yelled as he threw the diary on the ground. "Did it ever occur to you that maybe I needed to make that call because it might help me cope, as painful as it would be?"

Heidi sat in silence with her head down for a minute. "I didn't think of it that way. I'm sorry, Kid. I over-stepped my bounds, and I shouldn't have."

He headed for the stairwell. Even his legs felt like they were trembling and he stopped after a few steps. "You sure as hell did." He continued downstairs two steps at a time.

Kid's face was hot and his teeth were grinding as he reached the first floor. He stomped up the hall, too furious to soften his heavy footsteps.

Maria rushed out of the conference room and closed the door behind her. As she met him in the hall, she reached out. "Stop."

He tried to walk past, but she grabbed his arm.

He swung around to face her, pulling his arm away. He went to blurt something out, but stopped to compose himself for a second. "How could you go along with that? Did you know she was planning to call Mr. Hyland?"

"Yes, I did. Blame me, too," she said as she crossed her arms.

He shook his head and went to turn away.

She again grabbed his arm. "Listen, I know you miss Sara and probably do every minute of the day. But we didn't want to see you take the fall with Mr. Hyland so we called him. We didn't get to say much, but the important thing is that he knows about Sara."

"I have to face him sometime. He entrusted me with his daughter's life, and I let him down!" he yelled. He stood rigid as he stared at her.

"I'm sure you will face him, but hopefully after you've faced the facts and come to terms with what we already know, and that you know somewhere deep inside."

He gazed at her expectantly, his anger now coupled with curiosity. It was also a quick reminder that despite her wild and carefree persona, in those rare moments when she was serious, Maria was usually dead on. He had learned that when they were growing up, and knew she was far more observant and astute then she let on.

"And what is it you think you already know?" His challenge lacked conviction, and he again braced himself for a moment of realization.

She pounced before he even finished asking the question. "You didn't let Mr. Hyland down! He let Sara down!" Maria said with unusual force as she stepped toward him until she was just an inch from his face. "The monsters Mr. Hyland associates with did this to her, not you. They're the ones who aimed at her and pulled the trigger, not you. They're the ones who took the life of his daughter, and...." she hesitated.

Her words sank in and jolted his core. His eyes scanned the hall around him for something he would never find in his external visual field. Her words had flipped the version of the truth he had accepted on its side, forcing him to see it from a different angle.

Kid saw the pain in her eyes as she added, "...and stole your soulmate from you. He should be worried about confronting you."

His anger transitioned to grief, and he was unable to respond.

As she stared at him, Maria's fire also seemed to die down. "I'm sorry." She embraced him and whispered, "Please don't be too hard on Heidi. She meant well." She furrowed her brow and added, "I can't believe I'm actually saying that with how you guys used to hate each other, but she was really worried about you and didn't want you to take the fall."

"I know. But, she needs to understand how I operate," he said as they pulled apart.

"She will. You're a stand-up guy, Kid. You have a foundation based on things that most people just don't value enough anymore, like character and integrity. You're Mr. Old-Fashioned-Values. That's why you've always been a rock for people, including me." She put her arm around him as they walked up the hall.

He put his arm around her shoulder, his fury now subsiding. "You know me well enough to know how I would react, so why did you go along with Heidi and call Mr. Hyland?"

"Let's just say it was the lesser of two evils. Deal with your wrath, or deal with you taking the fall for something that wasn't your fault. I knew how hard we were stepping on your toes and how you would react, but I don't know if Heidi did. I'll bet she does now. Speaking of, let me go talk to her and bring her down. We'll fill you in on what Mr. Hyland said."

He stopped. "No, I'll go talk to her." She went to open her mouth, and he cut her off. "This is also my call to make."

Maria put up her hands and surrendered without hesitation.

Upstairs, Heidi faced the window but stared at the open arrowhead locket in her palm. Her tears dripped onto her hand. *I blew it. I don't know if he will ever forgive me.* Although she wanted so much more than just a friendship with Kid, she thought that saving him would at least solidify the relationship they had been building. Instead, her actions destroyed any progress and probably set her back to square one. *So much for Rome being built, ever...*

Kid walked up the stairs and entered the widow's walk. Heidi was facing away, and did not seem to know he was there. He watched her for a moment, feeling waves of guilt, pity, and even flickers of anger. She was sitting in the chair, holding her head up with her fist under her chin and her elbow on her knee. Her posture showed fatigue as she sat with an aura of sadness and solitude. True to its name and purpose, she looked like a widow up in her cupola, gazing upon the sea that claimed her spouse.

"Heidi?" he said in a soft voice.

She turned, startled, "Oh, hello. Is it your turn up here? I'll get out of your way." She stood up and stuck her hands into her front jean pockets. "I'm sure you don't want me around right now." Kid walked over, took her gently by the arm, and sat her down. "Or ever," she added with somber resignation while dropping her rear end onto the edge of the chair.

He crouched down on his knees and asked for silence with a single finger pressed to his lips. "What you did was not alright with me. For us to build a solid friendship, we have to understand what makes each other tick, and we need to respect those things. For me this was an issue of responsibility, and even accountability, and doing what I felt I needed to do, regardless of how much it would hurt me to do it, or how Mr. Hyland would react."

Tears started streaming down her cheeks as she nodded her head.

He added, "But I also know you were well-intentioned so let's work our way past it."

She fell into his arms and hugged him hard. "I'm so sorry, Kid."

"No more apologies. I've already forgiven you," he said as he wrapped his arms around her.

A few minutes later Heidi pulled strands of hair off of her tear-soaked cheeks. "We only talked to Mr. Hyland for a minute, but he gave us some important instructions. We need to get some medication to his Mom in Vermont. She was running out and can't survive without it, and it's only made at one place here in New Jersey."

"He also mentioned that in the diary entry he wrote for Sara," Kid noted as he stared at her, and then past her as he stood up. "Speaking of," he said and picked up the diary he had whipped on the ground earlier. He handed it to Heidi and she put it in her coat pocket.

Approaching a window, Kid faced the dark silhouette of the Tunney–Mathis Bridge.

"What are you thinking?" she asked.

"I'm thinking... tragic irony. Mr. Hyland influenced and manipulated everything so that those he loved the most would survive. Then his daughter perishes at the hands of his own soldiers, and now we have his mother. She survives, I assume she survived, a cataclysmic event only to die because she runs out of medication?"

"Sounds very Shakespearian," Heidi noted.

"It does... if it happens that way, and if there is another tragic ending. He already lost his daughter. I'll be damned if he is going to lose his mother too." He turned to her with a look of determination in his eyes. "Tell me everything we need to know. What medication, where do we get it..."

Kid devised a quick game plan in the conference room. He was exhausted, but every minute could make the difference in saving General Hyland's mother. He knew he had to sleep, but after mapping out the route they would take, he decided they needed to start off right away. They could sleep in the vehicle and take turns driving. Kid, Heidi, Jess, Maria, and 801 were all going, and they could fit into one vehicle. Kid wanted the entire group to stick together but Drex did not want to make such a long trip and said he would stay behind and track the movement and progress of the soldiers. They established a rendezvous point in Toms River where they would meet up if Drex had to flee from the Good Luck Marina.

Kid and Jess loaded the truck with supplies, food, and water. "Want me to drive?" Jess asked.

"I got it. I won't be able to close my eyes until we get the medication anyway. Why don't you sleep until we get to Rahway and then we can switch. With the road conditions, it'll probably take a couple of hours to get there. Come on everyone, let's get on the road." He then yelled up the stairwell to the current lookout, "Drex, we're leaving!"

Drex came into the conference room. "Hey Kid, since you are the captain of your crew, I designate you as the one responsible for bringing me back some genuine Vermont Maple Syrup."

"Why does everyone peg me as the leader?"

"I see it myself, but Maria here said you've always been the unofficial head of the group. When I asked why you were unofficial, she captured the entire essence in her simple response. She said because you don't try to be the leader, you just are."

Kid did not know what to say.

Jess waved to Drex. "See you later. Stay alert and don't let boredom get the best of you."

"I'll be alright. Hell, I could probably kill a few minutes drafting up the new legal doctrine Kid proposed when we were talking yesterday."

Kid thought for a second and then recalled, "You mean the doctrine of S.H.?"

"S.H.?" Jess asked.

"S.H.... shit happens," Drex answered and chuckled. "With such a doctrine, most of the court cases would've been thrown out immediately. What is the complaint? In accordance with the applicable legal doctrine, shit happens, move along. Next case..."

Maria strode over. "You'll be alright here alone, Drex?"

"I'm used to being alone. And I have heat, a hot shower, and food so I'm all set. I'm as comfortable as I was in my rickety old beach house. Maybe even more so." Maria opened her arms to hug him and started to smirk. He added, "I know what you're thinking, anything is a step up from that... dump?"

"I'm not saying a word." She laughed.

Kid shook Drex's hand and said, "We'll get back as soon as we can."

"Got it. I assume when you get back we will come up with a plan of our own? You seemed determined to, as you put it, awaken the humanity in the automatons on those ships?"

Kid and Heidi both nodded. "That's the idea, but we'll figure that out when we get back. For now, the priority is to save Evelyn Hyland," Kid noted.

Heidi waved good-bye and headed outside to the waiting vehicle.

The older man patted Kid's shoulder as he walked him out the door. "Good luck, and remember, real maple syrup. Up in Vermont you'll find the real deal, not imitations."

"In Vermont we'll find the real deal, not imitations," Kid repeated and paused for a moment. As he stepped outside, he said, "Oh, remember, we left the items the girls picked up at Mr. Hyland's house, including a laptop computer bag, in the conference room. The computer must be important to him so protect it at all costs."

"I will, but I wish I knew why. This General Hyland is a pretty mysterious guy. I hope to one day ask him how he pulled off what he did. How did he do it? And what was his plan after the smoke cleared?"

Kid climbed into the driver seat of the red pickup truck and rolled down the window. "So many revelations to come. But don't worry. I suspect that we will meet up with him one day." He hesitated. It was a stinging reminder that regardless of the shared responsibility for Sara's death, Kid would one day have to face the general, and would have much to explain.

Then again, so would General Hyland.

AUTHOR'S NOTES

First and foremost, thank you for reading this book and for sharing in the Utopia Project series journey! I am humbled and beyond appreciative.

Stay tuned! The story continues in the soon-to-be-released second book in the trilogy: **Utopia Project - The Frayed Threads of Hope**. What surprising twists and turns await Kid and the last remnants of humanity, and can they continue to survive against all odds?

To stay abreast of the release of the next installment, please check the utopiaproject.com website, follow us on Instagram (utopiaprojectseries) or Facebook (Utopia Project by Billy Dering).

Please, also consider posting a rating/review of this first book: **Utopia Project - Everyone Must Die**. Such ratings/reviews provide invaluable feedback for the author as well as other potential readers! Thank you.

Made in the USA
Columbia, SC
15 May 2021